Readers love JAMIE FESSENDEN

Small Town Sonata

"It was so incredibly easy to fall in love with Dean Cooper and that is down to the marvelous writing skills of author, Jamie Fessenden, and his uncanny ability to make a character so incredibly realistic and appealing."

—Joyfully Jay

"I recommend this well written and moving book and felt the men and their life challenges were genuine."

—Bayou Book Junkie

The Christmas Wager

"All in all, The Christmas Wager is a sweet Christmas tale that many will enjoy year after year—worthy of a reread despite a few fantastical moments, and definitely a well written historical romance for those who love the genre."

—The Novel Approach

Screwups

"I was completely sucked in and didn't come up for air until I was done."

—Prism Book Alliance

"Jamie Fessenden is such an amazing writer no matter what type of story he tackles, and this one hit me right in the gut."

—Mrs. Condit & Friends Read Books

By Jamie Fessenden

The Christmas Wager
Dogs of Cyberwar
The Healing Power of Eggnog
Penumbra – Delving into the Shadows
Saturn in Retrograde
Screwups

DREAMSPUN DESIRES
Small Town Sonata

Published by DSP Publications
By That Sin Fell the Angels
Murderous Requiem

Published by Dreamspinner Press
www.dreamspinnerpress.com

JAMIE
FESSENDEN

PENUMBRA

DELVING INTO THE SHADOWS

DREAMSPINNER
PRESS

Published by
DREAMSPINNER PRESS

5032 Capital Circle SW, Suite 2, PMB# 279, Tallahassee, FL 32305-7886 USA
www.dreamspinnerpress.com

Penumbra – Delving into the Shadows
© 2022 Jamie Fessenden

Cover Art
© 2022 L.C. Chase
http://www.lcchase.com
Cover content is for illustrative purposes only and any person depicted on the cover is a model.
Author Photo by C.H. Curtis

Trade Paperback ISBN: 978-1-64108-427-7
Digital ISBN: 978-1-64108-426-0
Trade Paperback published August 2022
v. 1.0
Watchworks originally published in Gothika: Stitch by Dreamspinner Press, April 2014.
The Book of St. Cyprian originally published in Gothika: Bones by Dreamspinner Press, October 2014.
Isolation originally published in Gothika: Claw by Dreamspinner Press, April 2015.
The Mill originally published in Gothika: Spirit by Dreamspinner Press, October 2015.
Abducted originally published in Gothika: Contact by Dreamspinner Press, October 2016.

Printed in the United States of America

This paper meets the requirements of
ANSI/NISO Z39.48-1992 (Permanence of Paper).

Table of Contents

Watchworks

Author's Note

THIS STORY was written for the first Gothika anthology. The theme for the anthology was "Frankenstein," but I found the idea of hacking up bodies too grisly. Instead, I let my fascination with Victorian automata—robotic dolls and figurines—take flight. I wanted to see just how far I could go with the technology available at the time. Plastics, batteries, and electronics were still much too crude for realistic animatronics, but with a bit of imagination, I think the story seems plausible.

London, 1900

HARLAND WALLACE stood at his second-floor bedroom window, watching as the coach pulled up in front of his Chelsea townhouse. The coachman jumped down to extend the footstep and open the door. The gentleman who stepped down was well turned-out and appeared young, though he moved with a certain stiffness, as though he suffered the effects of an accident or a childhood illness. He walked with the aid of a cane.

Harland waited until the man had been admitted to the house and Harland's butler came upstairs to present his card. *Mr. Luke Prescott.*

The visitor had been shown to the sitting room, though he was still standing when Harland entered. He was indeed young, perhaps in his twenties, and extremely handsome—one might even say "beautiful." He was very pale, with delicate features and a mouth as curved and sensual as a woman's. His hair was flaxen blond, short and combed back from a high forehead, and the eyes he turned upon Harland were wide and a startlingly vivid sky blue.

"Mr. Wallace," he said, smiling faintly and transferring his silk hat to the crook of his left arm, his left hand being occupied with the handle of his cane. He extended his gloved right hand and Harland moved to take it quickly, to avoid forcing the man to come to him. "I'm Mr. Luke Prescott."

"Mr. Harland Wallace."

"Please forgive the cane," the man said. "My balance is poor."

"Not at all. Shall we sit down?"

"Thank you, but I shan't take much of your time." There was something odd about the man's face. As strikingly beautiful as it was—Harland was troubled by how mesmerized he was by the man's features—his brief smile failed to move the rest of his face. No small crinkles about the eyes, no expansion of the cheeks. It was disturbingly still. "I am here on behalf of my employer, Dr. Mordecai Steward. He wishes to see you on an urgent matter, but I'm afraid he is unable to leave his house. He was hoping you might be persuaded to stop by."

"Might I ask what this is pertaining to?"

"I'm afraid I've been instructed to direct all questions to my employer."

"I am puzzled as to why the doctor should seek me out," Harland said. He gestured at a display case in one corner of the room. It contained some of the more elaborate watches he'd designed, along with others he'd collected over the years, including some particularly beautiful pieces he'd found during his travels in Germany and Switzerland. "He is aware that I am a watchmaker?"

"Indeed. Dr. Steward spent a considerable amount of time inquiring about skilled members of your profession in Great Britain and the Continent before deciding to approach you. He is looking forward to making your acquaintance."

Harland was flattered that Dr. Steward seemed to hold him in such high regard, but it also gave him pause. What could be so precious to the doctor that he would conduct such an exhaustive search? A family heirloom in need of repair, perhaps? Even that would hardly be deemed urgent. "I hope Dr. Steward finds me up to his expectations."

"I'm sure he will." Prescott withdrew another card from his waistcoat and extended it to Harland. "I've written our address on the back of his card. It's not far from here."

Harland took the card. The front was simple and elegant, with Dr. Steward's name embossed in a clean, legible typeface. Harland turned it over and saw the handwritten address of a townhouse in South Kensington. "Very well, Mr. Prescott. I'm intrigued. Will tomorrow morning be convenient?"

Prescott nodded and gave him that odd smile. "Quite. We look forward to seeing you, Mr. Wallace."

He took his leave, and Harland fretted for a few minutes about whether he should offer assistance. But though he relied upon the cane and walked stiffly, Prescott seemed able to navigate the hall and the front steps well enough. The coachman helped him up into the coach, and they drove away.

THE TOWNHOUSE of Dr. Steward was located in a block of nearly identical white-brick townhouses in a quiet neighborhood. Harland stepped down from the cab and paid the driver. The front door opened almost as soon as he'd knocked and a rather severe looking butler admitted him.

"Good morning," Harland said, "I believe Dr. Steward is expecting me. I'm Mr. Wallace."

"Yes, sir. Right this way, please."

The butler took Harland's coat and hat. Then he led the way to a side door and opened it, addressing someone inside the room. "Mr. Wallace has arrived, sir."

"Show him in, please, Bradley."

The parlor was dark, with walnut wainscoting and crimson wallpaper with a patterned silk trim, and a carpet of red and green. The chairs were of the same color scheme—dark walnut wood, upholstered in crimson. Though it was still light outside, the heavy curtains had been drawn and the gas lamps lit. A blazing fire made it extremely warm in the room, no doubt for the comfort of the gentleman seated near it, whose legs were covered in a knit shawl despite the fire.

Dr. Steward was quite elderly, his body seeming shrunken and withered with age. At one time, he might have been an imposing figure. He had a high forehead, now largely devoid of hair, and a strong patrician nose. The gray eyes that regarded Harland seemed to be sizing him up with a keen intelligence.

Mr. Prescott was standing beside Steward's chair and said with a nod in his direction, "Mr. Wallace, permit me to introduce my employer, Dr. Mordecai Steward."

"I'm honored to meet you, Doctor."

"Mr. Wallace." The doctor made a slight gesture toward Prescott. "You may leave us, Luke. Please wait outside until I call for you."

An odd thing occurred when Prescott attempted to leave the room. The butler was still standing in the doorway, as if awaiting further instruction, and when Prescott approached, Bradley continued to look past him, as if he wasn't there. He made no move to step aside, and Prescott was forced to turn sideways and slide past to go out into the hall.

The doctor frowned slightly at this but merely told the butler, "Bradley, will you please bring tea for our guest."

"Of course, sir."

The butler left, closing the door behind him.

"Please have a seat, Mr. Wallace. You may take one of the chairs away from the fire, if you wish. I realize not everyone enjoys roasting as much as I do these days."

Harland took a chair and the doctor asked him, "So, what do you think of Mr. Prescott?"

Harland was so taken aback that he merely blinked at the man for a moment. "I'm sorry?"

"Forgive me for being blunt," the doctor said, "but I dislike idle chitchat. I sent Luke to you so that you might observe him and see his condition."

"Observe… his condition?" Harland had to force himself not to fidget with the hem of his waistcoat. "I'm sorry, Dr. Steward, but perhaps there's been some sort of mistake. I'm not a doctor. I have no idea how to evaluate Mr. Prescott's medical state."

"I don't expect you to know anything about medicine, Mr. Wallace. I mean, how does he *appear* to you? Does he seem like a normal man?"

"I'm afraid I don't know how to answer that question."

Fortunately, they were interrupted by the return of the butler and a chambermaid with their tea. But it was a short diversion. After Bradley had poured for each of them, and then departed, Dr. Steward said, "When I was very young, my father took me to see a friend who had assembled a fascinating collection of automata—toys that moved under their own power. There were animals and people, some very elaborate. I absolutely fell in love with them."

"I felt the same way, the first time I saw a very elaborate German clock," Harland volunteered.

Dr. Steward nodded. "Quite. But you see, I was disappointed by their imperfections. They moved so stiffly. So I began to design my own. I made it my life's work, in fact, along with medicine."

"That's fascinating," Harland said, though he didn't really think so. But he felt one must indulge the elderly in their ramblings.

"My early experiments were crude, of course, but I soon surpassed the toys I'd been so taken with. As a schoolboy, I built a small dog that appeared quite lifelike. It ran about the house, navigating by means of lenses in the eyes, focused upon selenium wafers—are you familiar with the work of Charles Fitts, Mr. Wallace?"

"I'm afraid not."

"Well, I shan't bore you with all of the details of my experiments and inventions over the years. They made it necessary for me to acquire a considerable amount of knowledge in a wide variety of studies—electricity, hydraulics, pneumatics, physics, and of course mathematics.…"

"Of course."

Dr. Steward leaned forward and with excruciating slowness lifted his teacup to his lips. His hand shook so much that Harland worried he might spill the hot liquid in his lap. But he managed to take a sip and lower the cup back onto its saucer without mishap. "All of this leads to my purpose in bringing you here."

"I had assumed," Harland said, "that you had a watch in need of repair. But now I suspect it may have something to do with one of your inventions."

"Quite so. As you've no doubt observed, my hands are no longer as steady as they were. My last attempt at repair work was a dismal failure. I merely damaged the mechanism further in my fumblings. So I began this lengthy search to find someone skilled in working with minute mechanical parts—a man at the top of his profession, and with an honest and discreet reputation. For reasons which will become clear to you, I do not wish this… invention… to be gossiped about. You must give me your word, Mr. Wallace, that you will discuss it with no one."

Harland felt very uneasy making such a promise when had no idea what he was promising to keep secret. What could possibly warrant such a pledge? A toy dog? Some other innovative automaton? Was Dr. Steward afraid someone would lay claim to his invention? But surely he would have patented anything he felt it necessary to protect.

Still, Harland's curiosity was piqued. He could hardly leave after all this buildup without seeing the invention. "I give you my word, Dr. Steward."

"Excellent!" The doctor picked up a small handbell from the stand beside his chair and rang it. The door opened and Prescott entered. "Luke, would you be so good as to show Mr. Wallace your left hand?"

"Of course, sir."

Harland felt immensely uncomfortable as Prescott stepped toward him, removing his glove at the same time. If the man was injured or possessed some deformity, there would be little reason for Harland to look at it. He was generally squeamish about such things. It took all his willpower to keep his outward appearance calm as the hand was brought close for his inspection.

What he saw was more horrifying than he could have imagined. Underneath torn flesh, there lay not muscle and ligament, but what appeared to be metal rods. When the ring finger flexed slightly, one of the rods seemed to contract, and Harland realized it was actually sliding into a slightly larger metal tube, while behind it, a complex assortment of incredibly tiny, interlocking brass gears whirled about for a moment. But there was clearly something wrong, for an ugly clicking sound came from the mechanism, faint enough to have been muffled by the glove, and the gears rocked as if jolted. The finger stopped flexing, as if it were unable to move any farther.

Speechless, Harland lifted his gaze to Prescott's face. It must have been the cold chill of fear creeping into his brain that distorted his vision, for as his eyes beheld the man's face, Harland imagined he saw the cold, inhuman mask of a life-size doll—porcelain or painted wax—just before he fainted.

HARLAND AWOKE to find himself lying on a sofa in a different drawing room than the one he'd had his conversation with Dr. Steward in, but there was little doubt it was in the same house. The Morris-style wallpaper wasn't identical, but it was very similar. And the color scheme was still crimson and dark walnut. Again the curtains were drawn and the gas lamps were lit, but the fireplace was cold.

There was a damp cloth folded neatly upon his forehead, and Harland lifted a hand to remove it before tentatively sitting up.

"Mr. Wallace?" a voice said—that of Mr. Prescott. Harland was reluctant to look in the direction of the voice, in case the… hallucination… he'd had might turn out to be real after all. But he forced himself to turn his head.

Prescott sat as far away from him as the room permitted, in a chair by the door. He was sitting rather stiffly, his gloved hands in his lap. His face… well, from this distance, in the dim light of the gas lamps, his face appeared normal again. Quite handsome, in fact.

"Bradley and Dr. Steward's valet carried you in here," he said. "The doctor felt that you would be better off in a cooler room. I would not have felt it wise for me to… be the first thing you set eyes on when you woke. But Dr. Steward ordered me to come check on you."

Harland attempted to laugh it off. "That's quite all right. I don't know what came over me."

"One of the maids was tending you until I entered. I'm afraid none of the staff will remain alone in a room with me."

Harland had been about to place the cloth in the small bowl of water he saw on the table near the sofa, but this made him hesitate, the cloth momentarily forgotten. Truth be told, *he* would prefer not to be alone with Mr. Prescott. But he told himself he was being cruel. What he'd seen a short time earlier…. Dr. Steward's invention was no more than a mechanical hand, similar to those sometimes worn by men who'd suffered amputations in battle or other circumstances. Far more sophisticated than any Harland had ever seen, of course. But for people to avoid Prescott's presence due to his affliction was terribly unfair, and Harland was ashamed of himself for fainting. "Please forgive me," he said awkwardly. "It was… very warm in the drawing room. I feel like a complete fool."

Prescott regarded him silently for a long time. Then he stood, slowly and stiffly, leaning heavily upon his cane. "I shall tell Dr. Steward you've recovered. Alas, his health requires that he be kept warm…."

"I understand," Harland said. "Please permit me to join you. I feel fully recovered."

He followed Prescott across the hall to the doctor's drawing room. Once again, he felt the oppressive warmth of the fire as they entered, but he was certain he could endure it. The fire hadn't been the cause of his distress.

"Ah, Mr. Wallace!" the doctor said happily upon his return. "How are you feeling?"

"Quite well, thank you. Though frightfully embarrassed."

"Not at all."

Harland attempted to put on a professional demeanor, clapping his hands together, as if he couldn't wait to begin. "Now, then. Am I correct in assuming you'd like to engage my services in repairing Mr. Prescott's damaged hand?"

"That and more," Dr. Steward replied. "But perhaps we've all had enough excitement for the present. Might I suggest we go into the details tomorrow morning?"

Harland wanted to protest that he was completely recovered, but then it occurred to him that his host might be tiring. "Certainly, Doctor. Tomorrow would be fine."

He took his leave and, Bradley being oddly absent, Prescott escorted him to the door. The man was unable to assist Harland with his coat, but it wasn't difficult for Harland to manage on his own. As he retrieved his hat, Prescott surprised him by putting a gloved hand on his arm. Almost immediately, he withdrew it, as if realizing Harland might be bothered by the touch. Harland smiled at him in an attempt to undo some of the embarrassment he must have caused by his reaction earlier.

"Please come back, Mr. Wallace," Prescott said earnestly. "I beg you. The... situation is becoming more urgent every day."

Though his handsome face was still oddly impassive, he sounded distressed, and his startling blue eyes were pleading. Harland could not help but be moved. He told himself that what he felt was merely compassion. If the doctor had created a functional prosthesis to replace the hand Prescott lost, it would be agony to watch it fall into disrepair as its creator grew too decrepit to maintain it. What Christian man could turn his back on someone in this predicament if he had the power to help?

But too, Harland was disturbed by a resurgence of the old stirrings he'd felt in his youth—feelings he'd hoped he'd left behind in boys' school. As much as Prescott disturbed him, he also intrigued him in a way that was perhaps better left unexplored. It was, at best, inappropriate to dwell upon the sensual curve of another man's mouth. Harland forced the thought from his mind.

He smiled and gave Prescott a cheerful nod. "Rest assured, Mr. Prescott. With some guidance from the good doctor, I'm confident I can make the repairs. I will return tomorrow with the necessary tools for the job."

HARLAND DID return the next morning, his leather tool case in hand. If anything, Bradley seemed even more dour than he'd been the day before as he led the way into the same drawing room, where Dr. Stewart and Mr. Prescott were conferring about some matter. But Harland quickly forgot about the servant as the doctor greeted him.

"Mr. Wallace! You've returned!"

Harland nodded, holding his tool case in his gloved hands. "As promised, Doctor."

"Excellent. Please have a seat. Shall I ring for tea?" The butler had departed without a word.

Harland settled into a chair but shook his head. "Please don't trouble yourself on my behalf," he said. "I'm most anxious to learn more about the mechanism in Mr. Prescott's prosthesis."

Steward and Prescott exchanged a look that Harland couldn't interpret, but then the doctor smiled and said, "Luke, would you please open the curtains so Mr. Wallace can have better light?"

While Prescott was attending to that, Harland made a gesture as if to lay his tools upon the inlaid top of the coffee table. "May I?"

"Of course."

The leather of the case, when opened like a book, provided protection for the table so that none of the metal files or calipers would scratch it. Harland withdrew a monocle from its protective silk cloth and placed it in his right eye. "Would you mind sitting here, Mr. Prescott?" he said, waving a hand at the chair beside him, which would allow for the easiest access and the best light.

Prescott perched on the edge of chair, looking very stiff and formal. He removed the glove from his left hand and extended it.

For the first time, Harland took the hand in his own without gloves. The "skin" on the hand was disturbingly cool to the touch and felt a bit too much like human skin for his comfort. The effect was that the hand felt lifeless. When he turned it over to examine the palm, he saw that, although the major lines of the hand were present, giving it the appearance of a human hand at a glance, the tips of the fingers had strangely regular "fingerprints." They were formed of small concentric ridges, similar to the fingerprints on Harland's hand, but with no variation from finger to finger.

"Unfortunately," Steward said, "there have been some areas in which I simply had to rely upon the expertise of others. The skin was one such area. It was designed for me many years ago by a dear friend who worked with chemicals, Parkesine, and rubber. It consists of layers of silk, in different weaves, each saturated in some sort of artificial resin."

"It's very soft for a resin," Harland commented, prodding the palm of the hand with his fingers. Even Parkesine, he knew, was rather hard. This material flexed and bounced back into shape, just as a flesh-and-blood hand would do, and his poking caused the fingers to flex in a disturbingly realistic fashion.

"I'm afraid I don't know the formula, and my friend is no longer with us."

"Can it be repaired?"

The doctor shook his head. "Alas, no. It will have to be stitched together. I do have a small supply of it in my workroom, but we must be very conservative with it."

Harland glanced up to find Prescott watching him intently. Once again, he was struck by the perfection in the man's features, as if he were a life-size china doll, and part of Harland wondered if it were possible that Prescott's face could be made of the same material as his hand. Fortunately, the thought did not produce the same embarrassing reaction it had the previous day, and Harland quickly put it out of his mind. He was being fanciful. Prescott merely had very attractive features, and it would not benefit anyone for Harland to dwell on them.

He turned the hand over again and peered closely at the mechanism underneath the skin.

"YOU HAVE exceeded my expectations, sir!" Steward exclaimed, obviously delighted, as Prescott flexed the mechanical hand, testing the range of motion of each finger.

It had been an exhausting couple of hours. The mechanism had proven to be ingenious and quite the most complex thing Harland had ever worked with. Though the doctor had offered guidance, much of it had been a journey of exploration, delving into the intricacies of the gears and springs and tiny pneumatics. It had been indescribably beautiful. Harland was awed by Steward's genius. But his brain felt like a bread pudding—complete with brandy butter—and he wanted little at the moment but to sleep. "Thank you, Doctor. I feel honored to have had the opportunity."

Prescott looked at him with a small, almost shy smile, his eyes lit up with delight. "Oh, Mr. Wallace…!" He seemed at a loss for words, but the childlike joy in his expression forced Harland to look away or risk blushing.

"A job well done," Steward said. "But it is my hope, Mr. Wallace, that you will continue to assist us."

"Certainly. If the prosthesis breaks again—"

Steward waved a hand dismissively. "You misunderstand me. Your services in the continued maintenance of Luke's hand would be much appreciated. But surely you've noticed that he has difficulty walking?"

Harland glanced at Prescott, uncomfortable discussing his difficulties so openly in front of the man. "Forgive me, Mr. Prescott. I merely assumed an injury...."

"I'm afraid... both of my legs are mechanical, Mr. Wallace." He sounded apologetic, as if he were sorry to embarrass Harland with these intimate details. It disturbed Harland that he found this endearing.

"Oh." Harland looked away and busied himself packing up his tools. "Of course, I would be happy to help in any way that I can...."

"Perhaps later in the week?" the doctor persisted.

Harland did have a business to attend to. He couldn't spend all his time here, as fascinating as it was to poke into the doctor's inventions— and as much as part of him continued to be drawn to Prescott. But he did have time later in the week. "Would Friday morning be suitable?"

"That would do nicely," Steward replied happily.

Once more, Prescott escorted him to the door. And again, he stopped him with a hand on his forearm. This time, he appeared to be less afraid of rebuke, for he left it there a moment longer and pulled it away without hurry. "The doctor doesn't always think of these things.... His profession, of course. But I'm concerned that... in order for you to work on my hip.... Well, you understand...."

He gave Harland a pleading look, and then Harland *did* understand. In order for him to work on Prescott's hip, Prescott would have to remove his trousers. Depending upon where the damage was, things might get quite intimate. The thought made Harland blush a bit, and he desperately hoped it wasn't visible in the dim light of the hall.

"Of course, Mr. Prescott," he said. "It can't be helped. But we're all professionals." At least, he and the doctor were. And despite the fact that Harland had no medical expertise, Prescott was, in an odd sense, still his patient.

Prescott looked as though he had more to add, but after struggling with it for a bit, he merely smiled gratefully. "Thank you for understanding, Mr. Wallace. I look forward to seeing you."

FRIDAY WAS a miserable day, gray and raining. If Harland hadn't already given his word, he never would have gone visiting in this weather. Even traveling by coach, he arrived wet, dripping water from his coat and hat in Dr. Steward's entryway. Bradley seemed even more disapproving than usual as he took Harland's wet things.

"I'm sorry to say that Dr. Steward is under the weather this morning," the butler said.

"Should I come back another day, then?"

"The doctor has asked that you be taken to the workroom, so you may attend to your work there." Harland noticed that neither Prescott nor the nature of Harland's work were mentioned. Was the butler uninformed? Or was this another manifestation of the aversion the staff appeared to have toward Prescott?

Harland followed Bradley down the hall to a room he hadn't seen before. The butler opened the door and stepped back into the hall, telling him, "Here you are, sir. I shall send the maid with tea shortly. If you require anything else, please ring."

And then he left, as if he wished to be away from the room as quickly as possible. Harland entered to find Prescott sitting as he always did, perched on the edge of his chair in an almost feminine posture, his hands in his lap. He was without a coat today, though he wore a paisley waistcoat in hunter green over his shirt, and he had dispensed with his gloves. The injured "skin" on his left hand had still, to Harland's knowledge, not been repaired, but it was now discreetly covered by a bandage.

"Good morning, Mr. Prescott," Harland said, closing the door behind him. He noted that the room had a table off to one side, large enough to accommodate a man lying down. It was upholstered in leather, with a padded headrest and a ridge at the other end. Above the table, four Welsbach mantle lamps adorned the wall, hopefully providing enough light for Harland to work by. Beside the table was a workbench with various tools, and vise grips to hold components steady.

Prescott stood and came forward to greet him, walking with the aid of his cane. "Mr. Wallace. I apologize that the doctor cannot join us this morning. It was his hope that what you learned on Wednesday might enable you to work without his assistance."

"I shall do my best." He extended his hand to Prescott and was surprised at the feel of the man's right hand. It seemed cool, not unlike the artificial left hand. But Harland released it after their handshake and suppressed the impulse to examine it more closely. "Before we begin"—and before they were both subjected to what promised to be a very awkward and distracting situation—"perhaps you could describe the injury to me."

"It occurred when I fell on the front steps last December," Prescott said. "There was no visible damage, but clearly something is damaged inside the mechanism."

"Very well." Harland fished around for something else to forestall the inevitable—something he realized he was dreading, not merely for the embarrassment it might cause him and Prescott, but for the stirrings in his groin that grew stronger every time he thought of Prescott disrobing. Of course, the man might be... damaged. That seemed likely, in fact. The injury that cost Prescott two legs—and a hand—must have been quite horrid. The transitions between flesh and prosthetics might not be pleasant to look upon. Harland would have to be very careful how he reacted, in order to spare Prescott further embarrassment.

They were distracted by a soft knock on the door and a woman's voice saying, "Your tea, sir."

Harland bade her come in, but there was no response. Puzzled, he went to the door and opened it to discover that a tray containing a teapot and a single cup and saucer—clearly Prescott had not been taken into account—and a small plate of cucumber sandwiches had been left on the hall carpet. "What the deuce...?"

"I'm truly sorry," Prescott said as Harland carried the tray inside and set it upon a marble side table. "The staff will not enter a room with me in it unless the doctor is present."

Harland was appalled that the mild-mannered Prescott had to endure such indignities in his own household. Certainly he had no intention of drinking tea while Prescott went without. He returned to the door and closed it. The key was in the lock, so he turned it. "Perhaps we should simply get down to business."

"Of course."

Harland felt like a lecher, watching Prescott undo the buttons of his trousers and drop them. He clearly had difficulty bending at the knees, so Harland felt compelled to remove his shoes for him and help him step out of the trousers, rather than force Prescott to struggle with them. That left him in his socks and drawers from the waist down. There was little reason to remove his socks, but his cotton drawers extended down to his ankles and clearly would be in the way. Prescott unbuttoned them and let them fall.

His shirt and waistcoat hung low enough to cover his manhood, but Harland was nonetheless embarrassed to be crouching in front of him, helping Prescott step out of the undergarment. It was incredibly clean, as if it had only recently been removed from the laundry. Though it was vulgar to even think about, it did seem odd to him that there were no stains or discolorations on the fabric.

When he stood, Prescott was watching him with his characteristic impassive expression, but the corners of his mouth quirked up in a shy smile.

"Do you…. Will you need assistance getting up on the table?" Harland asked.

"No. The doctor would never have been able to lift me onto it—not in recent years. The table tilts."

And so it did. Harland found a lever that caused the end with the ridge to drop nearly to floor level. This enabled Prescott to step onto the ridge and lean back against the table. He handed Harland his cane. When Harland tilted the table back into a horizontal position, his "patient" was lying full-length upon it. "Clever," he said with a smile.

Then he noticed the seams, and his smile faltered. As with his hand, Prescott's leg prostheses were extremely lifelike. At a casual glance, they appeared no different than living human legs, albeit completely devoid of leg hair. However, there were several barely detectable seams in the artificial skin. It made sense, of course. It would have been impossible to effect repairs if the skin was one single sheath covering the entire leg. But it was unsettling, all the same. Harland would have to peel the skin away in order to get at the underlying mechanisms, and the thought made him squeamish.

"Where do you think the problem is located?" he asked.

"My right hip."

"Roll over onto your left side, please," Harland told Prescott. "Facing me."

The man did as Harland asked, and of course it was impossible for his… anatomy… to remain in place when he did so. It wasn't unusually large, but it still flopped obscenely against the back of Harland's hand where it rested at the edge of the table, causing him to jerk back involuntarily.

"I'm sorry," Prescott said, adjusting his shirt to cover himself.

"That's quite all right. I was… startled."

There was nothing Harland could do about the fact that he would have to touch Prescott's hip, however. He placed his hand on it and was surprised to find it warm. For a moment, he wondered if he were touching actual flesh—Prescott's body had to begin somewhere—but no. There was a seam just an inch above where his hand lay. Unable to stop himself, Harland slid his hand downward over the hip and onto the leg. He noticed that it grew cooler as he descended. He slid his hand back to the seam and traced it with a finger, until he encountered hair toward the front of Prescott's body—pubic hair. With a start, Harland yanked his hand away again.

"The seam follows my inguinal ligament," Prescott said.

"Your what?"

"That's what the doctor calls it. The crease between my stomach and my pelvis."

"Ah. Yes. I see that." What was disturbing Harland more than the touch of pubic hair was the involuntary swelling it had caused in his own trousers. He'd never thought of himself as… that type of man. It was true that he'd avoided women, preferring to live as a bachelor. But that didn't necessarily make him a mandrake, did it?

He had no choice but to return to his examination of the seam and hope he could prevent himself from becoming fully aroused. It would be impossible to hide that in the trousers he was wearing. But it wasn't going to be easy. As he followed the seam around to the back, he saw that it cut down alongside Prescott's buttocks and under them, following the crease there. Part of him was tempted to ask Prescott what the doctor's name for *that* crease was, but he thought better of it. The mere thought of being that close to Prescott's arse was making it difficult for him to breathe, and he felt his groin stiffening further.

"What's the best way to open the seam without damaging it?" he asked, attempting to focus on his task. His voice sounded ragged with arousal to his ears, and he prayed that Prescott didn't notice.

"It can be rolled down."

He did so, wincing when a slight tug with his fingers popped the seam open, exposing a dark gray substance underneath. Prescott apparently felt nothing, because he lay calmly on the table, his head resting on the headrest. He would be unable to see much in that position, but his blue eyes watched Harland with interest, as if gauging his ability to do the job.

Harland continued to roll the artificial skin down over the thigh, accidentally brushing his fingers against Prescott's scrotum in the process. A faint intake of breath made it apparent that Prescott had noticed, but both men pretended nothing had happened. When the skin was down to Prescott's knee, Harland realized that the gray material underneath was some kind of rubber, molded into pieces that resembled muscles. They were easily removed, and the gears and hydraulics they'd been protecting were indeed very similar to those in Prescott's hand. Harland felt reassured.

He also felt relieved that he could concentrate on something other than those tantalizing brushes against Prescott's anatomy.

It took longer without the doctor's guidance, but after what must have been hours of experimenting—asking Prescott to flex his leg and knee and foot, while observing the behavior of the mechanisms—Harland was finally able to determine what the primary cause of the problem was. One of the hydraulic pistons had a bent rod. Nothing more. Yet this had nearly crippled poor Prescott for months.

When he was certain he wouldn't be causing irreparable damage, Harland removed the piston and asked Prescott, "Are there replacement parts available?"

"I believe so," Prescott replied, "but I'm not certain where the doctor keeps them."

Waking Dr. Steward was probably out for the moment, so Harland set about repairing the piston, if he could. He anchored it in one of the vise grips and, using a pair of pliers, managed to bend the rod until it was straight again and slid in and out of its cylinder smoothly. Then he replaced it, put all the rubber padding back in place, and unrolled the artificial skin to cover everything up again. As he smoothed out the seam, he couldn't help but notice that Prescott's member was swelling as much as his own.

He finished quickly and turned away, embarrassment causing his neck and cheeks to flush. "Why don't we see if that does it? I'll help you down."

He didn't need to tilt the table again. Prescott sat up and scooted forward until he dropped off onto his feet. Then the man took a brief walk around the room, still naked from the waist down. It was somewhat improper, but since he would simply have to remove the trousers again and climb back onto the table if something was still malfunctioning, there was little sense putting them back on for the moment. His shirt hung low enough to cover him, but there was some obvious tenting in the front. Harland's manhood was likewise misbehaving, and Prescott had to have been aware of it. But they both pretended not to notice.

The leg repair appeared to be a complete success. Prescott walked a bit stiffly, but he assured Harland that he'd always walked that way, even when his legs had been at their peak performance. He positively beamed at the Harland as he moved around the room. "Thank you, Mr. Wallace!" he exclaimed. "You have no idea."

Harland found his childlike giddiness endearing, but when Prescott executed a small jump and caused his shirttails to flap up and reveal more than was proper, Harland hurriedly retrieved the man's trousers and undergarments.

"Let me help you dress," he said, wishing for a glass of water. His mouth had suddenly gone dry.

Prescott needed little help with his clothes. He perched on the edge of one of the chairs in order to slip his underwear over his stocking feet and pull them up past his knees. Then he did the same with his trousers. Inching them up his thighs and over his buttocks—one garment at a time—by rocking back and forth was a more arduous process, and Harland felt he was witnessing something private that he really shouldn't be watching. But Prescott seemed unselfconscious. When he had his trousers up at last, he stood and accepted Harland's assistance fastening his suspenders. He smiled at Harland, looking at him intently with eyes full of emotion. "Mr. Wallace… may I count on you, in the future?"

Harland shook his hand and smiled back at him, meeting Prescott's eyes as long as he dared. "You may, Mr. Prescott."

"Thank you."

Harland was exhausted, so he took his leave. Out in the hall, he encountered the butler, to his annoyance. His few encounters with Bradley had given him a dislike of the manservant. He allowed Bradley to retrieve his hat and coat, however, and responded politely to Bradley's inquiry into whether he'd had a pleasant afternoon. To his surprise, the butler said, "It's come to my attention, sir, that the maid who brought you tea left it on the carpet outside the door."

Harland felt uncomfortable responding, but really he had little reason to cover for the woman. Her behavior had been appalling. "I'm afraid that's correct."

"I do apologize, sir. She has been reprimanded."

"I see," Harland said noncommittally.

"Unfortunately, some of the staff have a rather irrational fear of the… invention."

Harland took his hat from Bradley and hesitated a moment. He knew he had no right to discipline another man's household staff, but he was unable to stop himself from saying, "The *invention*, Bradley? Are you referring to the prosthetics Dr. Steward constructed for Mr. Prescott?"

"Somewhat, sir…." Bradley appeared to be holding something back.

"Mr. Prescott is to be pitied for his infirmity, Bradley—not feared."

"'Mr. Prescott,' sir?" Bradley blinked at him, as if he couldn't comprehend. "I was led to believe that sir examined it."

"*It*?" Harland was extremely close to losing his temper.

"Forgive me, sir," Bradley said. "But surely sir has noticed that this 'Mr. Prescott' is a machine?"

"Mr. Prescott has prostheses, Bradley, but it's absurd to call him a 'machine'! He is still quite human."

"Ah. I believe I see where the miscommunication lies. I'm afraid, sir, that no part of the… I believe Dr. Steward prefers to call it an 'automaton'… is human."

IT WAS impossible. Harland had been attempting to dismiss Bradley's ridiculous statement on the coach ride from South Kensington to Chelsea. But every time he'd convinced himself that it was nonsense, odd things came to mind—the fact that Harland had been unable to discern the difference between the artificial "skin" below the seam at Prescott's hip and the supposedly real skin above it, the disturbing appearance of Prescott's face, as if it were a mask….

Prescott's face wasn't completely immobile, of course. It moved around the mouth and eyes. The man's eyebrows were part of what made his eyes so expressive. And Harland had spent little time examining the skin on Prescott's hip, buttocks, and groin, because he'd found it too arousing to do so.

That brought up other things Harland found disturbing. He disliked thinking of himself as a mandrake. The very word disgusted him. But even the memory of trailing his fingers through the hair at Prescott's groin was causing a stirring in his loins. Then again, wasn't Prescott's obvious reaction to Harland's touch proof that he was a man? Never mind what it might say about his inclinations. Surely a machine could not….

And even if it were possible for a machine to appear human on the surface, how could it talk and appear to think, as Prescott did? The very idea was absurd!

It was all making Harland feel ill. At dinner that evening, he found himself without an appetite and ate so little that he had to feign a stomach ailment to avoid insulting the cook. It wasn't far from the truth. He retired early—with a glass of hot barley water the cook foisted upon him— hoping sleep would soothe his troubled mind, but it eluded him. The image and feel of Prescott's smooth, sensuous buttocks plagued him, until he was finally forced to take himself in hand. Afterward, he was disgusted—both by the thought of reacting this passionately to another man, and by the possibility that he was reacting not just to a man, but to a *simulacrum* of a man.

Spent, Harland was able to at last drift off to sleep, but his rest was disturbed by confused nightmares, none of which he could remember the next morning. He desperately wanted to question Dr. Steward. Had the man deceived him about Prescott's… nature? Or had Bradley been passing along a bit of malicious gossip? Thinking back over the conversations he'd had with the doctor, Harland was unable to recall him ever referring to Prescott as a "man." But of course one would assume that to be the case.

He waited as long as he could stand it before sending a messenger to the doctor's house, inquiring if he was recovered enough to receive visitors. The reply was no, but the doctor would inform him when he was. There was little Harland could do but wait. He could hardly discuss the matter with Mr. Prescott.

It was three days before he received a message inviting him to South Kensington. Little had changed in that time. Harland was still eating little, and his staff had begun to nag him about seeing a doctor— something that amused him, even in his distracted state of mind. He'd also been tormented by thoughts of Prescott and visions of him naked and aroused, causing Harland to masturbate more often than he'd done since he was an adolescent. He hadn't had a strict upbringing, so he felt less disgust about the physical deed than others might have, perhaps. But his thoughts during it were repugnant to him once he was spent.

He wasn't certain if learning the truth about Prescott would lessen or increase his distress.

He sent a message to the doctor, specifying a time of arrival—after luncheon, of course, and well before afternoon tea—and requesting that Mr. Prescott not be present. He felt a twinge of guilt, as if he were betraying the man after they'd had a rather pleasant day together, but then, that was the issue. When he arrived and Bradley had shown him in, Harland was pleased to find the doctor had complied with his wishes. Prescott was absent.

"Your work on Friday was excellent, Mr. Wallace," Steward said congenially. He appeared even more frail than during their last conversation, and Harland hoped he wasn't taxing the man unduly. But his questions could not wait.

"Thank you, sir."

"The leg seems to be working perfectly. Luke was most pleased. Which reminds me—I've made certain he now knows where all the components I have on hand are located. It never occurred to me that he wouldn't know, after all these years. But I suppose he was used to waiting while I fetched them…."

Harland listened patiently while the old man rambled on. But as he was uncertain about his continued involvement in Prescott's… upkeep… he wasn't convinced any of this information mattered now. Eventually, when Steward seemed to be finished, Harland said, "I've come to ask you about Mr. Prescott."

"What about him?" the doctor asked. "Did he behave badly during your time with him?" It seemed an odd question to ask of an adult man. But then, Prescott appeared young enough to be Steward's son, or perhaps even his grandson.

"Not exactly. But you see… in order for me to adjust his leg, I had to peel down the artificial skin on it."

"Of course."

"There was a seam following the contours of his hip. I naturally assumed that this would separate the artificial skin from his real skin. Truthfully, I had expected to find straps of some sort…." He looked at the doctor hopefully, as if he might volunteer the information he was looking for, but Steward merely watched him curiously. "I don't wish to pry, but it seems like something I should know."

"What?"

Harland sighed. "How do Mr. Prescott's prostheses attach to his body, doctor?"

"I take it you didn't ask Luke to undress completely?"

"Of course not. It was hardly necessary for him to remove all his clothes to provide me with access to his hip and leg."

The doctor looked amused. "I suppose. But it would have answered your question."

"Perhaps, but it didn't seem appropriate at the time."

"Why don't I call Luke in here and have him undress for you?"

Good Lord! Harland felt himself turn scarlet. "No! Please. I see no reason to embarrass Mr. Prescott."

"I doubt Luke would be embarrassed. He's had to do that a great deal, as I've perfected his mechanisms over the years."

"I'm afraid *I* would be. Please remember that I am not a doctor."

Steward raised his eyebrows at him, as if he felt Harland was being unreasonable. "What you would have seen for yourself, had you asked him to undress, Mr. Wallace… is that Luke is flawless, apart from the seams you've observed."

"How is that possible?" Harland asked, a feeling of dread filling his chest and making it difficult to breathe. "The artificial skin is lifelike in appearance, but… it isn't *skin*. There must be places in which there are transitions from that to real skin…."

"No, Mr. Wallace, you've observed for yourself that the skin on both sides of the seams is the same."

Harland was on the verge of panic. He realized he'd made a mistake in coming here. He no longer wanted his suspicions confirmed. He wanted the doctor to tell him this was all a miscommunication, that Prescott was as human as either of them. "Surely it cannot cover his *entire* body…."

"It does."

Harland sat in silence for a very long time, and the doctor merely watched him without interrupting his swirling thoughts. At last, he asked, "Is there… any part of Mr. Prescott… that is flesh and blood, doctor?"

"No, Mr. Wallace," Steward replied calmly. "I tried to tell you this on your first visit, but there was all that fainting business. Luke is an automaton. The most sophisticated one ever built."

Harland felt like fainting again, but his stubborn brain wouldn't cooperate this time. It left him awake to deal with the horror of what he'd just been told. He stared blankly at the garish green-and-crimson carpet and said, "He isn't... alive...."

"Not in a strictly biological sense. But I maintain that biological life is not the essential aspect of a man. What makes a man is *consciousness*—awareness of his surroundings—and the ability to *think* and *feel*."

Harland looked up at him slowly. "How can a machine do any of those things?"

"I confess I'm uncertain whether Luke is truly conscious. He exhibits behavior that suggests it. But feelings.... Those came first in my experiments. Feelings are, at their simplest, extrapolations of the pleasure and pain felt by the body, abstracted and applied to models we hold in our minds. Luke can 'feel' through myriad minute sensors placed throughout his body. They sense pain, pressure, temperature, balance...." Harland had encountered small disks on the surface of the mechanisms in several locations. They appeared to correlate with metallic spots on the underside of the "skin," so he'd carefully worked around them. "I even gave him extra touch sensors in his sexual organs, to mimic the same functionality in the human body."

Harland must have looked shocked, because the doctor chuckled and shook his head. "No, Mr. Wallace, I have never used Luke in that manner. I did once pay a young woman to spend time with him—to test that particular functionality. He reported that it all seemed to work correctly, but I don't think he enjoyed it much. The woman's body was too alien to him. I believe he found her a bit repulsive."

Harland could no longer listen. His brain was screaming at him to get out of the house and run as far and as fast as he could to escape this madness. Fortunately, the doctor ended the conversation at that point.

"I'm very sorry," the old man said as he leaned forward stiffly to pick up the bell from the table and ring it twice. "I'm not currently up to long conversations. These few words have already tired me. Might we take up our discussion again in a day or two?"

As Bradley entered in response to the doctor's bell, Harland took his leave and slipped past the butler. He walked quickly to the door but stopped, his hand on the doorknob, when he heard Prescott say behind him, "Mr. Wallace? I wasn't aware you were visiting."

Harland stopped and turned around very slowly. Prescott was smiling and his eyes seemed lit up in delight. But Harland couldn't bring himself to say anything to him—to this artificial mockery of a man.

Something in his eyes must have given him away, because the light in Prescott's eyes faded and he glanced away.

"I see," he said.

Bradley had closed the door to the parlor and they were alone. Despite himself, Harland felt his heart aching in response to the sadness and loneliness that came over Prescott's features. Involuntarily, he walked nearer, until they were standing eye to eye in the front hall. Then he cleared his throat and said quietly, "Mr. Prescott. Forgive me... but I should like to touch your face a moment."

Prescott looked back at him, his eyes full of resignation. Silently, he nodded his assent.

Harland removed his glove and hesitantly lifted his hand until his fingers brushed against Prescott's cheek. As he had feared, it was cold. The work he'd done on Prescott's leg and hand had made him familiar with the feel of the synthetic "skin" covering those appendages, and that was what he felt now.

Prescott's entire face was synthetic.

Harland slowly withdrew his hand as a cold chill crawled up his spine and made the hair on the back of his neck feel as if it were standing on end. He could not avoid looking into Prescott's eyes, seeing the anxiety there.

"Please," Prescott said. But he fell silent after that, as if he had no idea what to say next.

Without a word, Harland spun about and left the townhouse.

SEVERAL DAYS went by, during which Harland attended to work he'd put aside for far too long while caught up in Dr. Steward's... project. During this time, he had horrifying dreams in which he saw Prescott standing in his bedroom, gazing out the window. He approached the man from behind and called his name, but there was no response. At last, he reached out to touch Prescott's shoulder, and the man turned. But when he did, Harland saw that his face was nothing but a mass of brass gears and copper wires.

Or worse, he would dream that Prescott was lying on his bed, apparently naked, though his body was covered in a linen sheet. These dreams were always disturbingly erotic in nature, and Harland felt his breath quicken as he approached the bed. Prescott smiled up at him with his perfect, china doll face and lifted the sheet to welcome him. But what lay under the sheet wasn't a beautiful male body. It was a hideous array of tubes and pistons, sparking and belching steam.

Harland frequently awoke screaming from these nightmares.

He could not get Prescott out of his mind. No matter how much he told himself the man was nothing more than a machine, it was impossible to think of him that way. He often found Prescott's beautiful face coming to mind when his thoughts were idle, or the perfection of his "body," of his… "manhood." Harland felt he must surely be ill. A healthy man would never have these thoughts about another man, let alone a mockery of a man made from metal, rubber, and resins. In daylight, when his will was at its strongest, he banished his daydreams and concentrated on his work or forced himself to read a book. But at night, lying in bed and waiting for sleep to take him, he was powerless to keep his mind from turning to fantasies that shamed him in the light of morning.

When two weeks had passed since he'd last visited Dr. Steward's residence, a message was delivered to Harland's townhouse. It read:

> *My Dear Mr. Wallace,*
> *I hope this letter finds you well. I have grown concerned that so much time has passed since our last meeting. I would very much like to invite you to discuss our business arrangement at your earliest convenience.*
> *Sincerely,*
> *Dr. Mordecai Steward*

Harland was tempted to go. It was absurd how much he longed to see Prescott again, even knowing what he did now. But his mind revolted at the thought. His fascination with Prescott had become a sick addiction. The best thing for him would be to stay away and never see that abomination again.

He sent a reply with the messenger, telling Dr. Steward that he was uncertain when he would be available. But of course, that would not resolve the problem, and he was unsurprised when another letter came from the doctor that afternoon, asking Harland to please contact him as soon as his schedule would permit a visit.

A week later, another message arrived, apologizing for the doctor's impatience, but reminding Harland that his health was failing. Harland again put him off with vague excuses about his schedule. He had to wonder just how long he would keep up this game. Until the doctor tired of inquiring? Until the man succumbed to his illness? It made Harland uncomfortable to think part of him was hoping for that eventuality. The decent thing to do would be to tell the doctor plainly that he would no longer work with Prescott. Yet when he sat down to write a letter to this effect, Harland stopped halfway through and tore it up.

The matter was decided for him two days later. Steward's message boy arrived panting, apparently having run most of the way. The letter he carried stated:

> *Dear Mr. Wallace,*
> *Please forgive me for pressing the matter, but the*
> *situation has become urgent. Luke has been injured, and*
> *I am simply not capable of handling the matter myself. I*
> *beg you to come at once.*
> *Most Sincerely,*
> *Dr. Mordecai Steward*

It was absurd that the words "Luke has been injured" should evoke such a strong feeling of fear in him—fear for Prescott—but he found himself telling the boy he would come at once.

WHEN HE arrived at Steward's residence and Bradley took his coat, Harland could not escape the feeling that the butler was disappointed in him for responding to the doctor's summons. There was nothing overt in his manner or the few words he spoke to Harland, but something in his eyes....

Harland found the doctor in his sitting room, as usual. The old man seemed to have grown smaller since the last time they'd met, and when he spoke, it was barely above a whisper. "Mr. Wallace, thank you so much for coming."

Harland was still uncertain exactly why he *had* come, but he smiled politely and said, "Of course, Dr. Steward. I was sorry to hear the situation has grown so dire."

"Forgive me," Steward said, "but I am not up to conversation. Luke is waiting in the workshop. He can inform you of the details."

"Of course, Doctor."

Bradley told Steward, "The nurse will be in shortly, sir." Then he escorted Harland to the workshop and left him there with little more than a curt bow. "Sir."

Harland entered, part of him afraid to see for himself how serious Prescott's injury was, and another part of him frightened by the prospect of seeing Prescott at all. But Prescott was sitting upon the workbench with his shirt off, looking as beautiful and perfect as he always had, and Harland felt the knot in the pit of his stomach unraveling itself. Then he mentally chastised himself. *Why should I be relieved that he doesn't appear seriously injured? He—it—is merely a machine!*

It was difficult to remember that when Prescott smiled at him and said, "Mr. Wallace! I'm delighted to see you again."

"Mr. Prescott. I understand...." He balked at saying "you," as if that would grant the automaton some measure of humanity that wasn't warranted, but it was simply impossible to avoid addressing Prescott directly. "...you've been injured."

Prescott didn't get off the table, which caused Harland to wonder if he'd done something to his leg again. But Prescott held out his left hand and said, "I grabbed a hot poker."

Harland closed the door behind him and approached, holding his bag of horological tools. He set the bag upon the table and took Prescott's hand in his, disturbed that the feel of Prescott's cool synthetic skin still quickened his pulse. But the sight of Prescott's palm made him cringe. It wasn't blistered, as one would expect of human skin, nor reddened, but the skin had melted on either side of a horrible, blackened tear. There was a soft, gray rubbery pad underneath, like the thicker pads Harland had seen under the skin on Prescott's leg. Thankfully, that wasn't damaged, beyond a shallow imprint from the poker, and likewise the mechanisms in the hand were undamaged. But the skin was beyond repair.

"I'm afraid, Mr. Prescott—"

"Please," Prescott interrupted. "I would like it if you called me Luke."

Harland regarded him thoughtfully. Then he said, "How is it you can 'like' anything? I've seen how your physical mechanisms work. They are works of genius and immensely complex. I would have thought them impossible a few months ago. Yet I can see how they work and understand them to some degree. But to give the appearance of thought...."

The smile on Prescott's face faltered, and he gently pulled his hand away from Harland's grasp. He said nothing as he placed the hand in his lap and shifted his gaze to the Oriental carpet.

"The automatons Dr. Steward spoke of the last time we conversed," Harland went on. "I've seen something similar. One used a cylinder like the one in a music box to guide its movements and give the appearance of autonomy. But that's all it was—appearance. Like a magician's trick. The automaton could not in actuality *think*. Yet you are so much more sophisticated than that. I still cannot fathom how you mimic human speech and actions so perfectly."

Prescott continued to stare at the carpet as he responded, "The doctor told me once that my brain was composed of several thousand thin sheets of silk, hand-painted with gold circuits and embedded with silicon wafers so small that it would take a watchmaker to sort them all out."

"I should like to see it," Harland said.

A look of what could only be fear passed across Prescott's face as he raised his eyes to Harland's. "It's all sealed together with resin. The layers cannot be peeled apart without destroying them."

The look in his eyes cut through Harland like a knife. He was forced to place a reassuring hand on Prescott's wrist. "I shall let it alone, then."

Prescott's soft sigh of relief disturbed him. *Can he really feel? It's impossible!* Yet Harland was afraid to test his assumption.

"I suppose this… unique situation would make it acceptable for us to use first names," he said. "I will call you Luke, if you will call me Harland."

Luke smiled bashfully at that and glanced away. "Thank you, Harland."

"Luke." Harland returned the smile briefly, but then he frowned as he ran his thumb over the damaged skin of Luke's palm. "I don't know what I can do to repair this," he said. "The mechanism isn't damaged. Merely the skin."

"I can show you where the replacements are kept," Luke suggested.

"Very well."

He helped Luke off the table, seeing little point in lowering the table with the lever when it was a mere few inches. Even so, he hadn't anticipated how intimate it would feel to have Luke's hands upon his shoulders, his hands on Luke's hips, and his palms against Luke's naked skin. He knew it wasn't actually skin, of course, but he'd grown so used to the feel of it that his mind played a cruel trick on him and made it *feel* like naked skin under his hands. Far worse, his body responded to the touch in a highly inappropriate manner, and he prayed that Luke wouldn't notice. Perhaps he shouldn't care if an automaton observed him stiffening in his trousers, but he was nevertheless embarrassed and glad to break the contact when Luke's feet touched the floor.

Luke led him across the room to a tall mahogany wardrobe against the far wall—one of four, placed side by side. It was locked, so Luke drew a ring of keys out of his pocket and selected one, saying, "There are only two sets of keys for the wardrobes—mine and the doctor's. Perhaps we could have another set made for you."

When he opened the doors wide, Harland could see instantly why the contents of the wardrobe would be so closely guarded. It was full of body parts. Luke's body parts, to be more precise. Though just the skin—hands and feet laid out on display racks like empty gloves and stockings, two dress forms with sections of buttocks and male genitalia attached, and stacks of thin wooden drawers with labels such as "Upper Right Arm" and "Lower Left Leg." The genitalia made Harland blush, but he found the face far more disturbing. There was only one, suspended on the back wall of the wardrobe, attached to a form that preserved its shape. Two similar forms were on the wall beside it, made of wood with several small metal nubs on their surface, but they weren't covered in the artificial skin. The solitary face was identical to Luke's but for one grisly feature—the eye sockets were empty. It looked as if a surgeon had removed the skin and mounted it, and it filled Harland with horror.

"I feel a bit light-headed," he said. There was a chair to one side of the wardrobe and he dropped into it, forcing himself to look elsewhere in the room, while he took slow breaths to calm himself.

Luke approached him, looking distressed. "Shall I fetch some water from the kitchen?"

Had he asked if he might ring for some water, Harland would have agreed. However, he realized Luke was unable to do that. None of the staff would respond to his summons. That thought forced Harland to rouse himself. He stood and said, "No, thank you. I'm fine."

He approached the wardrobe again, determined not to show further signs of distress. He avoided looking directly at the face but turned his attention to the hands. They did appear very much like gloves, although the synthetic skin was a bit thicker than leather. Only one pair remained, with an additional left hand. Harland wondered what happened to the other right hand skin.

"I damaged my hand with a pot of boiling water seven years ago," Luke observed, apparently sensing his curiosity. Then he added wistfully, "I must be very careful now."

Harland nodded, and then a thought occurred to him. "What about that gash you received on the back of your right hand?"

Luke held up the hand in question, so that Harland could see that it still sported a bandage on the back of it. "It doesn't seem worth using up the one I have left to replace it," he said.

"I see."

Harland lifted one of the left hand skins up gingerly and carried it over to the worktable, where the light was better. He set it off to one side and said to Luke, "Will you allow me to lift you back onto the table?"

"Of course."

It was disconcertingly like going in for an embrace. Luke was looking directly into his eyes with a serious expression as he placed his hands upon Harland's shoulders, and once more Harland felt as though he were holding a partially naked man as he placed his hands on Luke's waist and lifted him into position. The heaviness of his breath afterward wasn't entirely due to the strain.

Luke held out his left hand, and Harland saw the thin line of the seam between the hand and the forearm. He gently popped the seam open and separated it, folding the skin down as if he were removing a glove. He'd expected to be disturbed by the sight of the mechanical hand underneath, but he was not. In a way, it was very beautiful. Luke flexed the fingers slightly, and Harland watched the exquisitely smooth movement of the pistons and gears with fascination for a moment. Then he picked up the new molded hand skin and carefully stretched the wrist opening in order to slide it over the hand.

When it was done and the seam had sealed itself—the material along the seam adhered to itself somehow, without forming a permanent bond—the hand was nearly indistinguishable from a real human hand. Harland smoothed down the skin carefully, until he realized he'd been doing it for longer than necessary, and his touch was now more caressing than practical. He released Luke's hand and asked, "How does it feel?"

Luke flexed it. "Very good."

"How did you come to burn it?"

"I picked up a hot poker from the fireplace," Luke responded, as though the answer should be obvious.

It *was* obvious, but that wasn't quite what Harland had meant. "You didn't know it was hot?"

"I knew," Luke said. "That was the reason I picked it up."

"I don't understand."

"I picked up the poker to burn my hand."

Harland blinked at him in surprise. "Why on earth would you do that?"

"I hoped you would come if I was injured." There was no hint of guile in his voice or in his expression when he said this. If anything, he seemed delighted. "And you did."

It was true that Harland had needed something drastic to bring him back to this house, but he disliked being manipulated. And the smile on Luke's face angered him. "According to the doctor, these skins cannot be replaced, and what we see in that cabinet is the last of them. You cannot afford to deliberately destroy one. What were you thinking?"

"I needed to see you."

"There was no need to see me. You were uninjured!"

His harsh tone caused Luke's smile to fade. "Please don't be angry. The doctor has been so ill lately… and I've been so lonely…."

"Lonely!" The feeling of horror Harland had barely been keeping at bay welled up within him. "You can't be *lonely*! You can't feel anything! You're a *machine*!"

Luke stared at him openmouthed for a long moment, and then he slowly crumpled, lowering his eyes and hunching over, his shoulders sagging. He placed his repaired hand in his lap and rubbed the back of it with the fingers of his other hand.

At last he said in a very small, quiet voice, "I'm sorry."

Harland began to say something—something about talking to the doctor about this when he was feeling better—when he noticed Luke's cheeks were wet. He was crying.

He can't cry! It seemed impossible. What use could there be for an automaton to cry? *Perhaps it's merely a mechanism for lubricating the eye, so the lids can close smoothly*, he told himself. And that seemed a likely explanation. But it didn't matter. The sight of Luke crying was immensely disturbing. To all appearances, Luke was in his midtwenties and too old to be openly crying in front of another man. But he'd never been to school and had the lovely experience of being publicly humiliated for doing so.

"Please," he said. "Don't do that."

"Don't do what?"

"Cry."

Luke attempted to wipe the tears off his cheeks, but that merely served to make him look more vulnerable. "I thought you liked me."

He's a machine! I can't have hurt his feelings!

But even as Harland cursed himself for being a fool, he reached out and gently brushed Luke's cheek with his index finger. "I'm sorry, Luke. I do like you. Please don't cry."

DESPITE THE fact that there was little reason for him to come to Steward's townhouse if Luke was in good repair, Harland had been unable to escape without promising to return twice weekly—every Tuesday and every Friday. It wasn't the doctor who'd exacted this promise, but Luke. No matter how often Harland reminded himself that Luke was an automaton, his mind persisted in the belief that he was… if not human, then at least conscious and feeling.

Worse, Harland could not quench his physical desire for Luke, even after seeing the complex arrangement of gears and pistons and circuitry that made up his body. Harland continued to have intensely erotic dreams about Luke, of lying with him naked on the Oriental carpet in the workroom. But the dreams frequently turned nightmarish, with Luke's body falling into pieces like a china doll just as Harland climaxed. He awoke to find himself spilling his seed into the bed linens, at once aroused and confused and terrified, his heart pounding in his chest.

Still, he found himself enjoying the visits. He had the opportunity to speak briefly with Dr. Steward on his next visit about his concerns that simply keeping Luke company, when there was nothing in need of repair, seemed an abuse of their business arrangement. However, Steward dismissed this.

"I will pay you for your time, of course, Mr. Wallace."

Harland suddenly felt very uncomfortable. "That is not my concern, doctor. Luke… the automaton doesn't require anything from me at present—"

"He requires companionship," the doctor stated flatly. "I'm afraid my failing health no longer allows me to spend much time with him."

"I confess I'm having a difficult time with the concept of... the automaton... requiring anything so... emotional."

Dr. Steward regarded him thoughtfully before lifting a glass of water with a shaking hand to take a sip. "Mr. Wallace, it would require days to describe the complex mechanisms underlying what motivates Luke—weeks. Suffice to say, he has the ability to feel pleasure and pain on a physical level, and he has the ability to model that in his mind. Once these physical sensations become abstracted to a certain degree, and associated with, say, another *person* in his mind, then they effectively become what you call 'emotions.' You do him—and me—a great disservice by insisting that he cannot feel lonely or need human companionship."

The problem, Harland knew, was not that he couldn't believe Luke had feelings, but that he was *afraid* to believe it. "Very well, Doctor. If you wish me to act as a companion, I will do so."

Dr. Steward smiled. "Excellent! You may of course wish to take the opportunity to familiarize yourself with the contents of the other wardrobes. They contain replacement parts for all of Luke's systems."

Being a companion to Luke was far from a hardship. He was a pleasure to talk to. The doctor had apparently spent many long evenings giving him a rudimentary education in a number of fields of study, as well as the social niceties. He had little interest in politics, and Harland was unable to engage his enthusiasm on that topic, but he enjoyed hearing about the year Harland had spent traveling across the Continent. Luke longed to see the world outside London, since he'd never been permitted to leave the townhouse except for the shortest of errands, usually accompanied by the doctor. These excursions had all but vanished now that Steward was ill.

Luke was also fascinated by mythology, and many of their afternoons together were passed with Harland regaling him with the adventures of Hercules or Icarus or Persephone. Harland brought in the Mercier translation of *Twenty Thousand Leagues Under the Sea*—his grasp of French was poor and Luke's appeared to be nonexistent—so he could read it aloud on some afternoons. Luke listened intently, fascinated by such things as oceans and sharks and giant squids. Verne's description of the *Nautilus* provided Harland with the opportunity to inform Luke on the history of submersibles, though he found that only mildly interesting. What interested him was exploration. Perhaps, Harland thought, when they finished this novel, they could move on to Verne's *Journey to the Center of the Earth.*

HARLAND HAD learned, over the course of these visits, that Luke's body—and mind, for that matter—was powered by rows of nickel-cadmium batteries stored in his arms and legs, as well as several locations in his torso. They required charging every night in order for Luke to function.

One morning, after Bradley had silently removed his coat and hat—the butler rarely spoke to him these days, unless Harland directly addressed him—Harland entered the workshop to find Luke sitting on the sofa… completely nude. Some mechanical monstrosity Harland had never noticed before was belching steam in the corner. Harland stood in the doorway in shock a moment, before he came to his senses and hurriedly closed the door behind him. He locked it for good measure.

Luke seemed to find his distress amusing, because he smiled broadly and said, "Good morning, Harland," as if nothing were amiss.

"Good morning," Harland replied. He took a few steps into the room. "Might I inquire as to why you're naked?"

"I'm sorry. Is it upsetting you?"

What it was doing to Harland was arousing him, and *that* he found upsetting. "You haven't answered my question."

"The cable that charges my right leg must have been loose last night," Luke said. "It was barely responsive when I awoke." Luke did not "sleep" as a human would, Harland knew. But when his systems were charging, his body was largely dormant. "I reconnected it, and it appears to be charging now, but it will take several hours."

There was a thick cable leading to the sofa from the steam-driven machine in the corner, which Harland surmised must be an electrical generator.

"Do you always remove your clothes when you charge?"

"Yes," Luke answered matter-of-factly. "It's easier to reach the connectors that way."

As Harland drew near, he could see that Luke's right leg had the skin rolled down slightly on the inner thigh, up near his groin. It would indeed be difficult to reach that spot with clothing on. His manhood was casually pushed aside to make room for the electrical connector, and Harland felt himself flush at the sight of it. He forced himself to look away.

"Shall we pick up where we left off?" he asked, holding up his copy of the Verne novel.

"Please."

He read for perhaps an hour, doing his best to keep his eyes focused on the pages of the novel and avoid staring at Luke's naked body. Despite the fact that the seams were now clearly visible, Harland was still enthralled by its perfection. The situation was made worse by the fact that both he and Luke were becoming aroused. While it was somewhat possible for him to disguise his own arousal by crossing his legs, he suspected Luke was nonetheless aware of it, and there was no hiding Luke's arousal. If the young man—Harland had abandoned the conceit of referring to him as "it" or "the automaton"—seemed unconcerned about it, Harland found it far too distracting. He eventually gave up his attempts to read and closed the book.

"Is something wrong, Harland?"

"Luke… I understand that you don't feel embarrassment at being naked," Harland said awkwardly, "but even in front of a doctor or in a sporting club… one doesn't allow himself to…." If he hoped for Luke to fill in the obvious, he soon realized that wasn't going to happen. Luke hadn't the faintest idea what he was referring to. "It isn't considered proper for a man to be obviously aroused in front of another man," he finished.

Luke appeared to consider this. "Not even if we'd like to have coitus?"

Harland's eyebrows nearly crawled up into his hairline. *Is he propositioning me?* It was possible, considering Luke's lack of experience in these matters. Harland suddenly felt faint, and was glad that he was already seated. "That isn't something two men… would generally do together…."

"The doctor explained that to me," Luke said, "after my wretched experience with that woman." He screwed up his nose as if he smelled something unpleasant. "It felt somewhat pleasant in my genitals, but I didn't like the way she felt against my body and in my hands—too soft and… she didn't hold her shape well."

Harland found his description humorous, but Luke clearly did not, so he avoided smiling.

"I told the doctor that, if he wanted me to do it again, it would have to be with a man."

"I assume he ruled out that possibility."

To Harland's surprise, Luke shook his head. "He simply said it would be more difficult to arrange and perhaps a bit dangerous."

"One would think," Harland said, though he really had no idea. The thought of propositioning a man in a back alley somewhere and possibly being beaten or knifed for his trouble—or arrested—terrified him. "Is that all he told you about it?"

"He said it was something only a few men enjoyed doing with other men. But you...."

He seemed to think he'd said too much, and he allowed his last sentence to trail off. But Harland's heart was in his throat. Had Luke perceived something about him that even he was only vaguely aware of, that only haunted him in his dreams? "What about me, Luke?"

Luke stared hard at the carpet as he replied, "You become aroused when you touch me, and when I'm naked, you have difficulty looking away from my genitals."

Harland swallowed hard, finding his throat incredibly dry. He wished desperately for a glass of water, but that would require him to ring for a servant, and the last thing he wanted was for another person to enter the room at this moment. Perhaps he should leave, tell Luke he was being absurd, order him to never speak of it again. But Luke deserved a better response than that. "I suppose I do. I'm very sorry."

"If I'm likewise aroused by you," Luke said, "doesn't that mean we're attracted to each other?"

"I suppose so."

"Then why should you be sorry?"

Harland sighed and set the book down on the table beside him. "Society—other people—would not approve."

Luke leaned forward and gazed earnestly into Harland's eyes. "Harland... outside this door, everybody but the doctor hates me. I've overheard the servants talking about how I should be smashed into pieces and burned. What I do in this room... with you... won't affect that."

Harland felt nauseated by the thought of any harm coming to Luke. And perhaps that was what overrode his fears about what discovery could do to *him* and to the business he'd spent his life building. He glanced at the door, and then because he didn't trust his memory, he got up and walked over to make certain it was locked. It was impossible to hide his arousal while he did this, but there seemed little point.

He went back to stand in front of Luke and asked him, "What would you like us to do?"

Luke gave him a delighted smile, like a boy being offered a present. "May I see you without your clothes? I've never seen anyone, apart from myself in the mirror."

"You saw that woman," Harland pointed out, though he began to remove his tie. It would be difficult to get his clothes back in order without his manservant to assist him. He worried that he might leave the workshop looking obviously… disheveled… and give the servants more to gossip about. But it was evident that Luke dressed himself daily, since none of the servants would assist him. Harland would simply have to depend upon him.

"I saw very little," Luke said. "It had to be dark, so she wouldn't see my seams."

"I see."

Harland removed his tie and set it on the sofa. Then he removed his jacket and set it beside it. As he unbuttoned his vest, he asked, "Do you know how to… pleasure yourself?" He mimicked the motion in front of his crotch, which was tenting in a way he would have found highly embarrassing mere moments earlier.

"Yes. Would you like me to do that?"

It was making Harland uncomfortable to be the only one doing anything. "Does it feel good when you do it?"

"Of course."

"Then yes, I would like you to do that while I remove my clothing."

Luke laughed and began to stroke himself while he watched Harland undress. It was positively the most lewd and indecent act Harland had ever witnessed, and he found himself panting heavily with desire. At that moment, it didn't matter to him that he could see every seam in Luke's artificial body, and that an exact duplicate of Luke's beautiful face resided in a wardrobe not twenty feet from where Harland stood. It didn't matter that Luke was a machine. Harland wanted him as he had never wanted another human being.

After he'd removed his vest and lowered his suspenders to remove his shirt and undershirt, Harland sat down on the sofa to remove his shoes and socks. He'd never been aware of just how many layers of clothing he wore until he was in a hurry to remove them. At last he was able to stand again and slip both his trousers and his undergarments off in one motion. His manhood jutted out before him like the prow of a ship, bobbing as he stepped out of his things.

"May I touch it?" Luke asked.

"Of course." Harland stepped closer and allowed the young man to reach up and caress him. His touch was cool, as Harland had known it would be, but gentle and sensual enough to make Harland shudder. "You may do whatever you like," he offered.

Luke leaned forward and pressed his cheek to Harland's manhood, which throbbed at the touch. "I don't know what else to do," he said.

"Would you like me to teach you?" Harland was not overly experienced in such matters, but he had learned a thing or two from his fumblings in back rooms in boarding school.

Luke pulled away from him and looked up into his face. "Yes, please."

There was one thing in particular that Harland wanted—needed—to do. He placed a gentle hand under Luke's chin and leaned down until their mouths met in a kiss. Luke's lips were warmer than he'd expected, and moist, but he didn't move them under Harland's lips. At least, not at first. Harland persisted in sliding his lips along Luke's and nibbling at them gently, until Luke tentatively began to kiss back, mimicking his movements. When Harland pulled away, his entire body inflamed with by the touch of those lips, he asked breathlessly, "Did you like that? Or were you simply copying what I was doing?"

"Of course I copied you," Luke said. "But I liked it. Can we do it again?"

Harland obliged him. The cable charging Luke's leg was awkward, so he asked if it could be removed for a short time—Luke wouldn't have to use that leg for what he had planned. Once that was out of the way and the skin folded back into place on Luke's thigh, Harland climbed on top of him so that they could rub their bodies together and caress whatever was within reach of their hands and fingertips. Luke's body was warm under his, because it was more difficult for heat to dissipate from his core than from his extremities. But the technical explanation no longer mattered to Harland, and truthfully, it wasn't so different from the way heat was distributed in the human body. He simply chose to enjoy the sensation of it pressed against his flesh as they kissed.

When Luke moaned—a very human sound—Harland couldn't resist breaking the kiss and asking him in a breathless whisper, "Does this feel good to you? Is it what you'd hoped for?"

He was very much afraid Luke was merely mimicking his own behavior, cold and calculating like a machine. But Luke smiled up at him, and the expression he wore seemed blissful. "Very much. Nobody—not even that woman—has ever touched me all over my body, for no other purpose than to make me feel good. I don't ever want it to stop."

"I confess, my motivations aren't entirely selfless," Harland admitted. "I rather like touching your body."

Luke laughed. "Then please continue."

Harland obeyed, exploring every inch of Luke's body. He found himself doing things that would no doubt disturb him when he was less aroused—licking the seams that separated Luke's appendages from his torso, for instance. He had no wish to pop them open, but instead felt the need to show Luke that he accepted them and all they symbolized. He also found himself exploring Luke's fundament, inserting a finger to plumb its depths. He was disappointed to discover that it wasn't very deep—certainly not deep enough for the base act that had flashed through his mind as his finger slid inside—and Luke reported no particular sensation associated with the penetration.

The same could not be said of himself. Harland's explorations of Luke's body had put him in a position that placed his private parts within Luke's easy reach, and to his delight, Luke felt the need to explore as well. When he inserted his finger into Luke, the young man did the same to him. It hurt a bit, but the pleasure was far stronger, causing Harland to moan.

Luke laughed. "Yours is much deeper than mine," he said, sliding his finger in as far as he could manage.

Harland gasped, disgusted with himself at the same time he wished Luke could go deeper. "Yes, it's… very deep. Do you know what humans use it for?"

"Yes," Luke replied. "Elimination. The doctor gave me some anatomy lessons."

"It's rather disgusting."

"Not to me."

"I'm glad of that." It made Harland's wanton desire for more than Luke's finger a bit easier to accept, though he was still horribly embarrassed.

"The doctor told me about buggery," Luke continued, shocking Harland with the crude term. "When I told him I would rather be with a man than a woman, he told me that some men might want me to bugger them. Would you like me to bugger you?"

Harland was silent for a very long time, while Luke's finger continued to move gently inside him. He'd never done anything like that before, and though he could not deny that the sensations he was feeling now where nearly overwhelming his inhibitions, the disgust he felt whenever Luke used that filthy term was too strong. "I… I think not," he said reluctantly. "Perhaps some other time."

They returned to kissing, while Harland rubbed himself on Luke's body. It wasn't long before he was bucking his hips and panting heavily into Luke's mouth. Luke lifted his pelvis and writhed underneath him, moaning in response. They spent at the same moment, or at least Harland spent, spilling his fluid between their bodies while giving out one last strangled cry. Luke appeared to reach climax as well, gasping into Harland's mouth and clutching at his body for one endless moment, before collapsing into blissful exhaustion beneath him.

But when Harland lifted himself to examine the results of their lovemaking, he was surprised to discover that only his seed lay between them.

"Did you climax?" he asked.

"Yes," Luke said sleepily, and there was little doubt in Harland's mind that he was sated. Harland was a bit disappointed that he hadn't spilled the way a human man would, but that would have made little sense. Tears may have had a practical value for Luke, but semen clearly would not.

"Did you enjoy it?" Harland asked.

"More than anything I've ever done before."

Harland smiled. "I think I can say the same."

But in the dark recesses of his mind, the joy he'd felt in Luke's arms was tainted by feelings of disgust—that he could have done these things with a man, and furthermore with a "man" who was in fact not a man at all.

HARLAND AVOIDED going back to Steward's townhouse for the next week. It wasn't anything deliberate on his part—he was simply busy with other jobs. Although, if he were being honest, the thought of returning to the townhouse filled him with unease. He was perhaps easily distracted from his visits by things that might have been scheduled for another time. But he knew that, if he were to return, there would probably be a repeat of what had happened the last time. And the thought made him very uncomfortable.

He could no longer deny his desire for Luke. But outside the doors of the workshop, that desire seemed unhealthy and disturbing. He could not blame Luke. He had been created as a unique creature, and as such, he had no others like himself at which to direct his passions. But Harland was flesh and blood. There had to be something… twisted… diseased in his nature for him to be so strongly drawn to Luke.

It wasn't his intention to stay away forever. He knew that Luke needed repairs now and then, and Harland had promised to look after him. But perhaps if he kept his distance for a short time, his inflamed passion would subside and he would be better able to perform his duty.

A letter arrived from the townhouse on the ninth day, when he'd failed to show up for the second time. To Harland's surprise, it was not from the doctor, but from Luke. It read:

> *Dear Harland,*
> *Your continued absence is beginning to worry me.*
> *Are you ill, perhaps? Please let me know that you are*
> *well, and when I might expect to see you again.*
> *Your Dear Friend,*
> *Luke*

The desire to rush to Luke's side was nearly overwhelming. But it was the sheer strength of his need that frightened Harland enough to resist. While the messenger waited, he penned the following response:

> *Dear Luke,*
> *I am well, thank you, as I hope are you. Business*
> *has kept me away for a few days, but I shall see you*
> *soon. I promise. Please give my regards to the doctor.*
> *Your Friend,*
> *Harland*

It was distant but not utterly cold. Harland simply needed more time to sort himself out. He would have to go back eventually, perhaps even later in the week. He sent his reply and prayed that Luke would not be hurt by it.

Three days later, however, another visitor arrived at his door—a solicitor by the name of Mr. Dargan. It was with some trepidation that Harland invited the man into his sitting room.

"I'm afraid I'm the bearer of bad tidings, Mr. Wallace," Dargan said. He was a frail man, stooped and pale, with an agitated demeanor. He held an envelope in his hands that he continually rubbed and crinkled between his thumbs and forefingers.

"Would you like some tea, Mr. Dargan?" Harland offered.

"No, no thank you. I've come to tell you that an acquaintance of yours and a client of mine, Dr. Mordecai Steward, passed away a couple of days ago."

Harland felt the blood drain from his face. "Oh. That is… dreadful news, Mr. Dargan." He was thinking of Luke, however. Without the doctor, he would be lost. "Two days ago, did you say?"

"I'm afraid so."

That would have been just after Luke sent the letter. Why hadn't he sent another message with this news? Surely he hadn't felt that Harland had completely abandoned him.

"I understand you were a good friend of the doctor's," Dargan was saying.

"I… had a business arrangement with him."

Dargan looked surprised. "Oh? I was led to believe you were a close acquaintance." He opened the envelope with slow, quivering fingers. "He left you a considerable sum of money, as well as the entire contents of his townhouse." Dargan withdrew a stack of papers from the envelope, as well as another smaller envelope. This one was sealed. "The doctor met with me several weeks ago to draw up the paperwork. He also instructed me to give you this."

Dargan extended the envelope.

The envelope contained a key ring with several keys, and a short note:

> *My Dear Mr. Wallace,*
> *The contents of this envelope may come as a shock*
> *to you, as I don't know whether I shall have time to*
> *discuss the matter of my will with you before my passing.*
> *In any event, please accept these keys to my townhouse*

and various cabinets contained within, of which you will
know the purpose. I have made these arrangements in
the hope that you will look after our mutual interests.
Please, Mr. Wallace, I am depending upon you.
    Yours,
    Dr. Mordecai Steward

Harland fingered the key ring, while in the back of his mind a voice screamed, *What has become of Luke?* "Mr. Dargan," he asked, "do you know anything about a young man named Luke Prescott?"

Dargan shook his head. "No, sir. I cannot say I do."

"He wasn't mentioned in Dr. Steward's will?"

"No, sir."

"Has anyone been to the townhouse since the doctor passed away?"

Dargan looked uncomfortable being put on the spot like this. "I understand that the butler made arrangements for the… doctor to be… removed. Then the staff appears to have vacated the premises."

"The townhouse is empty?"

"It would seem so. I went to the house yesterday, but it was locked and nobody responded to the bell."

Harland felt a cold hand creeping up the back of his neck, and his breathing was becoming labored. "Didn't you have a key?"

"No, sir. Not without opening the envelope with which the doctor entrusted me."

HARLAND WENT to the townhouse alone, terrified of what he might find there. He opened the front door with one of the keys Mr. Dargan had given him and entered the front hall. The lighting was dim, so Harland couldn't see it at first. Then his eyes adjusted and he nearly screamed, but his breath caught in his throat.

Scraps of clothing, torn into shreds and tossed about the hall. In and of themselves, they were little enough, but Harland recognized them as Luke's. They appear to have been torn off and strewn about, but Luke wasn't there.

"Luke!"

There was no answer, so Harland checked the sitting room, where the fireplace now lay cold and the heavy curtains kept out nearly all light.

Harland crossed to one of the windows, his shoes crunching on a small porcelain figurine as he walked across the carpet. When he drew back the curtain, the light revealed that the room had been ransacked. Most items of value had been stolen—by the staff, Harland suspected, since he hadn't yet discovered signs of a break-in. He satisfied himself that Luke wasn't lying behind one of the sofas and went back out into the hall.

In the shadows at the far end of the hall, outside the workshop door, he discovered Luke.

He lay there completely motionless, collapsed in front of the door in a heap, like a horribly mutilated corpse. He was naked, apart from the torn remnants of some of his clothing, and covered in scuff marks from the boots that had obviously been kicking him as he attempted to crawl to safety. He was covered with spittle. His member had been torn off, leaving a gaping hole out of which rubber tubes jutted. But the worst was his face. Some wretched monster had taken a hot iron to it, leaving one entire side melted and scorched, and one of his beautiful sky blue eyes shattered from the heat.

Harland wanted to be sick. His stomach heaved, but somehow he willed himself not to vomit. Instead, he knelt down beside the pathetic ruin of Luke Prescott and reached out to touch him gingerly on the shoulder. "Luke," he said in a voice that quaked with fear. "Please...."

There was no response.

Harland sat on the carpet beside him for a long while, stroking Luke's hair, and trying to rouse himself to begin the long arduous task that lay before him.

But he could not stop crying.

THE SAVAGES who'd beaten, humiliated, burned, and mutilated Luke hadn't found the key to the workshop. Harland would uncover it later in the remnants of Luke's trousers. They had apparently not considered it worth their time to break down the heavy wooden door. *Thank God*, Harland thought, as he unlocked the door with one of the keys on the ring Mr. Dargan had given him and found the room untouched. He carried Luke's still form into the room and laid him out on the worktable, and then removed the shreds of clothing that still clung to him—the waistband of his trousers, his tie, the cuffs of his shirt, his stockings....

His leg didn't lie correctly on the table, confirming Harland's suspicion that Luke had taken a tumble down the stairs—shoved, most likely. The image of Luke attempting to crawl away as his attackers unleashed their hatred upon him made Harland's gorge rise, but he forced himself to focus on the job at hand.

He found a pot for water in the kitchen, along with some clean rags, so he could bathe Luke's body and at least remove the saliva and scuff marks and… good God… there were *teeth* marks! The skin was strong and hadn't been breached in many areas, but it took a lot of scrubbing to remove some of the scuff marks, and he had to be careful not to wear the skin down in those places.

He prayed that Luke was unresponsive because his batteries had completely discharged while he lay on the hall carpet for two days, unable to reach the haven of the workshop. The horrible image tormented him as he worked—decades later, it would still come to him in his nightmares— but he feared something might have been damaged in the fall, something he could not repair.

He removed all of Luke's skin, so that he might work unhindered by it. Especially that melted, burnt face. He couldn't bear to look upon it. The eye, he was relieved to discover, could be easily replaced by one he found in the wardrobes, and he did so. When he was finished, Luke lay before him, stripped of his illusion of humanity. There was no denying that this skeletal frame covered in pistons and hydraulics and gears was a machine. Yet something in Harland's vision had changed. Luke looked beautiful to him, even like this. And Harland knew now that no one else would ever look as beautiful to him, not until the day he died.

There were several connectors for the recharging cable at various locations in Luke's body. Harland found the one closest to the head and plugged it in. The other end was already connected to the steam-powered electrical generator in the corner of the room. When he lit the pilot, it took several minutes to heat the water in the generator's reservoir, but eventually steam began to cause an internal rotor wrapped in coils of wire to spin.

Nothing happened. Harland should have known that it would take hours to charge the batteries he'd connected, and Luke would require several of these locations in his body to be charged before he could function, yet still he felt a wave of despair threaten to overwhelm him.

Part of him had hoped Luke would immediately open his eyes and speak to him.

He pushed his feelings aside and settled down to work.

IT WAS an arduous undertaking. Luke's knee had broken in the fall, and although the framework of his leg was intact, several components were bent or broken. Harland found some replacement parts in the wardrobes, but now that he desperately needed them, he could see just how few of them remained. He was forced to scavenge some parts from the broken knee he was replacing and bend others back into shape as best he could.

Other parts of Luke's body were in better shape—some denting here and there from the blows he'd received, some jammed gears and flywheels—but there were so many repairs to be made, Harland despaired of ever completing the work. The day faded into night, and another day dawned.

He found tea and some bread in the kitchen—most of the food had been stolen—and that was his first meal since he'd arrived yesterday afternoon. He finally had to give in to his exhaustion and have a lie down on the sofa. How long he slept, he had no idea, but he woke to the sound of a human voice, speaking incoherently.

"Haaa-uuunnhhh…."

He bolted upright and looked around him. The sound was repeated, and he realized it was coming from Luke. He scrambled over the top of the sofa and rushed to the table, where he found Luke looking up at him with eyes that were lucid and focused. But when he tried to speak, his skeletal mouth was unable to form words.

"Don't speak," Harland told him. "Just a moment."

He went to the wardrobe and delicately removed the last remaining skin of Luke's face from its form. Then he carried it back to the worktable and told Luke, "Keep still."

It wasn't difficult to put the skin in place. It had been designed with tiny magnetic disks on its inside that lined up with similar disks of a reverse polarity embedded in Luke's facial structure. It merely required Harland to line everything up carefully, and then the magnets latched on to one another.

"Harland," Luke said softly.

Harland was unable to stop himself from kissing Luke tenderly on the mouth. Then he said, "I'm sorry, Luke. I'm sorry I wasn't here. I should never have let this happen." He saw a tear—his own tear—fall onto Luke's perfect cheek.

"I knew you would come for me."

"I don't know how," Harland responded, unable to prevent the tears from coming now. "I've been so horrible."

"You said you liked me."

"I do like you, Luke," Harland said adamantly. "My God, when I thought I'd lost you…. I've been such a fool for denying how I feel about you. I *love* you. Society be damned! You're the most important thing in the world to me."

And then Luke began to cry too, but he was smiling.

IT WAS only possible to charge one of Luke's systems at a time, and they'd all been thoroughly discharged, so it was a very long process to bring him back to "life." They spent the time with Jules Verne, and only when that novel was finished was Luke willing to talk about what the servants had done to him as they left the townhouse for the last time.

It had happened more or less as Harland had pieced together. As soon as the doctor's body had been removed, Mr. Bradley paid the staff their wages and told them their services would no longer be required. Then there was an argument about the amount being paid out to one of the kitchen staff, who felt she deserved more for her years of service, and someone brought up the possibility of "it" inheriting the doctor's estate.

Luke had been attempting to remain out of sight in the sitting room during all of this, but a couple of the younger boys felt it necessary to drag him into the front hall. Luke tried to tell them they could deal with Mr. Bradley for any wage disputes, but when he tried to go upstairs, one of the boys ran up to the landing and shoved him backward. The tumble down the stairs shattered his knee.

When the others saw him on the floor, it unleashed something in them and they began to shove and kick at him, and finally their contempt for him "masquerading" as a man and "putting on airs" led to them tearing at the expensive clothes he was wearing. He was stripped naked and beaten while Mr. Bradley looked on, heedless of Luke's pleas for help.

"I knew they hated me," Luke went on quietly, "but I thought their respect for the doctor…." He trailed off, falling silent for a long time, before continuing. "I tried to reach the workshop, though I knew it was hopeless. One of the boys spread my legs and pulled at me with both hands… tore it off, while the others laughed. Then the housekeeper brought out one of her irons…." He seemed to notice the horror in Harland's face and said, "I didn't feel pain. I'm not designed to."

He was lying, Harland knew. Dr. Steward had told him that Luke *could* feel pain. And the horror of it was almost too much to bear. But if Luke wanted to protect him, Harland would pretend to believe him. "Thank God!"

"But I was frightened," Luke went on. "Terrified. If they had broken open my head… they could have utterly destroyed me."

"Luke…. Luke…. Luke…." Harland couldn't think of anything to say beyond that, so he merely held Luke's hand and kissed it over and over again. Then at last, he said, "Nothing like that will ever happen to you again. I won't allow it!"

"Don't leave me here," Luke said, fear in his eyes.

Harland thought of Luke alone in this large townhouse, and his insides clenched. What if someone had held on to a key? Would they come back to steal more and find Luke there defenseless? Even if he had the locks changed, Harland knew he would never feel comfortable leaving Luke alone.

He would have to find a way for them to live together. Always.

London, Five Years Later

THE PACKAGE arrived via messenger, addressed to Mr. Harland Wallace and sent from Munich, Germany. Luke accepted it and carried it inside, but once the delivery boy was out of sight, he gave up all pretense of being a proper butler, tossing the package onto an upholstered chair in the hall and giving Harland a kiss instead.

"That might be important," Harland chided him, leaning over to retrieve the package.

"It is," Luke said. "It's the brass gears from Herr Baier."

"Ah. So it is." The elderly watchmaker was one of many contacts Harland had been reaching out to in Britain, the Continent, and the New

World, in order to have custom parts made for Luke. The special skin was still a problem, but he had sent small samples to some chemists he'd located, in the hopes that they could find a way to reproduce it.

Luke really was a very poor butler. But then, he only needed to convince the occasional visitor and two women who came in for a few hours a day to clean and do the cooking. Harland had reduced his staff as much as possible, fearing that live-in servants would soon notice something odd about Luke. And if not something about Luke in particular, then the fact that Luke spent all his nights in Harland's quarters.

Harland missed Flannagan, his old manservant—Luke wasn't particularly skilled with a tie—but it was a small price to pay for the privacy he and Luke now enjoyed after Mrs. Carmichael went home in the evenings.

He kissed Luke again but broke off when he remembered dinner would be served in less than an hour. Fortunately, the cleaning lady came and left in the early morning. "It's no good getting stirred up," he said regretfully. "We'll have to wait until evening."

"As you wish, sir."

Luke gave him a cheeky grin and slid a gloved hand up the back of his thigh to cup Harland's buttocks. Luke had found several uses for that particular bit of Harland's anatomy—uses that had made Harland a bit squeamish at first, but which he now enjoyed thoroughly.

He moaned slightly and gazed into those startling blue eyes. It was pointless telling himself that they were made of glass. He could see the desire in them and the love.

Luke was real in every way that mattered.

The Book of St. Cyprian

Author's Note

THE THEME for the second Gothika anthology was "voodoo." Fortunately, I knew Latinx people in Manchester, and there was a *botanica* there we could visit together. Taking my friends along turned out to be fortuitous, because the woman who ran the shop barely spoke to me. However, she entered into an animated discussion with my friends in Spanish, which they translated for me later. It gave me a lot more information about what running a *botanica* involved.

I did buy some holy water, Florida Water (which is very strong), and a can of what is to my New England Protestant upbringing somewhat baffling: Elegua spray. It's not exactly "God in an aerosol," which was my first thought. It's more of a scent that particular *loa* (pronounced "lwa") is attracted to, so if you spray it in your house, he'll protect it from evil.

One last thing: though I didn't plan it this way, the story ended up being YA. The two main characters are teenagers, and though I have no problem with the idea of writing realistic sex between teens, it ended up being mostly about the relationship and less about the hot and steamy.

Chapter One

THE BOOK was evil. It was said that to own it—or merely to *touch* it—was a great sin. An ancient tome attributed to St. Cyprian of Antioch, yet containing magical spells so dark that those who did own a copy took precautions to constrain its influence. Alejandro knew the moment he laid eyes on the intricately carved wooden box, wrapped with a metal chain in the shape of a cross and secured with a rusted padlock, that he'd stumbled across it: *El Gran Libro de San Cipriano.*

"Do you have a key to this lock?" he asked Miss Passebon.

The willowy young woman turned from surveying the rows of dusty shelves of books, candles, jars, and other items in the abandoned botanica to eye the box in his hands with disinterest. "I really don't know. I suppose it might be on the key chain." She searched in her purse for the keys she'd tossed into it after opening the front door. She fished them out and handed them to her guest, clearly indicating he could take the time to search for it, if he cared to.

Alejandro examined the keys closely while Miss Passebon walked down the aisle, an expression of dismay on her lovely face.

"Most of this will probably have to be thrown away," she muttered. She pointed at a row of saint figurines, some of them over a foot tall. "I suppose these will cause me all kinds of bad luck if I chuck them in the trash?"

"Definitely," Alejandro replied. He could tell she didn't believe, but he knew his grandmother would throw a fit if she heard anyone talking about throwing those figurines away. "We can pack them up and ship them back to Abuela if you can't sell them," he continued. He didn't have a fortune to ship the entire contents of the botanica back to New Hampshire, but he would salvage what he could. Old *Grand-père* Passebon had been a close friend of the family when Abuela had lived in New Orleans. Alejandro hadn't even been born then. But the old man had instructed his granddaughter to contact a number of his close acquaintances and allow them to take whatever they liked from his possessions. That included both his house and the botanica.

Alejandro hadn't been the first to arrive—the old man had known several people still living in New Orleans—so the truly valuable furniture and artwork had already been taken. Some specific items had been removed from the botanica. Alejandro wasn't sure what they'd been, but there were intriguing spots on the shelves where circular or square patterns in the dust indicated something had recently been carried off. Still, he felt a bit guilty grabbing something that could be very valuable. The others appear to have missed it because it had been tucked far back on a top shelf behind the counter. "Do you know what this is?"

Miss Passebon shook her head.

"Well, I'm not sure until I get it open…." One of the smaller keys fit the lock. He turned it and met resistance, but a slight pressure caused it to rotate with a scraping sound like fingernails on a chalkboard. Then the lock snapped open. He set the box on the countertop and pulled the chain away. Holding his breath, he lifted the wooden lid.

There it was, discolored and brittle with age, the cover made from paper glued onto cardboard, peeling away now, and bound to the pages with loose stitches of heavy cotton thread. Somebody had made this copy by hand a long time ago, crudely reproducing an illustration of a sorcerer surrounded by skeletons and devils on the cover. He'd seen a reproduction of that etching online, from the 1893 Portuguese edition in the Library of Lisbon. The fact that it was a copy was a little disappointing. It probably wouldn't be all that valuable to a bookseller. But what was really important was whether or not the spells inside had been copied down faithfully.

Alejandro lifted the cover carefully to look at the first page, a strange sensation going through his body when he did so, as if he'd eaten something that disagreed with him. The pages seemed to be… greasy somehow, though he knew that was impossible. Grease would make the paper translucent, and it wasn't. He knew what his grandmother would say about something making him cringe when he touched it, but at nineteen, he was still skeptical about some of her beliefs, even though he respected them. He shrugged the unpleasant feeling off.

The book was in Spanish, thank God, which possibly meant the person who copied it had also translated from Portuguese. Alejandro might be able to struggle his way through a Portuguese edition, but this was so much easier. His family spoke Spanish at home.

Miss Passebon peered over his shoulder and laughed. "It looks like something a kid put together," she observed.

"No," Alejandro said, shaking his head. "Somebody copied it by hand, and translated it, maybe. But I recognize some of it from fragments I've seen online. I think it may be complete."

"A complete what?"

"*The Great Book of St. Cyprian.* It's a very old book of magic—black magic. A lot of the spells are used today in hoodoo magic, but it's really unusual to come across a complete copy. Many people wouldn't *want* to see a complete copy."

She gave him a look of disbelief. "Why not?"

"They say you should never touch it, if you value your soul. And if you dare to read the whole thing from cover to cover, the devil will come for you."

She laughed, obviously not taking any of that seriously. "Oh well, then you'd better get it out of here!"

"Are you sure?" he asked. "You might be able to get a good price for it."

She put one hand on her slender hip and waved the other in the air to take in the shop that had been locked up since Grand-père Passebon passed away a month ago. "I just want to unload all of this stuff and get back to New York. Grand-père was a sweet old man and I want to carry out his wishes, but I don't have time to get appraisals or anything like that. Take what you like, and the others can take whatever they want. First come, first served."

Alejandro carefully closed the book and placed the cover back on the box. He'd been hearing about this book his entire life, but he'd never seen it. There were no more than fragments of it online. The feeling of excitement that welled up in him now was almost overwhelming. Still, he had enough presence of mind left to realize he had one big obstacle to overcome if he was going to bring this book home with him.

His grandmother would never allow it into the house.

MATTHEW HAD known the Varela family since he moved to New Hampshire six years ago. Alejandro had stood in the doorway of his apartment building, leaning against the weathered green frame as he watched the moving van being unloaded. He was barefoot and shirtless, his skin smooth and tanned, his torso thin but well-defined. And he was handsome. *Very* handsome. Short, dark brown hair and eyes so brown they seemed black, set under an angry-looking brow.

Matthew had just hit thirteen, but he already knew he preferred boys to girls. And it was only the fact that his new neighbor scared the crap out of him that prevented him from saying hello. Instead, he helped his mother and her current boyfriend, Frank, carry stuff into the building, watching the Latino boy out of the corner of his eye.

It was Alejandro who spoke first, when everyone but Matthew was inside, out of hearing. "Do you know what street you're moving in to?"

Matthew stopped and stared at him a moment before giving what he thought was the obvious answer. "Wilson Street."

The boy—Matthew didn't know his name yet—made a rude noise. He gestured at the doorway behind him. "This building has my family—the Varelas—and the Perezes living upstairs. *Your* building has the Riveras on the first floor and the Castillos on the third."

"So?"

"What's wrong with this picture?"

Matthew frowned at him and set the box he was carrying down on the walkway. "Nobody told my mom we had to be Hispanic to move in." What was obvious about the houses on the street was that they were all rundown and broken up into as many apartments as the landlords could fit. This was a poor neighborhood, and Matthew and his mom were poor. So why couldn't they live here too?

The boy shrugged. "You can live wherever you want."

"Fine," Matthew retorted. "I'll move into *your* place."

To his surprise, the boy burst out laughing. "You gonna sleep in my bed, *huero*?"

The word, Matthew would later learn, meant "blond boy." But all he could think about at the moment was the implication behind the question. He knew it was just teasing, but it still made his face feel hot. It was probably safest to just ignore it and go back to what he was doing, but he couldn't resist answering, "Only if I get to be on top."

Ugh. Did I just say that? He's gonna kick my ass!

Fortunately, the boy just laughed harder. Matthew quickly scooped up the box and hurried inside, dodging Frank on his way out the door. "Whoa, there, kid! Watch where you're going!"

Matthew ignored him. Frank was just some guy his mother had met at the diner she worked at. He'd be gone in a few months, just like all the boyfriends she'd had before him. Matthew only spoke to him when he had to.

MATTHEW'S PREDICTION about Frank came true even sooner than expected, when his mother caught one of the other waitresses at Frank's apartment a couple of weeks later. But the Latino boy next door stayed. For six years, they lived side by side while the neighbors on all sides of them came and went. Not surprisingly, almost all the new neighbors were Latino.

Matthew learned the boy's name was Alejandro Valera, and when he wasn't being a wiseass, he was a surprisingly cool guy. By the time they entered high school, they were best friends.

Alejandro was the first person Matthew came out to. Matthew had been a nervous wreck, but Alejandro was totally cool about it. About a year later, when they were both sixteen, Alejandro finally admitted *he* was gay too. Unfortunately, despite the fantasies that revelation stirred up in Matthew's lustful teenage mind, nothing happened between them. They remained friends, but Alejandro never showed any sexual interest in Matthew, so Matthew learned to accept that they would always just be friends.

Wilson Street wasn't strictly a Latino neighborhood, but it was close enough. If anyone had a problem with the huero and his mother living in their midst, however, it was never mentioned. Matthew suspected that might be due to his friendship with Alejandro and who the boy's grandmother was. Abuela, as Alejandro called her—as everybody called her, though it simply meant "grandmother" in Spanish—had lived in the neighborhood a very long time. More importantly, she ran St. Peter's Botanica a few blocks down, one of the few Santeria *botanicas* in the city.

Abuela was ancient—or at least she'd always seemed so to Matthew—tough, and generally cranky. She was also very tiny. Neither boy was particularly tall, but they'd towered over her since their second year of high school. She spoke very little English, and her face wore a perpetual scowl. Matthew had been convinced she hated him the first couple of years. But Alejandro began tutoring him informally in Spanish, starting with insults and obscenities and gradually moving on to more coherent phrases. Eventually, Matthew grew interested enough to take

Spanish in school. Alejandro helped him with his homework, and once Abuela saw that he was putting some effort into learning the language, she began to talk to him too. Matthew didn't always understand the first, or even the second, time she said something, but she was more patient than he'd expected. By his senior year in high school, Abuela treated him like a second grandson. She still scowled at him and her manner was still curt, but now there was an undercurrent of humor in it.

And that's how he came to be working in the botanica. Abuela didn't like strangers working in her shop, so she refused to hire anyone she didn't know. And she didn't know anyone—not really. She was known in the neighborhood and people respected her, but Matthew got the impression she made a lot of people nervous. Some would come to St. Peter's for herbs or protection sprays, floor washes to drive out dark magic, holy water, powders for money or love, or Florida Water—a cheap cologne Abuela was fond of that used to be common in the eighteen hundreds and was now used for spiritual cleansing. Many people consulted the old woman for advice, both magical and otherwise—she read cards, cowry shells, and coffee beans. But few people came to her apartment for just a friendly chat. So she worked the botanica alone and drafted her grandson, when he was old enough. By the time he was eighteen, Matthew was allowed behind the counter to help out.

HE WAS there in the back room, unpacking some boxes sent from New York, with Abuela tallying up the day's receipts in the front, when Alejandro called his cell phone.

"Yo."

"Are you alone?"

Matthew laughed. "Why?"

"I don't want Abuelita to hear this," Alejandro replied. He sounded dead serious.

"What is it, amigo?" Matthew lowered his voice and added, "She's out front. I'm in the storeroom."

"Good. Listen, I'm sending some stuff back through FedEx. Three boxes from Abuelita's friend. But there's something I don't want her to see. Can I send it to your house?"

"What is it? Porn?"

Alejandro didn't laugh. "No. It's a book. A very old book."

"Uh… sure." Now he was really curious. Alejandro didn't keep many secrets from his grandmother. What, apart from porn, could he be so anxious to hide? "Is it a present or something?"

"No. It's hard to explain over the phone. Just don't let her see it. And don't open it!"

"Why not?"

"Just do what I say, huero. Don't make me kick your ass."

"Don't you mean *lick* my ass?" Sadly, Matthew already knew the answer to that. Alejandro had never shown the slightest interest in him.

"You wish, *cara de culo*."

Matthew laughed. "That just means you'll lick my face." The insult translated to "butt face."

"In your dreams."

ALEJANDRO DISCONNECTED and put his phone back in his pocket, thinking about how much he really would like to lick Matthew's face… and ass, for that matter. And anything else the handsome blond boy offered him. He'd been attracted to him since the day Matthew moved in next door. Matthew had just been a skinny little white kid back then, but when Alejandro gave him shit, he gave it right back. Alejandro didn't know it at the time, but he fell a little in love with Matthew that day. He'd been falling more and more in love with him every day since then.

Only now he knew it. But it was too late. They'd grown too close. And the thought of actually *dating* Matthew felt… weird. Like thinking about dating his brother or something.

He walked back to the desk at the FedEx office and handed the clerk the fourth package he'd addressed. "This one's going to a different address." He thought about paying for it all with the money Abuela had given him, but on second thought, he said, "I'll pay for it separately."

Alejandro stepped out of the French Quarter Postal Emporium—a much smaller building than its name suggested—into a bright July afternoon. He wandered lazily down Bourbon Street, whistling the tune to Sting's "Moon Over Bourbon Street." He was done rummaging through Grand-père Passebon's dusty shop, there was a full day left until his flight home, and he was in one of the coolest cities he'd ever visited.

Time to do some sightseeing.

Chapter Two

THE PACKAGE arrived the next morning. Matthew wasn't expected at the botanica until after it arrived. He'd told Abuela he was waiting for a delivery that morning, though he didn't tell her who it was from. She didn't have a problem with him coming in late, because as far as she was concerned, she was doing *him* a favor by allowing him to work some hours there—not the other way around.

Matthew tossed the package onto his bed, kissed his mother goodbye, scratched his dog on the head, and ran out to the botanica. There, he found Abuela suspiciously eyeing three boxes the FedEx guy had dropped off.

"Alejandro sent these," she said in Spanish.

"He told me he was sending them yesterday. They're from the botanica in New Orleans."

"Sí, I remember he went down there," she said with exaggerated patience. "Do I look senile?"

"Sólo un poco."

"Mocoso!" ("Brat!") She pretended she was going to backhand him, though she'd never laid a finger on either him or Alejandro. "I have no idea where I'm going to find room for this much crap!"

It was a challenge. They spent the rest of the afternoon unpacking the boxes and trying to wedge icons of the saints, candles, and other things Alejandro had thought worth saving onto the overcrowded shelves of the tiny shop. Some of the saints could go in the window, on the other side of the heavy cloth that prevented curious outsiders from peering into the inner depths of the botanica. There they presented a fairly innocuous "front" for the shop that might pass for a Catholic religious display to strangers walking by.

Only people who worshipped the saints knew the icons weren't Catholic, or perhaps a devout Catholic might notice something off about them—that some had darker skin than most Catholic saint figurines or that the colors of the clothing seemed brighter. Some of the figurines resembled dolls more than the Catholic icons found in churches. Because these saints were really African gods—spirits would be more accurate—in a European guise. Back when slaves were first being brought to the Caribbean, they'd been forced to accept Catholicism, but they'd continued to honor the African spirits in secret. They'd simply hidden them behind the guises of the saints. St. Theresa became Oya, the queen of the dead. St. Barbara became Chango, the spirit of fire and thunder. Matthew's favorite was Eleggua, in the guise of St. Anthony. He was the patron of luck and destiny and something of a trickster, but Abuela had told him and Alejandro when they first came out to her that he was the guardian of gay men and women.

How, exactly, the worship of the saints found its way from Caribbean slaves brought to the United States to the Latino community, Matthew didn't know. Maybe he'd find the answer someday in the books on the botanica's shelves. For now, he was only mildly interested. His mother was more or less an atheist, which made his friendship with Alejandro and Abuela a little easier. At least she wasn't constantly freaking out about him losing his soul to the devil or anything like that. But that didn't mean Matthew was a believer himself. He just found it all kind of cool and interesting.

After they'd unpacked all the boxes and found places for everything, Abuela shooed him out of the shop. She always liked to be the last one there at night, so she could go around and make sure everything was in its place without the two boys "stumbling around like goats" and getting in her way. There were also a few altars set up in corners of the shop that needed to be tended.

Before he stepped out the door, the old woman insisted upon spritzing him with Florida Water, as she did every night. He hated the stuff. It smelled like cheap cologne—which, of course, it was. But he'd gotten used to the nightly ritual, just as Alejandro had. As always, Abuela muttered under her breath when she did it, "To keep you safe."

"Gracias, Abuelita."

Matthew went back to his apartment building and let himself in. Fifteen-year-old Gabriela Rojas was in the stairwell, making out with her boyfriend, but they ignored him as he climbed the stairs. His mother was working late, so it was just him and Spartacus. Spartacus was Matthew's pit bull, named after a character in a TV series his mother didn't like him watching. The dog was still kind of a puppy, though he was already massive. It was unlikely he'd be any good at protecting Matthew and his mom if a burglar broke in, since he was inclined to trust everybody, but Matthew had gotten him as a companion anyway. And he was great for that.

"Hey, pup!" Matthew laughed as he opened the door and the pit bull nearly knocked him back out onto the landing. "Hold on a second! Let me get the light."

He felt around for the light switch just inside the door, and a second later, the apartment lit up. The first thing Matthew saw was his muscular ball of puppy love making excited circles in front of him. The second thing he saw was the shredded paper and cardboard strewn across the living room carpet. It took him a moment to figure out what it was.

Then he remembered Alejandro's book.

"Oh shit!"

SPARTACUS HADN'T eaten the entire package. The external wrapping was pretty much destroyed, but once the dog had gotten through to the wooden box inside, he'd contented himself with gnawing on just one corner for a bit. Considering his powerful jaws could have made short work of the entire box, that was something, at least. But if the box was an antique, Alejandro was going to be furious.

Matthew sat on the couch, picking bits of the paper wrapping off the box, while Spartacus curled up beside him, happily gnawing on one of the immense rubber Kong toys he was *supposed* to chew on when he was bored, totally oblivious to how much distress he'd just caused his owner. The wooden box was damaged beyond repair. In addition to the corner, which simply wasn't there anymore, one side was splintered and there were several places where Spartacus's canines had punched holes all the way through the wood.

He's going to kill me.

Alejandro would never harm a hair on Spartacus's cast-iron head, of course. But Matthew would be in for it. He should have had the sense to put the package on the counter or a shelf out of the dog's reach.

The box had once had a carving on the lid. Matthew recognized it as a *veve*—a symbolic picture representing one of the African spirits. The elaborate crisscrossed veve on the cover represented Ogun, the smith, and was sometimes used for protection. But much of it had been chewed up, destroying any power it might have had. Matthew felt a slight chill of superstitious dread pass through him at the sight of it, as if whatever the lid had contained was now free to get out. The feeling wasn't helped by the bizarre chain wrapped around the box. It was fastened with a padlock, but thanks to the gnawed-off corner, the chain on that side was slipping off, so the entire thing could slide off the box without having to open the lock.

Matthew let the chain fall off and peered into the broken corner of the box. He could see what looked like a book in there, but he couldn't tell for certain that it hadn't been damaged. Alejandro had told him not to open it, but of course he hadn't anticipated this circumstance. It couldn't hurt to assess the damage, could it?

Matthew popped open the wooden cover of the box and looked at its contents.

It was a book, as Alejandro had told him. But it looked cheap, homemade, as if someone had written it by hand and then stitched the pages together. The cover was warped with age and apparently nothing more than cardboard with a hand-drawn paper cover glued to it. It was clearly old, though Matthew had no idea how old. The paper was yellowed and the edges were curled. The corners of the cover illustration were peeling away from the cardboard. The illustration itself was odd—an old man in a robe and a frankly silly-looking pointed hat, with skeletons and devils floating in the air around him. Maybe a hundred years ago, people would have thought it looked frightening, but in the light of modern horror movies, it was more goofy. Still, Matthew felt uneasy looking at the book, as if he was seeing something he shouldn't be.

El Gran Libro de San Cipriano. The Great Book of Saint…. *Cipriano*? He'd never heard of a saint by that name.

He glanced up and was startled to see Spartacus staring at the book too. It wasn't that the dog was growling or cowering or anything else particularly strange. He was just looking at it fixedly. But Matthew still found it unsettling.

He closed the wooden cover again and gathered the chain in one hand. "It's a good thing you didn't eat the book," Matthew told the pit bull, getting up off the couch. "Alejandro's gonna be pissed off enough when he sees the mess you made of the box. Don't expect me to take the blame."

Spartacus ignored him and went back to chewing on his Kong.

Matthew looked around for a place to put the box. For some reason he couldn't explain, he really didn't want the thing in his bedroom. He finally settled on the closet near the front door, hiding it behind the winter hats and mittens on the top shelf. Then he went back to the couch and put the DVD in for *Ip Man*, despite having watched it about twenty times already.

He thought about calling Alejandro about the damage done to the box, but he chickened out. It would be easier to explain when Alejandro got back. His flight was due in late that night, so Matthew would see him tomorrow.

Every once in a while as he watched the movie, and later, as he got up to bake himself a frozen pizza, he glanced at the closet. He didn't know why. It was stupid. Did he think the book was going to jump out of the closet and chase him around the room? The image that brought to mind, with the book flapping its covers through the air like a bat, made him laugh. But it didn't make him any less uneasy. He wasn't generally superstitious—at least, he didn't think so—but he'd feel better once the book was out of his apartment.

Chapter Three

THE DARK thing slithered down the wall and across the floor of the apartment, hugging the edge of the room, though all was still and dark. It avoided the splash of light near the wall, where some kind of cold blue flame flickered, but quickly returned to the comfort of the baseboard. It disliked being out in the open.

It was hungry.

It sensed food had been left for it on top of the counter, but when it climbed easily up the side to explore the surface on top, it found little to satisfy it—bread, cheese, and mashed tomato. Peasant food. It needed food with power—blood and flesh.

It sensed something... something nearby that could ease its hunger... and slithered back down to the floor. Following the contours of the room, it came to a closed door. There was a thin gap between the door and the floorboards, and the thing easily slipped through.

Inside, it found a bed, in which two warm bodies slept. The human was protected by a faint, lingering trace of magic—not much, but enough to make him unappealing. Yet the dog was not. The dark thing curled around the unsuspecting animal, which whimpered softly in its sleep, and then insinuated itself in through the nostrils, through the mouth, through the ears... claiming the animal with every breath, marking it as its own....

HIGH ABOVE the New England countryside, Alejandro started in his sleep and woke from the nightmare to the pilot announcing twenty minutes until landing at Manchester Airport. He shifted uncomfortably in his seat, wedged between an elderly woman who insisted on taking her smelly shoes off and a businessman who kept eyeing Alejandro as if he might make a grab for the man's wallet.

Something was wrong. He'd never considered himself to be particularly psychic, but the dream had been too vivid, too disturbing to ignore. He took his cell phone out of his pocket and verified the time he'd heard from the flight attendant. Just past one in the morning.

It was possible Matthew would be awake. He sometimes stayed up late watching a movie. He'd been sleeping in the dream, but hopefully that's all it had been—a dream. Hopefully, Matthew and Spartacus were all right. They *had* to be all right.

Twenty minutes, at least, until he'd be allowed to use his phone. He wasn't sure how he'd be able to stand it.

MATTHEW WOKE in semidarkness, with only a street light coming through his second-floor bedroom window to cut across his ceiling in a broad band of orange-yellow, and found Spartacus standing over him, looking down into his face. It wasn't something the dog had ever done before, and it was unnerving.

"What's up, pup?"

In response, the dog that had never once shown any aggression to his owner—or *anyone*, for that matter—lowered his ears and growled deep in his throat.

"Spartacus—"

That merely caused the pit bull to draw his lips back and growl louder, his canines clearly visible. A drop of saliva fell onto Matthew's shoulder.

THE MOMENT they were on the ground and the captain announced passengers could use cell phones, Alejandro flipped his out of airplane mode and dialed Matthew's number. It rang a few times but went to voicemail.

Shit.

"If you're still awake, huero, call me back. I just landed in Manchester."

He left the phone on vibrate and slipped it into his pocket. Then he waited, fretting, while the plane taxied to the gate. Everything was probably fine. Nightmares were usually just that. None of his dreams had ever come true before, so there was no reason to think this one would. Besides, it hadn't even made sense. Just a vague sense of something menacing loose in Matthew's apartment. Matthew would probably laugh at him if he told him about it.

Still, Alejandro knew he wouldn't be able to rest tonight until he checked on his friend.

SOMETHING WAS very wrong with Spartacus. He didn't appear to recognize Matthew at all. Was it possible for dogs to sleepwalk? Should Matthew try shouting at him to see if it would shake him out of it? Matthew was afraid to even move, never mind make loud noises. For the first time since he'd met the lovable pit bull at the shelter and wrestled with him, he was frightened by those sharp fangs and powerful jaws.

Was he bitten by something? Is he rabid?

The thought filled him with dread. Matthew couldn't remember encountering any animals recently when he'd walked Spartacus. Nothing that could have bitten him, anyway. Just some squirrels and chipmunks. Besides, he would have noticed if the dog had bite marks on him.

The buzzing of Matthew's cell phone in his pants pocket halfway across the room set the pit bull off. As soon as the phone broke the silence, Spartacus started barking ferociously, as if Matthew was an intruder. Instinctively, Matthew grabbed the dog's collar with one hand, shoving him back just long enough to yank the pillow out from behind his head and shove it in Spartacus's face. He rolled off the bed as the pit bull savaged the pillow, tearing it to shreds.

There wasn't time to sort things out. Matthew scrambled to his feet and bolted for the bedroom door as Spartacus launched his muscular body through the air. The dog landed at the door just as Matthew went through and slammed it behind him. A hundred pounds of muscle smashed into the wood while Matthew braced it with his body. Spartacus tore at it with his claws, snarling savagely, causing the door to bang loosely in its frame. The stupid thing had been put on backward before Matthew and his mother moved in six years ago, so it opened out into the living room. It also had no lock. Only the short latch bolt, rattling loosely against the metal strike plate, kept it from flying open as the dog slammed his massive paws against it.

Matthew's heart pounded in his chest, and his breath came in painful gasps. *This isn't happening!* He was terrified, but not so much for himself as for Spartacus. Why had the dog suddenly snapped like this?

Maybe it *was* rabies. Or a brain tumor or encephalitis. Unfortunately, it didn't matter. Because if Spartacus didn't calm down soon, somebody would take him away and have him put down. And that scared Matthew more than anything.

In between the barking and the slashing of claws against the wooden door, Matthew could faintly hear the phone buzzing insistently.

Damn it!

He'd left it in the room, along with all his clothes. It had to be Alejandro calling. His mother had already called before he went to bed, saying she'd be spending the night at her boyfriend's apartment, so it wasn't likely to be her. But Alejandro's plane was supposed to be landing tonight. Since he was coming in so late, the plan had been for him to get a taxi home, instead of pestering Matthew for a ride. But nobody else would call him at this hour, unless it was a wrong number.

It took a minute for Matthew to realize some of the pounding he was hearing was coming from the apartment door, rather than the bedroom door. *Terrific.* One of the neighbors had heard the noise, and the knocking was starting to get insistent.

"Quién es?" he shouted.

"Señor Rojas! Qué demonios estás haciendo ahí?" ("What the hell is going on in there?")

Matthew groaned. "Un minuto!"

The couch was nearby, so he took a chance that the door would hold for a moment against Spartacus's assault and ran across the small room. Putting his weight against the opposite end, he slid the couch across the wooden floor until the other arm was wedged firmly against the bedroom door. That would hopefully keep the damned thing closed for a few minutes.

When he opened the door to the second-floor landing, Mr. Rojas was standing there in his bathrobe, arms across his chest, glaring. Matthew himself was dressed in nothing but red-and-black checkered boxers. "I'm sorry if we woke you—" he began in Spanish. The man spoke English, Matthew knew, but it was rare to hear it in the apartment building.

"It's nearly two in the fucking morning!" Mr. Rojas snarled. His eyes were puffy, and his thinning black hair was sticking up in all directions. "Some of us have to work in the morning, you know! What the hell is going on in here?"

The sound of his voice seemed to rile Spartacus up even further, and the dog increased his attack against the bedroom door. Matthew knew the cheap pressed wood wouldn't hold up for much longer.

Mr. Rojas looked past the boy in horror. "What is that?"

Matthew didn't want to stand there chatting while there was a chance the dog could break out and come after him again. Or worse, get out of the apartment. He had no idea what to do, but he knew he needed to get out of there. At least until he could figure out a plan. Maybe the dog would calm down if nobody was in the apartment with him.

And he needed to call Alejandro. He couldn't think of anyone else. His mother would probably want to put Spartacus to sleep. It had taken her a long time to get over her fear of big dogs, but Spartacus's affectionate nature had gradually won her over. Her fragile trust in him wouldn't last long if she saw him like he was now. And the police would just shoot him. Matthew saw stories in the news all the time about police shooting big dogs at the slightest sign of aggression. Maybe not all police were like that, but he was too afraid to take the chance.

Alejandro loved Spartacus as much as Matthew did. He'd want to save him too. And maybe between the two of them, they could think of something.

"Mr. Rojas, can I use your phone?"

ALEJANDRO TRIED calling three times and then gave up. If Matthew was sleeping and the phone woke him up, he'd be pissed. Alejandro had left messages, but now he just needed to catch a cab and get home. He could poke his head in at Matthew's when he got there.

His phone vibrated while he was in the cab, and he anxiously fished it out of his pocket. To his surprise, it wasn't Matthew. The display read "Fernando Rojas."

"Sí, Señor Rojas?"

"It's Matthew," his friend said in English, sounding frantic. "I'm using Mr. Rojas's phone."

Alejandro wasn't sure whether he should feel relieved or not. Something was obviously off. "Why?"

"Where are you?" Matthew demanded, ignoring his question.

"I'm in a cab."

"You're heading home?"

"Yes."

"Come next door as soon as you get in. It's urgent!"

"What the hell?"

"I'll explain when you get here."

Chapter Four

MATTHEW FELT ridiculous, sitting in the Rojas's kitchen wrapped in a blanket like a victim of hypothermia. It was July and about eighty degrees out. But Mr. Rojas had insisted he cover up rather than sit there in his underwear. The man didn't want his daughters to wake up and see Matthew half naked.

So fine. At least he'd let Matthew call Alejandro. "Thank you," Matthew told him, handing the phone back.

"De nada," Rojas grunted. "I have to get some sleep. I have work in the morning. You can stay here until Alejandro comes, but don't make any noise."

"Gracias."

ALEJANDRO DIDN'T bother going to his own apartment when the cab dropped him off. All he had with him was a laptop case and a carry-on bag with wheels and an extendable handle. So he just wheeled it up to Matthew's apartment building. Before he could ring the buzzer, the front door swung open, and there was Matthew, standing there in nothing but a blanket.

"Don't ring the buzzer!" he hissed under his breath. "And keep your voice down. If I wake Mr. Rojas again, he'll kill me."

Alejandro struggled to keep his gaze from searching the gaps in the blanket, trying to see whether his friend was really naked under there. He knew Matthew slept in his underwear, so it seemed unlikely. But it was hard not to speculate. "What's going on?"

"Come into the stairwell."

Matthew stepped back so Alejandro could enter. He helped lift the luggage over the doorstep so it wouldn't bang against the wood, and while his hands were occupied, the blanket slipped off. Alejandro wasn't surprised to see the familiar red-and-black checked boxers, but he was certainly disappointed. He'd seen Matthew naked on occasion, changing clothes, but... not enough.

Once they were safely inside, Matthew wrapped the blanket around himself again, though he was sweating in the summer heat. "There's something wrong with Spartacus."

That snapped Alejandro back to reality and away from thoughts of Matthew's smooth butt. "What? What happened to him?" He remembered his bizarre dream on the plane. Had it been some kind of premonition, after all?

"I don't know. Suddenly he's acting like Cujo. I barely escaped from him without getting my face torn off." He was talking calmly, but his voice sounded strained, and Alejandro could tell he was close to tears. "I don't think he got bitten by anything…."

Alejandro felt a chill go through him. If Spartacus was rabid, that would be it. The poor pup would be put down. The thought horrified him—he'd never known a more awesome dog—and he knew it would kill Matthew. "When did it start?" He had no idea what that would tell them, but it seemed like a good question to ask.

"He was fine before bed…." Matthew hesitated a moment before adding, "Oh, he chewed up your package. I'm sorry."

"What?"

"He didn't destroy the book. But he chewed up the box pretty bad."

"The book?" It finally dawned on him what Matthew meant. *Oh shit.* Well, so much for owning his own copy of *El Gran Libro*. It hardly seemed important at the moment. "He attacked you, then chewed up the book?"

"No, the other way around," Matthew replied, clearly growing frustrated.

It took a few minutes, but Alejandro finally got the complete story. And the more he learned, the more he was disturbed by it. Not only because of what was happening to Spartacus, but because he was becoming more and more convinced it might have something to do with the book. Matthew often poked fun at him for being too superstitious—it was hard not to be, living with Abuela—but Alejandro knew the reputation of the book, and he knew how it had felt when he touched it. The way Matthew had described Spartacus staring intently at it, the way he'd felt about keeping it out of his bedroom… it seemed possible, at least.

Of course, when he explained his theory to Matthew, it didn't go over well. "Oh please! I said he was acting like Cujo. I didn't say we were actually living in a Stephen King novel."

"I had a dream," Alejandro said quickly, "when I was on the plane." He described seeing something coming out of the closet where Matthew had admitted hiding the book, slithering through the apartment, and then honing in on Spartacus.

Matthew stared at him openmouthed for a long time after that. At last he gasped, "You *fucker*!" He glanced at the door to the Rojas's apartment quickly and lowered his voice. "You sent me a cursed book!"

MATTHEW WAS furious. At least, at first. Alejandro was supposed to be the expert in this kind of thing. He was the one who'd grown up surrounded by all this stuff. He should have known better! True, Matthew had, by now, been around saints and floor washes and Florida Water nearly as much, but still....

Gradually, something occurred to him—something that caused his anger to evaporate. Or, nearly. "Wait a minute. If this is... possession or something... then it isn't permanent, right? All we have to do is force the spirit to leave Spartacus, and he'll be just like he was before!"

Alejandro looked uncertain. "Maybe. But I'm not sure how we can do that."

"There has to be something!" Matthew insisted.

His friend frowned and glanced up the staircase. "What's he doing now?"

"I don't know. It's been quiet for the last hour or so, but I think he got out of the bedroom. I thought I heard him pacing around up there while I was in the Rojas's kitchen. I'm afraid if I go up, he'll go nuts again. Even if he doesn't rip me to shreds, someone might hear him and call the police."

"Okay," Alejandro said, surprising Matthew by placing a hand over his. It was an unusually affectionate gesture, coming from him. "Let's go to the botanica. There are things there we can use."

Matthew nodded, his gaze still locked on his hand, held in Alejandro's. Then he recalled, "I need clothes. I can't walk across town in a blanket." Technically he could, but he didn't need the police harassing him.

Alejandro opened his suitcase and dug down past several shirts to a pair of shorts. "These are... well, I've worn them. But they're not that bad."

"You were wearing underwear, right?" Matthew asked, eyeing them dubiously.

"Yes. Don't be an idiot."

Matthew took them and slipped into them. They fit, as he'd known they would. He and his friend had worn each other's clothes more than once.

The shirts, however, were a lost cause. Alejandro sniffed them and grimaced. "You don't want these, huero. They reek."

"There's nothing clean?"

"No," Alejandro replied. "I just brought enough clothes for the trip."

"Fine." Matthew was happy with the shorts. It was hot enough to go shirtless, and he was relieved to get out from under the blanket. He folded it and quietly slipped it back into the Rojas's kitchen. Then he rejoined Alejandro in the stairwell and said, "Let's go."

Chapter Five

ALEJANDRO KNEW his grandmother wouldn't appreciate him raiding the supplies in the botanica. She wasn't a wealthy woman, and everything he took had come out of her own pocket—at least, the reserves she had in the business bank account. If she didn't sell it, she lost money. So he'd have to replace everything he took out of his salary.

But he was convinced what had happened to Spartacus was his fault. Or perhaps, like Matthew, he was *hoping* it was his fault… and that it could be undone. In any case, he had to try.

He started with the books on the shelves. He'd read about "duppies" in Jamaican voodoo—their word for malicious ghosts—but he didn't know if what had possessed Spartacus was one. Could a ghost be bound to a book the way this spirit seemed to have been? Some practitioners of voodoo and Santeria believed in demons, but the difference between demons and ghosts seemed vague in the books. And he was having trouble finding anything useful for getting rid of them, apart from prayers and offerings to the saints.

He really needed to talk to Abuela, but he was frankly more frightened of her than of the spirit, at the moment. She'd kill him for sending that book to Matthew's apartment. At any rate, he wasn't going to wake her up at three in the morning—not until he'd tried some things on his own.

The botanica had incense, sprays, and floor washes for cleansing a house of evil. Those seemed like a good place to start. He grabbed some of the ones he'd seen his grandmother pushing at customers and a couple of others that looked good.

But when he said, "Okay, let's go," Matthew stopped him.

"We can't! If we go into the apartment, he'll flip out again!" Matthew was still sounding like someone on the edge of a nervous breakdown. "They'll call the police and take him away!"

"Okay, okay," Alejandro said, caressing his back to soothe him. "We'll wait until Mr. Rojas goes to work. Then we'll tell Mrs. Rojas and the girls not to call the police if they hear Spartacus barking."

"That's not going to work!" Matthew protested.

It might not. But Alejandro was counting on the fact that few people in their neighborhood really liked dealing with the police. As long as they weren't keeping everyone awake in the middle of the night, the other people in the building might be more prone to look the other way. Or listen the other way, as the case may be. "We'll talk to the Torreses too."

"Don't you know a spell or something to put him to sleep? You know, without harming him?"

Alejandro waved his arm in a gesture that took in the whole shop. "You've been working here too. Do any of these powders and sprays claim they can do that?"

"I don't think so."

"I don't think so either. And the only spell I can remember is putting your nightie over your husband's face when he's asleep to keep him from waking up. I don't think that applies. Besides, you don't own a nightie, so you'd have to use your underwear." An image of Matthew stripping out of his underwear flashed into Alejandro's mind, making his mouth go dry, but he deliberately shoved it away.

Matthew frowned and said sullenly, "Fine."

"When does your mother get home?"

"She has to go directly to work from her boyfriend's house," Matthew replied. "She won't be back 'til tonight."

"Perfect! We'll just wait until about nine." That was five hours away.

It was Matthew who found the potential flaw in that plan. "We probably don't want to be here when Abuela opens the shop." He glanced at the small stack of supplies they'd "borrowed." It was going to be difficult to explain all of this.

"Why don't we go to my apartment?" Alejandro suggested. "Abuela's asleep now. We can sneak in and crash in my room until morning." They'd slept over at each other's apartments plenty of times over the years. Even if his grandmother saw them, she wouldn't think twice about it.

"Okay."

THEY SNUCK into Alejandro's apartment to avoid waking his grandmother. Matthew felt completely at home there, just as Alejandro felt in Matthew's apartment, so he quietly used the bathroom and grabbed a glass of orange juice from the kitchen while his friend stashed their ill-gotten booty in his bedroom. Matthew entered the room, juice in hand, to find Alejandro already stripped to his boxers and pulling down the blankets on his bed. The sight of so much smooth, warm beige skin was distracting enough to make Matthew hesitate a moment, the desire he'd been feeling for years welling up in him again. But he forced himself to ignore it, as he always did.

He sat in the chair next to Alejandro's desk and attempted to take another sip of juice. But his hand was shaking, and Alejandro noticed it.

"He'll be okay," Alejandro said softly.

Matthew wasn't convinced. All they had to work with was an assortment of powders and sprays he didn't have a lot of faith in. But he tried to smile as he set the glass down on the desk.

"I'll be right back," Alejandro said. He slipped out of the room for a moment—probably to use the bathroom.

Normally, when he stayed over, Matthew slept on the floor, on a mat and sleeping bag Alejandro had stowed in his closet. So he got up and went to the closet to fish those out. He unrolled the mat and then laid the sleeping bag down on top of it.

But when Alejandro returned, he glanced at the sleeping bag and asked, "Do you want to share the bed?" When Matthew's eyebrows shot up in surprise, Alejandro quickly added, "I'm not gonna make a pass at you. I just thought… you know… you might want to be… near someone tonight."

It was awkwardly phrased, and Alejandro seemed too embarrassed to look him in the eye as he climbed onto the bed. It wasn't something either of them would have been brave enough to say normally—they were too prone to teasing each other. Matthew couldn't even acknowledge the suggestion in words. He turned off the desk lamp, plunging the room into near darkness except for the faint light coming in the through the window blinds. Then he stepped out of the shorts he'd borrowed and slid under the sheet.

The moment Alejandro's arms wrapped around him, pulling him close, he felt as if he'd been so, so thirsty… dying of thirst… and Alejandro's embrace was pure, cool water, the only thing that could quench it. But he would only have a few hours to drink his fill.

When Alejandro kissed him gently on the back of the neck, Matthew felt a flood of warmth spread from the spot to fill his entire body. "I'll make it better," his friend whispered. "I promise."

Chapter Six

ALEJANDRO WASN'T sure if he slept or not. Maybe he did, because it seemed like Matthew had only just settled into his arms when the alarm clock went off. Matthew moaned softly in protest, and Alejandro quickly reached across him to silence the alarm. He was still stretched out half on top when Matthew snickered. "What?"

"Somebody has a boner."

It was true. Alejandro realized he'd been mashing it into Matthew's hip. He quickly rolled away. "Shut up. You probably do too."

Matthew didn't confirm the accusation… but he didn't deny it either. Instead, he turned red and glanced away. "Is Abuela still here?"

Alejandro forced his mind away from thoughts of Matthew's hard-on and glanced at the clock. It was just past nine. "She should be at the botanica by now."

Matthew slipped out of the bed, muttering something about needing to piss, and quickly left the room. Alejandro couldn't help but notice that he made sure to keep his front hidden while he did so. A short time later, he could hear his friend taking a leak in the bathroom.

Frustrated, Alejandro got up and dressed, thankful Matthew wasn't there to see how much his boxers were jutting out in front of him. It wasn't the first time they'd awoken with morning hard-ons and teased each other about it, but it was the first time they'd cuddled the night before. Everything felt different now—weird.

Did I actually kiss *him?* It wasn't that he minded the thought. Not at all. But…. Christ, where had he gotten the courage to do that?

By the time Matthew came back into the room, Alejandro was deflated enough to pretend there hadn't been any sexual overtones to sharing the bed. After all, it wasn't like anyone had done any groping in the night. It had just been one friend consoling another.

Yeah, that's all.

At any rate, they had more important things to worry about. "Get dressed," Alejandro said. He didn't bother suggesting Matthew borrow his clothes, because of course he would. "Then I have something I want you to do before we go over there."

The "something" was totally revolting, and he knew Matthew would give him shit over it.

"You're fucking kidding me," Matthew said, his face screwed up in disgust as Alejandro held out the raw meat from the fridge. It had been thawing in there last night. Alejandro had been happy to find it just before they went to sleep. But he had no idea how he'd explain to Abuela where a big chunk of it had gone.

"It's a very old spell," Alejandro explained again. "It will turn a dog away from its master and make him loyal to you."

"I *am* his master!"

"Not at the moment."

"Raw meat," Matthew said. "In my armpit."

"You have to hold it there for an hour."

"While it drips blood down my side. What the *fuck*, Alejandro? We don't have time for this!"

Alejandro shrugged. "I'm going to talk to the neighbors and try to convince them to ignore any noises coming from your apartment. Spartacus still has a crate in the living room, right?"

"Yeah. We never use it anymore, but it's there."

"Then we need to try to throw the meat into it so we can lock him up."

MATTHEW STOOD outside his apartment building as the morning grew hotter, feeling the squishy, raw steak slipping around under his armpit every time he moved. *He cursed my dog, and now he's making me do this. Why haven't I killed him yet?*

Matthew was shirtless, thank God. Wearing a shirt would have just made it worse. Alejandro had tucked a plastic grocery bag into the waistband of the shorts he was wearing—Alejandro's shorts, since there had seemed little point in putting on something clean—and although that kept some of the blood off the *outside* of the shorts, it caused it to pool in places along the waistband and dribble down the *inside*. The whole experience was beyond disgusting.

He thought back to Alejandro spooning him the night before. If he hadn't been falling apart, it might have been one of the best moments of his life. He'd fantasized about Alejandro holding him like that more times than he could remember. Though in his fantasies, the cuddling had just been the beginning, moving on to kissing and caressing and hot man-on-man action. But things would probably go back to normal when this was over—hopefully with Spartacus safely restored to his old self—back to just being good friends, horsing around, teasing each other. Caring about each other, but not… *loving* each other.

While he was wallowing in these dismal thoughts, Alejandro came out the front door of the building. "I've talked to everyone. I told them to stay inside until I give the all clear. I don't want one of their kids opening their apartment door and getting mauled by Spartacus if he gets out. And it sounds to me like he's still pacing back and forth in the living room. I listened at the door for a minute, and he growled at me."

"Terrific," Matthew muttered.

"I also called Abuelita to let her know I got back last night. But I told her I need to help you with something this morning." Alejandro checked his cell phone for the time. "We'll go in, in about fifteen minutes. Stay here a minute—I have to get dressed."

Matthew wasn't sure what he meant by that, since he was already wearing a T-shirt, pants, and sneakers, which was more than Matthew had on. But he waited while Alejandro went back into his apartment. A few minutes later, he returned in the most ridiculous getup Matthew could have imagined. Despite the fact that it was almost eighty degrees, Alejandro had put on his leather jacket and leather gloves. Most absurdly, he was wearing the hockey mask he'd worn in high school when he was on the team for a while. Matthew had to laugh. "How the hell can you breathe in that thing?"

"I'm dying," Alejandro admitted. He lifted the mask up to gasp in some air. "Jesus! We've gotta get this done fast or I'll pass out. Here's the plan. Do you have your key handy?"

"The apartment isn't locked," Matthew said. "There wasn't time to grab my pants, and that's where my keys are." He hadn't wanted to lock himself out.

Alejandro nodded. "All right. Fine. I'll throw open the door and rush in first. I'm gonna try to grab Spartacus by the collar. Once I've got him restrained, I need you to run to his crate and toss that delicious, underarm-sweat-soaked meat inside. Then get the fuck out of the room before he takes a bite out of your ass."

"And go where, exactly?"

"I don't know. Lock yourself in the bathroom if you have to. Once I get the crate closed, you can come back into the room."

It didn't sound like a brilliant plan, but Matthew didn't have a better one, so he agreed to it. By the time they'd gone into the building and climbed the stairs to the apartment, Alejandro's jet black hair was plastered to his face and dripping rivulets of sweat. He slipped the mask into place as he crept up to the door. They were afraid of alerting Spartacus, so Alejandro counted down silently with his fingers: three… two… one….

He burst into the apartment, and almost immediately Spartacus was upon him, barking ferociously. Then Alejandro cried out in pain. From his place on the landing, Matthew couldn't see clearly, but it looked as if the pit bull had sunk his teeth into Alejandro's arm. Matthew wondered fearfully whether the leather was tough enough to prevent the dog from ripping an enormous chunk of flesh out of his friend's forearm.

Then Alejandro shouted, "Matthew! Now!"

Matthew ran into the apartment and slammed the door behind him. Alejandro had Spartacus by the collar as he'd planned, holding it tightly in his left hand, but the dog hadn't released his death grip on his right arm. Blood was dripping out the end of the jacket sleeve.

Fuck!

The living room couch was still kitty-corner to the room, one end pressed up against Matthew's bedroom door. The door, surprisingly enough, wasn't smashed through, but Spartacus had apparently broken the latch and shoved the couch back far enough to make his escape. Matthew ran around the other end of the couch to where the dog's crate lay open in the far corner of the living room, but when he moved to toss the meat into it, he glanced back and realized Spartacus wasn't paying any attention to him at all. He was holding fast to Alejandro's arm, despite the boy trying to pull him off. Alejandro was managing not to scream, but he was grunting in obvious pain and swearing in a steady stream of Spanish.

"Spartacus!" Matthew tried waving the piece of meat in the air, but the dog didn't pay any attention.

This was a stupid plan!

Matthew scrambled over the top of the couch until he was close enough to shove the meat directly in front of the dog's nose. "Come on, you dumb dog! It's meat!"

"Matthew! Get away—"

Spartacus released Alejandro's arm and lunged for the chunk of steak faster than Matthew was prepared for. He came close to losing a finger as the pit bull sank his teeth into the meat.

"Fuck me!" Matthew had just enough presence of mind to keep a hold of his end of the steak. It tore in two, and Spartacus wolfed down his chunk in a single gulp. Then he lunged for the other half, still in Matthew's hand.

If he'd thought for two seconds, Matthew would have jumped back over the couch—it was the shortest route to the crate and might have slowed Spartacus down, since the dog was relatively short and squat. But he didn't think. He ran. Somewhere in the back of his mind, he saw a flash of an old silent movie where people were running at high speed with silly piano music playing, as he scrambled around the far end of the couch and looped around the coffee table before he remembered where he was supposed to be going. In one motion, he tossed the scrap of raw meat into the crate and jumped up on top of the thing.

He wasn't exactly safe there. It was strong, but nothing more than a wire mesh. His fingers and toes were sticking down into the crate, where Spartacus could easily bite them. But the dog took a minute to pounce on the meat and scarf it down. In that tiny interval, Matthew jumped down to close the door and throw the bolt.

Spartacus was trapped.

He didn't like it. The dog threw himself against the crate, but it was strong enough to hold him. While he clawed at it and snarled, Matthew scrambled out of reach. He turned back to Alejandro, who was still standing near the door, clutching his arm.

"I'm sorry," Alejandro said. "I was supposed to do that."

And then he collapsed.

Chapter Seven

ALEJANDRO WOKE to find himself lying on the floor with a pillow under his head and all his clothing gone. Well, he figured out after a second that his boxers were still on. But otherwise, he was naked. Matthew was wiping his chest and stomach down with a cool, damp washcloth.

"Um… where are my clothes?"

"In the bathtub," Matthew replied, looking a bit embarrassed. "They were all covered in blood."

"You had to take my pants off too?"

Matthew turned red, which Alejandro thought was adorable. "You bled all down your leg. Besides, you were sweating like a pig. I was afraid you'd get heatstroke or something, all bundled up like that in this weather. So I thought it was a good idea to cool you off."

Truthfully, Alejandro was incredibly relieved to be out of the leather jacket, gloves, and hockey mask. The rest… well, who was he to complain if Matthew wanted to undress him? "Did you at least have your way with me?" he asked. "It's been a while since I've gotten laid."

Matthew snorted. "Don't forget who you're talking to. Unless you had a really good time in New Orleans, I know you've never gotten laid—ever."

"Jose Garcia gave me a blowjob."

"I know. I was there, and he gave me a blowjob too. But that's not the same as getting laid."

Alejandro didn't argue. If he did, he might have to admit that Jose had come on to him a few days later, offering a lot more than just a blowjob. And Alejandro had turned him down, because he hadn't wanted his first time to be with someone he didn't feel anything for.

He'd wanted it to be with Matthew.

"Your arm is all chewed to shit," Matthew said, frowning. "I've been waiting to see if you turned into some kind of were-pit bull or something."

Alejandro rolled his eyes. "Don't be an idiot."

"I see," Matthew said, frowning at him. "Possession by evil spirits is totally realistic, but were-animals are silly. Got it."

"Fuck you, huero. I don't have the energy to argue. And my arm hurts."

Matthew didn't bother responding to the "fuck you" part—they said that to each other all the time, anyway—but he looked concerned about the rest of it. "We should probably get you to a doctor."

Alejandro lifted his arm to look at it, but Matthew had cleaned it and wrapped his entire forearm in bandaging. He couldn't see how bad the damage was. It was throbbing painfully, but not nearly as bad as it had felt when Spartacus had his teeth embedded in it. "Later. We have to do what we came to do." If he did go to a doctor, he'd have to lie about some "strange dog" biting him. If he mentioned Spartacus, someone might insist the dog be put down, regardless.

Alejandro struggled to sit up and Matthew helped him. For the first time, he noticed Matthew had cleaned the blood off himself and changed into some fresh shorts. "How is he?"

"He's gone kind of quiet," Matthew said, glancing in the general direction of the dog crate. They couldn't actually see it from down here on the floor because the couch was in the way. "But he's sure as hell not back to normal."

"Get the bag of stuff from the hall," Alejandro said. "Then we'll cleanse the apartment."

THE APARTMENT would have needed cleansing even if there hadn't been an evil spirit in it. Spartacus had crapped on the floor in a couple of spots and urinated God knew where. He'd also managed to get under the sink and drag the garbage out onto the floor. In eighty-degree weather, it wasn't surprising that the place reeked.

Matthew scooped up the poop with paper towels and flushed it down the toilet, while Alejandro did his best to clean up the garbage in the kitchen. Although he wasn't complaining, he was deathly slow at it, and Matthew could tell he was in a lot of pain. Matthew did most of the cleaning and then left his friend to fill the mop bucket with water and one of the cleansing washes from the botanica. He went around the apartment with a small black light that illuminated urine spots. He'd bought it when Spartacus was a puppy. He hadn't had to use it in a while, but he found a few spots now on the floor and furniture and cleaned them with an enzyme spray specifically designed for animal urine. Apparently, evil spirits weren't house-trained.

Matthew was having a hard time keeping it together. Every time he allowed himself to glance at the dog crate, he was shocked at how little the animal inside resembled his sweet puppy. Spartacus panted and watched him intently—perhaps suspiciously—with eyes that seemed glazed over, ears flattened against his head, drool mixed with blood from the raw steak hanging in ropes from his mouth....

Matthew focused on cleaning and prayed the washes and sprays Alejandro had brought would somehow bring Spartacus back from wherever he was.

The floor of the apartment was wood in all the rooms, including the living room, which made things a little easier. The wash had to be mixed with water and then used to mop the floor throughout the entire apartment. Since Alejandro couldn't do that effectively one-handed, Matthew did it. Alejandro opened a window and sprayed the place with Eleggua spray.

Eleggua spray was exactly what it sounded like—a spray to encourage the spirit Eleggua to manifest himself and chase away evil. The first time Matthew had seen that, and aerosols dedicated to other spirits, on the shelves of the botanica, he'd been flabbergasted. Spirit summoning in a can? The idea seemed beyond laughable. But Abuela had glared at him, and Alejandro had explained that it wasn't all that different from lighting incense at the beginning of a religious ritual. This particular scent—which frankly smelled a bit like Florida Water to Matthew, but sharper, more masculine—was pleasing to Eleggua, so the spirit was more likely to make his presence known where it had been sprayed.

Matthew still wasn't sure how much he believed, but he knew Abuela took these things very seriously, and her grandson... well, he suspected Alejandro took it more seriously than he let on. He might act dismissive of it when he was just talking to Matthew, but deep down he believed in it. And right now, if it would get Spartacus back, Matthew wanted to believe in it too.

While he sprayed the apartment, Alejandro was muttering under his breath in Spanish. Matthew couldn't hear him clearly, but he was pretty sure it was a prayer to Eleggua or his Santeria equivalent, St. Anthony.

Between the wash and the spray, it was getting hard to breathe in there, open window or not.

When Matthew had finished mopping, Alejandro approached him and dabbed some Florida Water on his neck and the middle of his forehead. Then he handed him a small plastic bottle of clear liquid. "Splash this on Spartacus."

Matthew looked at the label. "Holy water? This is *real*?" He'd seen it on the shelves at the shop but dismissed it, convinced it was… well, if not a joke, then at least something only gullible people believed in. He'd only ever seen people using holy water in horror movies to kill vampires.

Or… exorcisms. There was that.

"Of course it's real," Alejandro said impatiently. "It's water that's been blessed by a priest."

"It won't hurt him, will it?"

Alejandro hesitated. "Well… it's just water, so it's not like you have to worry about it getting in his eyes like Florida Water or something." Florida Water was highly alcoholic. They'd put some in a bowl and lit it on fire once. "But the spirit's not gonna like it."

Matthew nodded. He'd seen *The Exorcist*. He knew what that could mean. But that made him think of something else. "Do I have to say something? Like 'the power of Christ compels you,' or something like that?"

Alejandro clearly tried not to laugh, but he couldn't stop himself from snorting.

"Fuck you," Matthew said. He stalked off, holy water in hand, though he couldn't go far, since the living room was only about twenty feet across.

He approached Spartacus's crate and looked down at his beloved dog. The pit bull looked up at him expectantly, not growling but panting heavily. Maybe the stupid meat "spell" had worked, at least a little, because every time Alejandro had walked near him over the past hour, the dog had growled at him. But he hadn't been doing that with Matthew. He just watched his master, panting and… waiting.

"Dipshit over there tells me this won't hurt," Matthew told him in a quiet, soothing voice. "I don't want to hurt you. You know that, don't you, Spartacus? I just want you to come back to me."

With that, he opened the bottle and shook it back and forth over the crate, so that its contents rained down upon the dog. Whatever he'd hoped would happen, what he got was definitely not it. Spartacus threw himself against the door of the crate, barking and snarling in rage.

Matthew jumped back in terror, only to discover Alejandro standing there, blocking his retreat.

"It's not working!" Matthew said, feeling the sting of tears behind his eyes. "Nothing's working."

To his surprise, Alejandro wrapped his arms around his waist from behind, as if to comfort him. He pressed his cheek against Matthews neck and murmured, "It's okay. It's okay. We'll think of something else."

WHAT ELSE they could try, Alejandro had no idea. He'd brought some more things from the store, such as a small bottle of Cast Away Evil powder, a can of Go Away Evil spray, and a perfume called *Alcalado Kitamal* for chasing away evil. But he no longer had much confidence that they'd do any good. Perhaps sprinkling some Florida Water on Spartacus wouldn't be a bad idea after all....

"When you left the shop last night," he asked, "did Abuela spritz you with Florida Water?"

"Yes, of course. She always does."

In his dream, Alejandro had seen the spirit shy away from Matthew. Perhaps it had been the Florida Water. They could try it on Spartacus. But what if that just angered the spirit and made the situation worse? He simply didn't know what he was doing.

His thoughts were interrupted by his cell phone going off somewhere in the apartment. Since he was in his underwear, the phone wasn't on him, and he was busy anyway, so he was tempted to ignore it. But that ring tone was for his grandmother, and he didn't like to ignore her calls. "Is my phone still in my pants?"

"Yes."

Reluctantly, Alejandro withdrew his arms from around Matthew's waist and went into the bathroom. There he found his pants piled on top of the rest of his clothing in the bathtub. Matthew had been right—the right side of his jeans had a lot of blood dribbled down it. He couldn't get his phone out of the pocket without getting it on his hands, but he ignored it. "Sí."

"Alejandro! I've been robbed!"

"What?" he asked, alarmed. "What happened?" He was picturing some thug with a gun going into the botanica.

"I noticed that there were fewer bottles of Florida Water since last night," Abuela went on nervously. "One's missing! So I looked around the shop. A lot of things are missing! Some *pinche cabrón* broke in and robbed a poor old woman who can barely scrape by!"

Alejandro was simultaneously relieved and terrified to realize that the pinche cabrón was him. He'd intended to present her with a list of items he'd taken after this whole mess was over, along with a promise to pay for all of it. Now he was going to have to come clean when she was already worked up. Not exactly ideal.

"It's okay, Abuelita! Nobody stole anything. I took those things, and I'm going to pay for them."

There was shocked silence on the end of the line. Then she gasped, "You? *Idiota! Baboso!* You steal from your own grandmother! Scare me half to death! Didn't I raise you to have more respect?" The tirade went on for a considerable time before Alejandro was able to get a word in.

"Abuelita! I told you I'd pay for them!"

"What, in the name of all that is holy, could you possibly need that stuff for? Alcalado Kitamal? Eleggua spray?"

There was no way around it. He wasn't clever enough to come up with a lie that would make sense. So he told her the whole story, from finding the book all the way up to his and Matthew's failed attempt to cleanse the apartment and douse Spartacus with holy water.

"Estupido!" she spat out. "Just where did you expect the spirit to go, if you managed to chase it out? Downstairs to one of those sweet little girls?"

She normally had a somewhat harsher view of the "sweet" teenaged Rojas daughters, but Alejandro got her point. The spirit could easily have attempted to possess the next unprotected animal or person it came into contact with. "We were trying to chase it out the window," he said, realizing how lame that sounded.

"Tu eres un idiota!" Abuela told him. "Don't do anything more! You'll just make it worse. I'm coming over."

Chapter Eight

MATTHEW FOUND a pair of shorts for Alejandro so he wouldn't have to face the Wrath of Abuela in his boxers, and the two of them spent the next few minutes straightening up the rest of the living room. It didn't take Abuela long to get there, considering she normally walked pretty slow and the botanica was a few blocks away. When she knocked, the boys exchanged worried glances before Alejandro opened the door.

She stood on the landing, a tiny old Latina in a cerulean-blue blouse and pink slacks, clutching a worn, woven handbag, and scowling enough to wither the houseplants. She ignored her grandson, marching past him and directly into the living room, where she peered down at Spartacus.

The pit bull had quieted again, but he was still panting heavily and salivating. He looked ill.

"Poor boy," she told him, her voice surprisingly soft. "We'll make you well again, sí?"

Then she turned to Matthew, the stern mask falling back into place. "Close the window and draw the shades. It must be dark."

While he hurried to obey, the old woman ordered Alejandro to bring her a wooden chair from the kitchen so she wouldn't have to strain her bad knee kneeling on the floor. Then she handed him several black candles in small jars and some old-fashioned wooden matches. "Light these and place them on the floor in a circle."

Alejandro did so, forming the circle between his grandmother and the dog crate. Spartacus growled low in his throat whenever Alejandro got too close, but otherwise he remained quiet, as if fascinated by what Abuela might be up to.

Maybe he is, thought Matthew. *Or at least, maybe the spirit is.* The thought of something sinister watching them from behind Spartacus's eyes made him shiver.

Under Abuela's direction, Alejandro drew a pattern on the floor inside the circle of light created by the candles. He used white cornmeal to create the lines, and the pattern was one Matthew didn't recognize, though it looked similar to veves he was familiar with. When it was done, Abuela pulled a small glass bottle from her bag. It had a wide mouth and was filled with brand-new shiny nails, dried leaves of some thorny plant, and some gray-green spidery substance that might have been Spanish moss. The bottom had some kind of powder in it.

"What is that?" Alejandro asked quietly, but his grandmother shushed him with a curt gesture.

"Put this in the middle," she said, handing him the bottle. Then she took a small bottle of Jack Daniels and a cigar out of her handbag and set the bag on the floor. "Now help me up."

When she was standing, Abuela lit the cigar and began to sing, stopping now and then to puff on the cigar and lean down to blow the smoke at the bottle on the floor. Matthew could only hear bits of the song, since she was singing softly, half under her breath. It was in Spanish, of course, and what little bits he could catch seemed to be cajoling, calling the spirit to come drink and smoke with her. Once in a while, she would take a sip of the Jack Daniels—which shocked him, since Abuela never drank, as far as he knew—and then she would sprinkle some of the whiskey down onto the bottle.

Matthew crouched off to the side of the ritual circle, opposite Alejandro, and kept silent. He had no idea what was going on, but he knew interrupting would probably be extremely bad. In the flickering candlelight, Alejandro seemed to be watching his grandmother with rapt attention, and when Matthew dared to look at Spartacus, he was surprised to find the dog lying with his massive head on his paws, looking at the candles through half-closed lids, as if he were falling asleep.

Suddenly the room seemed to darken, and Matthew felt as if he was having trouble breathing. He looked at Alejandro in alarm and saw fear flicker across his face. Was something going wrong? The candle flames sputtered and appeared to be about to blow out. The smoke in the room was so thick, Matthew thought he was going to suffocate or vomit or both.

But Abuela remained calm. She continued to sing, slowly bending down to get close to the circle. Then with a single, swift motion, she reached out and shoved a broad cork into the opening of the bottle. She smiled slyly and said with a chuckle, "Got you!"

The air immediately felt lighter. It was still full of cigar smoke, but Matthew no longer felt as if he was suffocating. Nevertheless, he was relieved when Abuela told Alejandro, "Open the windows and let some light in. It is done."

A whimper came from Spartacus's crate, and Matthew turned to see his dog pawing at the floor and whining, the way he always did when he wanted to be let out. Matthew leaned closer, not yet daring to hope the ordeal was over. Spartacus looked up at him, tired and bedraggled, but his eyes finally clear. He barked once—not a ferocious sound, but the sound of a dog greeting his master—and wagged his tail.

"Spartacus!"

"I think he wants to come out," Abuela said behind him, her voice full of warm humor.

Matthew fumbled with the bolt on the crate, and Spartacus came charging out at him. But there was nothing savage in his "attack" as he bowled Matthew over onto the floor and began licking his face. "Ugh! You're drenched in spit! It's disgusting!"

But Matthew couldn't stop laughing, even though his eyes were brimming with tears.

To Alejandro, the sight of Matthew rolling on the floor with Spartacus, laughing after a night and morning of pure hell, was the most beautiful thing he'd ever seen. He wanted to join in their roughhousing, but his grandmother had other ideas.

"Where is the book?" she asked him, tapping the cigar out on the side of the whiskey bottle. She was scowling again.

Alejandro wasn't sure, but Matthew had said it was in the closet by the front door. He didn't feel like disturbing the happy reunion going on at the moment, so he walked over to the closet and peered inside. Up on the top shelf, he could see a spot in the corner where some packaging was half buried underneath hats and mittens, so he reached up to pull it out. Before he touched it, he asked his grandmother, "Is it safe now?"

"Sí."

He could tell that the moment he touched it. The sense of foreboding was gone, and when he removed the box from the shredded packaging and opened it to touch the book, the pages no longer felt greasy. They felt like dry, brittle paper.

He brought the book to his grandmother and held it out to her, but she made no move to take it. "Burn it," she said, her voice dripping with contempt. When Alejandro hesitated, some part of him still reluctant to destroy something so old, so rare, she added, "You can read parts of it, if you absolutely have to. It won't do you any harm now. But I won't have it in my house, and I doubt Matthew wants anything more to do with it."

"No!" Matthew affirmed from his spot on the floor. He was scratching Spartacus behind the ears, the pit bull lying against his leg, half-asleep from exhaustion but moaning contentedly at his master's touch. "I don't ever want to see that fucking thing again."

"Okay," Alejandro said.

He took it outside to the barbeque grill in the tiny backyard of the apartment building, intending to set it on top of the grill. But he changed his mind. Abuela was probably right about it being harmless—she would know, if anyone would—but the thought of putting it on a grill used for cooking hamburgers and hotdogs bothered him. He pictured the building being plagued by an outbreak of cursed cheeseburgers. So he laid it on the dirt in a corner of the yard instead, digging a small pit for it.

He flipped through the pages one last time, seeing invocations to the devil, curses for enemies, spells for forcing someone to love you or forcing them to leave their lovers, and then he closed it and doused it with charcoal starter. He lit a match, tossed it onto the book, and watched it go up in a ball of fire. He sat there for a long time watching it burn, dousing it with more charcoal lighter whenever the flames seemed about to go out. He made sure not a single scrap of paper was left unburned.

Then he buried it.

Chapter Nine

IT WASN'T easy to get into a cemetery in Manchester undetected at midnight. There were lights everywhere and cop cars patrolling the streets that bordered the low walls, on the lookout for vandals. But Matthew and Alejandro were teenagers living in one of the low-rent neighborhoods of the city. They were used to being regarded with suspicion, especially at night. And they were experts at dodging patrol cars.

Abuela had sent them on this mission. "Someone, a long time ago, bound this spirit to the book. Maybe to guard it—to keep fools like you two from messing with it. The spirit was a dead man with a troubled conscience. A criminal. Maybe a murderer. I lured it into the bottle, but now you must finish the job. Take it to the cemetery and bury it. And give the spirit some peace."

Matthew didn't really care much for giving the spirit some "peace." As far as he was concerned, the spirit could damn well suffer for what it did to Spartacus. But if this would get the goddamned thing out of his life forever, he'd go along with it.

They'd gone to the Elliot at River's Edge, the new urgent care center, to get Alejandro's arm seen to that afternoon. He wasn't going to die, but he'd definitely have some scars. The doctor had forced him to take a rabies shot, since Alejandro couldn't exactly tell her he knew the dog that'd bitten him wasn't infected. Matthew knew he wouldn't go back for the remaining four she wanted to give him.

He was still in pain, so Matthew had to do most of the work that night, digging the hole with a garden trowel. It wasn't actually in somebody's grave, but at the base of a tree, and Abuela had insisted it be three feet deep. The bottle was still corked, of course, and she'd threatened to kill both boys with her bare hands if they let the cork slip out. Matthew placed the bottle in the hole and buried it while Alejandro kept lookout.

When it was done, Alejandro recited some prayers his grandmother had taught him and placed a coin on the makeshift grave for the watcher of the cemetery, payment to keep the spirit there.

On their way out, a patrol car drove by, forcing them to duck down behind the stone wall at the boundary of the cemetery. While they were crouched, their heads close together, Alejandro whispered, "I'm sorry."

"You already said that. About ten times."

"I'll never be able to say it enough."

"Oh, stop it," Matthew said, reaching one hand up to cup behind Alejandro's neck. The affectionate gesture wasn't something Matthew would normally have done, but the past twenty-four hours seemed to have changed the boundaries a bit. "I shouldn't have left the package on the bed for Spartacus to tear apart. If it had just been a rare book, I'd be the one apologizing."

He moved to take his hand away, but Alejandro reached up to hold his wrist. Their faces were incredibly close together, and in the moonlight, Matthew could see the pain in his friend's eyes. Alejandro wasn't able to accept forgiveness this way—not through mere words. So Matthew leaned forward and forgave him with a kiss.

He would never have done it if he'd allowed a moment's thought before acting. There were a million reasons why kissing Alejandro could be the worst idea ever. A surge of panic rose up in him, and he tried to pull back, but it was too late. Alejandro enveloped him in his arms and practically devoured his mouth. The feeling of panic gave way to shock, and then slowly, tentatively, to joy. The feel of Alejandro's lips was softer than Matthew had imagined they would be, and so wonderfully warm. With their faces pressed together, the familiar scent of Alejandro's skin—musky, and smelling faintly of Ivory soap and the inescapable spice of Florida Water—overwhelmed him and filled him with a sense of coming home.

There was an odd light, somehow growing brighter, until Matthew realized someone was shining a flashlight down at them. A man's voice said gruffly, "All right, you two. Get up here where I can see you. I hope, for your sake, you've got pants on."

Shit.

They broke the clinch and stood awkwardly, blinking into the flashlight. The policeman was standing on the other side of the wall. If they'd really wanted, they probably could have made a break for it into the cemetery. It would have taken him a few seconds to get over the wall and come after them. They'd probably have been able to outrun him.

But when he said, "Come out here onto the sidewalk," they obeyed. The wall was only waist high, so it wasn't hard to just climb over it. The policeman turned the flashlight off once they were on the sidewalk in front of him, and Matthew could see that he was young—probably in his twenties. He didn't look threatening. More amused.

"Okay, I know doing it in a cemetery is a turn-on for some people, but it's public property. It's also locked up after dark, so you shouldn't be in there anyway."

"We weren't 'doing it,'" Alejandro said sullenly.

He had a tendency to mouth off to cops, teachers, anyone in authority—except for Abuela—and Matthew was afraid he'd get them into even more trouble than they were already in. But the policeman just nodded, as if conceding the point.

"Tell you what," he said. "If you promise to find someplace where you're not trespassing before you get back to whatever you *were* doing… we'll just call it good."

Alejandro looked like he was about to say something unpleasant, so Matthew jumped in. "Sure. Okay."

"All right," the policeman said, smiling and turning away. He didn't even bother asking their names. "You two have a nice night."

ALEJANDRO FUMED the entire walk home. The best moment of his entire life! Ruined by a cop! *Figures*. Gradually, though, it dawned on him that Matthew was still there, walking beside him. Maybe the best moment of his life wasn't *entirely* ruined.

"So…," he said, not sure if talking about it was a good idea. But he kind of had to. "Do you want to be my boyfriend now?"

"I guess so."

Alejandro stopped walking, unsure whether to feel elated or crushed. "You don't sound very enthusiastic."

Matthew turned back to him. They were in the shadows between streetlights, so it was hard to see his face. "We've been best friends for so long, it feels like my entire life. And I've been in love with you for just as long. You have no idea how desperate I've been to tell you I love you—"

"I think I know."

Matthew stopped for a second, as if he had to absorb that. Then he continued. "What if it all falls apart now? What if we break up and can't stand the sight of each other? I don't know if I could deal with not having you around anymore."

Alejandro stepped forward and put his hands on Matthew's waist, feeling the heat of his skin through the thin T-shirt he was wearing. "I'm scared of that too. But I know I love you—"

"I love *you*!"

"—and right now it's feeling like a good thing."

Matthew leaned closer until their foreheads bumped together and Alejandro could feel his soft breath on his face. "Yeah."

MATTHEW'S MOTHER had come back to the apartment earlier in the evening, after she'd gotten off work. She'd immediately insisted upon opening all the windows, saying, "What on earth happened while I was gone? It smells like a whorehouse in here! And were you *smoking*?"

Matthew had told her Abuela had come over and smoked a cigar, which killed any further discussion about it. Nobody told Abuela she couldn't smoke a cigar, if she wanted to.

Now, as the boys let themselves into the apartment, everything was quiet. Mrs. Shaw had long ago gone to bed. Of course, the moment he noticed the door opening, Spartacus launched himself at Matthew.

Spartacus was still a bit worn out from his ordeal, so rather than a full-on assault, Matthew merely had to deal with being circled and licked to death. Alejandro received the same treatment, and both boys ended up on the floor for a few minutes, nuzzling the beast. Matthew had cleaned him up that afternoon, so Spartacus was more or less back to normal now.

He would have nothing of being locked out of the bedroom, however, so Matthew had no choice but to let him in. Spartacus immediately jumped on the bed and curled up in his usual position at the foot of it.

"So much for a night of hot sex," Matthew muttered as he closed the door behind him.

Alejandro stood by the bed as he slipped out of his shirt, revealing the same lean, muscular chest Matthew had seen a million times before… though somehow it seemed much, much sexier now. "I suppose we can wait on that," he said, laughing. "As long as I get to hold you tonight."

Matthew approached him and ran a hand down his sternum, following the faint trail of dark hair that started there, down over the contours of his taut abdomen to hook his fingers into the waistband of his jeans. "Naked?"

Alejandro growled quietly, a low, lustful sound that made Matthew's cock swell. "Naked would be good."

Isolated

Author's Note

THOUGH I wrote this story for the third Gothika anthology, it was based upon a screenplay I wrote a decade earlier, when I was making microbudget horror films as a hobby. However, while I discovered it was relatively easy to make films with lots of blood splatters, corpse makeup, and community theater actors, it wasn't at all easy to make a film with a werewolf that wasn't laughable on camera. The screenplay required at least one close-up of the face, and we just weren't up to the task.

But I loved the story, so it was resurrected as *Isolated*. I would say that at least two-thirds of it is new, because a screenplay only shows the dialog and actions. A story has to bring the reader into the character's thoughts, drop in a little backstory, and rely upon description to convey what the camera would be showing. (And though I'd always intended for the film to have a fair amount of nudity, as my previous films did, it would never have gone as far during the sex scenes as it can in a story.)

It was fun. I learned a lot more about my characters in the process.

The ending was originally intended to be a classic '80s-style horror movie freeze-frame. I won't go into it more and spoil it. But if you'd like to find out what happened to Sean and Jack, they make a small appearance in my novel *Small Town Sonata*.

THE OLD Mazda shimmied so much on the dirt road that Sean could almost forget his hands were trembling. But not quite. It had been so long. Would Jack be happy to see him? Sean felt as if they'd had a fight, but they hadn't. Not really. Things had just gotten... weird. Four years apart hadn't seemed like that long when Sean had set out to find Jack, but the closer he got, the longer it seemed.

He passed something that could have been a turnoff. It hadn't looked like much more than a deer track, but Larry had said it was easy to miss. Sean slammed on the brakes, making his worn tires skid on the dirt and gravel, then backed up. There was no way he could turn around without ending up in the forest.

He saw wheel ruts going off into the trees. That had to be it.

Sean turned onto the road—if it could be called that. It was more a trail of deep tire ruts on either side of a low ridge of grass and rock. He prayed his car wouldn't bottom out. He'd also been fretting about the gas tank the last few miles. What if this wasn't the right road, after all? Would he end up stranded in the middle of nowhere with an empty tank of gas and the sun going down?

When he was a teenager, he and Jack had spent a ton of time in the woods. They'd learned how to build a shelter and start a campfire and get drinkable water. But that had been a long time ago. He wasn't anxious to see if his wilderness survival skills were still up to par.

He thought about turning back as the road narrowed and the brush seemed to be closing in on him. But just as he'd decided he couldn't risk going any farther, he rounded a bend, and there it was: a log cabin with a broad front porch, just as Larry had described it. The clincher was the beat-up old black pickup in the yard with the words "Jack of All Trades" stenciled on the side in yellow letters.

Cute.

Relieved, Sean pulled his car alongside the truck and stepped out. The summer air was hot and muggy, and his T-shirt was already clinging to his torso. Now that he was standing still, mosquitoes began to ravage his skin.

"Jack?" he called out, feeling the need to announce himself before walking up to the front door. He opened the trunk and hoisted his suitcase out.

Jack wasn't inside the house, anyway. After a minute, he came around from the back, wiping dirty hands on the red-checked flannel shirt he was holding. He looked good; Sean couldn't help but notice. He seemed a little taller than the last time they'd seen each other, when they were both twenty—though he'd always been a few inches taller than Sean. He also looked more muscular. Working as a handyman around town appeared to have kept him lean and added some definition to his stomach and chest. His dark brown hair was a bit on the shaggy side, but it suited him. Right then, sweat was running in tiny rivulets from his hairline. It streaked down his face and neck to pool in the hollows of his collarbones before spilling down his naked torso.

Jack looked at Sean for a long moment, as if he couldn't believe what he was seeing. Then he wiped the sweat off his face and tossed the shirt over one shoulder. "Hey."

"Hey."

Jack glanced down at the suitcase in Sean's hand. "You moving in?"

"Well," Sean replied uncomfortably, "I was kinda hoping I could stay with you for a few days."

Jesus! What was I thinking? It was an absurd request, considering how long it had been since they'd seen each other. But the old Jack would have had no problem with it. Sean realized then how much he'd been counting on that.

Fortunately, the "new" Jack didn't seem too bent out of shape about it, either. He just nodded and asked, "You have a fight with Denise?"

Sean shrugged. "No fight. Just a divorce."

THEY SAT out on the porch for the rest of the afternoon, catching up, while they killed off the six-pack and a half that Jack had in his fridge. Aided by a pleasant buzz brought on by the beer, the conversation was deceptively easy—just like the "old days," as long as they were able to dance around the subject of Denise and how Sean had screwed everything up between him and Jack.

But they couldn't dance forever.

"So," Jack said at last, casting a glance at the sun as it sank behind the pine trees, "I know this is none of my business—"

"Everything's your business, man," Sean said quickly. "We're best friends."

He immediately regretted saying it, seeing the way Jack frowned and glanced away in response.

"Yeah, well…. Are you gonna tell me what went wrong? Between you and Denise?"

Sean finished off the beer in his hand, then shrugged. "I don't know. Everything seemed okay. I mean, we weren't fighting, or anything. Things were just…."

"Just what?"

Sean mulled it over a long time before replying, "Cold."

Jack nodded, then opened another beer and handed it to him.

The wind sighed softly through the pines on all sides of the cabin. There was a small front yard where the truck and Sean's car were parked—mostly dirt and mud—but on the other side of that were more pines. They were completely cut off from the world. Not even the sounds of traffic reached them from the highway five miles to the south.

"Remember all those times you dragged me off to the woods to camp?" Sean asked, as if he expected Jack to have forgotten half their childhood.

"'Course."

"This is what you always wanted, isn't it? To be out in the woods where no one can find you…."

"You seem to have managed it."

"Yeah," Sean said, feeling a little defensive. "Well… your dad told me."

"I'm surprised he knew." Sean knew Jack and his father hadn't spoken in years—not since Jack came out. The old man hadn't been happy about his son being "one of them." He'd given Sean an earful about it that afternoon.

"He said Larry told him where to find you." Larry was the local sheriff and a long-standing friend of the family.

"Ah." Jack took a swig of his beer. "That figures." He didn't state the obvious—Jack's dad hadn't bothered using that information to contact his son. From what Sean knew, they hadn't spoken since Jack came out.

"Honestly, I was surprised to find you in a cabin," Sean rambled on. "I kind of pictured you in a tent or a teepee or… maybe a cave."

Jack snorted. "This was for sale and it was cheap. That cave sure sounds tempting, though."

Sean laughed, hating how nervous he sounded. *Are you wishing I hadn't been able to find you?* He didn't dare ask. But there was one thing he'd been wondering about over the past four years, so even though he knew he might not like the answer, he asked, "Have you.... Did you ever find...."

"A boyfriend?" Jack asked wryly.

Just hearing Jack say the word made Sean jealous. "Yeah."

"Relax, dipshit. There was never anyone but you."

Sean felt a surge of hope at those words—and guilt. He knew now he'd always felt the same about Jack, even though he'd been too dumb to know it. And he knew how miserable it would have made him to learn Jack had married someone else.

"I'm—"

He wasn't sure what he'd been about to say. An apology? Something brilliant that would make it all better? But Jack didn't give him the chance.

He stood abruptly and went to open the front door of the cabin, pausing in the doorway to look back at Sean and say, "You'd better come inside. It's getting pretty late."

Sean glanced at the sky, which had barely begun to fade from orange to gray. Then he looked at his iPhone. No reception, of course, but it still gave him the time. "It's not even nine o'clock yet!"

Jack seemed uncomfortable about something, glancing almost furtively at the sky. "I have to crash early these days. I do a lot of yard work for people early in the morning."

Then he went inside.

Why Jack needing to go to bed early meant Sean had to do likewise didn't make much sense. But Sean wasn't keen on sitting around by himself on the porch, so he got up to follow his friend into the cabin.

IT WAS a nice place, for a man living alone. There were really only two rooms—a big living room with a kitchenette in the back and a bedroom off to the right. Furnishings were minimal. The living room had a big fireplace, with a wide couch in front of it and a large oak chest serving as a coffee table and footrest. There were some bookshelves on the walls, and that was about it. No television—it was a pretty safe bet no cable company ran their lines out this far. Sean was surprised, though grateful, when Jack flicked a switch and an electric light went on overhead.

The small kitchen area had a sink with a pump handle and a small wood stove. The refrigerator was small, like something a college student might have in his dorm room. There was a chest freezer out on the porch for storing things, in case he got snowed in for a while—Jack had shown Sean its contents, as if to prove he hadn't lost his mind out there in the wild and started chopping up hikers or something. Near the window was a small aluminum table and a chair. At least Jack had an electric coffee maker on the counter.

Jack closed the front door behind them and, to Sean's surprise, threw the bolt on it. The door had a knob with a lock like any other house, and it was solid enough to keep anything shy of a rampaging bull moose out. Was he really that concerned about someone breaking in, way out here?

"The bathroom's over here," Jack said, walking past him and opening what Sean had thought was a closet door near the kitchenette. It contained a toilet and a shower stall. No room for a sink, but the kitchen sink wasn't far away.

Thank God it's not an outhouse.

"Cool."

As Jack went around the small space, pointing out where he kept towels and snacks and his favorite books, in case Sean felt like reading something, Sean watched the subtle shifting of the muscles underneath the tanned skin of Jack's naked torso. That old familiar feeling of arousal welled up inside him, making his crotch feel tight. Once upon a time, they would have played a bit before going to sleep. And though he knew it was wishful thinking, Sean couldn't help but feel anticipation at the thought of being invited into Jack's bed.

But the pleasant buzz Sean had gotten from the beer began to fade as he realized things just weren't going to be that easy. Jack was avoiding looking directly at him, and being careful to keep his distance. He had to have known what was on Sean's mind, but he didn't give any sign of interest.

When Jack opened the door to his own room, he stood in the doorway, blocking it, rather than holding it open for Sean to come in. "You can sleep on the couch. There are blankets in the chest. Or, if you want, there's a sleeping bag in there you can stretch out on the floor."

"You're making me sleep on the floor?"

"Or the couch." Jack hesitated and then gave him a wry smile. "Sorry. There's only one bed, and I'm used to sleeping alone these days."

Sean felt as if Jack had just dumped a pail of cold water over his head. It had felt, out on the porch, as if Jack had wanted the same thing he did—to be together, finally. But it looked as if he wasn't going to make that easy.

Sean knew he wasn't always the brightest bulb in the pack. He was still trying to figure out how *he* felt about things, never mind sorting out Jack's feelings. But he knew marrying Denise had fucked things up between them, and he at least owed Jack an apology for that.

"I'm sorry," he said. "For… what I did. You know… for marrying somebody else, when I should have known better…."

Jack stood very still for a long time, looking directly into his eyes. Then he gave Sean a single nod. "I know you are. I just wish it wasn't too late."

Sean felt his insides grow cold, as if his heart had been beamed out of his chest like in *Star Trek* and dispersed into space, leaving his blood still and coagulating in his veins. He didn't understand. Did Jack hate him now?

"There's more beer in the fridge," Jack continued. "Help yourself to anything you want to snack on." Then, just before he closed the door, he added, "But stay inside."

Sean's head was still churning with confused thoughts, but he managed to choke out, "Why?"

"I've had bears prowling around here lately," Jack replied. "I don't need to be scraping your innards off the porch tomorrow morning."

Sean might not have spent as much time in the woods as Jack, but a bear wandering by the tent now and then had never alarmed them as teenagers—not much. It hardly seemed cause for barricading themselves in the cabin as soon as it got dark.

But Sean didn't call him on it, even when Jack closed his bedroom door and Sean heard him throw another deadbolt on the other side.

Does he think I'll burst in and try to rape him in the middle of the night?

Things weren't going at all like Sean had hoped they would. He'd expected Jack to demand an apology, maybe even make him grovel a bit. But to say it was too late? Sean didn't know how to process that. They were both single now, and they were out there away from their families and friends—everyone who'd tried to keep them apart. How could it be too late?

Maybe Jack just didn't feel it anymore, that bond they'd shared—what they'd felt for each other. The thought was disheartening. But Sean refused to give up so soon. There had to be a way to remind him, to make him feel it again. There was time, as long as Jack didn't tell him to leave. Sean could afford to go to a hotel if he had to, but he had the uncomfortable feeling this visit might be his last chance to make things right.

SEAN SAT on the couch, staring at the cold fireplace while the sky outside the window darkened, irritated that there wasn't even a DVD player to help him pass the time. He glanced at the bookshelves on the wall, but didn't bother checking them out. He didn't feel like reading. He was lonely and watching Jack run around shirtless all day had made him horny as hell.

When things had been good between them—when the intense relationship they'd shared since high school had begun to grow obvious to everyone around them—Sean had panicked. He'd gone off to college, hooked up with Denise, and let Jack fade into the background. Somehow he'd thought they could still remain friends, but instead they'd just drifted further and further apart. Jack had agreed to be the best man at his wedding during his sophomore year at UNH, but that was the last time they'd seen each other.

Four years. Four years of trying to make his marriage work, when Sean knew deep down he'd made a mistake. He'd been an idiot. His fear of what was happening between him and Jack had caused him to drag a third person into the mess he was creating. He'd never meant to hurt Denise, but of course he had. His only excuse—and it wasn't much of one—was that he hadn't known he was doing it. And now here he was, foolishly trying to patch things up with Jack by making an imposition of himself.

God, I'm pathetic!

Sighing in frustration, Sean got up off the couch. He needed to take a leak, but he was feeling too contrary to heed Jack's paranoid warnings and stay inside. There was no reason he couldn't just use Jack's tiny bathroom, but he'd be damned if he was going to cower indoors all night just because there might possibly be the slightest chance of a bear wandering by the cabin. He could understand Jack being pissed at him, but there was no reason to treat him like he was five years old.

He quietly unbolted the front door and slipped out onto the porch. It was a beautiful night. The sky was somewhat overcast, but the moon illuminated the clouds from behind as they slowly drifted by. The late September air was starting to grow cool, though it hadn't yet taken on the chill of fall.

Sean walked to the far edge of the porch, unzipped, and started pissing on the grass below.

He was almost finished before he heard it—a sound like faint whispering in the woods. He'd heard it once before. Just once. And it had chilled him then, just as it chilled him now. Then there was another sound—something more concrete—the crisp rustle of footsteps at the edge of the woods. Sean zipped up and peered into the shadows, trying to see if there was something there. A breeze sprang up, causing the trees and underbrush to sway and making it impossible to tell which shadow might be a moving animal. The moonlight faded as heavier clouds rolled by, and Sean could no longer see the yard clearly. Snapping branches indicated that the animal was moving closer. It sounded large—perhaps a bear or a coyote—and Sean began to back up across the porch, reaching behind him for the door.

Suddenly, it growled low and ominous, sounding like nothing Sean could identify—and an enormous black shape lumbered across the yard toward him. Sean panicked and ran for the door, yanking it open and slamming it behind him. He threw the deadbolt and backed away, his heart pounding in his chest.

Whatever it was, the animal didn't attempt to break the door down. After listening for a couple minutes and peering out through one of the windows in a futile attempt to see into the darkness, Sean took a deep breath to steady himself and laughed at how frightened he'd allowed himself to get. He might even have imagined the shadow running toward him across the yard.

"Fuckin' coyote," he muttered before turning away to search for the blankets Jack had told him were in the chest.

HE DREAMT of that night when they were camping near Cedar Pond. They were both fifteen, both randy as hell, and their friendship was still burning with an intensity few adults could understand. So it was little wonder that here, isolated from the rest of the world, they finally gave in to what they'd both been wanting for such a long time. They didn't talk about it. Sean, especially, was afraid to. Talking might have given it a name, and he was terrified of that name, of the contempt his father and uncle would have had for him if they'd found out. So he and Jack just did... what they did. And when it was over, they held each other in the darkness of their tent, caressing and kissing until they drifted off to sleep.

Later he awoke and was disturbed to find himself alone in the tent. It was still dark, and without Jack's body heat warming the tent, Sean felt cold. He hoped Jack had just crawled outside for a minute to take a leak or something, but he waited and waited and his friend didn't return. Finally, with growing trepidation, Sean unzipped the tent door and peered outside. The moon provided a faint light, though the forest floor was thick with shadow.

"Jack?" His voice sounded quiet and a little fearful. He couldn't shake the feeling that something was very wrong.

He crawled out of the tent and stood, wrapping his arms around his naked body in a vain attempt to stave off the cold night air. Then he saw Jack, standing silent and still about fifty feet away. He was naked, beautifully illuminated by a shaft of blue-gray moonlight. But when Sean called to him again, there was no response.

Cautiously, Sean walked on bare feet through the ferns and pine needles blanketing the forest floor. When he drew near, and Jack still hadn't moved, he reached out to brush Jack's bare shoulder with his fingertips. Only then did Jack turn his head to give him a strange, enigmatic smile.

"Listen," he whispered.

Sean was shivering and wanted nothing more than to crawl back into the warmth of their sleeping bags—both him and Jack together—but he cocked an ear and tried to listen. At first he heard nothing. Nothing, that is, except the usual sounds of a forest at night—wind in the trees, the rustling of leaves, the occasional snap of a twig as a squirrel or deer slipped past in the shadows. But then he caught something—a faint sound like people whispering. The voices were elusive and impossible to pinpoint. He couldn't be certain what direction they came from, or even if he was really hearing them.

"What is it?" he whispered back.

Jack's smile was rapturous, as if he were hearing the voices of angels. "It's calling to us."
　　"What is?"
　　"The forest."

THE NEXT morning Sean woke to the sound of a vehicle pulling into the driveway. It was light out, and the clock on the fireplace mantle read nearly ten. Bright sunlight was streaming through the open curtains.

Before he could decide whether he was really awake yet, the door opened and Jack came in. Once again he was shirtless, which was a pleasant enough sight to wake up to, but the damp, sweaty T-shirt he tossed at Sean's head was a bit less pleasant.

"Hey, deadbeat! You ever gonna wake up? I've been working for hours already."

"Fuck you," Sean muttered, but he sat up, tossing the shirt on the floor. "What have you been doing?"

"Landscaping at the Donnelly's," Jack replied cheerfully. He crossed the living room to turn on the water in the kitchenette sink, then started scrubbing his filthy hands. "They want to rent their house out when they move to Florida."

"Oh." Sean stood up from the couch, still fuzzy and half-asleep. He was wearing just a pair of tight briefs, and when Jack turned back to him, rubbing his hands on the dish towel, Sean was pleased to notice Jack eyeing his package a bit before looking away.

"Come on. It's hot as hell, and I've got two hours 'til I have to deal with that old bitch, Mrs. Westcott, and her damned flower beds. Let's go for a swim."

"Where?"

"There's a pond, just down the path behind the cabin."

Sean rubbed his face with his hands and glanced down at himself. "I didn't bring a suit."

Jack quirked an eyebrow at him and tossed the dish towel onto the counter.

BATHING SUITS didn't appear to be standard issue this far away from civilization. Jack didn't bother with one, and apparently he didn't expect

Sean to, either, despite the wall he'd put up between them the night before. It was wonderful to see Jack naked again. He'd been making disconcerting appearances in Sean's masturbatory fantasies, even when Sean had thought he could make his sham of a marriage work. After the separation and divorce, Jack had moved to front and center. It was nice to see he'd improved over the past few years. His stomach was more sharply defined now, his arms corded with muscle.

It was a little embarrassing how quickly Sean got a semi after the clothes were tossed onto the rocks near the water's edge, but Jack didn't seem to mind. Once they'd waded out into waist-high water, Jack pounced and dragged him under. The pond was clean, but their bodies stirred up a cloud of silt when they hit bottom, so Sean quickly lost sight of his friend. But he could feel their bodies intertwined, rubbing hot skin against skin. The laughter died after they'd wrestled each other to the bottom a few times, and he could feel Jack's hard cock rubbing against his under the water, almost fucking, but not quite. Sean's frustration grew until he couldn't stand it. He tried to grasp Jack's cock with his hand, but Jack gently pushed him away.

Then he stood and squinted up at the sky.

"Is it noon yet?" he asked.

"How should I know? You want me to use my dick as a sundial?"

Jack sighed and rolled his eyes at him, then walked out of the water to go dig his cell phone out of his pocket. "I still have a few minutes," he said after glancing at it.

Rather than rejoin Sean in the water, he flopped down on his back on the grassy bank. Sean didn't see much point in swimming by himself, so he came out of the water to flop down beside him.

"Did you know my folks sold their place?" Sean asked.

Jack squinted up at the bright blue sky. "Yeah. I still run into your sister, now and then, when I'm in town. She keeps me up on what your folks are doing these days."

"It sucks," Sean said vehemently. "I loved the pond there. And the fields… and the old barn."

"Yeah."

Sean rolled over onto his side, giving Jack a sly smile. "Remember hanging out in the loft?"

Clearly, Jack did remember because his face grew flushed.

"You're turning red," Sean teased.

"Yes, I remember."

"I know *I* still remember."

Jack refused to look at him. "That's just… something kids do."

"Whatever you say, Dr. Freud. Think you can still beat me?"

Jack couldn't pretend he didn't know what Sean was talking about because he blushed even more. "I'm not in the mood."

He certainly had been in the mood a minute ago, judging by all the crotch grinding. And he still had a hard-on. "Why not?" Sean asked, grinning. "Nobody can see us."

"That's not the point."

"You're the one who wanted to get naked together and splash around in the pond."

"To cool off," Jack replied. "I wasn't trying to start anything."

It had certainly *felt* as if Jack was starting something. Maybe he hadn't thought it all the way through, but he'd been enjoying the eroticism of the situation as much as Sean. Still grinning, Sean slid his hand down the front of his body, and Jack seemed mesmerized as he watched it descend. Sean's breathing grew ragged as his fingers brushed through his blond pubic hair and slowly embraced the base of his swollen cock.

But apparently that was going too far because Jack suddenly jumped up and reached for his clothes. "I have to get back to work."

"I'm sorry. I just thought you were… holding back…." Hadn't Jack been horny just a minute ago? Hadn't they both been waving erections around?

Jack was fumbling to get his legs into his pants in a way that might have been comic, if Sean hadn't been so confused. "Maybe I *want* to hold back."

He took off for the house, still fastening his pants as if he were escaping a fate worse than death.

Sean growled in frustration and ran after him. "Why? Yes, I fucked up. I know that. I'll do anything you want—"

"I'm not trying to get you to grovel!" Jack protested, walking toward the house. "It's just… things are different now."

"I know! But I was hoping… I don't know. That we could *fix* it. That you'd *let* me fix it…."

"It's not that easy, Sean."

Sean opened his mouth to reply, but Jack jerked to a halt and Sean nearly collided with him. He looked up ahead and saw what Jack had reacted to.

There was a police cruiser parked in front of the cabin, and two officers were standing near it. Sean knew them both—Larry and Kelton. Larry had been elected sheriff when Sean was a kid, and he had yet to be unseated. He was a tall man with salt-and-pepper hair—a bit more salt than four years ago, but still pretty much the same. Kelton was short, darker-haired, and a bit on the rotund side. He'd come on board a bit later, but now it was hard to imagine the two not working together. They'd always reminded Sean of Abbott and Costello.

Kelton was regarding Sean and Jack—particularly Sean—with a startled expression, and that's when Sean realized he hadn't grabbed anything to put on when he'd chased after Jack.

Larry was unflappable, as always. He simply nodded at Jack. "Afternoon."

"Larry!" Jack said nervously. "Kelton. Hi."

Larry then said to Sean in an exaggerated country hick accent, "Yer *nekkid.*"

"Be right back," Sean said. He hadn't brought anything but his underwear down to the pond, and walking around in his tighty-whities in front of the cops didn't seem like a good idea, so he scampered up the steps and into the cabin to grab his jeans. It only took a moment, and he could hear the conversation through the open window.

"What can I do for you?" Jack asked.

Larry answered, "Well… really we just stopped by to warn you about some large animal sightings in this area."

"*This* area? Who's sighting things out here? I'm out in the middle of fucking nowhere."

Sean came back out onto the porch in time to see Larry nod, conceding the point. "Well, within a few miles. Ellie Jacobs saw something out at her farm last night—it was pokin' its nose in her dumpster. And later on, Ben Thompson took a shot at something sniffin' around near his chicken coop. But that's just a couple miles from here, and animals roam."

"Bears?"

"More like wolves, from what they were describing. Or maybe just one."

"In New Hampshire?" Jack asked, the disbelief clear in his voice. "Not likely." Wolves had been extinct in the state for over a century.

Larry shrugged. "A gray wolf was killed just twenty miles over the border into Canada a couple years ago, and hikers keep claiming they've seen them in the White Mountains. Probably just coyotes, but you never know."

Sean wondered for a moment if the animal noises he'd heard the night before could have been the animal Larry was talking about. Could it really have been a wolf? He opened his mouth to mention it, then thought better of it. Jack would be pissed if he found out Sean had gone outside despite his warning. And really, Sean hadn't seen anything. Most likely it had just been a coyote.

Jack laughed. "This is the part where some crazy old coot cries out, 'That weren't no wolf! I seen it, and it walked like a man. I tell ya... it was a *werewolf*!'"

"Maybe," Larry conceded. One corner of his mouth twitched up a bit—that was about as close to a smile as the man ever got. "My life sure feels like a horror movie at times." He turned and headed back to the cruiser, Kelton falling in behind him like a faithful dog, and called back over his shoulder, "Anyway, just be careful. And let us know if you see anything."

"Sure."

As they opened the cruiser doors, Sean heard Kelton mutter, "Somethin' there's gotta be illegal...."

"You wanna give 'em a ticket?"

"No."

"Well, all right, then."

They climbed into the cruiser and drove off.

SEAN SPENT a boring day at the cabin by himself while Jack did a bunch of jobs in town. He scrounged up some lunch and went skinny dipping again, but it wasn't as much fun without Jack. He jerked off this time, but that didn't take long. He didn't have much interest in reading, so he didn't even bother looking at the bookcase. He thumbed through the music on his iPhone—pretty much the only thing it was good for, this far off the grid—but couldn't find anything he was interested in listening to.

He thought about driving into town himself, but the gas in his tank was so low, he wasn't sure he'd make it. He'd have to ask Jack later if he had a gas can, or could make a gas station run for him. Anyway, he'd grown up in Dunkirk. It wasn't much more interesting than the cabin was.

Finally, in an act of desperation, he split wood. Jack had a bunch of cut logs piled up behind the cabin next to a woodpile covered with a tarp. Sean hadn't used a maul in years, but it came back to him quickly enough. And it gave him a way to pass the time and work off some of his frustration with the way things had been going. He understood why Jack was hesitant to let him back into his life, but that didn't make it any easier to deal with. He couldn't stay there forever, mooching off Jack's food. But he was afraid to leave again without resolving things between them. He couldn't escape the feeling he wouldn't get another shot at it.

JACK PULLED in just as it was getting dark and a beautiful crescent moon was rising above the pines. Sean was ecstatic to see him—even more so when Jack carried a large pizza and a twelve-pack up onto the porch. They spent another pleasant evening together, shooting the shit until mosquitoes drove them inside.

They'd dirtied a couple of plates eating the pizza, so Jack washed those in the sink. While he was doing that, Sean drifted back to the small bookcase. He'd glanced at it earlier but hadn't seen anything interesting. Mostly horror novels. Now he noticed something he hadn't before—a lot of them were about werewolves. Like more than half. And they weren't all novels, either. A lot of them seemed to be books *about* werewolves, with titles like *Werewolves in Western Culture: a Lycanthropy Reader* and *The Book of Werewolves, Being an Account of a Terrible Superstition.* There were also a bunch of dolls and figurines of the Lon Chaney Wolf Man and wolves in general.

"What is all this shit you're reading?" he asked, picking up a book called *The Werewolf* by Montague Summers and flipping it open to see a bunch of entries in the Table of Contents like The Werewolf: His Science and Practice.

Jack glanced over and then took the time to dry his hands on the dishtowel before replying, "I like horror."

"Especially werewolves. You've got three shelves on them."

Jack came close to him and peered over his shoulder at the book. They were both shirtless, thanks to the muggy summer evening, and Sean was intensely aware of the heat coming off Jack's skin and the mingling of their sweat as his chest brushed Sean's shoulder.

He could feel a soft puff of breath against his neck when Jack spoke. "When I was a kid, I used to think it would be so awesome to be a werewolf, running free in the forest." He chuckled, a low, sultry sound. "*Naked*. Far away from people…."

This was a childhood fantasy Sean had never been informed of. At least all the stuff about werewolves. He'd always known Jack had an affinity for the forest, even before that odd night of the whispering. They'd spent a lot of time camping together in the little pup tent Jack's father had given him for his eleventh birthday. During the summers they'd practically *lived* in the woods. Jack had seemed to belong there, and he'd talked about going off into the forest to live someday. Sean hadn't been quite so enthusiastic about that idea, but he'd always felt *he* belonged with Jack, wherever that might be… until he'd panicked and run away.

"Well, you figured out the 'far away from people' part, at any rate," Sean said with an awkward laugh, closing the book and slipping it back onto the shelf.

Jack wandered away and flopped down onto the couch, putting his feet up on the oak chest. "Not far enough when it comes to Mrs. Westcott and her goddamn flower bed. Bring me another beer, will you?"

"Yes, master." They'd stashed the remaining few beers from the twelve-pack in the fridge, so Sean grabbed a couple of those and brought them over to the couch. He handed one to Jack and flopped down on the couch beside him. "You were social enough when we were teenagers."

"Since when? *You* were social—sometimes. You went to parties, and I went to parties because I was hanging out with you. But I always hated them."

Sean knew that was true. They'd both always preferred to be alone. He'd just never thought of it that way because they'd always been alone *together*. Now Jack seemed to have forgotten the "together" part. It occurred to him for the first time that Jack really might not want him there at all. Maybe he'd just barreled in and set up house without noticing how uncomfortable Jack was with the idea.

"Am I making a pest of myself?" he asked. "Would you rather I stayed with my sister?" He braced himself for the answer.

Jack paused, his beer halfway to his lips. "Where did *that* come from?"

"I just…. Well, I just thought… I kind of showed up on your doorstep and expected you to take me in. Maybe you're feeling put on the spot."

"Are you drunk?"

"No," Sean said, frustrated. "I'm just asking."

Jack snorted and took a swig from his bottle. Then he carefully lowered it to his lap before responding. "You can be a little pushy, at times."

"So I *am* being a pest, then."

"You're not being a pest." Jack grinned. "Or maybe I should say you're always a pest. But I don't mind. Really. That's just the way you are."

That didn't exactly sound flattering. But Sean had asked, so he wouldn't piss and moan if that's how Jack really felt about him. He asked, "Would you like me to go stay with Julie?"

Jack appeared to think about it for a good long time. Then he rubbed his chin with one hand and said, "I don't think that's really what I want."

"Then why am I sleeping on the couch?"

Jack gave him a long, hard look then, directly in the eye. Then he sighed and stood up. "Look, what happened when we were teenagers…. We were different people back then. Don't you get it? You can't just expect to pick up where we left off."

"You told your father you were gay," Sean pointed out.

"What does that have to do with anything?"

"I'm just sayin' what happened between us wasn't just kids fooling around," Sean said. "You're gay, and so am I. It took me a while to realize it—"

"The fact that we're both gay doesn't mean we were meant for each other."

"No," Sean conceded, "but we *were* meant for each other. You know it as much as I do. I know I hurt you by… what I did…."

"You did." Jack looked Sean directly in the eye. "You have no fucking idea." For a moment Sean saw so much pain reflected in those smoky hazel eyes that he was forced to look away. And in doing so, he knew he'd failed yet again.

Jack finished off his beer and got up to go rinse out his bottle at the sink.

"I'm sorry," Sean said quietly.

"I know. And I forgive you. Really. But it doesn't matter." Jack set the bottle down on the counter and walked to his bedroom door. He turned in the doorway and spread his hands in a gesture of futility. "It's too late to fix it, Sean."

Then he went into the bedroom and closed the door. Sean heard the bolt latch.

SEAN DIDN'T know what to do. He knew he'd screwed up—big-time. But he kept apologizing, Jack kept saying he forgave him, and nothing was changing. What else could he do? Wait it out? Give it time? He could do that, if that's what it would take. But would Jack let him? Sean couldn't stay in the cabin forever. Certainly, not without a job.

Maybe he could talk to Jack about that in the morning—finding a job, pulling his own weight. Jack said he didn't want him to leave, and Sean sure as hell didn't want to leave. If he found something in town to help out with groceries, maybe that would help. It was something, at least.

Sean felt incredibly frustrated right then. He needed air. And another beer might not hurt. So he grabbed one of the last two in the fridge and quietly let himself out onto the front porch. Larry's warning about animals in the area was still fresh in his mind, but by then he'd convinced himself people were probably just seeing coyotes and freaking out about them. Certainly what he'd heard last night had to have been a coyote. They could be dangerous, of course. But he'd seen them often enough in the forest. Usually they just skittered off.

He stood on the porch in the darkness, listening to the soft sigh of the wind through the pine trees and birches as he drank his beer. He was still shirtless, and the breeze caressed his bare skin and tickled his nipples, causing them to stiffen involuntarily. It felt good. Almost without thinking about it, he reached up with his left hand and circled his right nipple lazily, encouraging it to grow even harder. By the time he'd drained the bottle, he decided a quick wank might help him relax. He would have felt weird doing it in the living room, where Jack could walk through at any moment, but out there in the dark....

Thoughts of Jack's naked body glistening with moisture as he lay on the grass that afternoon were all it took to make his jeans feel they were ready to burst at the crotch. Sean set the empty bottle down on the wooden boards at his feet and walked to the far edge. He unfastened the button on his jeans and opened the fly, then fished his hardened cock out of his boxers.

It felt good, stroking himself languidly in the muggy night, a gentle breeze bringing the mingled scents of pine and dirt and grass to his nostrils, and caressing his sweaty torso like cool fingers. It didn't take long before he felt his orgasm building, so he picked up the pace. He clenched his teeth as he exploded, squirting his seed out over the edge of the porch into the darkness. Hopefully, it wouldn't be visible in the morning.

When he'd finished, he stood there a moment longer, catching his breath. Then he tucked himself back into his boxers—not bothering to refasten his jeans, since he'd be taking them off in a minute—and went back inside.

"Do you still hear it?" Sean asked.

They were eighteen now, though their lives had changed little since that night when Sean heard the whispering. They still spent most of their free time together in the woods, they still kissed and caressed and explored in the dark, and they still spoke little about it. The whispering had frightened Sean, but Jack had seemed delighted by it.

"I do," Jack replied, lying naked on the grass, the sweat on his skin glistening in the moonlight. It was a hot night in July, and the heat had chased them out of their shelter. The old tent had long ago worn out and been sacrificed to use as material in lean-tos and other types of shelters they'd learned how to build. "It's still calling to us."

A chill ran down Sean's spine despite the heat. He'd heard the whispering himself, so he didn't think Jack was schizophrenic or anything. But that didn't make the situation any less disturbing. He sat cross-legged beside Jack, lightly tracing the contours of Jack's stomach muscles with his fingers.

"What does it want?"

"It wants us to join it."

"Where?"

"In the forest."

Sean shivered slightly. "You aren't thinking of going, are you? How would you survive? Especially in winter?"

"I'll go someday," Jack said, smiling serenely, "but not until you're ready to go with me."

Sean wasn't sure if he'd ever be ready. Yes, he loved being in the forest. He felt comfortable in the woods, at least when he was with Jack. But Jack knew so much more than he did about what was edible and what was poisonous. He never got lost or turned around. He could build a fire without matches, trap rabbits, and he'd even learned to hunt with bow and arrow—one of the few things he and his father enjoyed doing together. Sean wasn't like that. He'd be lost out here if Jack wasn't with him.

"I don't know if I'll ever be ready," Sean said.

"You'll have to be if we're going to stay together. I can't wait forever."

SEAN AWOKE to a sharp bang.

His heart was racing in his chest as he listened in the dark. But he had no idea where the sound had come from. The cabin was completely silent. Had he dreamed it?

Something massive slammed into the front door, making it shudder in its frame and jostling the framed picture of a sunset on the wall beside it.

"Oh, shit!" Sean gasped.

He had only a split second to remember he'd forgotten to latch the bolt before the door slammed open, banging against the wall. The picture crashed to the floor, glass shattering. Something half crouched, half stood in the doorway, hunched over but definitely balanced on two legs. It was silhouetted against a cloudy sky lit blue-gray by the moonlight.

Sean screamed and scrambled over the back of the couch without thinking. He fell hard onto the wooden floor behind it, landing on his back and getting the breath knocked out of him.

Then the wooden feet of the couch scraped against the floor as something bounded over it and landed on top of him—something massive and hairy and reeking of damp dog. Its breath was hot against his face, and an enormous paw with sharp claws pressed down on the center of his chest, pinning him. The thing growled, and in the faint moonlight coming through the windows, Sean could see it draw back its lips to expose ferocious canines. Hot saliva dribbled down onto his cheek.

Sean finally found breath enough to scream, but it had little effect on the animal. It lowered its face, and Sean waited for the searing pain of teeth tearing into his flesh. But it didn't come. Instead the creature sniffed at him a moment, and then, to his intense disgust, it licked his nose and mouth.

Sean turned his face away in revulsion, but the creature continued to lick him, switching to his ear. Sean whimpered.

Nice doggie, nice doggie. Please don't eat me....

Then as fast as it appeared, the creature was gone. Sean felt it jump off him, and when he dared to look, it was nowhere to be seen. He lay on the floor, panting and listening intently for the sounds of an enormous animal moving around the room. But he heard nothing.

He sat up tentatively, and his hand touched the floor in a puddle of warm liquid next to his ass. He'd pissed himself.

Fuck.

The door was still open, but it didn't take long to determine he was alone in the sparsely furnished room. Sean leapt to his feet and ran to the door. Slamming it shut, he threw the bolt. He flipped on all the lights he could find, and then ran to Jack's bedroom door to pound on it.

"Jack! Get up! Now!"

There was no answer, so he pounded again. It seemed like ages before he heard a sleepy "What the fuck?" coming from the other side. A moment later the door opened and a completely naked and sleep-tousled Jack glared at him. "What the fuck are you screaming about?"

Before Sean could answer, Jack glanced down at his boxers and made a face. "Jesus! You're dripping!"

SEAN TOOK a quick shower while Jack mopped the floor. He did feel a little guilty about pissing on the floor and dribbling it all over the place, but he was irritated that Jack hadn't taken his account of the beast seriously. It wasn't exactly that he hadn't believed him—that might have been reasonable.

Instead, he'd listened to Sean's account, frowned at him, and said, "I told you to stay inside and keep the door bolted."

What the fuck! "Because of a *bear*! You told me there was bear! That was no fucking bear!"

Jack had just glared at him and said, "Go take a shower. You're still dripping all over the place."

So he had. He left his wet boxers in the shower stall to deal with the next day and walked out of the bathroom naked. It didn't seem to matter—Jack hadn't bothered to put anything on either. But neither of them was in a mood to find it sexy.

Sean watched Jack empty the mop bucket into the sink, his frustration mounting, until finally he demanded, "Are you gonna tell me what the fuck's going on?"

"What makes you think I know?"

"The fact that I was just attacked by this thing—"

"You said it licked your face," Jack interrupted, smirking. "That's not much of an attack."

"Jesus! You don't even give a fuck! Which means you either don't care if I get eaten, or you already know what this thing is."

Jack opened the fridge and found only the one beer left. He magnanimously handed it to Sean. "Of course I don't want you to get eaten," he said. Then he surprised Sean by kissing him lightly on the cheek. "Come on."

Sean watched in disbelief as Jack crossed the room and threw back the bolt on the door.

"What the hell are you doing?"

"It's okay," Jack said, opening the door and gesturing for Sean to follow him. "It's gone now."

BY THE time Sean worked up the courage to follow his friend outside, he found Jack sitting on the front steps, gazing out into the forest as if it was a peaceful, serene night, instead of a night full of monsters. Sean looked around cautiously, but in the dark, he couldn't see well enough to tell what lurked in the underbrush.

"There's something magical about these woods," Jack said quietly. "You know that as well as I do."

Sean sat down beside him. He *did* know it, but he was too unnerved to wax philosophical. The creature hadn't been some cute little pixie. "If by 'magical,' you mean 'evil'...."

"I don't think the wolf is evil," Jack replied grimly. "Just... untamed."

Sean felt a chill crawl up the back of his neck. The bastard knew what it was. He'd known all along what was lurking out there. "The 'wolf'?"

Jack shrugged, then held out a hand for the beer Sean was drinking. Sean let him take a sip and hand it back.

"Well," Jack said, "I call it that. But it's not really a wolf. You saw for yourself."

"It was a fucking *monster*!"

"You said it didn't hurt you."

"It licked my face!"

Jack snorted. "Better than chewing on it."

"That's not funny. You knew that thing was out there, and you didn't warn me."

"I told you to bolt the door at night."

"Like I was gonna listen to that if I thought it was just a bear or something," Sean grumbled. "You should've told me what the fuck it was."

Jack nodded and gave him a conciliatory smile. "I'm sorry. You're right. I just... didn't know what to tell you that would make sense. I was hoping you'd have enough brains to take my warning seriously."

Sean huffed out a breath. "So if it isn't a wolf, what the hell is it?"

"I don't know. It started coming around about a year after I moved in here. I guess that would make it... two years back. The first time... I was terrified." He gave Sean a gentle nudge with his elbow. "Although I don't recall pissing myself."

"Fuck you."

Jack chuckled. "I put bolts on the doors. I picked up all those books on werewolves, because... well, that's what it seemed to be, from what little I knew of it."

"It stood up!" Sean remembered. "On two legs!"

"Yeah, I know. Anyway, I hoped the books might tell me how to... banish it... get rid of it. Chase it off."

"I'm guessing they didn't," Sean muttered sarcastically.

Jack laughed and held out his hand for another swig of beer. "Nope. I tried a bunch of stuff, but nothing worked."

"Did you try silver bullets?" Sean was racking his brain for different ways to kill werewolves. All he knew was what he'd seen in a few werewolf movies, and they were probably full of shit, anyway.

Jack snorted. "Who around here makes silver bullets? Besides, I didn't want to kill it—just make it go away. After all, it never hurt me. Never hurt anyone, as far as I know."

"It slobbered all over me!" Sean said indignantly, as though a more heinous crime had never been committed. What he really meant, of course, was that he'd been terrified. The thing had literally scared the piss out of him. But he didn't particularly want to bring that up again.

Jack was unmoved. "You'll survive." He paused a moment, then added, "If this thing really is a werewolf, then it's also a man, right? Or maybe a woman. But in any case, a human being. I can't kill a human being—not just for being scary-lookin'."

Sean really didn't get why Jack was so protective of some slavering monster. Sure, it might be human during the day, but that wouldn't matter so much if it decided to chow down on their intestines tomorrow night. Still, he knew Jack could be ridiculously stubborn, so he let that drop for now.

"Who do you think it is?" he asked.

Jack looked uncomfortable. "Well… in a town this size, it's pretty much gotta be someone we know."

Shit. Sean hadn't thought of that. He'd been assuming it was some stranger from out of town wandering through. But that couldn't be the case, if the creature had been coming by Jack's cabin for two years.

"It's probably Tommy Cooper," he muttered.

Jack laughed. "Yeah, it probably is." Tommy used to harass both of them in high school for no good reason. He was a jackass.

"Look," Jack continued more seriously, "if you're really all that scared of it, you can leave. Nobody's stopping you." He handed the beer back to Sean and stood up. "Otherwise, just stay inside at night and bolt the door. You'll be all right."

He clasped Sean's shoulder a minute, then turned and went inside the cabin, though he left the door open. The knowledge that his escape route was easily accessible gave Sean the courage to remain outside a bit longer.

You can leave. Nobody's stopping you. That stung. It didn't feel so much like Jack was trying to get rid of him as he just didn't care, one way or the other. Sean finished his beer and mulled over whether Jack really wanted him there or not, and why his lack of enthusiasm was hurting so much.

Maybe I should *leave*, Sean thought. He'd expected Jack to welcome him with open arms and for things to go back to the way they'd been before. Now Sean knew he'd been naïve. Jack had been hurt a lot more by his misguided attempt to lead a "normal" life than he'd realized. He'd said he didn't want Sean to leave, necessarily, but was that the same as wanting him to stay?

The sighing sound made by the wind no longer sounded peaceful to him. It just sounded forlorn. And he was afraid the whispering might start again if he listened too long. He got up and went inside.

THE NEXT morning, Jack fried up some bacon and eggs while Sean sat on the couch, reading one of the books on werewolves. The subject had never interested him when he thought it was fantasy, but now that he knew it was real—at least, it seemed like the most plausible explanation for what the creature was—he found it much more interesting.

"You know," Jack said over his shoulder, "if you keep hanging out here, I'm gonna start making you do some of the housework, you lazy bastard."

I'll clean the whole goddamn cabin with a toothbrush, if that's what it takes to get us back to normal, Sean thought. But out loud, he just said, "I can cook better than you."

"Fine. You can cook dinner."

Sean grunted, but he was still engrossed in the book. "This says some people *deliberately* become werewolves."

"Sometimes. Other times it just happens to them."

"It says they can do it by performing magic rituals or wearing wolf skins. How the hell could *that* work? People wear wolf skins all the time—or they did before they became endangered. They didn't all turn into werewolves."

"Don't ask me," Jack answered. "I didn't write the book. Bacon's done."

"Or you can drink rainwater out of a wolf's paw print. That sounds disgusting!"

"Then don't do it. Now put the book down and come get your breakfast."

Sean closed the book and set it on top of the oak chest. But before he could do more than stand up, he heard the sound of a car pulling into the driveway. He walked up to the front window and drew aside the curtain.

"Oh, for Chrissake," he muttered. "It's Larry and Kelton again."

FORTUNATELY, JACK had made more than enough food. Kelton scoffed down a plate of bacon and scrambled eggs while his boss stood across the room, glowering at him.

"Are you sure you don't want anything?" Jack asked Larry. "A cup of coffee, at least?"

The sheriff shook his head and managed a polite smile. "No, thanks. My daughter stuffed me—and Kelton—" This with another disapproving glance at his underling. "—with pancakes a couple hours ago."

Kelton either didn't hear the disapproval in his voice, or he was ignoring him.

Larry returned to the question he'd asked earlier. "You're sure you didn't see or hear anything last night?"

"Not a thing."

It took all of Sean's willpower not to say anything, or give Jack a significant glance that Larry would surely have noticed. He wasn't sure he was fully on board with Jack's desire to keep the werewolf a secret, but he'd betrayed Jack once, and he'd be damned if he'd do it again. At least, not until the werewolf proved dangerous. So far, Larry hadn't reported anything serious—no people had been hurt, and no pets or livestock had been attacked.

On the other hand, the phrase "fool for love" did come to mind....

"Whatever that thing is," Larry said, "people are startin' to get scared of it. It came close to town last night. Knocked over Ronnie Leclair's garbage cans and set his dogs off."

"If all it's done is knock over a few trashcans, I don't see why everyone's getting so bent out of shape over it."

Larry gave Jack a sour look. "It's big. That's why. It's big and nobody knows what the hell it is—not for sure."

He glanced down at Sean, who was sitting on the couch, leaning forward to get at the plate of food he'd set on the chest. Larry seemed to notice the book beside his plate for the first time and stepped forward to pick it up. *"The Werewolf?"*

Sean laughed and tried to sound offhand as he said, "That mention of werewolves yesterday got me interested."

"Yeah," Larry said. He looked over at the bookshelves and said to Jack, "You collect stuff on that, do you?"

"Tons," Jack replied. "I love horror movies—especially werewolves."

Larry looked back at the book in his hand. "Well... I hate to disappoint you, but I'm pretty sure we're dealing with a *real* wolf. Or more likely a wolf-dog hybrid. Did I tell you we found a paw print?"

"No." Jack's voice sounded unconcerned—perhaps mildly interested—but Sean saw the muscles in his jaw tighten.

Larry set the book back on the oak chest. Then he held up his hand, fingers splayed wide. "Big as my hand."

"That's... pretty big," Sean said, struggling to keep the fear out of his voice as he recalled the creature pinning him down the night before, one of those enormous paws in the center of his chest.

"For a wolf, it's *huge*. Some dog breeds get pretty big, but that paw.... That was a wolf. No doubt in my mind."

A silence fell over everyone for a moment, while Larry appeared to be waiting for them to react, and Sean once more debated the wisdom of staying silent about the creature he'd seen last night. He had no idea what the hell Jack was thinking.

Fortunately, Kelton knew exactly what was on *his* mind. "Hey, you mind if I steal some more bacon?"

Larry frowned at him, but Jack answered, "Help yourself." Then he asked Larry, "If you find this thing, are you planning on shooting it?"

Again Sean could sense the tension behind his expression of mild curiosity.

"I hate to kill anything for no good reason," Larry said. "But people in town want it out of their hair, and they don't issue us tranquilizer guns."

AFTER THE officers finally drove off, Sean and Jack finished their breakfast and went around to the back of the cabin to finish splitting the wood. Sean had made a sizable dent in the pile of logs, and Jack seemed impressed. But he wanted to get it all taken care of by the end of the day, so they teamed up, taking turns at the splitting.

"Why don't you just tell him what you know about the creature?" Sean asked.

Jack swung the maul and wedged it firmly into a log, then lifted the two together and smashed the whole thing down hard onto the stump he was using as a base. The log split apart with a tremendous *crack*, the pieces falling to the ground on either side.

"I'm not gonna help them track it down and kill it," he replied, gasping. "I told you—it's a human being."

"That's what I'm saying. If you can convince Larry of that, maybe he *won't* kill it."

Jack split another log before replying. "Let me put it this way. That thing keeps coming back to this cabin, for whatever reason. If Larry *doesn't* believe me about it being a werewolf, but he knows I've seen it a bunch of times, he'll set up a stakeout here. Then he'll shoot it, and I'll be the one who led him right to it."

Sean didn't have a reply to that. Jack was probably right. But what if the creature did finally kill somebody? Then *that* would be Jack's fault, too—at least, indirectly. And Sean's.

"I thought you said it showed up two years ago," Sean said.

"It did."

"Then why hasn't anyone seen it before now?"

Jack paused and looked thoughtful. "I've been wondering about that. The truth is, there's a lot of forest between here and town. I figure his home base is nearby, so he's been sticking to the woods near here for a while. Something must have… agitated him or something. So now he's roaming farther away."

He said this last while looking directly at Sean, as if he thought Sean's arrival must have something to do with it.

Sean laughed nervously. "Are you blaming me for upsetting the local werewolf?"

Jack snorted and looked away. He thunked the maul into the base to wedge it there and said, "I'm beat. You up for a swim?"

CLOUDS HAD begun to roll in from the southwest by the time they'd had their fill of splashing around in the nude, and Sean thought he heard a rumble of thunder. But it didn't sound close yet.

Jack climbed out of the water and flopped down on the grassy bank. He put his arms behind his head to pillow it and gazed up at the sky. "Looks like it's gonna rain soon."

Sean got out of the water, straddled him, and then fell to his hands and knees like a dog. He shook his head violently, spraying Jack's shoulders and face with drops of water from his blond hair.

Jack laughed and scrunched his eyes shut against the onslaught. "Stop it! You mongrel!"

"What do you care? You're wet already."

"You're such a dick."

"Sorry," Sean replied with a wicked grin. "You want me to clean the water off you?"

Without waiting for a reply, he lowered his face to Jack's chest and ran his tongue along his breastbone. He knew he was taking a big risk doing that. But as he'd hoped, Jack groaned—a sound full of arousal and pent-up sexual frustration. Jack might not want to go there—not yet—but that sound left little doubt in Sean's mind that there was still desire lurking under the surface, if nothing else.

"Will you knock it off?" Jack growled.

"If you tell me you don't like it."

Jack took a very long time to respond. "I never said I didn't like it."

"Then what's the problem?"

Jack sighed and fixed him with a look. "Tell me you love me."

Now it was Sean's turn to feel uncomfortable. Men didn't say things like that to each other. He'd had that drilled into him his entire life by his father, his uncle, his classmates…. He knew it was stupid to feel that way after coming out here determined to get Jack back. He knew he *wanted* Jack. He knew he *needed* him. He'd finally been able to say "I'm gay." But "I love you"? Even knowing how much Jack needed to hear those words from him, they still stuck in his throat.

"You know I care about you," he hedged. "You know I *want* you."

Jack frowned. "That was good enough when I was eighteen. It's not anymore."

"I used to say it to Denise. But it never meant anything—it was just what husbands are supposed to say to their wives, and I knew it's what she wanted to hear…." It didn't feel right to think of saying those words to Jack, who meant everything to him. Not when they'd become tainted by so many years of falsehood. He hadn't wanted to lie to Denise. He'd *wanted* to feel what the words were saying. But he couldn't. And when he'd finally admitted it, she'd been so hurt....

He opened his mouth, trying to find a way to articulate what he was feeling, but he stopped when he heard another rumble of thunder. It was ominously close. "Shit," he said quietly, "I guess we better get inside."

Jack merely looked back at him with a sadness in his eyes that tugged at Sean's gut. *I don't want to hurt you*, Sean thought. But it was exactly that thought that prevented him from saying what he knew Jack wanted to hear. Those words had hurt Denise a lot when she'd discovered they weren't true.

He got up and began walking toward the house as the rain came down in a light summer shower. When he didn't hear Jack following, he turned to look back. Jack was still lying on the grass, his eyes closed, rainwater sprinkling against his face.

Sean waited for a while, until it was clear Jack needed some time alone. Then he turned and walked to the cabin.

Sometimes, he really hated himself.

EVEN AFTER Jack came inside and the rain began to pour down around them like a waterfall, things remained uncomfortable between them. Not exactly hostile—they spoke to each other and the conversation was friendly. But it wasn't easy. Sean was almost glad when Jack said good night and locked himself away in his room. It still irked him that Jack seemed to think he couldn't be trusted not to sneak in during the night, but he figured they both needed a little time alone to think.

He stripped to his shorts, turned off all the lights, and lay on the couch for an hour or so in the dark, mulling things over and listening to the rain battering the shingled roof of the cabin until he finally drifted off.

THEY WERE nineteen, and the summer was coming to an end. Sean would be leaving for college in a week. It wasn't more than twenty miles away, but he'd be living in a dorm and he didn't have a car. He'd be back for holidays, but... it wouldn't be enough.

They lay in their shelter on a bed of moss and leaves, arms and legs intertwined, skin against skin. It was a chilly night, but they were warm. This was the closest Sean would ever come to heaven, and he knew it.

But he was going to leave it behind because his family wanted him to go to college. He had no idea what he would study. He didn't even want to go. But he was going anyway.

"I don't know what I'll do without you here," Jack whispered.

"I won't be gone forever."

"You'll meet someone there," Jack prophesied. "You'll probably get married and have twenty kids, and I'll never see you again."

Sean laughed, but it was an awkward sound. Jack was perilously close to saying things they'd never said, and it was making him uncomfortable. He tried to make a joke out of it. "I'll name all of the kids after you—Jack, Jacqueline, Jackie, Jack Frost, Jack the Ripper...."

"I love you," Jack said suddenly.

Sean fell silent. He knew Jack wanted him to say it back, but when he opened his mouth to respond, he heard the voice of his Uncle Greg in his mind, telling him how disgusting fags were, and he shut it again. He couldn't say it. Men didn't say it to other men.

But he leaned over and kissed Jack on the mouth. He could do that.

HE WOKE to another loud bang on the door.

His first thought—felt more than articulated—was that the creature was trying to break in again. His body trembled all over as he listened for another bang, wondering if the wooden door could hold if the thing really wanted to get inside. The bolt was fastened, at least. He could see that, even in the darkened room. The rain had died down, so some moonlight was filtering through the windowpanes.

There was another bang, which made him jump, and it was followed by the door latch rattling. Then, to his surprise, he heard Larry's voice. "Jack! Sean! Are you in there?"

Jesus! Are you trying to give me a heart attack?

He jumped up, only dimly aware he was in his boxers, and unbolted the door. When he opened it, Larry burst in so fast he almost knocked him over. The officer whirled around and shined his flashlight directly in Sean's face—which caused him physical pain this soon after waking—and then spun around to scan the room with it.

"Where's Jack?"

He sounded frantic. He was also soaking wet, just like Kelton, who'd followed him inside.

"Sleeping," Sean said, pointing to the bedroom door.

Larry rushed to the door and pounded on it with his fist. "Jack! Are you okay in there?"

"Why the hell wouldn't he be?" Sean was back to being alarmed.

While Larry continued to pound on the door and shout for Jack to open up, Kelton explained breathlessly, "We came across that thing in the woods near here and shot it! Then it took off in this direction. We caught up to it just as it jumped through one of the cabin windows!"

"What?" Sean gasped.

But there wasn't time to think about the implications of that before Larry kicked the bedroom door hard with a muddy boot and splintered the bolt. The door swung inward, and all three men rushed to see what lay on the other side.

Sean was terrified they'd find Jack torn to shreds, the creature hunched over him with gore dripping from its fangs. But apart from the wide open window, and the water all over the sill and the floor near it, nothing seemed amiss. Jack was there, lying naked on the bed, the sheets and blankets kicked off in his sleep.

He was facing away from them, but as they entered, he turned his head to look over his shoulder and asked sleepily, "What the hell are you guys doing in here?"

"Oh, jeez!" Kelton whined, shielding his eyes with one hand.

Larry looked back and forth between Jack and the open window, dumbfounded. Sean wasn't sure he knew what to make of the situation either, especially the fact that Jack was still lying there as if two police officers bursting into his room was nothing unusual. He wasn't making any move to cover himself, or jumping up and shouting for them to get the fuck out, or anything.

Why is he just lying there?

"Sorry," Kelton said uncomfortably. "Uh… maybe we should go…."

Larry ignored him. He swept the flashlight beam around the room, bringing it to rest on the windowsill. There was something dark there.

"Uh…. Larry?"

Larry moved into the room, his eyes focused on the windowsill, and Sean followed him, a knot of dread growing in his chest. The smudge on the sill was mud. Sean was no detective, but he knew there was no way it could have gotten there without someone—or some*thing*—coming in from the outside.

Larry directed the light to the floor, where it revealed massive muddy paw prints. Worse, there were spatters of blood on the floor around them. As the sheriff moved the light along the floor, it became clear that the trail of prints led directly to the bed. Larry and Sean approached the bed until the flashlight clearly illuminated Jack. From this angle, he was unable to hide the blood that pooled around his body on the mattress.

The three men stared at each other silently—Sean, and probably Larry as well, struck dumb by the sheer horror of the situation, and Jack trembling in obvious fear.

Fear of us, Sean thought. Afraid Larry would raise his gun and empty the magazine into Jack's gut. *He's the monster!* Sean felt his world spinning, and he had to brace himself against the dresser to keep from falling over. Even at that, his knees still threatened to give out underneath him.

Finally, Larry spoke, his voice quiet and surprisingly gentle. "Is everything all right, son?"

Jack glanced at Sean, his eyes pleading, though for what, Sean wasn't sure. "Yes."

"You sure?"

"Yes. Everything's fine." He was gritting his teeth against the pain, making his voice sound strained and clipped.

Larry gave him a long, evaluating look. Abruptly, he said, "Sorry for disturbing you. We'll let you sleep."

He gripped Sean's elbow and yanked him away from the dresser, forcibly steering him around the bed toward the door. The two of them practically ran over Kelton in the doorway.

When the door was closed behind them, Larry pulled Sean away from it and asked in a low voice, "Do you want a lift into town, son?"

Kelton looked completely baffled. From his vantage point in the doorway, he couldn't have seen the blood or Jack's injured state. "Why would he want that in the middle of the night?"

Larry was looking intently into Sean's eyes. They knew. They both knew. And while Sean's head reeled with the knowledge that Jack and the beast were somehow—impossibly—one and the same, and Jack was now seriously wounded and possibly dying in the next room, he had enough presence of mind to recognize what Larry was really asking.

Do you want to escape before he changes again and maybe kills you?

Would Jack really kill him? He'd been lying to Sean for the past few days—pretending he had no idea who the werewolf was. Had he also lied about it being harmless? Was he capable of killing people? Had he *already* killed people?

Is he planning on killing me?

Even as the question flashed through his mind, Sean knew he didn't believe it. Not Jack. They'd been best friends all their lives. *Lovers* ever since that fateful camping trip. Sure, things were strained between them at the moment, but…. Jack? A killer? It didn't register.

It must not have made sense to Larry either, or he wouldn't have left the bedroom without arresting Jack. Or at least doing *something*. Instead he'd hid it from Kelton, protected Jack. He'd known Jack and Sean for their entire lives, and right then he seemed to be gambling on what he knew of Jack's character. But he also seemed to be assuming Sean was an innocent bystander in this little horror movie drama, and he was offering Sean a chance to escape, if he wanted it.

"Thanks," Sean heard himself saying, almost as if it was somebody else talking, "but I think I'm okay."

Am I?

Larry nodded slowly and turned to walk out of the cabin. Kelton still seemed baffled by his partner's behavior, but he gave Sean an embarrassed wave and said, "Sorry to disturb you."

"No problem."

Sean stood in the open doorway a moment, watching the two policemen get into their cruiser and drive off. He needed to get back to Jack, see what he could do to help him, but it was hard to move from that spot. He was acutely aware that there was no cell phone reception out there, no landline, and his car probably didn't have enough gas to make it to town if he needed to escape.

WHEN HE returned to Jack's bedroom, Sean found Jack sitting up in the bed with the reading lamp on the nightstand turned on. He was sitting in a pool of blood, and it was more or less all over his body and hands, but he was conscious, examining the wound in the lamplight.

He looked up when Sean approached and said, "I think I need some help."

Sean gazed back at him, the horror of the scene making his skin prickle, before the more practical part of his brain was able to assert itself and send him running for a clean washcloth and a bowl of warm water. And maybe some rubbing alcohol and bandages.

The wound turned out to be far less severe than it seemed. Once the blood was washed off, Sean discovered it was just one gash in Jack's side. It was deep and probably needed stitches, but he was able to sterilize it somewhat with the alcohol, making Jack gasp in pain, and then put a large bandage over it with antiseptic ointment on the inner side. He fastened that in place with gauze bandaging, wrapped around Jack's middle.

While he was taping that in place, Sean tried to joke about the whole situation. "I thought werewolves couldn't be harmed by regular bullets."

"That would be incorrect," Jack said, wincing. Then, after a long uncomfortable silence, he added, "You seem to be taking this well."

"Am I? I suppose this is better than having a giant monster chase me around the cabin until I piss myself."

Jack grunted and looked away, as if embarrassed. "I'm sorry about that."

"Why did you lie to me?" There was a note of shrillness in Sean's voice. He felt as if he might lose it at any second.

"I guess I was hoping I could introduce you to the idea gradually. I didn't want to scare you."

"Well I'm scared *now*, okay?" Sean snapped. "I have no idea how dangerous you are when you change into that thing."

"I could never hurt you, Sean. You saw that for yourself."

"Maybe you just weren't hungry that night."

"Or maybe I just *love you*," Jack said impatiently, "and I would never hurt you."

For all of Sean's agonizing about not being able to say those words himself, he realized this was the first time *Jack* had said them since he'd arrived here. It was good to hear.

"How did this happen, Jack? Did you learn some kind of magic spell from those books?"

Jack shook his head. "No. It was the forest. I told you it was calling to us. All those years camping out in the woods when we were kids, I could hear it calling to me—to both of us—and there were some nights when it felt like the only thing keeping me from getting up and just walkin'… never coming back… was I didn't want to leave you."

Sean felt a twinge of fear at that—at the thought of Jack disappearing from his life forever. He realized he'd always been afraid of that, of Jack just walking into the forest and never coming back.

"Then I ended up out here on my own," Jack went on. "And I was more or less completely isolated. I barely saw anyone except for the work I did now and then to get a little cash—that, and Larry swinging by to make sure I hadn't shot myself in the head or something."

"I'm sorry," Sean said.

Jack quirked up a corner of his mouth at him and shook his head. "No. That's the thing. I didn't mind it. I felt at home out here. At peace. And at some point… it was like it took me over. When I said the creature started showing up a couple years ago, what I really meant was… that's when I started to *change*."

"How?" Sean asked.

"I don't know. But I'd go to bed and wake up outside, naked. At first I didn't remember anything the next morning. But eventually things started coming back to me, like remembering a dream."

Jack's face lit up while he talked about it, as if he were describing a religious experience. And maybe, for him, it was. The spirit of the forest had finally revealed itself to him and made him one of its own.

"Are you fully conscious now, when you're the wolf?" Sean asked.

Jack shook his head. "Not really. Nothing real clear, or I wouldn't have come in and scared you that night. I just… wanted to be with you."

Sean laughed. "Jesus." That was oddly sweet, though still terrifying.

He stood up and began to pull the bloody sheets off the bed, more for something to do than anything else. He felt as if his brain was overloading with all of this. Jack lifted his ass so Sean could get the sheets out from under him.

"In the beginning," Jack went on, "I was pretty frightened. That's when I bought most of those books, hoping I could find a way to cure it. But most of them say the only cure is death, or permanent maiming."

"Maiming?"

"In folklore, a hunter often cuts off the paw of a wolf, only to find the wolf transforming into a naked human being—missing a hand, of course."

"That would suck."

"Pretty much," Jack agreed. He hesitated, then said, "After a while I stopped looking for a cure. I wasn't killing people, and I enjoyed being a wolf."

"Why?"

Jack's face took on that vaguely religious look again. "It's wonderful, Sean. You have no idea! The things you can see, the smells on the wind, the strength and energy flowing through you! The *freedom*!"

"The bullet wounds," Sean replied sarcastically.

Jack raised a hand to touch the bandage, a bit more subdued. "It barely grazed me."

Part of Sean understood. He'd always loved the time they'd spent in the forest when they were boys. Partly because he'd been with Jack, of course, but also he'd loved the scents of pine and earth, the sounds of wind in the trees and the streams near their camping places. And the peace he'd always felt there.

Sean lifted the bloody sheets in his arms. "Look at this!" he exclaimed, trying to shift the conversation back to something less ethereal. "How can you call yourself a gay man, when you don't even care your best sheets have been ruined!"

Jack laughed. "I'm not that kind of gay man. Are you?"

Sean smiled back a little ruefully. "Probably not. But I've been fucking around with you since we were fifteen. I guess that makes me *some* kind of gay man."

"It never mattered to me what we called it," Jack said. "But there's one thing I want stated out loud, and you know what it is."

Sean did. And he thought maybe he could say it now. But the moment he opened his mouth, there was a knock on the front door.

SEAN DARTED out into the living room and peered through the curtains at the window. "Shit! Larry's back!" He turned to see Jack standing naked in the bedroom doorway, clutching his bandaged side. He was still pretty bloody, despite Sean's attempts at wiping him off. "You'd better cover that bandage up."

Jack shook his head stubbornly. "No."

"Well, at least put some pants on, dumbass. Larry probably doesn't want to see your dork twice in one night."

While Jack disappeared back into the bedroom, Sean went to the door and opened it. Larry was caught in the act of raising his hand to knock again. He hesitated, then put his hand down.

"Evenin'."

"Hi," Sean replied.

"Sorry to bother you again at this hour, but somehow I figured you'd still be up."

Sean nodded and stepped aside. "Come on in."

"Thank you."

Larry entered as Jack came out of the bedroom, still shirtless, but at least wearing jeans. They glanced at each other uncomfortably, and Jack started to raise a hand to the bandage, but stopped himself. Larry nodded at him, as if everything was normal. But all three men knew things had shifted radically that evening.

"What can we do for you, Larry?" Jack asked.

"I told Kelton I was going home after I dropped him off," Larry said, "but I thought maybe you and I should have a little talk instead."

"About what?"

Larry glanced at Sean, and then his attention seemed to be caught by Sean's hands. Sean looked down to discover they were still covered in Jack's blood. "Uh… excuse me."

He walked over to the sink in the kitchenette while Larry continued, "I shot something tonight—something I know wasn't a man. It was dark, sure, and it was raining. But… that thing wasn't human." As he spoke, he began to drift around the living room, glancing at the couch, the oak chest, as if he were taking in the décor. "I followed it right to this cabin here. I saw it jump in through the window. But you know what I found when I went inside? Not an animal. Not a… *monster*. Just my good friend, Jack." He paused when he reached the bookcase. "Who happens to have a pretty impressive collection of stuff about werewolves. And who, coincidentally, has somehow been injured in his left side—the exact same spot I could swear my bullet grazed that animal."

Jack did bring his hand up then to rest on the bandage. "It's just a nick. I'll be fine."

Larry picked up one of the figurines on the bookshelf, a werewolf that appeared to be lunging and snarling ferociously. "I'm glad to hear that."

"Larry…." Jack took a step toward the sheriff. "You've known me my entire life. You know I'd never hurt anyone."

Larry's attention appeared to be occupied by the figurine's vicious countenance. "Not under normal circumstances...."

"*Never.*"

Larry placed the figurine back on the shelf and turned to face Jack. "This is a rural area, son. Everybody and his kid brother owns a gun. Even if Kelton and I stop hunting... this thing... sooner or later, if it keeps showin' its face around here, somebody's gonna put a bullet in it." He paused, distracted by Sean tossing the towel he was drying his hands on down and coming to join them. Then he looked back at Jack. "If this thing really is harmless, then that would be pretty tragic. Don't you think?"

Sean felt a twinge of fear at that. Larry was right. Jack didn't appear to have any supernatural healing abilities or immunities to weapons. If that bullet had hit him in the head....

Jack nodded slowly. "Yes. I do."

Larry sighed and walked to the front door. He placed a hand on the handle but paused to say, "I don't know what can be done about that. It's just what I'm thinking about right now." He smiled sadly. "Anyway, I should be getting home to bed. You two have a nice night."

"Good night," Jack said.

A moment later, the sheriff was gone.

"WELL, THAT was fucked-up," Sean muttered.

"He's right. People are on the alert now. I'm gambling with my life every night I stay in the area." He turned and walked into the bedroom.

Sean called after him, "Can't you just stick close to the cabin?" When Jack didn't reply, he followed him into the room. He found Jack trying to lift the edge of the mattress, but not having an easy time of it. "Stop that, you jackass! You're gonna make yourself bleed again!"

Jack eased up, wincing against the pain. "I'm just trying to flip it over, so I don't have to sleep in a pool of blood."

"Get out of the way. I'll do it."

Wrestling with the mattress was really a two-man job—it was more of a heavy futon than a mattress, and annoyingly floppy—so it was a pain in the ass doing it by himself. But better that than Jack bleeding all over the place and dying. So Sean managed.

Jack stood there watching him, looking frustrated. "No, I can't just stick close to the cabin. If I had that much control over what the beast does, I wouldn't be rooting through people's garbage at night."

"Dude! That's disgusting."

Jack shrugged as if to say, "A werewolf's gotta do what a werewolf's gotta do."

"You just started doing that," Sean pointed out. "Ever since… well I guess since I showed up."

Jack kept his expression blank, but he glanced away guiltily, and Sean knew he'd been thinking the same thing.

Sean didn't want to say it, but he had to. "Maybe if I go away…. Maybe that will calm the wolf down, so he'll stop roaming."

"No," Jack said adamantly. "It won't."

"How do you know?"

"Okay. Yes. Maybe you showing up put me off balance," Jack said. "But it'll just get worse, if you leave now."

"You don't—"

"Sean!" Jack practically snarled. "Do you really think the wolf will be happy if you walk out on me… *again*?"

That brought Sean up short. He looked away, embarrassed. In the uncomfortable silence that fell between them, Jack went to the closet and pulled some fresh sheets off a shelf.

"I just… I thought you loved this place," Sean said quietly.

"What I love is the forest. I only love the cabin because it's in the forest." Jack tossed the sheets on the bed. "The forest has been calling to me since we were kids. You know that. I kept asking you to come with me. After you left… I wanted to just give in, run off into the woods and never come back."

The thought of Jack disappearing—really disappearing, forever—made Sean's stomach clench. "That's pretty much what you did, isn't it?"

"No. I bought a cabin in the woods, but it's not the same. As long as I stay here, I still have ties to people in Dunkirk."

"That's not so—"

"I kept those ties because of *you*," Jack interrupted, sounding impatient, almost angry. "I was afraid to go somewhere you could never find me again, because I was stupid enough to think you'd come back for me someday."

That revelation dropped between them, cold and hard like a stone, causing both men to fall silent again. Jack busied himself with flipping the sheets open onto the bed. It wasn't that Sean hadn't known how much Jack needed him. They'd just never laid it out like this, raw and exposed. Sean felt his face stinging as if he'd been slapped.

But I did *come back, even if it took me a while. I'm here!*

Jack said gruffly, "Help me with this."

Sean obeyed, finding a corner of the fitted sheet and hooking it over one corner of the mattress, while Jack did the same with the opposite corner. They fastened down the remaining corners, and then Jack picked up the top sheet. He held on to one corner and tossed another to Sean, but when he moved to tuck it under the mattress, Sean pulled on his end, drawing the sheet taut between them.

"What are you doing?" Jack asked.

Sean's gaze fixed on his, and he said softly, "I want to sleep in here tonight."

Jack was silent for a long time before finally wrenching his gaze away from Sean's. He let out a breath and replied, "God, Sean. You don't know how much I want that. But I can't. The change tends to come over me while I'm sleeping...."

Sean pulled gently on the sheet, reeling it in until Jack was forced to kneel on the mattress to avoid falling face forward onto it. Sean met him halfway across. "Then how about I go back to the couch after I've had my way with you," he said, trying to sound lighthearted, though he felt as if he'd fall apart if Jack locked him out one more time.

"I'm injured."

"I'll be gentle."

Jack gave him a tolerant smile. "You're such an asshole."

Then he leaned forward and kissed Sean on the mouth.

SEAN TRIED to do all the work. He laid Jack out on the mattress and kissed and caressed every inch of his smooth, sun-bronzed skin, wanting to keep him still so he wouldn't make the injury worse. But when he took Jack's thick, hardened cock into his mouth, relishing the familiarity of it, Jack grabbed his hips and pulled him around so Sean could straddle his head. Sean felt the hot dampness of Jack's mouth engulf him, and he moaned.

God, I've missed you. How could I have ever thought I'd be happy without this?

As teenagers, it had been enough to bring each other off with their mouths or their hands, but Sean yearned for more now. They caressed each other's thighs and hips and asses, but the touch wasn't enough. Sean could feel a hollowness in his belly, a longing to merge their two bodies together. It was so powerful it ached.

He let Jack's cock slip from his mouth in order to lick farther down, bathing Jack's tightened ball sac with his tongue. When Jack lifted his legs on either side of Sean's head, Sean didn't hesitate to move lower, lapping along the hardened muscle there until his tongue plunged into Jack's puckered hole. Jack's moan vibrated his cock and rippled up the length of his body. Sean plunged his tongue in deeper, savoring the sweet muskiness he found there.

It wasn't the first time they'd done this. Both had tasted the other intimately. But there was one thing they'd never done with each other. It had seemed too forbidden.

But now Jack pulled his mouth off Sean's cock for a moment to gasp, "Fuck me."

"Have you ever done it?" He felt a surge of jealousy at the thought of Jack with another man—especially doing *that*. But he could hardly have blamed him.

"No," Jack sighed. "But I've always wanted you to do it. I've fantasized about it forever."

Sean had never done it either, but he was fine with the idea of trying, if it would make Jack happy. He licked his forefinger and slowly slid it into Jack's slicked hole, eliciting another moan.

"Yes," Jack breathed.

They did that for a while, Sean uncertain how much preparation Jack would need to take something as thick as a penis. He tried adding fingers, but discovered saliva didn't quite make it slippery enough.

"Do you have any lube?" he asked.

"No. See what you can find in the kitchen."

It was hard to stay aroused while searching cupboards, but fortunately it didn't take long to locate a bottle of vegetable oil. Soon Sean was back in the bedroom, his cock quickly hardening again in Jack's mouth while he slid two greased fingers into his friend's backside.

After he'd worked his way up to three fingers, he figured Jack should be able to take him.

Since Jack was already lying on his back, Sean simply kneeled between his legs, then moved forward until Jack's thighs were draped over his and Jack's ass was lifted slightly, his hole positioned near Sean's crotch. Sean entered easily, grunting as Jack's body squeezed his shaft tightly. Jack gritted his teeth and hissed.

"Are you okay?"

"Yes," Jack said. "Give me more."

Sean pushed in deeper, moving slowly, watching Jack's face closely as he tried to keep him on the thin line between pleasure and pain without going over it. Every time he paused, Jack would breathe a moment and tell him to keep going, until Sean was completely inside. Then Sean began to move.

It was amazing. Yes, Sean had fucked before, but it had never felt like this. It had been something physical, and it had felt good, but nothing more. Now he felt a surge of energy and emotion building in every part of his body, spreading from his groin into his torso, filling up his chest with a warmth and so much joy and love—yes, love!—for this man it was almost agonizing. It spilled over and flooded his limbs, making his arms quiver as he balanced on one hand and stroked Jack's cock with his other.

Jack erupted first, crying out as he sprayed his stomach and Sean's arm, coating Sean's hand with thick cum. They hadn't used a condom. Neither had even thought about it. So when Sean shuddered a moment later with his own release, it felt as if he were flooding Jack's insides and claiming him.

I love you! I will always love you!

But he couldn't speak it. He was unable to speak at all.

LATER THEY lay together in the dark, the sheets thrown off skin damp from making love on a muggy summer night, but arms and legs intertwined because the contact mattered more than the heat. Sean had been craving Jack's touch ever since he'd arrived—ever since the last time they'd been together in the forest, really. Though maturity and awareness of his feelings had lent an intensity to this night that he'd never felt before.

He hadn't known what he was doing, fumbling around with Jack as a teenager. Now he knew. And it was so much better, knowing.

"Don't fall asleep," Jack warned.

"You're the one who can't fall asleep, Fido."

Jack snorted. "Jackass."

"Spot."

"Asshole."

"Tintin."

"Tintin's human. I think you mean Rin Tin."

"That too," Sean said, giggling like a little kid.

Jack ended the game by leaning in to kiss him. Sean savored the kiss for as long as possible before Jack pulled away.

Then Sean whispered as he trailed his fingers along the curve of Jack's naked hip, "You didn't make me say it."

Jack didn't pretend not to know what Sean meant. The moonlight coming through the window illuminated his face as he gazed back at Sean. "It doesn't matter now."

"Why not?"

"Because what I wanted when I told you to say it… I know I'll never have that now."

"What did you want?"

"For you to come with me."

Sean didn't know if he could do that. It was one thing to live in the woods for a summer. Sure, that could be fun. But all the time? "Can't we just move somewhere else?" he asked.

Jack shook his head.

"Or maybe I could lock you up at night," Sean said, "so you couldn't get out."

Jack looked appalled at that. "Every goddamn night? Chained up while the forest is calling to me? You don't know what you're asking."

"Then…." There wasn't any other option. Sean knew that. He didn't want to lose Jack again—certainly not forever—and he sure as hell didn't want some idiot putting a bullet through his skull. "Fine," he said. "Take me with you."

Jack looked at him for a very long time. Then he climbed out of the bed and walked over to the window. It was still open, and he stood, looking out at the woodpile behind the cabin and the forest beyond.

At last he said, "I want to. But you've never been out there in the winter. You don't know how rough it can get."

"You haven't been out in the winter either."

"Yes, I have," Jack replied, turning back to look at him. "Not for more than a week or so at a stretch, but I've done that much."

"So you'll teach me what you know, and we'll figure out the rest. But at least we'll be together." When Jack still seemed uncertain, he added, "I love you, Jack."

Jack didn't react the way he'd hoped he would. There was no rushing into his arms, no ecstatic "I love you" in return, no tears of joy. Just a noncommittal "huh" as Jack directed his gaze out the window again.

"What do you mean, 'huh'? I thought you wanted me to say it."

"Only if you meant it."

Sean growled in frustration. "I *do* mean it, you idiot!"

"We just had sex," Jack replied. "Everybody loves you after you fuck them—or let them fuck *you*. Wait until morning, and then see how you feel."

"I don't need to wait. I know how I feel." Sean sat up on the edge of the bed. "Look, Jack. I'm sorry I panicked when you asked me to say it down by the pond. But for four years I slept with a woman I *thought* I loved, except that it never felt right. We never connected. I thought for a while it was her fault—that she didn't love me. But it wasn't her." He stood up and took a couple tentative steps forward, feeling as if Jack might leap out the window and bolt if he didn't approach slowly. He gestured back toward the bed. "Laying there with you tonight… I was in heaven. I wanted to stay there forever, pressed up against you. I'm not confused at all anymore. I know I'm in love with you. I was in love with you when we were nineteen. I was just too stupid to know it."

He was close enough now to see Jack's face in profile as he smiled sadly and shook his head. "Even if… that's true… I'm talkin' about going way up north, Sean, deep into the forest, as far away from people as I can get. And half the time I'll be an animal. If you came along, you'd be isolated from everybody—even from me, a good bit of the time. It would be a lonely, miserable life for you."

"What if I was like you?" Sean asked in a last fit of desperation.

"Like me?"

"A werewolf. Can't you make me one? Then we'd both change at night, and you wouldn't have to leave me behind when you hunted."

"You've lost your mind."

"Why?" Sean asked. "Didn't you say it was wonderful?"

"It is."

"Then let me experience it!"

Jack sighed and frowned. "I don't know how, even if I wanted to. I already told you, nobody made me a werewolf. It just happened. I have no idea how to make you one too."

"You could try, couldn't you?" Sean pleaded. "You could bite me or something." He wasn't a total coward. He could handle a single bite wound.

Jack seemed to be mulling it over. In the silence that fell between them, Sean became aware of the sounds of the forest outside the window—the wind in the trees, the hooting of an owl, even the sound of water still dripping off branches. And beneath it he could hear the faint whispering again. Would this be the soundtrack of his life from now on? The music of the forest replacing the music he had on his iPhone? Forever?

Will we never have beer*?* That was almost incomprehensible.

"You're not ready," Jack said, as if he'd been reading Sean's mind and watching the doubts scroll by.

But that just made Sean stubborn. "That's my decision, isn't it?"

"I suppose," Jack said doubtfully. "But it isn't easy, Sean. Becoming a wolf…. That scared the shit out of me, even though I always thought I'd like the idea."

"So you'll help me through it."

"You're just being contrary."

"You bet your sweet ass," Sean said. "Now change me into a werewolf before I punch you."

That made Jack laugh and broke some of the tension. He groaned and leaned forward to rest his forehead against Sean's. "I want to…."

"Then do it."

NEITHER OF them really thought it would work for Jack to bite Sean when he was human, but they decided to try it anyway. Jack brushed his teeth first to hopefully decrease the chance of infection. It felt ludicrous.

The whole thing did. But Sean knew it was the only way they'd be able to stay together.

It hurt like a son-of-a-bitch. Jack bit him on his left forearm, where it would be easy for Sean to clean and dress the wound, and he bit *hard*. There was no point in being half-assed about it. It bled a lot, and even after they'd cleaned the bite with rubbing alcohol and covered it with bandages, Sean could feel it throbbing.

But he didn't change.

"Maybe I have to sleep on it," he suggested.

"Maybe," Jack said dubiously. "Or maybe it just didn't work."

"Have you ever read anything in those books about someone becoming a werewolf like this?" Sean asked. "By being bitten by someone who's a werewolf, but when they're in human form?"

Jack sighed and shook his head. It was beginning to grow light outside, and they were both getting tired. Not to mention the fact that they were now *both* injured and in pain. "Not that I remember. People in the folktales are always bitten by an animal and then discover afterward that the animal was a werewolf."

"Then you'll have to change."

Jack seemed to be thinking it over for a bit before he said, "I might be able to. I tried a couple times, and it seemed like the change *started*, at any rate. But I'm afraid I might hurt you."

Sean was afraid of that too. But he didn't want Jack to know that. "You said you remember things from when you're... transformed. Do you remember the night you licked my face?"

"Yeah," Jack said, smiling. "I remember that."

"What was going through your head then? Did you want to hurt me?"

Jack shook his head adamantly. "No. I was curious about you. You seemed familiar. And I liked the smell of you."

"Then doesn't that mean you won't hurt me?"

Jack gazed intently into his eyes, perhaps trying to divine how much faith Sean really did have in his ability to keep him safe. They'd turned on the table lamp earlier, so they could see to tend to the bite wound, but now he leaned over and flicked it off.

"Go stand near the window," he said.

Sean obeyed, a nervous quivering welling up in his stomach as he stared out into the gray predawn light. The bullfrogs had gone silent, but some of the morning birds had begun chirping. There was a thick mist hanging over everything. He felt as if he'd just agreed to surgery without anesthetic. Had he really asked Jack to turn into a monster and *bite* him? He remembered the sight of that mouthful of fangs snarling at him just before the creature—Jack—had licked his face. Knowing that it had been Jack only made the memory slightly less terrifying.

I must be insane.

Jack came up behind him and said in a low voice, "Try not to move. I need to sort of… meditate. Don't make any noise."

It wasn't like any meditation Sean had ever heard of. He could hear Jack breathing behind him, slow and deep, but while he was doing that, he was pacing slowly back and forth. He was very close to Sean, and his warm, naked body frequently brushed against Sean's ass or back. When it did, Jack seemed to be sniffing him, running his nose along Sean's shoulders and up Sean's neck into his hair. It was intensely erotic, and Sean's cock grew harder with each featherlight touch. Almost against his will, Sean closed his eyes, carried off into a meditation of his own, a trance induced by gentle caresses.

Jack ran his tongue along the base of Sean's neck, and Sean couldn't help shivering. "Is that part of the meditation?"

"Shh…."

Chastised, Sean shut his mouth against the desire to moan as Jack licked him again.

Jack began to run his fingers along Sean's arms, tracing paths along them with his fingertips… or rather his fingernails… while he nuzzled Sean's neck. It felt good, even when the nails began to scrape a bit, as if they were lengthening, growing sharper. Jack's breathing grew stronger, more like panting.

A low, soft rumbling behind Sean set his hair on end. It wasn't a human sound. It was the sound an animal like a wolf or a dog made deep within its chest, a menacing sound, a warning before the attack. Jack's breath was hot against his bare flesh, but it no longer felt sexual.

It felt hungry.

The creature snarled, and Sean wrenched himself away, screaming in terror. There was no place to go. He slammed into the wall beside the window and turned, quivering with fear, expecting fangs and claws to fall on him and rend his flesh.

Jack stood still in the moonlight, his hands clenched into fists as hair grew *into* his body, withdrawing into his naked skin like the hair on the giant doll's head Sean's sister had played with as a kid. Sean might have found that thought funny, but his heart was racing, and he was too horrified by what was happening to Jack's *face*.

A second ago, it had probably looked more like a wolf, but now it was in the process of retreating back to the visage of a man. The resultant half-wolf, half-man he saw now nauseated Sean more than the twisted things he'd once seen in jars at a freak show—made worse by the fact that it was *changing*, contorting as he watched, making him want to scream in the most primal depths of his consciousness....

Then it was over. Jack was Jack again, naked and glistening with sweat in the moonlight. He was panting, and when he took a step forward, he staggered and had to grasp the window frame to keep from collapsing.

I failed. The realization washed over Sean with a sickening certainty. He'd had the chance, but he'd lost his nerve. His voice was small and defeated when he said, "I'm sorry...."

"It's okay."

"I'm so sorry—"

"I understand." Jack took a deep breath and steadied himself. Then he reached out a hand.

Sean took his hand, but when Jack tried to pull him forward, he held back, trembling. Jack gave him a wounded look, and that broke through the fear. He folded himself into Jack's arms and buried his face in Jack's shoulder.

"I'm sorry," he whispered, his eyes stinging with tears.

"Shh," Jack hushed him, petting his hair affectionately. "It's okay."

But Sean knew it wasn't okay. It was goodbye.

SEAN WOKE to discover the sunlight coming into the room was almost directly under the window, which meant it had to be nearly noon. He and Jack had fallen asleep just as the sky had turned rosy at sunrise. He still felt as if he could sleep several more hours, but a vague sense of alarm filtered through his grogginess and jolted him wide-awake.

He was alone in the bed.

"Jack!"

No answer. Sean sat upright and called again, but he knew—the cabin was empty. He could *feel* it. The small trash can beside the bed held the bandages he'd used on Jack's wound the night before, balled up and spattered with dried blood.

Then he saw the note on the night table.

> *Sean, I'm sorry. I have to go, and we both know you can't come with me. I love you—you know that, right? More than I can put into words. But I can feel the forest calling me. I can feel the wolf pacing inside me, wanting to be let out. I think it might take me over completely someday. And if that happens, I don't think I'll mind.*
>
> *But it means we can't be together. I know it's cowardly to disappear without saying goodbye, but I knew I'd never be able to do it if you woke up and begged me to stay.*
>
> *Don't feel guilty anymore. I forgive you, and I know how you feel about me.*
>
> *I'll always love you. Nobody but you.*
> *Jack*

Sean ran out into the living area, and then flung open the door to burst naked out onto the porch, shouting though he knew it was futile. Jack's truck was still parked in the driveway, but nothing came back from the surrounding forest but the songs of birds and the nattering of squirrels. Jack was gone. The bastard had left him behind.

The pond! He didn't know why he thought Jack might be there. It made little sense. But maybe he'd stopped to get a drink of water or… something….

Holding on to that ridiculously scant fragment of hope, Sean ran down the path, his bare feet slipping in the mud. Everything was wet from last night's rain—the earth, the leaves that whipped his naked body as he ran, the grass near the water's edge.

Jack wasn't there. Of course not. Why would he be? By now he was probably miles away, running on all fours.

Sean collapsed on his knees, despair overwhelming him. *Why was I such a fucking coward?*

He'd had the chance, and he'd blown it. A few seconds longer, the pain of one bite—that's all it might have taken. And then he'd be with Jack right now.

Jack, who'd always been the center of his life, even when Sean was too stupid to see it, the one person Sean had thought he could always come home to. Sean knew he was self-centered, a bit of an asshole. But Jack had always been there for him—even this time, when Sean had shown up on his doorstep unannounced, not having talked to him for almost four years. The thought of him being gone forever was excruciating.

The one time I tried to sacrifice my own needs for his, and I failed.

Perhaps it was his self-centered nature, but Sean refused to accept this. He refused to believe it was over, less than twenty-four hours after he'd finally wrapped his head around the fact that he was in love with Jack—that he'd always been in love with him.

The books.

People didn't have to get bitten to become werewolves. There were all kinds of ways. Some of them were pretty much impossible for Sean— he wasn't likely to find a wolf skin to wear or make a belt out of. At least not in a reasonable amount of time. He needed to do it fast, if he were to have any hope of finding Jack before he disappeared up north into hundreds of miles of forest in New Hampshire or Maine or the thousands of miles of forest in Canada.

He took a step on the rain-drenched grass, and the answer came into his head immediately. Turning, he raced back to the cabin.

It was there, in the mud near the woodpile—one massive footprint. Or rather, paw print. Just as Larry had described it—as large as Sean's hand with the fingers splayed out. There were other prints, of course, running between the forest and the open window to Jack's bedroom, but this one was clear and unmistakable. It could be nothing other than a massive wolf.

And it was full of rainwater.

Still naked, Sean fell to his knees, and then leaned over the print on all fours. Part of his mind was yelling at him to get up out of the mud, clean himself up, and put some goddamn clothes on, but he forced himself to ignore it. He'd chickened out once too often. Not this time.

The rainwater tasted exactly as he'd expected it to. Muddy. But he drank as much as he could. He felt ridiculous, but he kept at it until he was licking up more mud than water.

He lifted his head, unsure what to do next, but he didn't have to think about that for long. Something was different. He was hit with a wave of smells, as if he'd opened a window and a fresh breeze had carried the scents of mud and pine and cut wood and... *everything*... to his nostrils. It was overwhelming at first, making him dizzy.

Then the sounds. He heard a cardinal flutter down onto the woodpile, then take off again. A chipmunk scurried along the base of the pile and *chittered* at him a moment. The wind in the branches, the rainwater still dripping off the eaves of the cabin roof, the drone of a plane high overhead, the cawing of crows in the front of the cabin, the cabin door softly banging in its frame because Sean hadn't closed it properly and the wind was agitating it....

And the whispering, growing in volume until it was louder than he'd ever heard it before. It came from the forest on all sides of him, and now he could distinguish words—*Come, Sean! This is your home! It has always been your home!* He'd never heard voices so beautiful. They seemed to reach into his soul and tug on it. This is what Jack had been hearing all this time. It was what he'd been feeling. Sean finally understood.

As he lowered his head again, he detected a scent to the paw print. It had been hidden beneath the smell of mud and water before, but now it came to Sean's nostrils as clear as strong perfume—the smell of Jack, the smell of the *wolf.*

Sean was barely conscious of his nasal passages lengthening as he inhaled the scent, of his face elongating. He was too excited by the smell. He could smell it coming from the bedroom window, and it was all around the area near the woodpile. He moved to follow it, his gait becoming more fluid as his arms and legs evened out, as the muscles grew larger in his shoulders and hips, and fingers withdrew to make forepaws more suitable for running.

He ran then, around the woodpile, following the scent. At the edge of the forest, he paused, snuffling around on the ground until he found it—a trail of odors leading off to the north. The scent of Jack's paws on the ground, of his fur brushing against the witch hazel bushes, of a spray of urine where he'd marked an oak tree. Without a second's thought, Sean plunged into the undergrowth. He ran, exhilarated, sniffing frantically at everything he passed, the path Jack took as clear to him as if it had been marked by blazing torches.

There was little thought in the mind of the wolf that had been Sean. All else had faded away, leaving just the one driving need—a need no longer able to be expressed in complex human terms.

Find Jack.

Abducted

Author's Note

I RECALL reading "true" stories of alien abduction and UFO sightings when I was in middle school and being utterly fascinated by them. In the library, I still have a stack of books that I collected back then. I'm afraid I find them a bit cheesy now. Though I don't dismiss the possibility and still listen with rapt attention to new accounts, I don't find many plausible. I read Whitley Strieber's *Communion* and… well, let's just say I wasn't persuaded.

However, I do believe in life out there somewhere in the universe. It seems absurd to insist our little planet is the only one upon which space-faring species could evolve. But even if they've reached space, they may not have found us yet.

In *Abduction*, the aliens have good reason to safeguard Earth, which means making an appearance now and then, but I won't give it away.

Part One

Chapter One

THE FARM wasn't hard to find, even with Cody's barely coherent directions, because there was literally nothing else along Brickyard Pond Road for almost two miles. At one time the farm had sprawled across the countryside, keeping its neighbors at bay. Now most of that acreage had reverted back to forest. I'd learned all that from a phone conversation with Cody months ago, when he first bought the place. Back then, he'd described the property as beautiful and peaceful—just what he'd been looking for after living in Boston for years. But as I pulled into the cul-de-sac in front of the house, those words weren't the first that came to mind.

The house itself was in decent shape, I supposed, though its gray paint was peeling and the porch sagged a bit on one side. Two of the lower-floor windows were boarded up, and the mesh in the screen door was torn. A bicycle I felt sure must have come with the house lay in a rusted heap on the overgrown front lawn.

Cody was a computer programmer—a private consultant—and he worked from home these days, so he could afford to live off the beaten path. Still, this seemed a bit much.

He must have heard my car pull in, because he stepped out onto the porch as I parked and climbed out of the car. My first sight of him in over a year was disturbing. He was pretty much naked except for a tattered red flannel bathrobe, which hung open and did nothing to cover a body I'd once salivated over. Now he looked emaciated. I doubted I would have recognized his face at first glance if I hadn't known he was the only one living there. He'd always been clean-shaven and had kept his dark brown hair in a short, nerdy style reminiscent of a man in a fifties sitcom. Now he was bearded, and his hair was long and unkempt. I suspected he hadn't bathed in a very long time.

"Marc," he gasped, staggering down the front steps in his slippers.

I didn't object when he threw his arms around me, despite the nudity. It was weird for a man who always dressed fastidiously, but even though our relationship had never really gone beyond friendship, we'd slept together a couple of times. And we'd shared a dorm room in college. I'd seen him naked often enough. Harder to ignore was the rather funky body odor. But I embraced him anyway, disliking how thin and breakable he felt in my arms. Then I stepped back to examine him more closely. He looked pale, and his face was drawn. His gentle brown eyes blinked back tears, as if we hadn't seen each other in a decade.

"Are you all right?" I asked. He'd told me next to nothing over the phone—just that he needed me, and please, please, *please* come.

His breath was foul. "Oh, Marc…. You have no idea…."

Then he burst into tears.

I HELD Cody until he stopped crying and then gently guided him indoors.

The inside of the house was just as dreary as the outside. Apparently he'd inherited the furnishings from a previous owner. The paisley upholstery on the sofa and chairs in the living room was a sickly green color, faded and worn through on the arms. Stuffing peeked out in places. If I'd been the one living there, I would have burned them all for fear of fleas or bedbugs in the cushions.

The kitchen was a bit better, though God knew when he'd last taken out the trash. The bin was overflowing and smelled of something rotten. Fortunately the clutter on the table was mostly coffee cups—quite possibly every cup he owned. There were a few dishes in the sink, but not many. Had he been eating? I suspected not much.

Another odd thing, simply because it was so contrary to Cody's nature to leave things like this unattended to—the kitchen clock was either stopped or completely out of sync. It read three twenty-five. But I knew it couldn't be past noon. The clock on the stove was blinking at ten fourteen. As I watched, the clock changed to ten fifteen, though it kept blinking. Obviously, it had lost power at some point and needed to be reset.

This was so different from the anal-retentive and unashamedly nerdy man I'd once roomed with, I didn't know how to process it. Could he be suffering from some kind of mental illness? Depression, perhaps? Or schizophrenia? I wasn't a psychologist, so I had no idea what to look for.

"I need to talk," he said roughly.

I took both his hands in mine and looked him directly in the eye. "Cody… I'm going to listen to everything you have to say. But first I want you to do something for me. It'll just take a minute."

"What?"

"Do you have hot water?"

"Yes."

"Then I want you to take a shower."

His eyes drifted away from mine, and he pulled his hands away. "I guess... I must smell pretty bad."

"This isn't for my sake—it's for yours. You haven't showered in a long time, have you?"

He shook his head. "I don't remember."

"Then shower now. And brush your teeth." I added, "Trust me, you'll feel a lot better. And by the time you're done, I'll have some coffee ready."

The first thing I did, after he'd left the kitchen, was take out the trash. I wasn't exactly a neat freak, but Jesus! It was disgusting. I could have sworn there were maggots crawling around in it, but I didn't look too closely. I just tied it up and hauled it out the kitchen door. There wasn't anything like a dumpster or a trash can to put it in, so I just set it on the back porch. Obviously it would have to be moved before nightfall or we'd find it torn open by raccoons in the morning, but that could wait.

I washed my hands in the sink, hoping I wasn't making the water ice-cold for Cody—I could hear the shower running upstairs now—but there was no way I'd prepare food after touching that disgusting garbage without scrubbing down.

I was unsurprised to find the refrigerator devoid of anything like milk, cream, or half-and-half. They probably would have been spoiled anyway. But there was a little coffee left in the can, and some sugar. The coffee maker could have used some scouring, but I figured we'd survive using it. By the time I heard the shower turn off, I had a pot brewing, and the warm, comforting scent of it was almost enough to mask the residual odor left by the trash.

How the fuck am I going to stay here? Cody had begged me to come for the entire weekend, and it hadn't seemed an unreasonable promise when we'd been on the phone. Now, I wasn't so sure. I shuddered to think what condition the beds were in. Did he even have a guest bedroom?

In the hope I'd find some nondairy creamer, I rummaged through his kitchen cupboards. That turned out to be a lost cause, but I did turn up several cans of soup. There were clean pans under the sideboard, so I put some minestrone on one of the gas burners. I made up my mind that Cody was going to eat it, if I had to hold him down and pour it into him.

He shuffled into the kitchen in a pair of sweatpants and his slippers. I wasn't sure if the sweatpants were clean, but they looked less grubby than the robe. His hair was wet and combed. He still had the beard, but I hadn't expected him to shave. I noticed a small Band-Aid on his left forearm, but it looked dry and clean. He must have put it on after the shower.

"Sit," I ordered, and when he'd obeyed, I set the bowl of soup in front of him. "Eat."

"I'm not hungry."

I folded my arms in front of my chest and raised my eyebrows. "When's the last time you ate something?"

"I don't know."

"Then eat. And don't give me any shit."

The old Cody would have told me to fuck off if I'd hovered over him like that, but now he just sighed and picked up the spoon. I poured myself a cup of black coffee, spooned in extra sugar to compensate for not having any cream, and then took a seat opposite him.

We didn't talk for a while. I was curious about why he was in this state. More than curious, to be honest—freaked out. But I was worried he'd forget to eat if we talked. So I just sipped my coffee and tried not to make faces at the bitter taste, while he slowly and silently spooned the soup into his mouth.

God, he looked awful. Like a man withering away from some horrible disease. It hurt to look at him.

Finally he set the spoon down and pushed the bowl away. "I can't eat any more."

There was still a bit of soup left in the bowl, but I didn't press. I sat back in my chair and said, "All right. So… what's going on, Cody? You look like shit."

"You won't believe me."

I gave him a sour look. "Fuck that shit. You called me, remember? You wanted me to come out here. So tell me what's happening."

"It started… about a month ago," he said slowly.

And then he proceeded to tell me a story that was disturbing, somewhat frightening… and completely insane.

Chapter Two

"I BOUGHT this property, say… about eight months ago," Cody began. I knew that part, of course, but I let him continue without interrupting. "It had been in the Corwin family for generations, but the last owner didn't have any children of her own, and her brother had moved away. She lived here by herself, with just a friend driving out from town a couple times a week to check on her, until she passed away from… I don't know. Natural causes. She was in her eighties. Her daughter lives out in California and didn't want the house, so she listed it on the market."

He paused to take the cup of coffee I handed him and sip it. "It was a great deal. All these acres and acres of land—almost six hundred! For next to nothing!"

I was skeptical about how much good all those acres would do him if the house was falling apart, but I didn't say anything. Where he wanted to live was his business. At least, it would be under normal circumstances.

"I managed to get it financed," Cody went on. "And I closed last January. Everything was great for the first six months or so. I mean, yeah, the house needs work. But the roof is good, the boiler works fine, and I have electricity and internet. Then… in the early summer… things started happening…."

What he described seemed at first like a ghost story. He kept finding his bedroom window open in the morning, no matter how careful he was to shut it at night. And there were weird power glitches that set every clock in the house blinking.

"But it was more than just a power outage," he insisted. "*Everything* went dead. My Kindle, my iPad—even the clocks that ran on batteries." He pointed up at the kitchen clock I'd noticed earlier. "I recharged them, replaced the batteries on the clocks. Then a few nights later, it would happen again."

"So… you think you have a… poltergeist?" I didn't really believe in them, but I'd watched some episodes of *Ghost Hunters*. Last I knew, Cody had never believed in anything supernatural. But this wasn't the Cody I knew.

"It's not a goddamn poltergeist," he said, glaring at his coffee cup. "I wish it was. Then I could just… call an exorcist or something."

"What is it, then?"

He looked away and said nothing for a long moment. Then he appeared to change the subject. "I started getting headaches. Awful, awful headaches, like my skull was trying to split open. Then the dreams started…."

"What dreams?" This conversation was making me nervous. I'd been afraid Cody might be suffering from some kind of mental illness, and now he was describing headaches and nightmares. Could these be symptoms of schizophrenia? Or worse, a brain tumor?

"They didn't make sense!" he said angrily. "I kept seeing a room—an operating room—but I was strapped down, so I couldn't see much. And they kept poking me and… and stabbing me, and… *cutting* me!"

I tried to sip my coffee, but my hand was shaking, so I set it down again. I had no idea what I should say at this point, but he was glaring at me as if it—whatever *it* was—was all my fault. So I asked, "Who are 'they,' Cody?"

"Look!" He jumped up so fast he startled me and made me jerk back in my chair. For a second I thought he was going to hit me. But he just thrust his bare arm out for my inspection. "*Look!*"

My God. I hadn't looked closely enough to see earlier, but there were needle marks in it, all along the veins. Christ. He was doing drugs. My sweet, nerdy computer programmer friend was an addict. He also had small cuts up and down his arms, some healed and barely visible, but others just recently scabbed over. Then, of course, there was that fresh Band-Aid.

My voice quavered when I asked, "What are… what are you taking, Cody? Heroin? Cocaine?"

"*What?*" His face turned red with anger. "No, you fucking idiot! They did this!" He slapped his arm repeatedly with his hand. "*They* did it! They keep doing it! And I can't make them stop!"

"*Who* is 'they,' Cody?" Frustrated now, and unable to stop myself, I added in a mocking tone, "The *government?*"

He shook his head violently. "No! No! No! This is way beyond them! It's the fucking *aliens!*"

I DIDN'T know what the hell to do. At that moment I was convinced what Cody needed was therapy and rehab—not a friend's shoulder to cry on. It wasn't just the talk about aliens. A lot of people believed in alien abduction without it preventing them from living normal lives. Though, honestly, I never would have expected him to be one of them. He'd always been an atheist, and he'd rolled his eyes at shows like *Finding Bigfoot* and *Ancient Aliens*. Even so, I could deal with a new interest in alien abductions. He was an adult, and he could believe what he liked. But this was more than an obsession with silly reality shows. He was insisting aliens were experimenting on *him*. And he seemed to be having some kind of nervous breakdown over it.

"Cody," I said slowly, "I need you to calm down and explain this to me. What exactly do you think is happening?"

He leaned forward, balling up his fists against his knees in frustration and gritting his teeth. "*Augh!*" he groaned. "You don't get it!" Then he straightened up and held out a hand to me. "Come on. Let me show you."

Against my better judgment, I took his hand and let him lead me upstairs. On the way up, I glimpsed something worrisome between his shoulder blades—a small lump over a half inch in diameter. It wasn't red and inflamed like a boil. It looked as if there were something just under the skin.

His bedroom was at the end of a short hall, past a bathroom and a couple of side rooms. I'd been afraid I'd find he was living in squalor up there, surrounded by piles of dirty clothes and remnants of meals, but fortunately that wasn't the case. The room was messier than Cody used to keep his room, certainly—a few articles of clothing strewn about, some books scattered on the floor, and more dirty coffee cups by the head of the bed. But it wasn't unlivable.

Cody closed the door behind us, as if to keep people from listening in—though of course we were alone in the house. Then he left me for a moment to fetch something out of the top drawer of his dresser. While he was doing that, I picked up a paperback lying on the floor near where I was standing. *Incident at Exeter: Unidentified Flying Objects Over America Now* by John G. Fuller. It appeared to be about Betty and Barney Hill, who'd claimed to be abducted for a few hours while driving through a remote part of New Hampshire in 1961. I'd heard of the case, since I lived near Exeter. There was a yearly UFO festival in the town.

"Look at this," Cody said, pulling something out of the drawer. He brought it over to show me.

It was a small Altoids Peppermint tin. But when he opened it, what it contained turned my stomach. They looked a bit like human teeth—blobby and bone-colored, though lacking any roots or sharp edges. In the crevices, there was a pinkish substance that looked far too much like skin. The tin contained nine or ten of them. "What... the hell...?"

"I don't know," Cody said. "I think they could be transmitters or something."

"Transmitters?" They certainly didn't look electronic, though I'd seen hearing aids that looked vaguely like them. But not nearly as... disgusting.

Cody thrust out his arm again. "I keep finding them imbedded in my skin," he said matter-of-factly, as though that wasn't totally insane. "Some on my arms, some on my legs and other places. I've been cutting them out as soon as I find them, but there's one I can't reach." He turned around and pointed over his shoulder to the lump I'd seen between his shoulder blades. "They're getting more clever about it."

I could feel spiders crawling around in my brain, like the feeling of hair standing on end. But it went deeper than that. I'd stepped into a world completely off-kilter, and I knew I needed to escape. Now. What was wrong with Cody was far beyond my ability to help.

I stepped back slowly. "Cody... maybe you should have a doctor look at that. I can drive—"

"No!" He whirled back around to face me. "Don't you think I've thought of that? But they wouldn't believe me. They'd assume I was schizophrenic or something—hallucinating—just like you're probably thinking now. They'd put me in the hospital and give me medication. But it wouldn't help." He stepped forward, then snapped the tin shut with his thumb and rattled it in my face. "This isn't in my mind, Marc. Something is implanting these things in my body."

"They could be... anything, Cody. Tumors, maybe. Or calcium deposits...."

"No!"

I took another step back and bumped into the closed door.

Fuck.

Was he dangerous? For the first time, I wondered if he was capable of hurting me. It was impossible to reconcile that notion with the Cody I'd known, but this man standing in front of me was very different.

"Don't you think I considered that idea?" Cody demanded. "If they were tumors, they would start small and grow larger. These don't do that. The first one stayed the same size for a week before I finally had the balls to cut it out."

"The hospital could protect you," I said weakly. "The aliens wouldn't be able to get at you... there." I'd almost said, "If you were locked up."

He seemed to consider this, looking intently at the mint tin and pressing his lips together in a thin line. "I don't know. Maybe. But eventually they'd let me out of the hospital, and I'd have to come back here."

Over my dead body, I thought. Even if the doctors managed to control his delusions with medication and therapy, allowing him to live out here completely isolated from friends and family seemed like a very bad idea. I wasn't sure what the solution was. As much as I cared about him, I couldn't see myself living with him or anything like that. But I couldn't just turn my back on him.

All this could be dealt with later, though. What I needed to do right now was get Cody out of this fucking house and into a hospital. He seemed open to the idea, so I pressed my advantage. "Cody... you know I care about you. I don't want anything to hurt you. Which is why I think we should go to the hospital."

"I knew you'd say that." He didn't sound angry. But he didn't give in either. "Not yet."

He turned away from me and walked to the dresser. There, he placed the tin carefully back in the top drawer and then slid the drawer closed. I could have made my escape while his back was turned, but I still had hope that the fear coursing through my body was an overreaction. Cody couldn't really be dangerous. It seemed impossible.

"Why not now, Cody?"

"There are some things I need you to do first."

"What?"

"First, you need to cut that thing out of me."

My stomach threatened to turn over at the thought of it. Not just how disgusting it would be, but how absolutely psychotic the whole situation was. Then I had a sudden moment of clarity. "Was this it? Was this why you called me?"

"Yes. I can't reach it. So I needed someone I could trust to come here and do it."

The spiders were working overtime in my skull. "Cody, I'm not cutting into you."

He turned back to me and folded his arms across his chest stubbornly. "If you want me to go to the hospital, you will. I know *they* won't do it—the doctors at the hospital. They'll want to take X-rays and run tests and all that shit before they do anything. And I'm not going to just let it sit there, doing... whatever the fuck it's doing. Broadcasting my location, trying to control my thoughts... I don't know. I just want it out. Then we can talk about going to the hospital."

I swallowed nervously. Could I actually do something like that? Cut into someone's skin? This was far more than removing a splinter. It would hurt him, it would bleed—a lot—and a cut that deep could get seriously infected. Besides, wouldn't it just reinforce his paranoia? I doubted I'd be able to explain my actions to any psychologist examining him later.

"What other things did you want me to do?" I asked finally. "You said there were 'things.' Plural."

"I need you to stay the night."

Chapter Three

I WON'T describe what it was like cutting into Cody's back with a scalpel he provided. It was repulsive, and I still feel nauseated thinking about it. Not only did it bleed profusely, but the way the object popped out, as if it hadn't been attached to…. Never mind. It was unpleasant. And, of course, he added the horrid thing to his collection. I refused to think it was an alien implant. Perhaps his body was somehow producing them—a nasty idea, but at least a more reasonable one.

The scalpel bothered me. Apparently Cody had ordered it online. Not that there was anything particularly wrong with someone owning a scalpel, but it put me in mind of serial killers carving up their victims. I'd agreed to spend the night, extracting a promise that he'd let me drive him to the hospital the next morning, assuming I didn't see anything to convince me he was right about aliens harassing him. But was he really safe to spend the night with? What if he decided to use that scalpel on my throat while I slept?

It turned out, though, he didn't *want* me to sleep.

"You have to stay awake," he insisted. "Promise me!"

"Why?"

"I have to sleep," he said. "They won't come if I'm awake. I've tried to stay up all night and catch them breaking in, but… no. They only come when I'm sleeping. That's why I need you to hide and keep watch."

I looked at him dubiously. "And what am I supposed to do if I see them? Photograph them? Fight them off?"

"Everything electronic goes dead when they show up," he replied. "I gave up replacing batteries and recharging things. I haven't used my cell phone in weeks."

I pulled my cell phone out of my pocket and looked at it. The battery was still at 80 percent, since none of these mysterious outages had occurred in my presence. But there was no signal at all.

"How did you manage to call me?" I asked.

"I have an internet connection. I had to get it for work. So I use an internet phone when I have to call out."

That made me feel a little better. Though it didn't mean I had access to the internet phone—not if it was on *his* computer, protected by *his* password. I could see his laptop on the desk, but it was currently closed. "I want you to give me the use of your laptop tonight."

He looked at me suspiciously. "Why? Who do you want to call?"

"At the moment, nobody. But if I'm going to stay, I need to know I *can* call somebody if I need to." I left out the reason for this—my concerns about his mental stability. I was sure he knew that.

He looked at the laptop for a long moment, his face petulant, like a child told he couldn't have everything he wanted. "If they come, you won't be able to use it. It'll shut down. So will the router and everything else in the house."

"Understood. But I want access to the phone up until that point." He still looked reticent, so I added, "I'm not going to call the hospital or the police. Not as long as I feel we're both safe. It's either that, or I leave now. Your choice."

He turned to look me in the eye. "All right. I'll trust you."

CODY WAS afraid any light in the room might prevent the aliens from coming, so I agreed to sit in one of the spare rooms with just the light from the laptop and a thermos full of hot coffee to comfort me. The doors to both rooms were left open, so I could hear if anybody or any*thing* went into Cody's room. The rest of the house was dark.

I couldn't believe I was doing this. I'd probably be berated by the hospital for reinforcing his delusions, if I did manage to get him there. But my other options were to abandon him—which I simply couldn't do—or call the police and hope things didn't get violent as they dragged him bodily into a squad car. I just hoped, if I stuck it out for one night and nothing happened, he'd be reasonable about going to the hospital with me in the morning.

The spare room had a bed in it, but Cody had said it came with the house. There'd been a recent outbreak of bedbugs in southern New Hampshire, traced to people buying used mattresses and upholstered furniture, so I was leery of it. At any rate, lying or even sitting on a bed would be unwise if I wanted to stay awake all night. So I sat in the wooden chair by the desk in my underwear and a T-shirt and browsed the web. I was disconcerted to see how many sites about aliens and UFOs

Cody had bookmarked, and a quick glance at some of them did nothing to put my mind at ease. I decided it was better to read posts on Facebook or play mah-jongg.

By two in the morning, I'd run out of coffee and really needed to piss. I was also starting to nod a bit. I could hear Cody snoring quietly, so I figured it was safe to venture down to the kitchen and brew another pot. I knew Cody would be annoyed if he discovered I'd abandoned my post, but it would only take a couple of minutes, and it had to be preferable to me falling asleep.

Down in the kitchen, I had to fumble around for water and ground coffee without violating Cody's "no lights" rule. Fortunately there was a crescent moon that night, and it shone in through the windows, giving me a small amount of light. Not much, but a little. The most challenging part was judging how much water I'd put into the coffee maker, but I managed. As soon as I had the coffee brewing, I stepped out onto the porch so I could take a quick piss off it into the grass.

That was when the aliens came.

The first thing I noticed was a massive shadow moving slowly across the front yard, heading directly for the house. Startled, I jerked my eyes upward. It would be inaccurate to say I saw a spaceship. What I saw was blackness—an enormous triangular shape blotting out the stars and the moon as it drifted silently overhead. I couldn't tell how high up it was, but even if it were just a few feet above the nearest treetops, it would still have been massive.

Only dimly aware I'd just pissed on myself, I spun around and rushed back inside. The coffee maker was no longer brewing. The stove clock wasn't blinking. Everything was dark and deathly silent.

I ran for the stairs and tried to take them two at a time, but in the darkness, I stumbled and slammed down hard. I cried out in pain. Above me, coming from the direction of Cody's room, a bright bluish light spilled out into the upper hall like headlights from a car. It had to be moving, because the shadows cast by the stair railings drifted slowly across the wall over my head. No longer caring if I made any noise, I scrambled up the stairs, using my hands as much as my feet.

Fuck! Why did I leave the room! Idiot!

I was going so fast when I reached the top, I slammed into the door frame of the room I'd been camping out in. I pushed myself away from it and flung myself through the open door of Cody's room.

Then, for a second, I froze.

He was *floating*. His body was naked, since he slept that way, and he appeared to still be sound asleep. But the covers had slipped off, and he was a good foot or so from the bed, still in a reclining position. To my horror, he was moving slowly but steadily toward the open window. Beyond that, I could see nothing but that glaring bluish light.

"Cody!" I forced myself to move, though I felt as if I were dreaming—struggling to run through air the consistency of pudding. "Cody!"

He was moving so slowly, it seemed impossible that I couldn't reach him before he went through the window. But by the time I grabbed his ankles, his head and shoulders had already slipped through. No matter how hard I pulled, he continued sliding farther out the window, getting sucked into the light.

"Cody!"

Then he was through, and I followed him, literally yanked off my feet. I panicked and lost my grip on his ankles as I grabbed for the window ledge. Cody vanished, lost in the blinding blue-white glare. I continued to float through the air, not falling, but tumbling like an uncoordinated trapeze artist, grabbing at nothingness.

Then something exploded, searing my eyes, and I fell.

Part Two

Part Two

Chapter Four

THE DREAM was disjointed.

I was in some kind of operating room, lying naked on a table, the hard, cold metal surface chilling me wherever my body pressed against it. Overhead, the ceiling was lost in a sea of bright spotlights shining directly down upon me. But the "doctors" hovering over me were the stuff of nightmares—human in shape, but with large heads and enormous, bulbous black eyes. They were silhouetted against the light, so the details of their faces were in shadow, but as they worked, they moved in and out of the light. Their skin was gray and leathery, like that of a lizard, and their noses and mouths were just small slits. I was terrified and wanted to scream, but I was also groggy, as though under the influence of a powerful sedative, and the best I could manage was a whimper.

That caught the attention of the creatures, however. One turned to me and said something in a language I couldn't understand. One of the others—there were four—responded with a curt, single word and a dismissive wave of his hand. Their mouths didn't appear to move as they spoke.

The first turned away for a moment, and when he turned back, he was holding a thin syringe. As I watched in horror, the creature lowered the syringe toward my body. I tried to pull away, but I was strapped down. I couldn't move my head to see where the needle went, but a second later, I felt a sharp prick in my upper arm. I gasped.

Then a wave of dizziness washed over me, and everything went black.

THE FIRST thing I became aware of, as I clawed my way back to consciousness, was a low, pervasive hum. Not so much an audible sound as a sensation I could feel with my entire body. I opened my eyes to find myself lying in a strange room on a bed of some kind. But nothing was familiar. The walls and ceiling seemed to be made of some kind of webbing—not quite like a spider web, but more like a dark gray-green mesh that covered nearly every surface, including the floor. Where the walls ended and the ceiling and floor began was indistinct. Everything was rounded, as if I were inside a cocoon of some sort. But it was large enough for a man to stand and move around in, and a portal in the far wall appeared to be a door, though it was currently closed.

The bed I was lying on seemed to be made of something like memory foam. It conformed to the shape of my body and was very comfortable. My head was propped up on some kind of pillow, and I was covered by a thin blanket. When I moved under the blanket, my hand brushed against the skin of my hip. I was stark naked.

Terrific.

I sat up and swung my feet out of the bed to rest on the floor. It was hard, perhaps made out of metal, but not at all cold. If anything, the temperature in the room was a bit warm.

Where the light was coming from, I couldn't determine. The room wasn't dark. The ambient light was similar to afternoon sunlight coming in through a window, except that there was no window, and the shadows my body cast on the bed and the floor were diffuse and indistinct.

The doorway dilated like the iris of an eye, and I grabbed the blanket to make sure my crotch was covered. God knew why. My captors had stripped me and ogled my private parts to their hearts' content when I was unconscious. Of course, that didn't mean I had to give them a free show *now*.

It didn't matter. As soon as I saw the two creatures entering the room, I scrambled backward on the bed in fear to cower naked and terrified against the mesh wall. I was no longer even vaguely aware of the blanket or what it might or might not be covering.

They were tall, though not particularly taller than some human men. I couldn't tell if they were naked or clothed in leatherlike suits, but I wasn't really looking at their bodies. I was looking at those horrible *faces*. Their heads were larger than any man's, and they had two enormous eyes, black and as featureless as glass orbs. Between these, where a human nose would be, there was a slight bump with a small horizontal slit near the bottom. A bit lower there was a "mouth" that likewise was nothing more than a small slit.

"What… the fuck… are you?" I managed to say, my voice quivering.

"Wee… weel… noht… hoort… yoo…."

I blinked at them for a long moment. Then I realized what I'd heard wasn't an alien language. It was English. Sort of. It sounded like someone from Eastern Europe trying to pronounce English words, very slowly and carefully, and not quite getting the vowels right. There was also a vaguely electronic overtone to it.

His—was it a he?—companion gripped his shoulder briefly and then stepped forward.

"Do you understand me?" the second one said. His voice was much clearer. Still accented oddly, but definitely understandable. Like the first, his voice sounded slightly electronic, as if he were talking through a speaker.

"Yes," I replied.

"We will not hurt you."

"Glad to hear it."

He tapped his companion on the shoulder again and said something I didn't understand at all. The latter nodded, and with a slight nod toward me, he turned and left the room. The door silently constricted, leaving me alone with the one who spoke English more coherently.

He—his voice sounded kind of male, so I decided to go with that until I learned otherwise—made a gesture with his hand, as if he were lifting something, and the floor in front of him bulged upward, forming a sort of stool. He moved in front of it and sat down.

Then he took off his head.

It wasn't actually his head, or I would have pissed myself. As it was, I gasped when he gripped it on both sides, and I heard a *crack* like the breaking of a seal. Then he lifted it up to reveal a very ordinary-looking head underneath what I now knew to be a mask or helmet.

I gaped at him. "You're human!"

As soon as I'd spoken, I knew I was wrong. For one thing, his eyes were a shade I'd never seen in a human eye—sort of a gunmetal blue. His features were more or less human, but his skin was mottled in an odd way. The overall skin tone was what I would have called "olive"—kind of Mediterranean—but he had indistinct mahogany spots forming lines down his face. One in the center, down the bridge of his nose, and two trailing down under his eyes like lines of tears. He was bald and had no eyebrows, but his features weren't unattractive. In fact, once I got over my initial surprise at his appearance, I could acknowledge that he was fairly handsome.

"By some definitions of your word 'human,' I would qualify," he said, his voice a pleasant baritone, without any hint of the electronic quality the mask had given it. He spoke very slowly and deliberately, and he was easy enough to understand, even with the accent. "But we are not of the same species, and I do not originate from your planet."

Though I'd expected it, by this point, his words chilled me. Where the fuck *did* he originate from? I suddenly realized I was flashing my genitals at him, and reached out to tug the flimsy blanket over my legs and waist.

"Everything Cody told me was real," I said, still having trouble grasping it. "You've been kidnapping people, experimenting on them...."

"No," he said. "We have not experimented on any of your species."

"You experimented on *me*! I remember... getting injected with something, and...."

He shook his head. "We were not conducting an experiment on you. I am sorry if you were hurt or frightened, but it was necessary to be sure you had no diseases that were communicable to us."

I supposed that made sense, though I wasn't willing to give in so easily—not after they'd scared the shit out of me in their... operating room, or whatever it was. "If you aren't experimenting on us, why are there so many reports of people being abducted and having probes inserted into their... various orifices?"

"We have not conducted experiments upon members of your species," he insisted. "We have, however, taken samples for testing."

"Why? What are you testing for?"

He straightened up and pointed at his face. "Look at me. We have explored twenty-four solar systems with planets similar to our own, yet your species is the only one we've discovered that is nearly our biological twin. *How* similar we are, and how this circumstance came about... this is of great interest to our scientists."

"But you're kidnapping us in the middle of the night!" I snapped, my anger overriding some of my fear. "We have no idea what's happening! Do you have any idea how *terrifying* that is?"

"I am sorry."

"*Where is Cody*? Where are you keeping him? I want to see him!"

"Cody is... the other of your species?"

"Yes!"

He frowned and glanced at the floor for a second. Then he looked up at me and said, "He is not here. We rescued you, but the Karazhen took him."

"What do you mean?" The hair on the back of my arms was standing on end. "What is a... kara... karajen...?"

"Karazhen. They are our enemies. And they have your friend."

Chapter Five

HE REFUSED to tell me anything more about Cody until he'd had a chance to fill me in on the whole situation, so I bit my lip and tried to listen as he explained.

"The Karazhen and the Alzhen—my people—have been at war for what would be over one thousand of your years. The war has been brutal but far away from here, until now."

"So you came here to suck us into some intergalactic war?" I muttered.

He shook his head. "We did not come here to do that. We came here to study your species. How could we not?" He set his helmet on the floor, and I couldn't help but glance at those bulbous black "eyes" again. The thing gave me the creeps, even knowing what it was now. "Unfortunately the Karazhen discovered our interest in you, and for them your species provided an opportunity."

"For what?"

"To experiment. To find potential weaknesses in us. In all this time, they have failed to capture any of our kind alive. Those who are captured know to end their lives quickly, before the Karazhen have a chance to vivisect them. You are so biologically similar to us, it is possible for the Karazhen to use you to develop biological weapons—viruses—to use against us."

I clutched the thin blanket and felt the hair on my arms pricking up again. This time the sensation traveled all the way up my neck into my scalp. "Is that what they're doing? Testing viruses on us to see if they'll work against you?"

"Yes."

Cody! "Oh my God. They've been doing it to Cody for *months*!"

My host—I still had no idea what his name was—surprised me by getting up and moving to sit near me on the bed. Perhaps he was trying to be comforting, though I think I would have screamed if he'd touched me. Not that he was hideous, but my brain was on overload by this point—

aliens, bug-eyed monster helmets, the fact that I was possibly inside a spaceship, Cody kidnapped, biological weapons....

"If they had tested anything deadly on your friend," the alien said, "he would already be dead. It's possible they were testing some viruses that proved ineffective, but we suspect they've been taking samples and running harmless tests on his body, so far—"

"*Harmless*? Cody's been falling apart! They've been embedding these... disgusting *things* in his skin...." I shuddered, completely believing Cody's version of events at last. He wasn't insane—not unless he'd been driven crazy by those motherfuckers.

"Transmitters, perhaps. Chemical delivery devices. Or biological monitors. The Karazhen are not like us. They are closer to your insects or arachnids. They have absolutely no understanding of our biology. While they have no doubt captured many of your people, studying you in your natural habitat also—"

"How do we get Cody back from them?" I demanded.

I hadn't thought it possible to be more frightened than I already was, but when he sighed and shook his head, I felt a tremor go through my entire body. I realized I'd been holding on to the faint hope that *these* aliens might be able to help me against *those* aliens—the giant bugs or whatever that had Cody. They were aliens, after all. Weren't they supposed to have unworldly healing powers and make things fly with their minds? Didn't they have any giant robots? Couldn't they time travel?

What the hell were they good for?

"As soon as we detected the energy signature of their transport beam, we attempted to intercept it. We succeeded in freeing you, but your friend was already inside their ship. The best we can do now is pursue them."

"To where?"

Again, he shook his head. "Hopefully, not out of your solar system. We have learned of a refueling base orbiting one of your gas giants—the one with the highly visible rings—"

"Saturn?" I asked weakly. He couldn't be saying what I thought he was saying....

"Ah! Yes. We hope they will stop there. If so, we may catch up to them in about thirty-six of your hours."

I pulled the blanket up under my chin like a child afraid of the dark. "Thirty-six hours… to Saturn…. Where are we now?"

"We passed the orbit of your moon not long before you woke."

MY HOST appeared to understand how overwhelmed I was, because he decided to leave me alone to rest for a while. I didn't object. But as he stood to leave, I asked, "Can I get some clothes, please?"

He gave me a blank look for a moment, as if he couldn't imagine why I would want such a thing. But goddammit, *he* was wearing clothes. Why did *I* have to be naked?

"I'm sorry," he said at last, "but your clothing was destroyed after we brought you on board."

"What? Why?" I hadn't been wearing anything irreplaceable—just boxer briefs and a *Big Bang Theory* T-shirt—but Jesus! They'd belonged to me. Did these guys make a habit of trashing other people's belongings?

"Most of the Alzhen on this ship haven't yet been exposed to the microbes and viruses in your environment and on your body," he explained. He picked up the creepy helmet and added, "They're forced to wear environmental suits whenever they have contact with your atmosphere—not because our atmosphere is significantly different from yours, apart from a bit more nitrogen and a slightly different balance of trace gases, but because of the risk of contamination."

I felt vaguely insulted, though I knew it wasn't the sort of thing that could be helped. "Why aren't *you* afraid of viruses and jock itch and whatever?"

"What is 'jock itch'?"

I rolled my eyes. "Never mind. I don't have it. I'm just saying…."

"I have been to your planet several times, and I've been inoculated many times." He smiled. "I've even caught what you call a 'cold.' It was extremely unpleasant."

"Yes," I said unsympathetically. "We don't like it either." Then something else occurred to me. "Wait a minute. What if *I* catch something from *you*?"

He cocked an eyebrow at me. Or rather, he raised the skin over his right eye, since there wasn't actually an eyebrow there. "Anyone entering or leaving this room is sterilized by ultraviolet radiation."

"But that just sterilizes the outside of your suits, right?" I persisted. "You just removed your helmet and breathed all over me."

"The risk to you is slight. All microbes in my body are catalogued, and can easily be removed from your system if you are infected."

I wasn't entirely convinced, but it seemed pointless to argue. I'd already been exposed. I just hoped he was right, and I wouldn't die an agonizing death from Alzhen pinkeye or something.

He turned as if to leave, but I stopped him again. "Can't you at least give me *something* to wear? It makes me really uncomfortable sitting here naked while you have clothes on."

"Should I take my clothes off the next time I visit you?" he asked.

That shut me up for a minute. I couldn't help but wonder what he actually looked like under that suit. Was he exactly like a human male? Or did he have some weird anime crotch with gelatinous tentacles? I shuddered at the thought. But now he had me curious.

I finally managed to stammer out, "Um… no, I don't think that's necessary. I was just hoping you could find me some pants or something."

"I will see what I can do."

"By the way," I said, "my name is Marc. Thanks for asking. What's yours?"

He blinked at me again. Then he said, "You may call me Dalsing. It means 'major,' more or less. Like your military title."

"Is your real name too difficult for me to pronounce?"

That elicited another smile. "No, Marc. Our mouths are roughly equivalent, so what I can pronounce, you should be able to pronounce. But our names are used only in intimate contexts. We prefer titles. Is that suitable?"

I shrugged. "I…. Sure."

"Good."

"Are you in command of this ship, then?"

He shook his head. "No. I am merely in command of the exploratory team. And I will be leading the foray into the Karazhen base, when we arrive there."

Then, with a slight bow, he turned and left.

Out of curiosity, I got up and padded across the chamber to see if the door was locked. Not that I'd be in any position to escape if it wasn't. What was I going to do? Find an escape pod, jump in stark naked, and hope I could figure out how to direct it a couple hundred thousand miles back to my planet? If I didn't accidentally spiral into the sun, I'd probably drift off into the void until my oxygen ran out.

Ultimately, all this speculation turned out to be moot. The damned door didn't have any controls on it. It didn't matter if it was locked or not; I couldn't figure out how to open it.

ONCE I'D been left on my own, I quickly discovered I had nothing to do. I curled up under the blanket, and even though I thought it would be impossible to sleep with all the chaos going on in my head—worry about Cody, terror at the idea of the Karazhen building biological weapons that would work on humans as well as the Alzhen, my mind being blown by the fact that I was in *outer space*, wondering what an alien looked like naked, wondering if I was going to return to Earth and find out everyone was fifty years older because of relativity—I must have eventually dozed off. The dreams I had were bizarre and frightening, with a dash of eroticism thrown in.

Frankly, I might have been better off if the first alien I'd met hadn't been male and good-looking.

I awoke to find the room dimly lit, but as I sat up, the light increased. A moment later the door dilated and one of the aliens in suits entered, carrying a covered tray. I think it was female, judging from the shape of the chest, and when it spoke, it sounded like a woman.

"Ahrrr… yoo… huhngahree?"

I pondered that a moment and then replied, "Yes, thank you. I'm starving."

She bowed slightly and waved her hand at the floor. A portion near the bed slid up to form a sort of table. The Alzhen woman placed the tray on this, bowed again, and then left.

I scooted forward on the bed to lift the cover off the tray. What it revealed was… presumably food. It was hard to tell. Some kind of blue-green mush in a bowl, with what looked like crackers stacked beside it. There was also a cup full of yellow liquid that looked disconcertingly like urine. Not just Gatorade-yellow, but a more muted piss-yellow, and kind of cloudy, with a disturbing froth on the top. It was a testament to how thirsty I was that I dared lift the cup to my nose and sniff it. Fortunately the odor wasn't unappealing. Kind of citrusy. I sipped it and actually found it very refreshing.

Thank God.

I downed most of it but left a little in the cup to wash down the "food." I tentatively nibbled one of the crackers and discovered that it tasted pretty much like… a cracker. Kind of an odd aftertaste, sort of like peas, but not bad. I ate one and then followed it up with a dab of the mush on the tip of my finger. This was the consistency of buttercream frosting and kind of sweet. But again, it tasted more like some kind of vegetable than a dessert. Not bad. I discovered I was hungry enough to eat the mush and all the crackers without paying attention to what it looked like. Then I downed the rest of my drink-that-wasn't-urine. Despite the fact that I hadn't been given large portions of anything, I was thoroughly sated.

I was just placing the cover back over the empty dish when the door opened again and Dalsing entered. To my surprised, he was dressed very informally in something like a white bathrobe, as if he were spending the day at a spa. This revealed his feet, which were wearing sandals, his hands, and parts of his arms and legs. Apart from the fact that the skin on his extremities matched the coloring on his face—olive with lines of brownish spots trailing along his shin bones and the contours of his arms—he looked human enough. Though like his head and face, his arms and legs were utterly hairless.

He had a pair of sandals in one hand and another white robe draped over his arm.

"Good waking, Marc," he said with a bow. "Are you rested?"

"Well enough, I guess."

He glanced at the tray. "And have you eaten?"

"Yes. It was good. Thank you."

"That is good." He held out his arm. "I have brought you something to cover your body, and I am wearing the same garment. I hope this will put you at ease."

"Thank you." I took the robe from him and stood to slip it on. This, of course, resulted in me flashing him again. I'd considered for a split second asking him to turn around but decided I was being foolish. If I could shower with strangers at the gym, I could manage to change into a robe in front of Dalsing.

The robe didn't have a belt, but when I closed it, the soft material stuck together like Velcro. Dalsing handed me the sandals, and I dropped them on the floor so I could step into them.

"Do you mind if we sit?" he asked, gesturing toward the bed.

"Uh… no. Not at all."

We sat cross-legged on the bed, and I was startled to get a brief glimpse of the bare skin of his inner thigh as he adjusted his robe. Was he *naked* under there? That would be taking this whole "making the guest comfortable" thing really seriously. I couldn't imagine a ship's officer on Earth doing the same for a passenger from another country.

"We still have an Earth day before we reach Saturn," Dalsing said. "I would like to speak with you further, if you do not object. Though I have visited your planet several times, I rarely have much opportunity to speak your language with a native."

I raised my eyebrows in surprise. "You speak it very well."

"Thank you."

"You are aware that our… species… speaks a lot of languages? I mean, *thousands* of languages."

"Yes."

"Do you speak languages other than English?"

He shifted again, and I glimpsed more skin under his robe. I willed myself to look away. It was bad enough I was beginning to think impure thoughts about a space alien. I didn't need to be a lech on top of it.

"No," he replied. "I focus on English, because I have explored the region near your home more than other regions. And the people I've encountered to date have all spoken this language."

That took me aback until I realized he meant Cody's farmhouse. He didn't actually know where *my* home was. How could he?

"Can you read it too?"

"Yes. One of the first of your kind I encountered was a teacher. She taught me much and gave me books to continue my studies. It has become a passion of mine."

"Where is this teacher now?" I asked.

He smiled sadly. "She died many years ago on my home world. She was very old by then. I counted her among my dearest friends."

"So… just how long have your people been visiting Earth?"

Dalsing looked thoughtful as he leaned back against the wall, lifting his knees up to brace himself. This gave me a pretty clear view of the underside of his thighs and a little ass crack. There was no doubt about the fact he was naked under the robe. Was he deliberately flashing me? Or did he just not give a fuck? I honestly didn't object—he was very nice to look at. But I was finding it very distracting.

"My people first discovered your planet about two of your centuries ago. I, personally, have been studying your species for perhaps seventy-five years."

"Seventy-five *years*?" I gaped at him. "Just how old *are* you?" I realized too late how rude the question might be considered.

He didn't seem to mind. "I will soon be a hundred and twenty-four Earth years old. I was rather young when I joined my first expedition. Our life expectancy is approximately three hundred years."

Jesus.

"Is this another expedition, then?" I asked. "To study us?"

"Yes."

"You said you were in command of the exploratory team," I commented, recalling the conversation we'd had earlier.

"Yes," he replied, "but I answer to Terkang. That is her title. It might be translated as 'general.' She commands this vessel."

General? "Are we on some kind of military ship?"

"There is no other kind for us. Our society is what I believe you would call a military dictatorship. Our mission to your planet is to study your race for scientific purposes—we mean you no harm. But we are still a military vessel."

I was curious about this "military dictatorship" he mentioned. Generally I considered a dictatorship to be bad, but his tone was matter-of-fact, as if he had no problem with this form of government. Maybe he didn't, if he'd lived with it his entire life.

Before I could think of another question, he asked one. "Would you like me to remove my robe?"

Chapter Six

THE QUESTION had been so casual, I thought I'd misheard him. "What?"

"You have been trying to appear uninterested, but you seem curious about my body."

"I can't help it!" I exclaimed. I pointed at his crotch. "You keep flashing me!"

"Flashing? Isn't that something involving bright light or explosives?"

"It also means letting your clothing slip open so other people can see your... private parts."

He looked at me curiously. "Private parts?"

Oh, for fuck's sake. "Your genitals, your crotch, your... sex organs—whatever you call them. You've seen mine, dangling between my legs—not that I *asked* you to look at them."

"Oh yes." He smiled. "Of course." Then his expression turned to one of concern. "I apologize if removing your clothing violated one of your cultural taboos. Our anatomy is a bit different, so... it isn't the same for us."

That piqued my interest again. For all I knew, he was just an outer space pervert who got off on waving his ding-a-ling at the natives, but that didn't really bother me. I just didn't like the implication that *I* was a pervert. Still, if he was offering....

"How is your anatomy different?"

"Would you like to see? Or would you prefer I simply describe it?"

"You can show me if you want," I replied, trying to sound nonchalant. I guess I was just a *little* perverted, because I was already stiffening up at the thought of what might be under that robe. Fortunately *my* dick was safely tucked away under *my* robe.

He stood and let his robe slip from his shoulders.

My jaw must have hit the floor. Not because he had some hideous tentacle-monster thing writhing in his crotch or anything like that, but because it was just the opposite. There was *nothing* there. He had a pubic mound like a human, which was as hairless as the rest of him, but it was completely smooth. No dick, no nothing. It was completely featureless, apart from a thin brown line traveling up from between his legs to his navel. His body was muscular and pretty much a work of art, even with the four nipples, but… well, so much for alien porn. He was a *Ken doll*!

I tried not to look disappointed. No point in creating an intergalactic incident over penis size. Or… lack of penis altogether. "It's very nice," I said diplomatically.

Dalsing laughed. "If you are referring to my 'private parts,' you can't see them. They are here." He cupped his crotch in what would have been a lewd gesture for a human male. "Inside. This is why clothing for us is merely functional."

"I see." I pictured that thin line splitting open like a seam. "So it… comes out, when you need it to?"

"Yes. We reproduce the same way your species does. One carries the egg inside her body—we call our females *ba-len*—and the male, the *ba-ti*, inseminates it."

"And you are… *ba-ti*?" I asked, just to be clear. He *looked* male, but I could have been wrong.

"Yes. Unfortunately I cannot easily show you my 'private parts.' I must be aroused in order for them to emerge."

This was beginning to sound like the lead-in to a cheesy porn film. *"Let me show you how my species mates, earthling."* Boom chicka wow wow…. But although I was, in fact, still curious about his anatomy, I discovered I'd hit my limit for how crass I could be with a space alien. We weren't even on a first-name basis.

"That's okay," I said. "I've satisfied my curiosity."

Sort of.

"Very well." He picked up his robe, giving me a brief glimpse of his back, which seemed oddly segmented, as if he had interlocking plates underneath the skin. Clearly, Alzhen and humans weren't *completely* alike. Then again, I'd read that bonobo DNA is 99 percent identical to human DNA, but we don't look much like bonobos. The Alzhen must be even more closely related… somehow.

After he'd tied the robe around himself, Dalsing said, "If you would be willing to wear one of our suits—the ones you've seen with the helmets—I could take you on a tour of the ship. Unfortunately both you and the crew might be endangered if you walked around our living quarters without protection."

The suits didn't look very comfortable to me, but how could I pass up the opportunity to see the inside of a spaceship from another solar system?

"Okay!" I said.

WE HAD to wait for someone to bring the suit. I have no idea how Dalsing communicated the request to his crew, but it wasn't long before someone appeared at the door, dressed in one of the suits himself. He left one for me and departed, bowing slightly to Dalsing.

I had to drop my robe in order to slip into it, and I thought about asking Dalsing to turn around, but by now that seemed rather pointless. I just tossed the robe aside and tried to ignore the fact that I was naked as he helped me into the suit. The damned thing was *snug* and hugged my body like a wet suit. It was also made of some kind of material not too far removed from silver lamé, which didn't do much to stop me from feeling naked in front of my host. It might have been sufficient for a species that didn't have external genitalia, but not for a human. My dick and testicles were clearly visible through the fabric—and it was obvious I was circumcised.

I pointed this out to Dalsing, but he was unconcerned. "My people might find it curious, but it won't disturb them."

Well, okay, then. As long as *they* were all fine.

The large helmet was a bit claustrophobic, since it sealed at the neck, but some kind of apparatus in the nose area kept fresh air coming in and prevented it from getting too warm inside. I was surprised to find that the large, round eye lenses didn't distort my view, and sound wasn't at all muffled when it reached my ears.

"This way," Dalsing said when I was adequately sealed in. He led me to the door, and it dilated to allow us through.

My first view of the outside of my quarters was disappointing. It was a short, tubelike corridor with another door at the opposite end. But I soon discovered this was simply an airlock. It wasn't that the ship had a different kind of air or a different pressure than my quarters; it was that they didn't want my diseases. Even though my germ-ridden body was sealed inside the suit, I'd still fondled the outside of the suit and breathed all over Dalsing. We both had to be decontaminated with a flash of blue UV light.

Then the second door opened, and I passed into the ship proper.

THE CORRIDOR was shaped like a hexagonal tube, and I soon realized that was because it was designed to be functional in zero gravity—or "microgravity," as my college physics professor would have insisted I call it. There were handholds on all surfaces, including the one we were walking on.

I hadn't thought to ask about the gravity on the ship, so I did now.

"It isn't gravity," Dalsing replied, "but acceleration. The ship is moving in that direction"—he pointed straight up—"accelerating at a rate that approximates our gravity, both on your world and mine."

"Won't we be going insanely fast when we get to Saturn, then?"

He smiled and shook his head. "Halfway through the journey, the ship will flip over and begin decelerating. You will need to be secured when that happens, or you'll fly around the chamber and probably injure yourself."

"You'll warn me when that's about to happen, right?"

For the first time since I'd met him, I saw something akin to mischief in his eyes. "I will try to remember."

We stepped into a chamber similar to the airlock outside my quarters, but smaller, and with no exit other than the door we'd entered. The floor shook for a moment, and then the door opened to reveal a different corridor. Then I felt like an idiot for not realizing the little room was an elevator.

One end of the second corridor opened into a vast chamber with a dome overhead. At the floor level, people milled around or sat at tables where dim red lighting illuminated them. Over their heads, the dome looked out upon a sea of stars, and only the seams, laid out in triangular patterns like those found in a geodesic dome on Earth, indicated there was *anything* between the people and the void of space. I had a sudden attack of vertigo and grabbed Dalsing's arm without thinking. He made no move to push me away.

"This is the center of the ship," he explained. "We are on the top level, which is why we have this dome over our heads." He pointed upward. "If you look toward the center, you can see Saturn. That is our destination."

The helmet gave me limited head movement, so I had to lean back as far as I could in order to see what he was pointing at. It might have been Saturn. I couldn't tell. It looked like a bright dot among a kazillion other dots, slightly brighter than the rest. "It doesn't look like we're moving."

"We are moving very fast, but there is nothing nearby to gauge our speed by. Perhaps I will bring you here when we approach the planet and its moons. Then you can watch them approach."

"What are we going to do when we get there?" I asked.

He didn't answer right away. Instead, he placed a hand over mine on his arm and led me into the chamber. "Let us sit. Unfortunately the suit will prevent you from eating or drinking, but we can talk."

I'd been wondering if Dalsing would be underdressed for wandering around his ship, since he still wore nothing but the robe and sandals. But as we passed other men and women, some of whom nodded to us, I quickly learned that wasn't the case. If anything, he was *over*dressed. None of the Alzhen in this… I suppose it would be called a lounge on Earth… were wearing the creepy suits. The suits weren't too uncomfortable, but they were a far cry from casual clothes to relax in. Instead, the Alzhen there were dressed in a variety of clothes ranging from colorful kimono-like robes to diaphanous cloaks that revealed pretty much everything. A disconcerting number of them weren't wearing anything at all, or had nothing more than jeweled stoles draped around their shoulders, or various kinds of hats. Some seemed to have on nothing more than phosphorescent makeup, which made the lines of spots on their bodies glow a bright orange or a smoldering red. At least, I assumed it was makeup. Perhaps their spots could be made to glow like that naturally.

This was my first view of naked Alzhen females. They were nearly identical to the men, except for their breasts. Even these weren't exactly like human women's breasts, since they were more integrated with the chest. Picture Mystique in the X-Men movies, but with slightly smaller breasts. The breasts *had* to be smaller, since there were two sets of them, one above the other.

I noticed a third type of Alzhen that baffled me. They had no nipples at all. Even Dalsing had nipples, just as human men do. He had four of them, true, but they were still unmistakably nipples. These Alzhen also seemed a bit thinner than either the men or the women. The men tended to have broader chests, and the women to have broader hips, just as with humans, but these seemed… I guess the word "androgynous" might fit.

I wanted to ask about them, though it seemed kind of rude. On the other hand, Dalsing had stripped naked for me to ogle him—largely because he'd earlier gotten an eyeful of *my* naughty bits. So perhaps it would be okay.

We took a seat at one of those odd tables that rose up out of the floor, and he asked, "Do you mind if I drink something?"

"No, go ahead."

"Thank you." He motioned to some kind of floating sphere—it must have been a robotic bartender—and when it approached, he said something to it in what I assumed was Alzhenese. It burbled at him and then lowered itself onto the table a moment. When it lifted up again, there was a cup of blue liquid on the table. I tried not to think of a chicken laying an egg… and failed.

The bartender-thing flew off, and Dalsing told me, "If you are thirsty, touch your tongue to the panel in front of your mouth. You will be supplied with water."

"Thanks."

"And if you feel the need to relieve yourself, the suit is designed to handle liquid waste."

"Uh… thanks. I'm good." I couldn't imagine having a conversation with him while I was peeing my pants. I changed the subject and asked my question about the Alzhen without nipples.

"I never said we had just two genders," he replied, giving me that mischievous smile again. "They are what we call *ba*—I suppose it could be translated as 'undifferentiated.' We are all born *ba*, but some of us choose to become *ba-ti* or *ba-len*, if we would like to produce offspring."

It took me a moment to wrap my head around this. "Then those Alzhen I've seen are children?"

"No. Some are older than I am. We don't all choose to differentiate. Gender isn't always necessary for us. *Ba* are perfectly able to experience sexual pleasure, for instance."

"Then you *chose* to be *ba-ti*?"

"Yes."

"Because you and your… wife… wanted children?" I was far more disappointed to learn Dalsing had a wife than I had any reason to be. Had

I been secretly hoping our little game of I'll-show-you-mine-if-you-show-me-yours would become more sexual? That was a disturbing thought.

"In my case," Dalsing replied casually, as if it were perfectly normal to be explaining his genitals to a total stranger again, "no. I chose *ba-ti* because I planned on interacting with your species. If I had been female, this would have been more problematic. Your people do not respect females as much as males."

Ouch.

I decided now would be a good time to change the subject. "So how are we going to rescue Cody?"

"*We,*" he said with a smile, "are not. My people will deal with the situation when we arrive at the Karazhen base. You will remain in your quarters until we return."

He couldn't see the sour look I gave him, but my silence must have made it clear I was displeased.

"You are not here on this ship to participate in our attack on the Karazhen base," Dalsing said, his voice gentle. "You are here because we did not want you to be taken by them, and we did not have time to return you to your home. We were in pursuit of their ship. Our choice was to take you on board or let you fall to your death."

"Well, thanks for not dropping me." I had a hard time keeping the sarcasm out of my voice, but I hoped he wouldn't pick up on it.

"You are welcome." He drained his cup of blue liquid and set it on the table. "Come. Let me show you the rest of the ship."

Chapter Seven

I COULDN'T honestly say it made sense for me to be part of Operation Rescue Cody. I had no military training. I'd never been in space before, never mind encountered arachnid-like aliens. I'd probably scream and wet myself if I even saw one. And it made perfect sense to leave things to the professionals, while I stayed out of the way, and avoid turning the whole thing into a Three Stooges routine.

But I was still pissed off. Cody was my friend, and I felt responsible for him. Especially since I'd passed up my one chance to knock him over the head and drag him to safety before the Karazhen nabbed him. It didn't help that I'd been taking a leak outside when they abducted him, rather than manning my post as he'd asked me to. I'd dropped the ball, and now he might be suffering unspeakable horrors because of it.

Still, I knew there was no way of convincing Dalsing to take me into the Karazhen base. He wasn't an idiot. So I didn't try.

The ship was enormous and saucer shaped, with five levels. We didn't visit every inch of it, of course. Dalsing took me to the control room, the engine room, the mess hall—which was basically like the lounge, but with a ceiling instead of a dome—and several other rooms I quickly forgot the purpose of. I don't generally think of myself as stupid, but when everything is alien, it all starts to blur together. The engine room was the most impressive, since it featured massive cylindrical columns that went up through four levels of the ship. My entire body vibrated with the low hum they emitted, and cold purple light sparked up and down their ribbed metal surfaces.

I had no idea how they worked, but they were certainly cool.

I discovered that my "quarters" were in what Earth naval ships would call "the brig." Not exactly a prison, since they weren't keeping anyone prisoner there, according to Dalsing. I just had to take his word for that. I couldn't see into the other rooms. But they were used to isolate aliens like me when we were brought on board.

"Do you do that a lot?" I asked.

"Yes," Dalsing replied. "Though they are generally unaware of it. We bring them in, study them for a short time, clear their memory, and then return them to where we found them."

We were walking along one of the interminable corridors, and this comment made me stop dead in my tracks. "You wipe their memories?"

"Most are unable to understand who we are or what we're doing, and they find their encounter with us very stressful. We clear their memories to be merciful."

"Except that it doesn't *work*!" I growled. "We *do* remember. Not the whole thing, maybe, but bits and pieces. Just enough to torment us. Have you seen Cody? He's falling apart!"

Dalsing frowned. "That appears to be a recent phenomenon. We are uncertain as to the cause. It may be that, with the recent advances in your technology, your minds are more accepting of the concept of space travel and contact with other worlds."

"Yes," I muttered darkly, "we've all seen *Close Encounters* and *E.T.*"

"What is that?"

"Never mind." We walked without talking for a while until I finally broke the silence. "I have to go to the bathroom. And I mean *now*." I hadn't been able to do so since coming on board, and that had to have been eight or nine hours ago. As far as I knew, there wasn't a toilet in my quarters.

"You can relieve yourself in the suit."

That didn't make me any less irritable. "I have no intention of peeing my pants like a five-year-old. And that isn't all I have to do. I'm not going into detail—I assume you have an alimentary canal, and if not, you've been probing both ends of ours for centuries."

"Ah yes. Don't *golshu* in your suit—it isn't equipped for that."

I'd just picked up a new vocabulary word. Oh goody.

"My crew will be distressed if I allow you to use one of our communal *golsha-ren*," he continued. "You would have to remove the isolation suit to do so, and that could be dangerous for them. But I was about to suggest we visit my quarters so you can see how one of us lives. I have no concerns about you relieving yourself there."

"Thanks."

MY FIRST view of an Alzhen living space wasn't very spectacular, because it was dark, and I really didn't give a fuck. I just asked him to take me to the *golsha-ren* or whatever it was called and give me a quick—*very* quick—rundown of how to operate the horrifying suction-cup thing that stuck out of one wall. I stripped out of the suit while he was explaining it all and then practically shoved him out of the room. I could cope with being naked around him, but I wasn't going to let him watch me relieve myself. Nobody did *that* at the gym.

"You don't need to put the suit back on," he said, standing in the doorway. "I will find you a robe." Then the door constricted, leaving me alone to do my business.

I'm not going to go into the gory details of the next few minutes, though I'll mention that the toilet was designed for microgravity. It kind of latched on to my body between my legs, covering both the front and back—though the front was a tight fit, since my anatomy was, well... *existent*. Then the suction started.

And then... other things happened.

When I was done, I washed up in a basin that was thankfully not hard to operate, though the "water" behaved oddly. It evaporated quickly, leaving my hands clean and the basin completely dry. Bizarre.

I walked out into Dalsing's living quarters and then stopped dead, gaping in awe.

I wasn't sure what I'd expected. Gleaming chrome and fluorescent lights, maybe. Or more of the malleable greenish mesh I'd been seeing in other parts of the ship. The last thing I'd expected was a forest. By that, I mean trees. A lot of trees. Though not Earth trees. In the relatively dark space, bioluminescent lines of blue-green and pink highlighted the rough edges of their bark and created swirls around knotholes and the bases of branches. Under my feet, a carpet of moss sparkled with shimmering silver, and glowing orange cones four or five inches high shot up in clusters like mushrooms.

"This is beautiful," I said, whispering, afraid to disturb the stillness.

"It is my home world."

I turned to find Dalsing standing behind me, naked again and holding out his robe to me.

"I am sorry," he continued, "but I was unable to find a robe. You may wear mine, if this isn't taboo in your culture, or you may look at my other clothing to see if anything else might suit you."

I took the robe and smirked at him. "Are you sure you don't get off on running around naked in front of me?"

"Get off?" He seemed genuinely puzzled.

I slipped the robe on and closed it at the waist. Like the robe I'd worn earlier, the soft material adhered to itself like Velcro. "It means to get turned on—become sexually aroused. I've known guys who get turned on by being naked in front of other people."

"Why is that?"

I thought about that for a second. "Well, I suppose it only works in a culture where being naked in front of other people is a rare thing. That doesn't seem to apply here."

"If I become sexually aroused," Dalsing said, taking my hand and leading me deeper into the forest, "you will know. It will be obvious." This was the first time we'd touched, skin to skin, and his hand was disconcertingly warm.

He was walking sideways so he could look back at me as he spoke, and I couldn't help but glance down at his crotch. "Why? Because your… genitals will pop out?"

"Eventually. But before that, my *shiri* will glow." He stroked the darkly pigmented spots on his face with his free hand.

"Oh!" I exclaimed. "I remember! Some of the… Alzhen in the lounge were doing that." I felt my face flush as it occurred to me those people must have been aroused. And they just walked around like that? In public?

But Dalsing laughed and shook his head. "That is just a paste some of us wear on social occasions to mimic arousal. Mostly younger Alzhen. My generation generally considers it… I am uncertain what the word is in your language…."

"Crass? Tacky?"

"Perhaps. You understand my meaning? It is something the young do."

I couldn't help but smile at that, imagining all the 150-year-old Alzhens shaking their heads in dismay at the way the younger generation dressed. They probably disapproved of their music too.

THE FOREST seemed to be infinite. It stretched ahead of us as far as I could see, with tiny streams and waterfalls and man-made—*Alzhen*-made—bridges with beautifully carved enameled railings arching across them. Over our heads the trees seemed to be as tall as redwoods, and although it was shadowy down on the forest floor, I thought I could see the sun peeking through the leaves high above us. At last we came to a broad clearing, where fairly ordinary-looking grass made a soft bed in a small patch of sunlight. Here, Dalsing sat and invited me to sit beside him.

"This can't be real," I said. "The ship isn't big enough to hold a forest like this!"

"Sadly, no. This is a re-creation of a park in our largest city, Chaikun. There are no wild places like this on our world—not anymore. But each city has its own park, where the plants and animals are allowed to grow, and the citizens can remember the beauty that once dominated our planet." He smiled wistfully. "Not everyone feels as I do about it… but I have always been a rebel. Look there."

I followed his gaze and saw an animal not unlike a deer, though with two parallel rows of spikes along its head and neck forming a crest. It saw us and started, jumping away into the undergrowth. In a second it was gone.

"When you say this is a re-creation," I persisted, "do you mean a physical re-creation, or some kind of… I don't know… hologram or something? Like the holodeck on *Star Trek*?" I touched the grass we were sitting on, picked a blade, and held it between my fingers. It certainly felt real. But how could this park be taking up as much space as it appeared to be?

"Holodeck?"

He'd never seen *Star Trek*, of course. I spent an unproductive few minutes trying to explain television and movies to him and finally gave up. It wasn't that he couldn't understand the concept of moving pictures telling a story. He simply didn't seem to understand why we would like such a thing. And the idea of science fiction seemed uninteresting to him. He spent his life traveling between solar systems, encountering aliens, and battling hideous insect creatures. Why would he want to read about it or watch it?

"As for the plants and animals in this space," he said, "the computer places the images in our minds simultaneously, so we share in the experience, as if we were dreaming the same dream. Is that like the 'holodeck' you mentioned?"

"I don't think so. I think that's supposed to create physical objects with replicator technology or something." I saw him blinking at me again, so I waved my hand in the air. "Don't ask."

"I was hoping to show you some of *our* entertainment, if you are interested."

"Yes, absolutely."

He snapped his fingers and a stage appeared in the center of the clearing, complete with actors in brightly colored robes and hats, similar to those worn by some comic book supervillains.

"This is one of our most famous plays," Dalsing told me. "I confess I chose it partly because the romantic pairing in it is *ba-ti* to *ba-ti*, which is my preference. If this is not to your liking, I can choose something else. Perhaps one that does not have any romance in it at all."

I was a little surprised to learn Dalsing preferred romances with two males. I thought back over the conversations we'd had and couldn't recall whether we'd discussed his orientation—or mine, for that matter. But I certainly didn't object to his choice of entertainment, in that case. "That will be fine," I said.

"Good." He leaned in close to me and said quietly, his warm breath brushing my ear, "The computer does not know your language, so I will translate what the actors are saying."

I hadn't realized until that moment that I found Dalsing sexy. Erotic, yes. He was exotic and clearly well put together—and he was naked. But that wasn't quite the same as being attracted to him personally. Perhaps it was the husky tone to his voice as he spoke just above a whisper, combined with our physical closeness and what was admittedly a romantic setting, but when I turned to glance at him and saw those startling gunmetal blue eyes looking back at me, I had a strong desire to lean in and kiss him.

I didn't. Instead, I took a deep breath and forced myself to look at the stage.

Chapter Eight

THE PLAY was… different. I doubt I would have been able to follow it, even if I'd understood the language, because there was very little dialog. Most of it was pantomimed to ethereal music played on a flute, accompanied by a harp-like instrument, bells, and something like a wide drum laid flat so metal balls of various sizes could roll around on it and clang into each other as the drummer tapped out gentle rhythms. Occasionally, during fight scenes, he banged on it, and the balls clattered around noisily.

I gathered it was one of those stories everybody in Dalsing's region knew, so detailed explanations were unnecessary. The audience had no trouble understanding that when an actor donned a blue headband, he was declaring war on his enemies. And when he raised his pinky in the air, it meant he was accusing someone of lying.

Dalsing kept up a steady stream of explanations in my ear, so I was able to follow the story. For a "romance," it was pretty violent. I counted seven deaths by the intermission. One guy got decapitated right on stage, and I jumped in horror until Dalsing assured me it was all simulated by the computer—and even when the play was performed live, that particular moment was simulated these days.

"These days?" I asked, feeling queasy.

"In ancient times, the part would be played by a criminal who volunteered to die on stage in exchange for one night of freedom beforehand."

I felt ill. But Dalsing assured me there would be nothing that explicitly violent in the rest of the play.

"That doesn't bother you?" I asked. "Even if it was simulated, it looked real!" I was being a bit hypocritical. Modern movies often had violence and realistic gore in them. But it had felt so much more visceral when it appeared to be a real person kneeling not ten yards away from me.

Dalsing shrugged. "I have seen this play many, many times. I knew it wasn't real, even as a child."

As a child?

Fortunately the second half of the play was the romantic part. And as Dalsing whispered into my ear, I found myself caught up in it. The story was a bit like Romeo and Juliet—or Romeo and Julius—with two warriors caught up in a feud between rival clans. One was called Hinsing, and it was his clan that had decapitated the brother of Mahzhing. Mahzhing challenged Hinsing to a duel. Actually, there were several duels. But with each one, the two men grew to respect each other more. And eventually this turned into a secret love affair.

I found the story interesting, and the actors were sexy together. But I was surprised when they actually began to have *sex* on stage. The kissing was fine. Kind of hot, in fact. But then Hinsing began to kiss his way down Mahzhing's chest. Mahzhing arched his back and his… I struggled to remember the word… *shiri* began to shimmer with a smoldering red light. When Hinsing moved lower to lick along Mahzhing's crotch, I drew a sharp breath.

"*Tegu!*" Dalsing said hurriedly, and everything froze as if we were looking at a still image.

"What is it?" I asked, turning to him.

He'd clearly been affected by what was happening on stage, since his *shiri* were also glowing red. Though as I watched, they dimmed.

"I am sorry," he said. "I wanted you to experience something from my culture—something I find very beautiful. But it did not occur to me until just now that this would be considered 'crass' in your culture. Please forgive me. I can move the play forward and start it after this scene."

I was a little annoyed by the implication I was some kind of intergalactic sexual prude, but he wasn't that far off. Sexual behavior in a lot of contexts did make me uncomfortable. But I wasn't uncomfortable now. I was turned on. And I was just kinky enough to want to see how two *ba-ti* had sex.

"It's okay," I assured him. "You don't have to skip this scene. I'd like to see it."

That sounded a little lecherous, but I wasn't the one taking an alien stranger out to a porno. Or perhaps "performance art" would be the more generous term. But it seemed to me it was disingenuous to have sex in front of an audience and not expect the audience to be aroused by it. I suppose it had artistic value—perhaps more so in his culture than I was aware of—but it wasn't just "art" making Dalsing's *shiri* glow.

"Very well." He spoke again in his language, and the action on stage continued.

We watched the performance in silence, since what the actors were doing didn't require much explanation—not when our two species were so similar. I did finally have my curiosity about male Alzhen anatomy satisfied when the actor playing Mahzhing groaned and shuddered, and a rather large, erect cock seemed to split his crotch open at the seam. It slid out in one smooth motion, testicles and all. If it had resembled an animal penis, I would have been immediately turned off, but it looked very human. It appeared to be uncircumcised, though I was too far away to see for certain.

After a considerable amount of foreplay, the other actor revealed his cock, and I discovered something else unique to their culture: size didn't appear to matter. In other words, he wasn't terribly well-endowed. That doesn't normally matter to me, honestly, but how often did gay porn stars on Earth have small dicks? Perhaps it was because these actors *weren't* porn stars—they were actors. Maybe acting ability trumped dick size for the Alzhen.

I glanced at Dalsing several times during the scene, wondering if he was going to… pop. He didn't. His *shiri* turned a fierce red, and I could hear him breathing heavily into my ear, but he didn't go past the point of no return, or whatever he would call it—not even when the scene finished with impressive geysers from both *ba-ti* on stage. I myself was hard as a rock and beginning to leak a bit. But I kept that to myself, bunching up the robe in front of my crotch to hide my arousal.

I realized I was disappointed when the action of the play continued and Dalsing's *shiri* faded to their normal color. Perhaps part of me had hoped to experience what it would be like to be ravished by an extraterrestrial. Well… *gently* "ravished," at any rate. I never got into the whole forced, scary sex thing. But if he'd hoped to plant the idea of us having sex in my head… it worked.

Still, we'd only known each other for nine or ten hours. I didn't know how that played out in his culture, but that was moving pretty fast for mine.

IN THE middle of yet another dueling scene—this play was *long*, not that I wasn't enjoying it—there was an odd chime. It didn't sound as if it had come from the stage but from the forest around us. Dalsing stopped everything again and sat up. "There is a small case inside the pocket of the robe. You should open it and swallow the pill inside."

"Why? What's happening?"

"The ship is about to flip over. The pill will prevent you from vomiting."

That sounded like a plan. I fished around in the pocket and found the pillbox. Then, after I'd swallowed the capsule inside, he had me lie down flat on the grass. He didn't bother lying down himself, however.

For a long time, nothing happened. Then the chime rang out again, three times in rapid succession. A split second later, the world turned upside down. It was disorientating, but I suppose it wasn't too much different from some amusement park rides. I seemed to be pulled to the right, then straight up, then to the left, and finally down again, all in the space of about two seconds.

What really amazed me was that I didn't fall, despite the fact that nothing was holding me down. Neither did Dalsing. The stage and the actors, all the plants and animals in the forest around us—none of them tumbled ass-over-teakettle to end up as one huge pile of broken, bleeding rubbish. I recalled that most of these things were virtual or somehow implanted in our minds, but Dalsing wasn't, as far as I could tell. And I certainly wasn't. So why hadn't I tumbled around the clearing like a ragdoll? Was there some kind of force field holding everything in place?

"Do you feel well?" Dalsing asked as he helped me sit up again.

I was a little nauseated, but the pill seemed to be doing its job, and I didn't think I'd actually puke. I gave him a wan smile and a thumbs-up.

THE PLAY ended with Hinsing and Mahzhing committing mutual suicide as their clans went to war for the fifteenth or sixteenth time. Very Shakespearean, with a touch of Japanese Noh theater. And it had me blubbering like a baby.

Dalsing looked at my tears with curiosity. "Does this mean you liked it?"

"Yes," I replied, dabbing at my eyes in embarrassment. "Don't you cry when a story like this moves you?" He looked baffled, so I added, "That is, when it makes you feel strong emotions?"

I was afraid for a moment he'd say he never felt emotions and that his species had discarded them as inferior. Except for Mr. Spock, aliens without emotion seemed best avoided. But he smiled and said, "I see. Yes, I do cry at plays. But I have seen this one many, many times. It saddens me, but it does not make me cry. I find it very beautiful that they love each other so much."

"Me too."

"Are you hungry now?" he asked. "You have not eaten in several hours."

The nausea from the ship flipping over had long ago faded. "Yes, I'm starving."

"Starving?" He looked alarmed. "Does your species require food more frequently than we realized?"

Chapter Nine

FOR DINNER, we traveled to the top of a skyscraper in the center of Chai-kun, via the computer. It was unnerving to watch the forest dissolve around us and discover I was now perched high above a vast cityscape stretching to the horizon in all directions. The platform was inside a transparent dome, and we were surrounded by tables with other Alzhen dining at them. The quiet murmur of conversation reached my ears, but nobody seemed to notice our sudden appearance.

"This is my home city," Dalsing said. "We are in my favorite restaurant."

I was curious how far above the ground we were but decided I was better off not knowing. It might be a simulation in our minds, but it was still giving me vertigo. I focused on the table in front of me. "Are we going to eat virtual food?" I asked.

"Virtual? Oh. No. I will have food delivered to my quarters. If you'll excuse me for just a moment...."

He wandered toward the edge of the restaurant, and I caught my breath as he appeared to walk through the glass dome and drop off the edge. *It's just an illusion.*

To keep myself occupied, I got up from the table and tried to see how close to the edge of the dome I could get without passing out. I was self-conscious, at first, about bracing myself against other people's tables, but I quickly discovered they didn't even notice me. They were, after all, just holograms... or something like that.

The view was definitely spectacular. There were wispy clouds drifting by *underneath* the platform, and through these I could see a city lit by millions of lights in blue and green and orange and crimson. It wasn't yet night, but the sun had set, and the sky above me was a pale whitish-orange on the horizon, fading to indigo directly overhead. In the center of each table, a small brazier flickered to life.

By the time Dalsing returned, the stars had come out. It was breathtaking, but I was happy to get back to the table where I could feel a bit safer.

He apologized for taking so long, saying, "Since I've been in close proximity to you, I was required to go through sterilization procedures before I could interact with a member of the crew."

I didn't say anything, but I suspect I didn't exactly look flattered, because he hastily added, "You will have to do the same when we send you back to your people, due to your contact with me."

"I understand."

He'd brought several brightly colored boxes with him, and as he laid them out upon the table between us, I realized they were the Alzhen equivalent of Chinese takeout. Each contained something different: pink noodles that had an odd metallic sheen to them, gelatinous black cubes, something like green pudding with white beads in it, a pile of red flowers....

"This could be a bad idea," Dalsing said. "We initially gave you food we were certain your system could digest. Have you had any intestinal discomfort from it?"

I squirmed in embarrassment. "No, I'm fine, thanks."

"Good." Dalsing waved his hand over the buffet. "These are, I think, much more palatable, and hopefully they will not cause you any nausea or intestinal distress."

Okay. Got it. Can we stop talking about my digestive tract now?

The food was good. Weird, yes. Nothing tasted like I expected it to. The iridescent pink noodles were very sweet, a bit like yams. And the green pudding was good, though it tasted oddly like roast beef. I didn't like the black cubes. They were fishy, and Dalsing confirmed my suspicion they were made from something roughly equivalent to squid ink.

I nibbled the petals off one of the red flowers, liking the vague hint of cinnamon. "I'm beginning to feel like I'm on a date," I commented.

"A date?" Dalsing asked, looking confused. He held up two fingers as if he were pinching something small. "A... tiny fruit?"

I laughed. "No. That's one definition of the word. But a 'date' can also be when two people go out to a play or something together, and then have dinner—just like we're doing."

"Oh. Then I guess we are doing a date."

"We say '*on* a date.' But it isn't really a date if it's just two friends. 'Date' has the implication that we're romantically interested in each other—or hope to be."

Dalsing took a sip of a dark, coffee-like liquid and gave me a mischievous smile. In the flickering light of the brazier, he looked vaguely demonic… very *sexy* and demonic. The kind of demon who could definitely tempt me to sin. "Then are we on a date or not?"

I stopped nibbling. "I… don't know. We're two different species.…"

"Two compatible species," he replied. "Not that you and I would be capable of breeding. But… breeding is possible between our species."

"Really?" I had a sudden idea what that might mean and narrowed my eyes at him. I was picturing a lot of B sci-fi horror movies I'd seen, as well as a bunch of supposedly true abduction stories. "You mean you— your species—has raped human women?"

He knew what *that* word meant. I could see it in his eyes. "I have raped no one. And I am not aware of anyone on this ship forcing sexual intercourse with one of your species. But my female human friend—her name was Maria—had a *ba-ti* lover when she lived on my planet. They produced two children."

"I apologize. The stories I've read about… alien encounters… often involve the aliens doing sexual things to us while we're semiconscious."

Dalsing sighed and put his drink down. Then he surprised me by reaching around the brazier and placing a hand over the one I was resting on the table. "I cannot say whether these things have happened with other Alzhen exploratory teams, but I will not allow it. I confess, my team has run tests on human subjects that were probably not pleasant to them. Not all of our scientists are convinced of your intelligence— they regard humans the same way many humans regard apes—and many believe wiping your memories after the tests is sufficient. I am sorry for this. I have tried to convince them to be more… humane. But they have not known humans as I have."

"You just said Maria lived on your planet, among your people."

Dalsing removed his hand from mine and leaned back. I instantly missed the warmth of his palm, and I couldn't help but notice the *shiri* on the back of his hand flickering slightly. "Maria used to jokingly refer to herself as Pocahontas. Do you know the reference?"

"Pocahontas was a Native American—one of the indigenous people of my country who lived there before my ancestors came to it. There's a story about her pleading for the life of a man named John Smith when her father wanted to kill him. Though I think that's considered to be a myth."

Dalsing nodded. "According to Maria, Pocahontas traveled to the continent of Europe and became very popular in the royal courts. But despite her popularity, she was still regarded as something exotic, a curiosity. None of the Europeans considered her to be as… sophisticated… as they were. Maria often felt this way on our planet. She was charming and well-liked by my people, but they regarded her as, in her words, 'a talking monkey.'"

"Did you see her that way?" I asked.

"No. I saw her as a fascinating and intelligent friend, as did Qitsing, her mate. But we remain a minority."

I lifted my own glass, wondering at the technology that had kept it piping hot while we ate and talked. I supposed batteries could do it, though I preferred to think it was some incomprehensible alien tech. Perhaps I wasn't immune to the attraction to the exotic that Dalsing had been describing. "So… are you saying you find me attractive? Or is it just that it would be hot to screw an alien?"

He laughed. Then he leaned forward and fixed me with his gaze. The odd metallic hue of his irises seemed to be shimmering, though perhaps it was just the flames in the brazier between us. "Perhaps my long friendship with Maria has opened me to the possibility of mating with someone of your species, but I have met many of you in the seventy-five years I've been stationed in your system. Some of the men were attractive, but of those I conversed with, most were uninteresting. Some did seem unintelligent, insisting I was a 'commie spy' or 'government spook,' despite my efforts to persuade them otherwise. I never learned what those terms meant, at any rate. Others were simply too frightened to speak coherently."

"Being abducted by extraterrestrials is a lot to wrap your head around," I said, feeling defensive about my fellow humans.

"I understand," Dalsing said with a nod. "But you are different. You share Maria's inquisitiveness—she was a scientist herself, an anthropologist—and our conversation has been most satisfying."

I snorted. "I'm no scientist. I barely made it through algebra."

"Nonetheless, you are intelligent and interesting. And physically… yes, you are very attractive to me."

I took a deep breath and met his gaze. "I guess I'd have to say I'm attracted to you too. It just seems… we've only known each other for one day…."

"I think I understand. Maria often said Alzhen moved very fast in their approach to sex."

I shook my head and smirked. "I wouldn't say humans are necessarily slower. I mean, not if all we're looking for is a quick fuck. But I've kind of outgrown the quick fuck thing. It's fun, but it usually leaves me feeling lonely and depressed afterward…."

Dalsing regarded me thoughtfully, his brow furrowed with concern. "I fear I haven't been clear. I have enjoyed our conversation very much. I have enjoyed sharing my culture with you and learning more about yours. I am also erotically attracted to you. If you would like to have sex with me, I would like that also. But if it will make you unhappy, I do not want it."

"Sorry," I said quickly. "I didn't mean to get maudlin. Yes, I would love to have sex with you. How could I pass up the opportunity to have sex with an extraterrestrial? I'd never forgive myself. I understand we aren't going to run off to Alpha Centauri together, and I'm okay with that. I won't be sad. I promise."

I suspected I was lying, but he didn't need to know that. He couldn't live on my world, and I doubted I'd want to live on his, though I did find it fascinating. And how do you manage a long-distance relationship when the distance separating you is measured in light-years? I still had no idea how they traveled from one solar system to another. For all I knew, it would be decades before we saw each other again, if that ever happened.

Dalsing blinked at me. "Alpha Centauri doesn't have any habitable planets."

"Just… fuck me."

Chapter Ten

DALSING CHANGED the setting back to the forest, though there was no stage now, and it was night. Small fireflies flitted through the clearing, and high overhead two reddish moons hung in the sky. A warm breeze caressed our skin, and the scent of cinnamon reached my nose. Perhaps some of those red flowers were blooming nearby.

Dalsing was already naked, so he stretched out upon the grass and waited for me to join him. The situation felt a little awkward, since I'd begun to get used to him walking around like that, and the absence of genitalia made him seem almost clothed. After all, I'd seen plenty of movies with aliens or superheroes or whatever who didn't appear all that different—except for the multiple nipples. But it wasn't like I'd never had sex before. So I shucked the robe, my only article of clothing, and lay down beside him.

The grass was soft and cool against my skin, and I stretched, luxuriating in it. "Mmm... I could get used to this."

"Perhaps we can visit this place on my world someday," he said, moving closer. "May I touch your skin?"

I was intrigued by the idea of visiting his world, but I let that slide by for now. "Please."

He ran his fingers over my chest, stopping briefly to tug gently on my chest hair. I didn't have much, by human standards, but he had none at all.

I laughed. "That tickles."

"It's fascinating," he said. "I have always found your *hair* interesting. It doesn't appear to keep you warm, as it does with other species on your planet."

"We have a lot of things in our bodies that might be holdovers from ancient times—body hair, the appendix, fingernails... I don't know much about it. I think it's interesting that you don't have any hair at all."

"Would you like to touch me?"

I didn't need any further prompting. I rolled toward him, and we lay side by side for a time, just running our hands along each other's bodies, exploring. I rubbed the top of his bald head and drew a thumb along the ridges above his eyes, where humans usually have eyebrows. His skin otherwise felt human. I think I'd been afraid it might feel lizardlike or something, but that wasn't the case. In the warm air, I even felt a trace of sweat. I was fascinated by the plated appearance of his back. It resembled armor, but the plates slipped easily underneath his warm skin. I suspected they were like human ribs, but broader and heavier.

At last, I gave in to what I'd being wanting to do for hours—I traced the lines of his *shiri*, causing them to phosphoresce a warm orange. On an impulse, I leaned forward and drew my tongue along one that formed a trail from his shoulder to his elbow. I liked the taste of his skin. His sweat lent a slight saltiness to it, just as human sweat did, but underneath that was a faint, musky taste that was very masculine.

He drew his breath in sharply as the *shiri* turned a bright red, and I felt a slight tingle in my tongue, as if those shimmering lights were electrical.

"I'm sorry," I said. "Was that too familiar?"

His mouth quirked up at one corner. "It was… nice. We are very sensitive there."

"I have this perverse desire to lick all of them," I confessed, hoping I wasn't sounding… I wasn't sure. Too aggressive, maybe. But that one lick had given me a huge boner.

"Please. I would like that very much."

So I did. I loved the way the *shiri* responded to my licking, flickering under my tongue until his entire body was streaked with lines of red light. And the way it felt on my tongue was mesmerizing. I just hoped it wasn't some kind of drug I was ingesting. Overdosing during sex would be embarrassing, never mind the health risks. I raised my head to ask him about it but discovered he was in the middle of what looked like an orgasm. His head was tilted back, and his breathing was coming in short gasps.

Suddenly, he groaned and arched his back. "I… I'm going to…."

Then his crotch kind of popped, and his cock emerged. It's difficult to describe, but it reminded me of a swordfish breaching the surface of the ocean, arcing up in the air in a graceful curve. Though of course it stayed there, once it was out. This close up, I could see it was neither circumcised nor uncircumcised—it just didn't have a foreskin. Which made sense, now that I thought about it. Why would it need one? It was protected at all times, except when he wanted to have sex.

It was wet, as if covered in some kind of natural lubrication. Otherwise, as I'd observed with the two actors in the play, it looked like a human cock, and a very nice one at that. I'm not a size queen, but it was moderately large and thick, which I found appealing, and just... beautiful. Some cocks are lumpy and not terribly attractive to me, but Dalsing's was smooth and graceful and just a work of art.

"Now I'm jealous," I said.

"Why?"

"Because that looked like it felt *really* good."

He laughed and looked at me with half-closed lids. "It does."

"Can I touch it?"

"Please. But I'd like to touch yours as well."

So we sixty-nined for a bit. The moisture that covered his cock's surface, including his balls, was very much like precome and just a bit sweet. I loved it. But he was doing too good a job sucking on my cock, and I was afraid I was about to explode. I was also afraid *he* would explode. I didn't want that to happen—not until he'd buried that beautiful cock in my ass. I'd meant it when I told him to fuck me.

I pulled away and rotated my body so we were face-to-face again. We hadn't actually kissed yet. I guess I'd been nervous about it. What if he had multiple tongues? Or weird alien breath? But now I was too worked up to care about any of that, and I took his mouth with mine, devouring him with fervor. Fortunately his breath smelled like the flowers we'd eaten at dinner—like cinnamon—and the tongue that wrestled with mine felt "normal" enough. I almost laughed at the thought that anything I was doing right now fell into the category of "normal."

I pulled away for a second.

"Do you... does your species practice anal sex?" I asked breathlessly.

"You mean inserting my *tisha*—" He gripped his cock to illustrate. "—into another *ba-ti*'s—man's—*golsha*?" He lifted one leg and pointed again. I couldn't see the opening in question from this angle, but I knew what he meant.

"Um... I know it doesn't sound appealing, when you describe it like that...."

He laughed again. "Yes. We do. Would you like to do that to me?"

That was an interesting idea. But I shook my head. "Maybe some other time, but right now I really want to feel you inside me."

"I would be happy to go inside you."

I grimaced. It was odd how slight differences in wording could change the tone so much. "The term we use is 'fuck.' At least when we're horny and being a little crude. I want you to fuck me."

"Then I will fuck you."

We didn't have any lube, but that didn't seem to matter. He produced his own. And the sleek design of his cock allowed it to slide in with next to no preparation. It was amazing. We fucked face-to-face with me lying on the grass, my ankles over his shoulders, and he penetrated me deeply with every thrust.

"Go faster," I breathed.

Dalsing picked up his rhythm until he was slamming into my ass harder than I'd ever let anyone else do it. But he seemed to fit so perfectly, I couldn't get enough of it. I'd never been particularly noisy in bed either, but I couldn't stop myself from gasping in pleasure with every thrust. My own cock was dripping so much, the precome was forming a trail down my side.

When he came, I felt his cock moving inside me, squirting over and over again. I'd never felt a man come that much. It went on and on without stopping, while Dalsing's entire body went rigid. His eyes were squeezed shut and his mouth was set in a grimace, but his *shiri* were lit up like strings of lights on a Christmas tree.

I watched his face in fascination and felt him filling me, so enthralled I forgot I hadn't yet attended to my own orgasm. My body was tingling all over, and my cock was painfully hard, but I didn't think to touch it. Then Dalsing exhaled a long breath and opened his eyes. He gazed down at me with a kind of dopey, fully sated smile on his face.

Then he seemed to realize the state I was in, and his eyes widened. "What about you? What should I do for you?" He gripped my cock, perhaps intending to jack me off.

But that was all it took. I grunted and shot so far it splattered against my chin and neck and then continued to douse my chest and stomach. I didn't come anywhere near as much as he had, but it was a damned good come. One for the scrapbooks.

Chapter Eleven

WE CLEANED up, and then we must have drifted off, because I woke to another one of those damned chimes. Dalsing grumbled and unwrapped his arms from my torso in order to sit up. At some point the forest had vanished, and we were now lying on a bed. I suspected it might be a real bed, and that the virtual reality program had simply shut off while we slept.

"Is the ship going to flip over again?" I asked sleepily.

"No. We're approaching Saturn. We must prepare for the attack."

My grogginess vanished, and I sat bolt upright. "What do we do?"

"You do nothing," he said, giving me a kiss on the cheek and then climbing out of the bed. "There is nothing you *can* do."

I knew that was true, but it still galled me to sit around on my ass while Dalsing and his people risked their lives to rescue my friend. I also knew that wasn't their sole purpose, but Dalsing had promised he'd bring Cody back alive—if he *was* still alive.

Oh God. Cody....

"You must not leave these quarters while I'm gone," Dalsing said sternly. "My crew knows you are here, so if something happens to me, someone will come for you. You will not be allowed to starve."

That alarmed me for a number of reasons. Now I was not only picturing myself clawing at the door, desperate for food while the Alzhen outside ignored my scraping, I was picturing Dalsing *dead*. The first was probably unlikely. I hoped. But the second....

"Just how dangerous is this?" I asked.

He gave me a look that suggested I might not be nearly as intelligent as he'd previously thought. "I will be leading the advance into the Karazhen base. One of the advances, at any rate. They will, of course, resist us. And the Karazhen warriors are quite lethal."

He leaned down to kiss me again, this time on the mouth. I wondered if he'd have to brush his teeth to get rid of my germs before speaking with his crew. Probably. On the other hand, one would hope Alzhen brushed their teeth in the morning, regardless of alien cooties....

"Look," I said, trying to be reasonable, "I know you have to do this. It's the only chance Cody has—"

Dalsing startled me by gripping my shoulders fiercely. "This is not about your friend. You need to understand that. I want to rescue him, for your sake, but if we cannot find him in a reasonable amount of time…."

"What?" I wasn't sure I wanted to know the answer.

"We have to blow the base up. It aids the Karazhen in their travels to and from this system, and we suspect there is also a scientific outpost there. Under no circumstances can any physical traces of their research or any of their scientists be allowed to survive."

I'd been right. I didn't want to know the answer. But there was a brutal logic to it. This was about the survival of the Alzhen. One human life was ultimately insignificant, even if they hoped they could save him.

"Do you… do you even know what Cody looks like?" I asked weakly.

"No."

"I don't have any pictures…." Perhaps I'd had one in my wallet—I wasn't sure—but that was hundreds of millions of miles away now.

"We will try to rescue any humans we find."

"Could you broadcast an image to me or something, if you find human prisoners?"

"Why? Wouldn't you want us to rescue them all?"

"Well, of course. But…." I didn't want to say it out loud, but if they were running out of time, and there were a hundred human prisoners… I wanted to make sure Cody was one of the ones who got out.

Perhaps Dalsing knew what I was thinking. "We will try to rescue all humans we come across. That is the best I can promise. I'm sorry."

"What if I could *see*?" I persisted. "You must have… dash cam technology, or something like that…."

"What is a dash cam?"

"A small camera that attaches to… well, it would be more like your helmet or clothing, if you intend to wear any—"

"I will be wearing armor."

"Exactly! So you'd have a camera attached to it, and I could see what you're seeing while I stay back here on the ship. Then, if you come across Cody, I could tell you!"

Dalsing held up a hand to stop my rambling. "Have you been to war?" he asked.

"No."

"Are you certain you wish to see it?"

IT WAS horrifying. I knew it would be, and Dalsing had warned me, but no amount of discussing it could have prepared me.

I, of course, was perfectly safe, watching from his quarters in total comfort, but the technology of his holographic projector—or whatever it was—put me in the middle of it. It was more than watching a flat image on a screen. I was *there*, running through the corridors of the Karazhen base, surrounded by armored Alzhen soldiers, though I was unable to actually do anything. The camera was mounted on Dalsing's helmet, at roughly eye level, so I saw everything from his point of view, but I was powerless to affect what I saw. He moved where he needed to move, and I seemed to be floating in the air, drifting along with him.

In point of fact, I *was* floating in the air. The ship was no longer accelerating through space, so I was drifting in microgravity, along with everyone on board. Fortunately Dalsing had given me another dose of the antinausea medication before he left.

The Alzhen camera had an advantage over our technology, in that I saw everything in the space around him in all directions, and I could look places he wasn't necessarily looking. I could talk to him, to alert him if I saw Cody, but he'd made me swear to keep my mouth shut otherwise. If I kept jabbering at him or screamed whenever something came out of the shadows, he could be endangered by the distraction.

It wasn't easy to stay quiet. The Karazhen base was like a horror movie set. It was really more of a nest than a base. They'd tunneled out a network of tubes in the bottom of the deepest crater of Janus, Saturn's tenth moon. These tubes had no flat surfaces to speak of, being roughly cylindrical and coated with a thick layer of webbing. They wormed their way deep into the moon's icy crust, crisscrossing haphazardly, with no rhyme or reason I could determine, unlit and seemingly empty.

The Alzhen themselves would have given me nightmares, if I hadn't known what they were. Their pressurized armor suits didn't resemble the suits I'd seen and worn. The heads were covered by low black domes that were transparent from the inside but not the outside. Dalsing had assured me the material was as strong as thick steel. The bodies of the suits were heavily armored with interlocking plates on the back and chest, and the arms and legs appeared to have pneumatic pistons strengthening the joints. This was confirmed when the Alzhen came across a doorway that was sealed by a metal partition. They sliced through it with lasers, and then two men grabbed ahold of the pieces with their gloved hands to wrench it open.

Janus did have gravity—about one-tenth that of Earth. Which meant that although the Alzhen were very light by comparison to their weight aboard the ship, they weren't in freefall. There was a definite "up" and "down," and unfortunately the Karazhen hadn't built the tunnels with that in mind. In places tunnels turned abruptly downward, creating a pit that would have killed anyone jumping down it, even in that low gravitational field. This required the Alzhen to belay down on cables.

The first attack came very suddenly, as Dalsing and his team dropped to the bottom of a particularly deep pit. The Karazhen came at them from all sides, and it was all I could do to keep myself from screaming in terror. They were hideous creatures, larger than a man, whose bodies seemed to be made of swords and knives, somehow held together by pinkish-gray tendons and tufts of gray bristles. If they had eyes, I couldn't see them. They moved swiftly, with their multiple legs stabbing furiously at the ground in a blur like mechanical sewing machines.

They were upon the Alzhen so fast, one man was literally shredded before he could raise his weapon. Then I could make sense of nothing for a while as jagged legs, laser blasts, and spurts of Alzhen blood and Karazhen ichor filled my vision. The monsters came from above as well as the sides, skittering down the vertical tube above the Alzhen warriors with ease. The Alzhen appeared to be adept at blasting them into fragments of bone and slime, but the creatures kept coming, and there was nowhere to retreat.

There was no atmosphere in the tunnels to carry sound, so the nightmare was utterly silent except for Dalsing's frantic breathing and muttered exclamations. I couldn't understand a word until he whipped around several times, his gun at the ready, and said in English, clearly for my benefit, "I think that's the last of them... for now."

I realized I was whimpering, so I swallowed and said weakly, "I'm sorry. I'll be quiet."

"I am glad you are safe."

Then he seemed to forget about me as he barked out orders over the com link and the others responded. Dalsing walked among the wreckage

of bodies, and I counted silently to myself. Sixty-five dead Karazhen...
and eighteen dead Alzhen, torn to pieces, their skin and blood already
frozen where it was exposed to the vacuum of space. I'd never seen a
sight that sickening before—not outside of a horror movie. These were
real. They were *people*, even if they were a different species than I was.
I began to get tunnel vision, so I had to close my eyes for a minute. My
stomach was threatening to heave.

There were only forty-two people still alive on Dalsing's team. If
they went up against a few more attacks like that, I didn't see how they
could possibly survive.

Chapter Twelve

SOMEHOW DALSING'S team survived a dozen more encounters with the Karazhen, though the losses were heavy. No one battle cost them as much as that first one—perhaps because the Karazhen had thrown the bulk of their forces at the intruders and were now reduced to smaller skirmishes throughout the base—but Alzhen warriors continued to fall. There were only sixteen still alive as they drew near what seemed to be the heart of the base.

The Alzhen came to a door with a window in it. When Dalsing looked through it, there was another door just a short distance away.

"An airlock," he told me. He said something I couldn't understand to his crew and then stepped back. While they gathered around the door, he said in English, "The Karazhen warriors do not breathe oxygen. They metabolize salt water and are able to store some reserves in their bodies for a considerable amount of time. This allows them to operate outside the pressurized zones of the base and conserves resources."

I had actually been wondering about that. The Karazhen didn't look very technological. How could they build spaceships and bases in the first place? Did they even have hands? Since we had a quiet moment and he'd been speaking to me, I ventured to ask about that.

"These are the warriors," he replied. "Savage, lethal, and coordinated but not particularly intelligent. The ruling class and scientists are quite different."

In a couple of minutes, the Alzhen had cut through the outer door of the lock, but they'd set up some kind of force field at the entrance, which glowed with a cold blue light. The Alzhen walked through it without a problem, but I guessed it somehow kept air in. I couldn't ask about it because Dalsing was occupied again, but it wasn't really important for me to know.

When the Alzhen blew the door on the other side of the lock—they didn't bother to cut through it—they were immediately set upon by more of the Karazhen warriors. Fortunately they dispatched these without any losses on their side.

The first room was very different from the tunnels on the other side of the airlock. There was no doubt the equipment there had been created by a technologically advanced race—more advanced than humans. They had interstellar travel, after all. I had no idea what any of the equipment did, but it didn't seem to be relevant to Dalsing's mission. After a brief look around, he and his team proceeded to the next room.

They went through several rooms like this, sometimes finding nothing, other times coming across a token resistance. But nothing like the first attack.

"This makes me nervous," Dalsing told me quietly. "They are holding back, amassing for one final strike. And we could easily be trapped in these rooms."

Jesus. That was the last thing I wanted to hear. But it was impossible for me to be more terrified for him than I already was.

Then the team entered the specimen room.

That's the best name I can think of for it. The room was an enormous cavern containing row upon row of sealed pods with clear glass panels on top. There were various illuminated displays and rows of LEDs throughout the room, but most of the light came from the pods themselves, shining up through the panels from their interiors. And thanks to the three-dimensional panoramic view the camera on Dalsing's helmet gave me, I could look down into the pods, even when he was facing in a different direction. What I saw sickened me. Naked human beings—mostly *dead* human beings, in various stages of decay. Of the corpses that were still recognizable, many showed the ravages of horrific, disfiguring diseases. Others had been cut or burned.

Dalsing had been right. The Karazhen were experimenting on us.

"This one is still alive," Dalsing told me as he peered into one of the pods.

It wasn't Cody. The young man inside the pod looked barely out of high school. The thought that if I told the truth, he might be abandoned to die alone in this alien death camp, probably enduring unimaginable torment at their hands, nearly prevented me from speaking. But I was the only champion Cody had, and I couldn't let him down. "I… I hope you can save him," I said at last. "But he's not Cody."

Dalsing barked a command into his com link. "I've told them to fan out and locate every survivor. We must do this quickly."

We looked at over a dozen of them and failed to find Cody. They were all unconscious inside their prisons, awaiting a miserable fate or, at best, a quick death. The Alzhen had been planting explosives throughout the tunnels and inside the pressurized part of the base. They were primed to go off at a signal from the ship, as soon as Dalsing's team had retreated.

It occurred to me that Dalsing could kill those survivors I was forced to admit weren't Cody. At least that would assure they were put out of their misery. But I couldn't even suggest such a thing. I clung to the hope they might still be saved, somehow.

We hadn't examined even half the pods when someone shouted over Dalsing's com link. I spun around to see… *things* moving in the shadows at the far end of the chamber. Things with seemingly millions of sharp blades stabbing at the floor, scurrying between the pods. Karazhen warriors. I whipped around, but they were coming from all sides now, flooding into the chamber through the doors at either end and rapidly spreading out. All avenues of retreat were cut off.

"*Fuck!*"

If Dalsing heard my exclamation, he didn't acknowledge it. There was no need. He saw exactly what I saw and probably knew better what the odds of survival were. I watched helplessly as he shouted commands to his team and blasted the Karazhen bearing down on him. Off to his left, an Alzhen who might have been his second-in-command was torn in two. In this pressurized chamber, the battle wasn't silent. I heard the explosions of the lasers, the chilling screeching of the Karazhen, and even more horrifying, the screams of Alzhen warriors being sliced to ribbons.

The odds seemed hopeless. It was hard to see in the darkness, but there seemed to be *hundreds* of Karazhen. And there were so few Alzhen left. I was tempted to close my eyes against it, but I forced myself to stay alert. There might be nothing I could do, but I refused to stick my head in the sand while Dalsing and his team might be facing their last moments.

When one of the hideous bugs leapt at Dalsing from behind, I violated our agreement and shouted, "Behind you!"

Dalsing whipped around and cut the thing in half with his laser.

Then I saw something where the creature had been—a pod we hadn't looked at yet. All I could see, at first, was a tuft of unruly dark brown hair. But I moved in my virtual bubble to get a closer look. It was Cody, looking ghastly in the bluish light inside the pod. He might have been alive; he might have been dead. I had no way of knowing.

"That's him!" I exclaimed.

Then, with a horrible screech and what seemed like a thousand flailing, swordlike legs, the world tumbled around me and went black.

Dalsing had been hit.

Chapter Thirteen

I DON'T know how long I was trapped in Dalsing's living quarters. It might have been a few days, though it seemed like weeks. The "gravity" returned, which meant we were traveling again, but I had no idea where we were going. To Earth? To Dalsing's home planet?

At first I tried to obey his directive to stay inside, no matter what happened. He'd assured me I wouldn't be allowed to starve to death, hadn't he? But after I'd slept several times, and still nobody had come to let me out or even spoken to me through any kind of sound system, I decided I couldn't risk the possibility that I'd been forgotten. I donned the protective suit before leaving—I wasn't a total asshole—but I knew the outside of the suit would be contaminated by my touch.

I discovered a small room in the back of the bathroom that basically operated like a shower, though it had more of that weird water-like substance that vanished shortly after it touched me. It sprayed against the outside of the suit, but as it trickled down my body, it disappeared. The floor remained dry.

That would have to do.

It turned out to all be for nothing, however. Nothing I did got that goddamned door-iris-thingy to dilate and let me through. I was trapped.

I wasn't starving. The computer was apparently set to provide food and water at regular intervals, because containers kept appearing on the small table near the bed. So I ate, drank, relieved myself in the bathroom occasionally, and slept a lot. Eventually, when I could no longer stand the smell of my armpits, I tentatively stuck a finger under the shower spray. It didn't make my skin dissolve, so I risked dousing my entire body. It cleaned me better than soap and water, and I suspect it killed the bacteria that makes underarms smell, because I didn't have any underarm odor at all for a day or so after that.

At some point I heard the chimes sounding, and only remembered what it was signaling a split second before the ship turned over. Once again I somehow managed not to fly all over the room, and neither did the objects resting on tabletops and other surfaces. I did, however, upchuck on myself this time, forcing me to make another foray into the shower.

All this time, I fretted about the fate of Dalsing and Cody, and sometimes I cried over them. It seemed likely they were both dead. Even if Dalsing had somehow survived, he probably hadn't been in any shape to rescue Cody. He might not have even heard my shout.

If Cody hadn't been rescued, I prayed the Alzhen had blown up the entire base. Better that than to leave him in the... pincers... of those hideous monsters.

I WOKE to noise coming from the corridor outside the doorway. It sounded for all the world like somebody was doing construction out there—drilling or riveting and metal scraping against metal. I leaped out of the bed and ran to the door.

"Hey!" I shouted, pounding on it.

Everything went silent for a moment. Then a voice, muffled by the door, said, "Eyvreeteeng... ees... ohkay. Poot... awn... yoo-ur... soot."

After I'd sussed that out, I went into the bathroom and returned a short time later dressed in the suit. I'd even showered for good measure.

I had to wait a long time. Long enough that I was forced to choose between taking the goddamned suit off again, so I could relieve myself, or testing out its supposed ability to handle liquid waste. I finally decided I'd rather leave with a damp crotch than delay leaving by a single second. I wanted *out. Now.*

Luckily, Dalsing hadn't exaggerated the suit's ability to handle bodily functions. After the deed was done, I didn't feel any dampness down there at all.

Eventually, the door dilated, and an Alzhen in an isolation suit stepped inside. "Cohm... weet... mee."

He led me out into a small airlock that hadn't been there when Dalsing brought me into his quarters. When both doors were closed, we were sprayed down and illuminated with blue light. Then the outer door opened and we stepped out into the corridor. I would have been delighted to escape my temporary prison, but the fact that I was tightly wrapped up in the suit put a damper on that. I doubted I'd be allowed to remove it again unless I was either back in Dalsing's quarters or the room I'd occupied earlier, which was far smaller.

Even though there had to have been more than one Alzhen working on the airlock, no one greeted us in the corridor. I followed my guide into the elevator and down a level. After a few twists and turns, we entered a corridor bustling with activity, and at last we came to a large complex that appeared to be an infirmary. We passed through numerous glass sliding doors, and on either side of us, there were rooms with Alzhen lying in beds or, more disturbing, floating in midair. Perhaps they were suspended in some kind of force field. I didn't really care. If we were in a hospital, that meant we had to be on our way to see either Dalsing or Cody, and that was all I could process. My stomach was in knots.

When I tried to ask my guide about it, all I got was "Faw... loh... mee."

Ugh. I decided then that, if I *was* being taken to the Alzhen planet, I would have to learn their language. Listening to them mutilate English for much longer would drive me insane. Of course, I'd probably end up mutilating Alzhenese or whatever it was called, but turnabout was fair play.

We entered a less frenetic wing of the hospital, where the patients seemed to be in worse shape than the ones we'd passed. Most were unconscious. Many were bandaged so much, hardly any skin could be seen. I had a very bad feeling about it.

At last my guide stopped at a closed door and turned to face me. "Doo... noht... bee... lawn-guh." Then he gestured to the door. Apparently he intended to wait outside.

Nervously, I stepped forward, and the door opened with a faint puffing sound, as if the air inside was at a slightly different pressure from the air in the corridor—but not enough to warrant an airlock. The room beyond was dark, although a dim light illuminated a bed with an Alzhen *ba-ti* lying in it. I hadn't grown so accustomed to the Alzhen gender distinctions that I could tell a *ba-ti* from a *ba* when the Alzhen was covered by a blanket, but there was little difficulty in this case.

It was Dalsing.

Chapter Fourteen

I STEPPED inside the room, and the door constricted. Then a hiss informed me air was being pumped back in to readjust the pressure. I'd read once that Earth astronauts sometimes had to accustom themselves to working at a slightly lower pressure than sea level on Earth. Perhaps the Alzhen on board the spaceship were doing the same thing, but the pressure was increased in some of the hospital rooms to aid the patients' recovery. I'd have to ask about it some other time.

At the moment I had other concerns. Dalsing looked awful. As I approached his bedside, I could see his head and the left side of his face were covered by something resembling sky blue plastic, and the eye that peered back at me was cloudy, as if he were heavily drugged. His left arm below the elbow was *missing*.

"My God," I said quietly.

His eye blinked several times, and he smiled faintly. "I needed to see you. I am sorry if the sight of me is disturbing."

"Don't be ridiculous!" I said, irritated. "I'm not some delicate little flower." He looked confused by that, so I added, "I'm worried about you. That's all that matters to me right now."

"Thank you." He sighed and closed his eyes. I was afraid he'd slipped into unconsciousness, but when I said his name softly, he opened them again. "Please take off your helmet," he whispered.

"Won't your doctors have a fit if I do?"

"I do not care. Please... I want to see your face."

I reached up and popped the seal around the neck of the suit, praying I wouldn't be exposing him to any germs his body couldn't handle. We'd made love, and as far as I knew he hadn't suffered any unpleasant consequences from that intimate contact, but he was so weak now....

I remembered, as I removed the helmet, that I hadn't actually had time to wash my hair that morning before I'd been escorted out of his quarters. It was probably sticking up all over the place.

But he smiled again. "Of all the humans I have seen in the past seventy-five years, you are the most beautiful."

"Sweet-talker."

"I want to feel your skin against mine," he said softly.

He was in absolutely no condition to have sex, but I didn't think that was really what he wanted anyway. He just wanted contact, affection. Unfortunately I had no idea how to get the gloves off the isolation suit, if that was even possible. So instead I leaned down and pressed my cheek to the right side of his face. It was warm and soft, and when he sighed gently into my ear, I found myself growing hard. The warmth that had flooded through me when we'd made love swelled in my chest again.

"You can't die," I whispered. "We're just getting to know each other."

"I know."

When at last I pulled away, his *shiri* were glowing scarlet. "Thank you," he said. "But I didn't bring you here just for selfish reasons. I need to tell you about your friend…."

I took a breath, steeling myself for the news. "Is he…? Is he dead?"

"No," Dalsing replied. His head moved slightly, as if he'd wanted to shake it but was unable to. "He is… not well. But he is alive. I was able to identify him to my people, after the battle… before I lost consciousness. Kaising will take you to him when you leave here."

I assumed Kaising was my guide. Dalsing seemed to be struggling to talk, however, so I didn't waste his time clarifying that point.

"Will *you*… recover?" I asked, my voice breaking on the final word. I glanced at the stump where his arm had been and then looked quickly away.

"I do not know…."

I planted a kiss on his lips, and then another on his forehead. "Listen," I told him. "I don't know if they're taking me back to Earth or not. But I'm not leaving. I refuse. I'm not going anywhere until you're better."

What would happen after that, I had no idea. But I couldn't go the rest of my life not knowing whether Dalsing was alive or not.

He didn't argue. He smiled and said, "I will not let anyone force you to leave me."

OVER THE next several hours, with the help of Kaising, I learned something of that final battle with the Karazhen. I won't report the entire conversation, since it was torturously slow.

Most of Dalsing's team had perished in that attack, but one of the last commands he'd managed to give before losing consciousness was a call for a retrieval team. The new team was small, and they had to retrace the route Dalsing's team had taken, but fortunately they encountered little resistance. They barely made it in time, but with their help, the last five members of Dalsing's team managed to destroy what turned out to be the final wave of Karazhen in the base. Dalsing and three others were transported to the ship for medical care, one dying before she reached the ship. The base had been blown up as soon as we'd left orbit.

All the living human subjects had been retrieved, to my intense relief, though some had died in the meantime. There were twenty-seven still alive. A few might not survive much longer.

But Cody's prognosis was good. He was being kept in a stasis tube similar to the ones I'd seen in the Karazhen base, but of Alzhen design. He was unconscious, and he looked ghastly, floating naked in some kind of amber fluid like a fetal pig in a specimen jar. Only the constantly fluctuating displays nearby indicated he was still alive. I couldn't read the displays, of course, but Kaising told me the values were good. And he didn't appear to have been cut up like some of the others. I gathered he'd been infected with some kind of virus, but the Alzhen doctors had already cured him of it. Now his body just needed time to recover.

I found the young man I'd first seen when Dalsing examined the pods in the base. He was alive, and again Kaising assured me he would survive. I was relieved not to have his death on my conscience.

But I had to wonder what was in store for him when he woke at last—what was in store for all of them. Including Cody. A lifetime of waking up screaming in the night? Insanity? Doctors, psychologists, and hospitals—an array of antipsychotics and antidepressants? Suicide?

Oh, Cody….

Maybe the memory-wipe thing was a good idea after all. But as Dalsing and I had discussed, that didn't always seem to work. I didn't know what the answer was.

I just knew I hated the Karazhen with every part of my being.

Chapter Fifteen

I'D BEEN wrong about them taking us back to Earth. If that had been the case, we would have reached Earth orbit while I was still locked in Dalsing's quarters. We were heading to Alzhen-Ai, which basically translates to "world of the Alzhen." Considering that the name of our planet is basically "dirt" and we call our moon "moon," I couldn't criticize their lack of originality.

I don't know what star system Alzhen-Ai was in—not from an Earth perspective. Kaising knew nothing of Earth astronomy. I gathered it was something like twenty-six light-years away. This meant that even if the ship we were on could go as fast as the speed of light, we wouldn't get there until I was approaching sixty years old. That would have sucked.

Fortunately the Alzhen had figured out a shortcut long ago, or their exploration of solar systems would have been extremely slow. Again, I had no idea how it worked, but some kind of quantum jiggery-pokery let them skip through empty space as if it literally wasn't there. The upshot of this being that, by the time I found out we were on our way to Alzhen-Ai… we were already approaching orbit.

I went up to the lounge with Kaising and got my first look at an alien world—one that wasn't just a dead rock, at any rate. The enormous curved edge of Alzhen-Ai took up one half of the view through the dome, a beautiful blue-green planet streaked with white clouds, not unlike Earth. I was, in fact, looking at it as it seemed to roll away from us. The engines under my feet were swinging around to aim at the planet as we braked in orbit.

Dalsing had told me Alzhen-Ai was a bit larger than Earth, with a slightly higher gravity, though he assured me I would have no trouble adapting if I went to the surface. The air had some trace gases not found in Earth's atmosphere, but none that would harm me. Alzhen scientists speculated that the similarities between our planets might have led to our similar evolutionary paths, though some still clung to the belief that our species were "seeded" by an even more ancient race neither of us had yet encountered.

"If you believe that sort of thing," Dalsing had said, his tone making it clear he did not.

Unfortunately, even if I did want to visit the planet, that wouldn't occur for several weeks. Our ship was a plague ship. Not only were humans on board with all the myriad diseases and microscopic organisms we normally carried, but most of us were infected with unknown viruses designed to kill Alzhen. Doctors were flying up to the ship from the planet's surface in order to give medical aid to the survivors of the assault on Janus and to assist with the isolation and study of the aforementioned superviruses, but until such time as they declared it safe, we were under strict planetary quarantine.

I made the mistake of asking Dalsing what would happen if one of the viruses proved resistant to treatment.

"Then," he said grimly, "they will have to destroy us."

I felt the blood drain from my face. "I suppose that makes sense. Even with the doctors on board—the ones who flew up from the surface?"

"Yes. Those medical personnel knew what they were volunteering for. The government cannot risk a deadly epidemic." He nodded toward the drinking bottle on the table, partially filled with more of that urine-yellow liquid. Apparently it was a nutrient mixture filled with vitamins, though knowing that didn't make it look any more appetizing. I held it up so he could drink from the spout. He sucked some down and then released the spout with a gasp, as if that simple act had exhausted him. "That is a last resort," he continued. "We need to know what the Karazhen have been working on, and we need defenses against it."

Another of those goddamn chimes sounded. I'd been learning to distinguish the different tones and what they meant. This one meant I had to leave. Under the care of his new doctors, Dalsing was recovering, but he was still very weak. He could sit up and talk to me now and then, but never for long.

"I'll see you tomorrow," I said, leaning over to kiss him. The fact that I still took my helmet off when I was in his room upset the staff, but Dalsing had insisted upon it, and even as wounded as he was, he could still throw his weight around.

He returned the kiss, nibbling my lower lip a bit before I pulled away. His *shiri* flickered dimly to life, and I couldn't resist licking the line of them along the bridge of his nose. I drew back, pleased to see that line shimmering with fire.

"Consider that a promise," I said huskily. "For when you're better."

As THE resident human on the ship—and it probably didn't hurt that I was Dalsing's… whatever I was to him—I was consulted when some of the humans were considered safe to be released from their stasis pods. Apparently there was some concern about how my planet-mates might react when they awoke from their induced comas. God knew how long some of them had been unconscious. They could have been abducted by the Karazhen *decades* ago. Of course, there was no guarantee they all spoke English. I might not even be able to speak to them. But at least having a human around when they woke might keep them from flipping out a bit. The last thing they needed was to open their eyes and see an Alzhen in an isolation suit looming over them.

Because of my personal connection to him, Cody was brought out first. I had him taken to a holding cell like the one I'd first awoken in. Then, after they'd administered something to wake him, I asked the medical staff to wait outside.

They'd dressed him in a jumpsuit—something nobody had thought to offer me when I first came on board—and I was dressed in my isolation suit, minus the helmet, so I wouldn't freak him out. I'd have to be leaving eventually, so it made sense to wear it. Besides, I'd grown used to it by now.

It took a minute for him to come out of it. When he did, he screamed and sat bolt upright on the bed.

"Cody," I said quietly.

He jerked his head around at the sound of my voice, his eyes open wide in terror.

"It's okay, Cody. You're safe."

The first sound he made was an inarticulate scream as he flailed his arms in front of his face.

"Cody! Cody… it's okay. You're safe now. Nobody's going to hurt you."

After a minute he stopped screaming and began to rock back and forth, his arms still held in front of his face. He lowered his head until his forehead rested against his wrists and began to sob.

I knew it would be a mistake to touch him. I had no idea what I *should* do, but I continued to speak to him in a quiet, soothing tone of voice. I was afraid it was too late, that he was completely insane now. But after a long, long time of this, he said in a pitifully small voice, "Marc?"

"I'm here, Cody. You're safe."

"It couldn't have been a nightmare.... It felt.... It was *real*! I know it was real!"

"It was. I'm sorry. We got you out of there as soon as we could."

He wasn't really listening. He began wailing, "My God! My God! They cut... and they.... There were dead people.... Oh God! It hurt! It hurt so much!"

Chapter Sixteen

WE WERE in orbit around Alzhen-Ai for months, by Earth reckoning.

During that time, I learned to be something of a therapist for my fellow humans as they woke one by one. Not that I had any idea what I was doing. But they needed another human being to reach out to in a world that had gone completely insane—and I was it.

Some of them, perhaps, couldn't be saved. They never stopped crying and screaming long enough for me to talk to them. Worse, some of them kept clawing at themselves or hitting their heads against the wall. These people needed to be sedated. What would happen to them if they didn't eventually come back to themselves, I didn't know. Others eventually calmed down and talked to me, or if they didn't know English, they'd write things down for me to take to the Alzhen translators. There were translators for most languages on Earth, it turned out. They would give me the English equivalent, and I'd give them answers to translate back into German or Swahili or whatever language the human spoke.

One of them—the teenage boy I'd first seen—just wanted to be held. It was a little awkward at first. The boy was American, I eventually learned, with a thick Texan accent. He was also younger than I'd thought. About sixteen. He wasn't gay—he wanted to make very sure I was clear on that point—but he had nightmares. And the only way he could calm down after the really bad ones was to wrap himself up in my arms while I talked in a low, calm voice about stupid shit that had nothing to do with aliens and spaceships and outer space.

Cody eventually recovered enough for us to have conversations about what had happened, though he went into a panic attack, hyperventilating and cowering in the corner, when one of the Alzhen attempted to bring him food. It took me hours to calm him, and he made me promise to keep "them" away from him. From that point on, I brought his food in to him, making sure to leave my helmet in the airlock, as I did with all the others.

I tried to talk to him about the Alzhen, but it was hopeless. His experiences with the Karazhen had made him paranoid, even before he'd been taken to their base.

"You have to understand," I insisted, "these aren't the same people who experimented on you. The Alzhen *rescued* you."

"Why?" he asked, narrowing his eyes suspiciously.

"Because I asked them to. And because they're basically decent people."

"They're plotting something, Marc. I don't know what. But you can't buy into their bullshit."

"Cody...."

"How do you know they're what they tell you, Marc?" he demanded. "Huh? How do you know they aren't planning on taking over the world and farming us like goddamn cattle?"

I frowned at him. "Because they don't eat people. And I've gotten to know them, Cody. They aren't like the... bug creatures. Not at all." I refrained from mentioning some of the more "alien" things about the Alzhen, such as the fact that they let their children attend plays with beheadings and sexual intercourse in them. That was a cultural thing, I supposed. But by now I'd learned to trust them, at least as much as I trusted any group of people I'd known for less than a year. And I trusted Dalsing.

Cody just gave me a wide-eyed look and shook his head sadly. "You drank the Kool-Aid, man."

I gave up trying to persuade him the Alzhen weren't his enemies. Considering what he'd been through, I supposed I was lucky he hadn't gone completely insane. But I'd had to draw the line at his conviction that his food was poisoned. That had been one of our first arguments.

"Goddammit!" I snapped. "I'm not going to let you starve when there's perfectly good food sitting right in front of you! I know it looks weird, but I've eaten it a million times, and it hasn't done me any harm."

He glared at me. The Alzhen had shaved all the hair off his body to aid in the sterilization process, and now he looked like a pissed-off, younger Charles Manson, except for the absence of an upside-down cross tattooed on his forehead. "If you want me to eat it, you eat it first. Right in front of me. Every single thing on that tray."

"Christ!" I did what he asked, sampling a bit of everything, and had to do the same thing every day from that day on. He never got to trust me enough to just eat the fucking food.

OVER THOSE months, I found myself increasingly "going native." I was living in Dalsing's quarters, and as long as I wore my suit and went through the airlock sterilization procedure when I stepped out, I was free to roam about the ship. Apart from the medical bays, where some of the humans were still being kept in stasis and the medical staff struggled to analyze all the horrible things infesting their bodies, I wasn't prevented from accessing anything. I even wandered up into the command center occasionally.

With Dalsing's and Kaising's help, I began to learn the language, and the crew was patient with my attempts to communicate. They all knew me by now, and I was treated with indulgence, like a pet or a mascot. It soon became clear that they thought of me as belonging in some way to Dalsing. I wasn't sure if I should be concerned about that, but Dalsing assured me I wasn't his property.

"They know of my... fondness for you," he told me.

He was doing much better now, walking around his hospital room with no more than thin, semitransparent casings around his knees and on his hips to aid him. I gathered they were miniature hydraulic devices to reinforce his joints while they healed. Since he was otherwise naked, I could clearly see how he was healing, at least externally. He looked good. The plastic-like substance that had sealed the wounds on his head and face had been removed, and though there were scars, they weren't disfiguring. I actually thought they were kind of sexy.

"Fondness?" I asked. We hadn't really clarified what our relationship meant. After all, we'd only slept together once.

"I have told them you are my mate," he said casually. But he seemed to be watching me for a reaction.

"Humans don't really use that word about ourselves," I said. "We tend to think of animals as 'mating,' and humans as... well, a lot of things. What do you mean when you say it?"

He glanced at the floor uncomfortably and then walked unsteadily around the bed to come closer to me. "I intended no offense...."

"I wasn't offended. I'd just like to know what you meant."

He lifted his face to look me in the eye. "I meant… we have engaged in sexual acts, and I have grown fond of you."

"How fond?"

"I do not understand the question."

I sighed but smiled at him. "How strong is this 'fond' feeling you have for me? Do you mean you enjoy sex with me and would like to do it again—?"

"Of course," he replied. Then he quickly added, "Though I would understand if you do not want to be… physically close to me now…."

I snorted and ducked in to kiss him on his scarred cheek, hoping my touch wouldn't hurt him. "If you have some dumb idea that I won't want to have sex with you because you're wounded, get rid of it. I'm *desperate* to have sex with you. As soon as your doctor says you're up to it, I'll throw myself down in front of you with my legs spread." I was pleased to see his *shiri* flash briefly at that. "But what I'm asking you is, do you think of me as more than just a sex toy? More than just a *friend*, even?"

He stepped forward, the hydraulics surrounding his joints making faint hissing sounds. His jaw was set and the uncertainty he'd displayed a moment ago was gone. He pinned me with his gaze. "I am uncertain what you mean by 'sex toy'—though I can guess. You are more to me than merely someone with whom I enjoy sex. I believe we are becoming friends, but if by that you mean a relationship without passion, I do not want to restrict it to that."

"We call friends who have sex 'friends with benefits,'" I said. "And that sounds good to me. But do you understand the English word 'love'?"

"I do," Dalsing replied without hesitation. "Our word is *ba-la*, but it is the same. And I feel it unfolding in me when you are near, or when I think of you."

I liked that idea. "Unfolding…."

"Yes." He raised his hand in a fist. "Our symbol for *ba-la* is the *shirsha* flower—we shared some the night we mated. Or 'had sex,' if you prefer. They smell beautiful when they blossom." He spread his fingers outward.

"You sly dog," I said, smirking at him. "Were you coming on to me when you served me those flowers as part of our dinner?" He cocked his head, clearly unable to parse my question. "Don't worry about it," I continued. "They were delicious, and they do smell beautiful. And I feel *ba-la* unfolding in me for you as well."

Then, despite my concerns about his strength, I couldn't resist wrapping my arms around his waist—gently—and kissing him. He returned the kiss with the fervor of a man denied any sexual release for several months. I confess I'd masturbated often during that time, thinking of our night together and what I'd like to do when Dalsing was finally able to return to his quarters, but that might not be so easy to get away with in a hospital bed, with machinery and nurses monitoring every heartbeat.

He was still weak, as I realized when he slumped against me. The hydraulic joints seemed to have difficulty keeping him upright with my added weight knocking his body off-kilter. But he didn't show any sign of wanting to stop, so I just held him up, bracing us both with my shoulder against the wall. I wasn't even aware of my hand caressing his crotch until I heard him moan and felt his body shudder, and suddenly my hand was cradling a very hot, wet, and hard Alzhen cock. It throbbed against my palm in time with his pounding heartbeat.

Dalsing broke the kiss and gasped, "I'm sorry."

"I am so *not* sorry. God, that feels good!"

"I don't think I have the strength—"

"Lie down," I ordered him. "I'll take care of everything."

I'd always loved the taste and scent of a man's cock. I could happily give a blowjob for hours. Dalsing's cock had a similar musky smell, though a bit stronger than a man's, and I was growing to love the sweetish taste of his precome. I licked him up and down his thick shaft and all around the bulge of his scrotum. He writhed on the bed and ran the fingers of his right hand through my hair as he panted my name and other things in his language that I couldn't understand.

At some point I think we might have been discovered. I'll never be sure. But I could swear I heard the door open briefly, then close softly. If that was the case, the Alzhen were more understanding of these things than most human hospital staff would be.

When Dalsing moaned and came, I had him deep in my throat. But I was selfish and didn't want to swallow it all without tasting it, so I pulled back and let the hot liquid flood my mouth. It was not unlike human semen. A little different. But I couldn't pinpoint just how the taste differed. Just... enough to make it interesting.

I quickly learned that if I intended to give many more blowjobs to this man, I'd have to work on my stamina. He came a *lot*. I loved every drop of it, but… yeah. It took a lot of swallowing.

He finally finished and lay there breathing heavily, stroking my hair.

"I don't know if I can do the same for you, *balanai*," he said sleepily. "But I will try."

I laughed and licked his cock one final time before it slipped quietly back into place. "You just rest and sleep if you need to. I'm fine."

In fact, I was in the middle of coming. I hoped my suit could handle it.

Epilogue

Five Years Later

WE WERE eventually released from quarantine and allowed to land on Alzhen-Ai. My first view of it from Dalsing's quarters was breathtaking, though also a bit disturbing. It provided a hint of what Earth might someday become—overpopulated and covered with sprawling cities to the point where one was impossible to distinguish from the other, the wild spaces reduced to mountains and remote forests where few people wanted to live. As he'd told me the first night we spent together, each of the large cities had parks where the ancient landscape was allowed to thrive, but they were ultimately zoos.

After a time I was allowed to walk among the Alzhen without the use of an isolation suit. Their doctors had declared me free of any dangerous microbes. By this point I'd been surviving on their food and breathing their air for so long, my body had acclimated. The gravity difference wore me out for the first year, but I got used to it.

I also adapted to the Alzhen lifestyle, which meant, among other things, far less clothing than I typically wore on Earth. However, I'd discovered even before landing that nudity for me was somewhat different than it was for the Alzhen. After being told I no longer needed the suit, I decided to brave the central lounge—naked. It didn't go over well. Since I was now widely known as Dalsing's *balanai*, nobody said anything, but they were clearly having difficulty looking at me. The problem was my penis. An Alzhen *ba-ti* who walked around with his dick hanging out was committing a pretty severe breach of etiquette. They knew, of course, that mine didn't retract. But still… it was awkward.

So from that point on, I tended to wear shorts in public. At home, of course, Dalsing was rather fond of my penis.

The Alzhen equivalent to marriage, as it was practiced on Earth—specifically in the USA—was generally much more polyamorous than I would have been happy with. Fortunately Dalsing understood the way I felt and assured me he had no interest in bringing in others. So two years after he'd stepped down as Dalsing, we were… well, basically married.

That was another thing. His name wasn't Dalsing. As he'd told me when I first asked him his name, "dalsing" was a rank, like the way Spock always called Kirk "Captain" on *Star Trek*. Now that he was more or less retired, I called him by his actual name at home. However, names are very private in Alzhen culture, so I don't feel comfortable writing it in this account. I continued to call him Dalsing in public. And a year later, he was pulled out of retirement anyway, to act as the Alzhen ambassador to Earth.

But I'll get to that in a minute.

The humans who'd been rescued all opted to return to Earth, including Cody. He sold the farm—thank God—and moved into his parents' house in Greenfield, Massachusetts. I checked in on him now and then during the year Dalsing and I spent as ambassadors to the United States, and then the United Nations. Cody seemed to be better now that he had people looking out for him, and was seeing a psychologist and getting medication for his anxiety. It helped, I think, that his therapist believed his stories. After all the uproar the appearance of an alien ambassador—accompanied by a human—caused, how could she not?

The decision to make contact had been long overdue. The government on Alzhen-Ai—there was only one government for the entire planet—initially resisted the idea, since it would inevitably entail passing some Alzhen technology along to Earth. That sort of thing always happened. But the Earth was now in danger from the Karazhen, so leaving humans in the dark would have been cruel.

I hated all the commotion surrounding our appearance at the UN. We might as well have been declaring war on the planet to judge by the reception we got. There were nut jobs on television insisting we'd come to destroy humanity, or that we were the sign of the coming apocalypse. And of course the governments were all trying to get in bed with the Alzhen so they could get access to interstellar travel and better weapons. Dalsing and I needed a security detachment at all times the entire time we were on the planet.

I was pretty disgusted with my species that year.

Fortunately Alzhen-Ai sent another team to take over as ambassadors once we'd laid the groundwork. I had no desire to be trapped there forever.

"It's strange," I commented as our ship left orbit for the return to Alzhen-Ai. "I should feel like Earth is my home. After all, I was born there and lived there my entire life until I got abducted."

Dalsing scoffed at that and put his robotic left arm around my shoulders. It was nearly indistinguishable from his flesh-and-blood arm, and he claimed he could feel things just as well with the "skin" on it. "The Karazhen were abducting you. We simply intervened."

We were standing in the lounge, watching the horizon of the Earth dip down as the ship turned away. "At any rate," I said, "I don't belong there. Not anymore." It occurred to me that we were speaking Alzhenut. That was what they actually called the language—not "Alzhenese." We rarely spoke in English anymore when away from other humans.

"Where do you belong?" he asked, his blue eyes twinkling.

"Right now I'm thinking I belong in our bed."

"Then I think I belong there too."

He lowered his face to mine and kissed me. I couldn't stop myself from tracing a finger along the seam of his crotch, but I stopped short of caressing it. I'd developed something of a fetish for watching him pop out. But that wouldn't have been appropriate public behavior in either of our cultures.

With a reluctant groan, Dalsing broke the kiss. We were both panting, but I was distracted from my lecherous thoughts by the brilliantly lit crescent moon coming into view above us. It wasn't really any larger than it looked from the surface of the Earth, but outside the atmosphere, it was brighter. And it was gorgeous. I realized this could easily be the last time I'd ever see it, and the thought saddened me. But I'd found my happiness elsewhere, and I was prepared to leave my old life behind in order to grasp it.

Dalsing seemed to sense I needed a minute. So we watched the stars slowly rotate over our heads while the ship's navigational computers plotted a course for the Alzhen-Ai system. Only when the moon completely disappeared from view did I turn my head to smile at him. Then without a word, my husband took my hand and escorted me to our quarters.

The Sheriff of Para Siempre

Author's Note

THIS WAS originally written for Kim Fielding's wonderful anthology *Once Upon a Time in the Weird West*, and is, so far, my only attempt at a western. It ended up being one of my favorite novellas. I adore Billy and Joe. I believe it's one of the most emotional stories I've written. Few of my stories bring me to tears. This one does.

I lived in New Mexico as a teenager, so I'm very familiar with camping in the desert. If you can take the heat, it's beautiful and much slower-paced than New England, where I live now. I also visited more than one ghost town, usually attached to mines that were exhausted. And yes, they were creepy.

However, I was surprised to discover that New Mexico wasn't actually a state until 1912. It was a territory annexed from Mexico at the conclusion of the Mexican-American War (1848) called the New Mexico Territory, which was twice as large as New Mexico today. In 1897, that territory was divided into the Arizona Territory and the New Mexico Territory.

Billy and Joe are roaming around in the middle of all that, in 1875.

New Mexico Territory, 1875

IT WAS about ten years after Robert E. Lee surrendered at Appomattox. Course, I wasn't there to see it. I was way out in the New Mexico territory. I kinda remembered the territory bein' split in two to form the Arizona territory, but mostly I just remember the gold and silver miners travelin' through on their way to newly discovered mines in the territories—mines that often closed just as fast.

But Billy and me, we had our own problems. We'd stayed too long in Golden. We were dumb enough to think we were makin' real friends, and maybe we might settle there. Big mistake.

But before I go into all that, let me tell you about Billy. He was probably the prettiest man I've ever seen, before or since. Not pretty like a girl, really. If he took off his shirt, you could see he was fairly rugged for someone so thin. But he had a pretty face. Long lashes, wide eyes the color of turquoise, a delicate nose, and soft, full lips that had no business bein' on a man. Billy always kept his blond hair cut short, on account of everyone teasin' him if it got too long. Soon as he let it grow, it got as curly and soft as a newborn baby's.

He was beautiful, all right. And I loved him. Which made things kind of difficult, 'cause, you see, I'm a man too.

My name is Joe. And I reckon I'm all right to look at—nothin' special. Brown hair, brown eyes, probably kind of plain by most people's definitions. But Billy saw something in me, 'cause he loved me right back. If there's nothing else in the whole universe I'm sure of, I'm sure of that. Billy loved me. And after I'm done tellin' this, you'll see why I ain't never doubted that.

I was a little beefier than Billy at the time, I reckon. Maybe a little stronger. And I could handle myself in a fight. But make no mistake— Billy was the one lookin' out for us. That's 'cause he'd come into possession of a Colt Single Action Army revolver—I ain't gonna say how—and that thing was like a natural part of his body. Somehow he always managed to hit his target, and he could fire off all six shots faster than any man. When Billy drew that gun, he was like an avenging angel. Nothin' could stop him.

A man with that kind of skill with a firearm could've run roughshod over the farmers and miners in those parts. There weren't no lawmen in most of the small towns. Hell, some of 'em didn't even have main streets. They were just clusters of houses and farms. But me and Billy, we weren't the type of men to do that. We knew these people were barely scraping by, and we had no desire to make their lives harder. Billy got it into his head we were some kind of heroes, protectin' good folk from thugs and bandits.

For a little bit of *dinero*, of course. We had to eat.

Anyway, we were staying at a ranch house just outside of Golden, after taking care of a little land dispute between two neighboring ranches. The family was nice, though I wasn't thrilled with the way the oldest daughter kept making cow eyes at Billy. I think her parents were hoping he'd marry her. But that all went south the night Billy and I got a little loud in bed. Mr. Tanner kicked that door in and stuck a shotgun in our faces. We scrambled out of bed so fast, Billy barely had time to grab his gun belt from the bedpost before we tumbled out the open window. A blast of buckshot just missed my bare ass, and I landed hard on Billy. Fortunately it wasn't a long fall, and we scurried out of the yard as the bastard fired off another shot over our heads.

Billy was fit to be tied. We had nothin'—no clothes, no money, no food. Worse, Tanner had just insulted us, after we'd done so much for him. Billy ran around to the front of the house and pounded on the door. A minute later, Tanner opened it with his gun half raised. But he froze when he came face-to-face with the barrel of Billy's revolver.

"I got half a mind to give you a third eye," Billy said. Even though he was talkin' quiet-like, I could tell he was angry enough to do it. "Joe. Take his gun."

I did what he said.

Tanner held both hands up in surrender. "Don't get excited. I didn't hit either of ya."

"You couldn't hit a cow standin' still," Billy spat. "Now I'll give Ellie to the count o' twenty to toss all our shit out to us, if she don't want to be a widow. One… two… three…."

He didn't hit ten before a big heap of clothing came tumbling out the door from between Tanner's legs. I scooped it all up and held it against my chest, which was awkward, on account of the two pair of boots. I figured we could dress when we were away from those ungrateful grangers. A second later, the sacks Billy and I used to carry our meager possessions tumbled out.

I heard Ellie say something from inside, but it was too faint for me to make out. Billy asked, "What was that?"

"I said, 'Now take your filth off our land!'"

Tanner eyed the barrel of Billy's gun nervously. "Don't rile him, Ellie...."

"A gun won't help them come Judgment Day," Ellie hissed. "They've traded their immortal souls for the sins of the flesh."

"Ellie!"

She shut up, but I doubted Billy woulda shot Tanner, even if she'd kept squawkin'—tempting as it might've been. I never saw him kill anybody just for shootin' their mouth off, and we got what we needed. I grabbed one of the bags, and he grabbed the other. Then we backed away from the door, Billy keeping his revolver aimed at Tanner's head until the door closed.

Then we hightailed it off the ranch, stopping just a little ways down the road to pull our clothes on. I was pleased to see I still had my wallet on my belt, and Ellie had either been too decent—or more likely too rushed—to clean it out.

THE DESERT in midsummer wasn't a bad place to spend the night. It was warm and dry, and as long as you didn't accidentally step on a rattler, they usually wouldn't bother you. There was enough yucca and mesquite around to make a small fire, so we built one, more to cheer ourselves up than to keep warm.

Billy and I lay down on the ground next to each other with our bags tucked under our heads, and he draped one of his long arms across my belly. But I was too upset to sleep. Not just about being kicked out of a comfortable bed, but... I'd been feelin' kind of cozy living with the Tanners. They'd seemed like real nice folks. I weren't at all happy about the way things had turned out.

"What's wrong?" Billy asked.

"Nothin'," I said, not really knowing what there was to say about it. What was done was done.

"We just need to find a place of our own, where no one will bother us."

"You wanna build a house right here in the desert?"

He laughed. "We don't got much by way of food. We're gonna have to go into town tomorrow."

I knew that. My stomach was already unhappy about being awake at this time of night without something to eat. I shifted and asked, "Do you ever wonder about all that Bible stuff?"

"Not much."

"You don't think we're endangerin' our immortal souls, or whatever the heck Ellie said?"

Billy snorted. Then he kissed me nice and sweet on the mouth. When he was done, he said, "I ain't worried about it. If God don't want my soul, when I die, you can have it."

That made me nervous. Billy and I weren't real religious, but still… you didn't joke about stuff like that. "You can't give someone your soul. It's either God's or it's the devil's."

"It's my soul," Billy insisted, "so I should be able to do what I like with it. And I'm givin' it to you."

I was pretty sure that was blasphemy, but it made me feel warm inside to hear him say it. So I kissed him and said, "All right, then. I promise to take good care of it."

BILLY AND I walked to the center of Golden the next morning, stopping in at the general store for some supplies—some cornbread and sourdough biscuits, buffalo jerky, and a few apples. The apples wouldn't keep long in the desert, but they'd be good for a day or so. We also grabbed a box of Arbuckle's, since we had an old can we used to brew the coffee in. Mr. Lyttle smiled at us, just like normal, so I figured he hadn't heard anything from the Tanners yet. But that wouldn't last long. We knew we had to get outta there afore word spread about how degenerate we was.

"You boys plannin' on leaving us?" he asked.

"Yessir," Billy replied. "We done what we came to do."

"Where you gonna go now?"

"Not sure. Know any place that's looking for a hired gun?"

Lyttle shook his head, but one of the younger fellas sitting in the corner with his buddies—Tommy Harris—spit his tobacco in the brass spittoon and said, "There's a mining town up north—place called Para Siempre."

"Para Siempre!" Lyttle said with a laugh. "Thought that place'd be a ghost town by now."

"Near enough," Tommy said, tipping back to balance on the rear legs of the chair. "Silver vein played out, oh… five, six years back. Most of the miners've up and left. Don't think they got more'n a general store and a saloon up there now. But ever' once in a while, someone finds a little more silver—not much, but enough to keep the diehards diggin' away at it."

"We ain't miners," I said.

He snorted. "Didn't ya hear what I said? They don't need miners. What they need is someone like Billy here, who's good with a sidearm, to protect the miners is left from being robbed. Or *killed* and robbed. They had a sheriff, but he had a run-in last year. Someone shot him in the back." Tommy shook his head sadly. "Nobody else is dumb enough to take the job."

Billy was. I could tell by the way his eyes kinda narrowed and his mouth quirked up on one side. He was the best around with a gun, and he weren't afraid o' nothing. I had a bad feelin' about Para Siempre, but I knew that's where we were going.

We filled our canteens at the pump in front of the store. Then we walked south on the road out of town 'til we got to the crossroads. There a road headed northwest to the Rio Grande. The river was a day's walk from town, but we figured it would be better to stick close to water. Tommy said this mining town was a fair ways to the north, and it would take us a few days to reach it—'specially without horses.

We rested a spell when we came across a shady spot near the cliffs, taking a short nap until the sun passed by overhead. But we reached the Rio by nightfall and set up camp near the bank. That first night, we were so exhausted we barely had the strength to build a fire, but Billy wanted to boil up some Arbuckle's. He was the only man I knew who could down a mug o' coffee and fall asleep right after.

I stretched out on the ground behind him, while he sat close to the fire, swirling the black sludge in the pan around with a stick. I was feelin' a mite horny, so I stuck my hand up the back of Billy's shirt. He ignored me, but he didn't stop me from caressin' his smooth skin. He didn't say anything when I put my hand inside the waistband of his trousers either, but when I tried to slide around to the front, he slapped me through the canvas.

"Get that tarantula outta there afore I stab it with my knife."

"You can stab me, if'n you want," I said, sliding my hand around a bit more 'til I could grab holt of him.

He grunted, but he stopped trying to push me away. "Ain't you tired? I am."

"This don't feel tired to me," I said, giving his hard cock a squeeze.

"Well… the *rest* of me is. I just wanna drink my coffee and fall over."

"Fall over on top o' me, then."

Billy snickered, but he went back to ignoring me. So I just kept strokin' him. He acted like he had no idea I was there, 'cept for unbuttonin' his trousers a little in the front to give me more room. Suddenly he stopped stirring the coffee and jumped up on his knees, yankin' hisself away from my hand. But it was too late. He pulled open the rest of the buttons in his fly, letting his hard cock flop out just as it started spurting.

"Well, don't *waste* it!" I scooted forward and took him in my mouth as he was still spewin'. I swallowed it all 'til he was spent. Then he pulled away and sat down hard on his rump.

"You don't have to *eat* it," he said.

"I like it," I said, tellin' the truth. I couldn't say it tasted good, exactly, but I liked it. I knew nobody else had ever tasted him like that, and that made it sweet. "The Arbuckle's is boilin' over."

While Billy turned back to tend to that, his spit-slicked cock still pokin' out of his fly, I lay back and popped open my buttons so I could take care of myself. I knew it wouldn't take long—not with the taste of him still in my mouth. But Billy had different ideas. He set the pan off to one side of the fire and then got on his hands and knees. He batted my hand out of the way and sucked me into his mouth. I knew he didn't like the taste like I did, so I tried to warn him. But all I got out was a strangled grunt, and then I was floodin' his mouth. He swallowed it all.

"There," he said, comin' up to kiss me. I tasted myself on his lips, and the flavor mixed with his taste in my mouth. That made it even better. "You happy now?" he asked.

"Not as happy as I'd be if we was unshucked."

"Land's sakes," Billy said with a shake of his head. "Let me drink some coffee first. Then we can do that, if'n it'll make you happy."

I took off my boots while he drank some of the thick brew right out o' the pan. Then I shucked my shirt and trousers. Neither of us owned any underthings. I walked to the river's edge and took a piss, and by the time I got back, Billy was unshucked hisself and diggin' through his bag for the one blanket we owned. It was pretty worn, and the wool even had a hole in it near one corner, but it did for us. He laid it down on the ground and stretched out on it. I crawled on top of him, pressing our bodies together in all the right places, and Billy tossed part of the blanket over my back, so we were snug like a burrito. I laid my head on his shoulder, and he wrapped his arms around me, and that's how we fell asleep.

I DIDN'T lay on top of him all night, or he probably woulda suffocated. I woke up lying on my side, with him pressed up against my back and his hard cock wedged between my asscheeks. He woke up as soon as I shifted, and before I knew it, he was kissing the back of my neck and sliding his hand up and down my front. I didn't have to coax him into anything that morning. He started rockin' his hips, inching that cock deeper and deeper between my cheeks, 'til it was bumping against my hole. Fortunately for me, the end of that thing tended to get real slick when he was horny. It was better if we could do it with butter or lard, but we had to make do.

"Put it in me," I whispered.

Billy gave out this soft little whimper, and then I felt him pressing harder at my hole. I saw stars for a second when his shaft popped inside and slid in all the way. But having him in me was the best feelin' in the world, and I was happy to trade a little pain for it. Tanner had interrupted it the night before. For that alone I coulda made him bite the ground. But having Billy inside me made everything right again.

The sun was rising and starting to make things pretty sweaty under the blanket, so we threw it off. I rolled onto my belly, and Billy climbed on top of me, pushing my legs apart so he could thrust in deeper.

"I wish we could always be joined like this," Billy whispered into my ear. Then he shoved in one last time, and I felt him filling me with spurts of liquid heat.

I ground myself into the blanket and cried out as I squirted into it. I was beyond talking at that point, but in my head I answered him.

We are. Forever.

PARA SIEMPRE barely counted as a town. One long dirt road snaked its way up into the foothills where the miners dug holes like ants, and along that was a bunch of rickety buildings that looked like they'd fall over the first time a strong wind hit 'em. Most of 'em was boarded up, including an abandoned hotel and what mighta been a bank. Billy and I passed a shack that mighta been a saloon and another that looked like a general store. The store had a sign in the window. Billy and I, we couldn't read, but we knew the word Closed when we saw it. We kept going 'til we found what we thought might be a sheriff's office and town jail, judgin' by the bars in some of the windows, but it was locked up tight. All the other buildings along the street that weren't boarded up—and there weren't many of 'em—looked like houses.

So we backtracked to the saloon and stepped inside. It was dark and nearly empty, but there was a bar, and the place reeked of old whiskey, tobacco, and vomit. The wooden floor was covered in straw, which could cover up all kinds o' things a man might not wanna step in.

"What can I do for you gentlemen?" a fella asked from behind the bar, grinnin' at us with a mouthful o' brown teeth, like he'd been chewin' since he was a baby.

"Who runs this place?" Billy asked.

"Runs the saloon? Well, I do."

"I mean, who runs the town?"

The man snorted. "Nobody. We ain't got a mayor or nothin' like that. Not anymore. I run this here saloon—name's Eugene—and Teddy Wilcox has a general store a few houses down, if he ain't up at the mine. Anyone finds some ore, Teddy can assay it for 'em. Once a month, a coupla the boys take a wagon into Santa Fe to pick up supplies and mail. That's about it."

We didn't have much money left, after what we bought in Golden, but Billy sidled up to the bar and tossed a quarter down.

"That'll get you two shots," the barkeep said, snatchin' the coin up afore it even had time to stop rattling. "Your buddy want one too?"

"Sure he does."

There weren't no seats at the bar, so I just leaned my elbows on it, making sure to stay out of the wet spots. The barkeep slapped a couple glasses down in front of us, then splashed some brown liquid into 'em from a bottle. The smell of it kinda curled my nose hairs when I lifted it to my mouth, but I threw it back. We paid for it, after all. It burned all the way down and tasted like goat piss, but I wished Billy would toss another quarter on the bar. A man might feel pretty good after a few drinks o' that.

"I heard," Billy said, "this town might be lookin' for a new sheriff."

That got a big ol' belly laugh. Eugene stoppered the bottle and wiped it off with a dirty rag. Then he put it up on a shelf behind the bar, next to a few others. "*Lookin'* is kind of a strong word. We don't have a sheriff, 'cause the last one got shot trying to stop the Cassidy brothers from taking their fair share o' Ben Wilder's ore. He got hisself shot, and he got poor Ben shot too."

"What do you mean 'their fair share'?" Billy asked.

The barkeep shrugged and tossed the rag under the bar. "Well, they got more men and more guns than anybody else in town, so they feel it's only fair they get a percentage of all the ore that comes out of those hills."

"So you don't want a sheriff, then?" Billy asked.

"You ever been a sheriff before?"

"Naw," Billy said, shaking his head. "But I can shoot the scales off a sleepin' rattler without waking him."

Eugene spread his hands like it weren't no big concern of his. "I s'pose we could use someone to deal with the drunks when they get outta hand. Not that we want you to *shoot* 'em, necessarily. But we ain't lookin' for someone who wants to stir up trouble."

"By 'trouble,' you mean upsettin' the Cassidys."

"That's right."

"What if these Cassidys up and kill someone?" Billy asked.

Eugene looked uncomfortable. "Well… long as a man don't rile 'em, he won't have to worry 'bout that."

"But if he does rile 'em?"

"Look, friend," Eugene said patiently, "if you got any ideas about messin' with the Cassidys, you'd best move on. We don't need troublemakers. Understand?"

Billy glanced at me. He understood, all right. And I could tell he weren't too keen on the idea of ignorin' lawbreakers, if he was s'posed to be the sheriff. But he asked, "Does the job pay?"

"There ain't much money exchangin' hands these days. We paid the last fella in credit at the general store."

Billy and I looked at each other. That wasn't a terrific deal, but food was food. And there might be other things we could get in the store— things we could use. Billy could handle a drunk now and then. Heck, I could probably do that much. Sounded like the worst thing in town were the Cassidy brothers, but if nobody wanted us to mess with 'em... well, we could probably manage that.

"Where would we stay?" Billy asked.

"At the sheriff's office. There's a cot in the front for you. Your buddy can sleep in the cell—long as nobody else needs it." Eugene looked at us closely a moment, then added, "By the way, if you two are hoping to go pirootin' about with the ladies in town... we ain't got none."

I'd been afraid he was gonna accuse us o' something—maybe chase us outta town afore we even settled in. But that didn't seem to be what he was gettin' at. "You ain't got no ladies?"

"Not a one. We had a cat wagon come by last spring on its way south, but it didn't stay long. The bawdy house closed down a coupla years back. So you'll just have to make do on your own." He snickered in a way that made me wanna take a bath.

I had to wonder if, in a town without no womenfolk, the men might be doing what Billy and I did. But even if they were, they'd probably be all secretive about it. Which meant we'd have to be just as careful here as anywhere else. Maybe more. Men got strange about stuff like that. They might start feelin' guilty and looking for someone to blame for it.

But Billy smiled at Eugene and said, "That ain't a problem. Who do I talk to about the job?"

"There ain't really no one to talk to," Eugene said with a shrug, "so I reckon I can hire you. I s'pose we should clear it with Teddy when he gets back, seein' as how he'll be feeding you. But I can give you the key to the sheriff's office." He reached for a ribbon stuck up on a nail in the wall. A key was dangling from the end of it. He didn't seem inclined to take us there hisself. He just held the key out and said, "Five doors down. The one with the cell bars in the back window."

Billy took the key. "You got yourself a sheriff."

THE SHERIFF'S office was grubby, sad, and smelled like an outhouse. Didn't look like nobody had been inside since the last sheriff—we never got his name—so there was a layer of dust over everything. A metal plate of something unrecognizable, turned black with mold and dried to the enamel, sat on the desk, and a bucket in the cell had been used as a piss pot—though what was in it weren't piss. It was mostly dry but still reeked to high heaven.

"Welcome to our new home," Billy said, disgusted.

I saw a brown canvas duster hanging on a peg and reached out to touch it. Then I realized it belonged to a dead man, so I yanked my hand away. "We'd be better off sleepin' outside."

"Won't be so bad," Billy said, "once we clean it up a bit."

"Just what I wanted to spend my day doing—cleaning up month-old shit."

Billy laughed and snagged me with one hand, pulling me close. He noticed the open curtain and dragged me outta sight of anyone walkin' by. "I'd kiss you," he said, "but all I can think about right now is that smell."

So we cleaned the place up. Not like we had a choice, if we was gonna sleep there that night. We tossed the nasty bucket and the plate into the alley behind the jail, along with a sack of what might've been apples once. The alley was full of trash, anyway. The windows didn't open, but we propped the door open to let air in. Though it was a hot day, so it didn't do much good.

We didn't know what to do with the old sheriff's belongings, not that he had much—some clothes folded up all tidy in a corner, a whiskey flask, a book with a title we couldn't cipher.... It felt wrong to throw these things away—'specially the book—but we had no use for 'em. Not like we was gonna wear his clothes. We tucked them under a chair for now. Then Billy swept the floor and called it good enough.

"Where the heck are we gonna sleep?" I asked when the place was about as clean as it was gonna get. There was a cot by one wall, but it weren't big enough for the both of us.

"I reckon one of us will have to sleep in the cell, like Eugene said."

"Have you seen that cot?" I asked. "The drunks in this town've been sweatin' all over it. It's probably full of bugs."

"We cain't be sure this sheriff was any cleaner," Billy pointed out.

"His cot sure *looks* cleaner," I insisted. To be fair, after four days on the road, me and Billy weren't so clean ourselves. But Billy would have to be pretty bad afore I refused to snuggle up to him. A filthy, bug-infested cot slept on by a bunch of drunk strangers... well, that was another thing.

"All right," Billy said, giving in. "I'll sleep in the cell. You take this one out here."

It still meant I'd be sleeping alone, which I hated, but I s'posed it was the best I could do. I felt a little guilty making Billy take the dirtier cot, but then I reminded myself he was the one wanted to be sheriff—not me.

OUR FIRST few days in Para Siempre was pretty uneventful. By the end of the second day, Billy and me was getting' pretty hungry. We'd run outta jerky and apples. We still had a few coins left, but Eugene didn't have much for us to buy but whiskey, and Teddy hadn't come back from where he was camping in the hills to open the general store up.

Eugene gave us some of his own grub that night, but he clearly didn't like partin' with it. So the next morning, he broke into the general store and let us grab about a week's worth of supplies.

"Teddy better not give me any guff o'er this," he muttered. "If he can't mind his own store while the sheriff starves to death, it's his own get-out."

Course, Teddy hadn't exactly agreed to hire Billy on as sheriff. But we wasn't gonna argue.

Men wandered in and out of town during the week, generally stopping at Eugene's saloon, and he kept tellin' everyone Billy was the new sheriff. None of 'em got too excited about it. They was polite. But they probably figured he wouldn't be around long. The last sheriff hadn't lasted more'n a month.

But when Eugene told 'em Billy was a crack shot… well, that was somethin' they wanted to see. Billy was more than happy to oblige. We all went outta the saloon into the street, and he said, "Pick a target."

"How 'bout that turkey vulture up yonder?" someone asked, pointing to the bird circling overhead.

"I'm not gonna kill somethin' for no good reason," Billy said. "Pick somethin' that ain't living."

They probably thought he was afraid to try for something that far away, but I knew better. I'd seen him shoot cattle rustlers and bandits dead in their tracks, but he wouldn't shoot a dog 'less it was rabid, and he only killed other animals if he planned to cook 'em.

Another man pointed at a rusted weather vane on what looked to be an abandoned house at the far end of the road. The roof was half caved in, so the weather vane stuck up at a funny angle, and the cock on the end swayed back and forth in the wind. At that distance it'd be pretty hard to hit.

But Billy grinned and said, "Shoot! That's 'n easy one!"

He drew his pistol and fired, quicker'n I could say it, and that rusty ol' bird flew off with a clang. Everyone stood there a minute, jaws hangin' open. Then someone hooted, and they all laughed. For the next hour or so, they pointed out targets and Billy shot 'em all. He never missed once.

Finally they all admitted they was impressed, and Billy said he didn't wanna waste no more bullets. So they took us inside, and somebody bought him a drink. Billy swilled it down, and Eugene filled the shot glass up again as soon as it hit the bar. Billy slid it my way, and I snatched it up, so Eugene shook his head and poured Billy another one.

For a few days after that, everything was pretty good. All the men were friendly to us on the street, we got the sheriff's office mopped and at least tolerable to live in, and Teddy finally showed up to open the general store. He was a friendly-lookin' man—bald and round-faced with a bushy white mustache, and kinda thick about the middle. He weren't too happy to find out we'd been rootin' through his stock, but Eugene smoothed that over. Then Billy and me was able to take what we needed—within reason. That included a couple o' decent blankets for the cots.

I still wasn't happy with the sleepin' arrangements. Even with the curtains pulled and the door locked, there weren't no way we could sleep together, and it weren't easy to have more'n a tiff in one of the cots or on that wooden floor.

"We won't stay here long," Billy kept tellin' me. "Not less'n we build ourselves our own house."

"In this ugly dirt hole?" I said, disgusted. "Who'd wanna live here? If'n you wanna play sheriff for a while, you go right ahead. But I don't wanna stick around long."

"You ain't gonna leave me, are ya?" Billy looked really upset at that thought.

I tossed my shirt at him. "Heck, no! Anywhere I go, you're comin' with me."

BILLY'S DUTIES as sheriff weren't much. A coupla times some of the fellas in Eugene's got a little rowdy, so me and Billy had to break it up. It weren't too hard—they didn't give us much trouble. But the night Billy brought one of 'em back to the jail to sleep it off, he ended up having to sleep in the desk chair, since the drunk man passed out in his cot. I offered to let Billy take my cot, or at least trade off during the night, but he just told me to go to sleep.

"You wake me after a few hours," I said. "Then we can switch."

"Sure, Joe."

But he didn't wake me. Next thing I knew, the drunk fella was shouting, "Hey!"

I opened my eyes to see sunlight comin' through the gap between the curtains and spillin' across the wooden floorboards. I squinted up at Billy, but he was asleep in the chair, the brim of his slouch hat covering his eyes.

"Hey! Deputy!"

It was the man in the cell. I sat up and tried to focus on him. "What?"

"I gotta piss."

"So? Use the bucket."

"There ain't no bucket." He rattled the cell door. "And ya locked me in!"

We'd forgotten to replace the nasty bucket we'd tossed out back. I stood and fetched the keyring off the nail over my head. Billy stirred and yawned, liftin' his hat up to see what all the ruckus was about.

"Sorry, friend," I told the man as I unlocked the cell door.

"This mean I'm free to go?"

I glanced at Billy who nodded.

"Long as you keep outta trouble," I said, trying to sound official-like.

"I will, deputy. Word of honor." He tipped his hat at Billy as he hurried out. "Sheriff."

When we was alone, Billy snickered and stood up to stretch. "Deputy?"

"You got anyone else lined up for the job?"

"Nope."

So that's how I became the deputy sheriff of Para Siempre.

Turned out, everyone more or less already thought I was, 'cept Billy and me. We were the last to know. But that was fine. Can't say I minded. It gave me some authority in the town, and the work weren't too hard. Better yet, nobody questioned me and Billy stickin' to each other like glue.

So things went along just fine for a while.

'Til the day it all came apart, 'til the worst day of my whole life—the day that made me wish I'd never even heard the name Para Siempre.

IT STARTED with the first big rain of the season. It poured down so heavy, hardly anyone left their houses, 'cept to run to the saloon. Teddy didn't even bother openin' the store. Billy and I was hanging out in the saloon, leaning against the bar and drinkin' some of the swill Eugene passed off as whiskey and watchin' some of the fellas play a game of poker at the only table in the room. We never played ourselves. For one thing, we had no money. And even if we had, cards just wasn't our thing. But we liked to be sociable.

It was getting pretty late, though, and we were thinkin' of turning in. That's when the door opened and two big men came in, drippin' wet.

Eugene nudged Billy and said in a low voice, "The Cassidys."

Jed and Nick Cassidy were twins, so we'd been told. And they looked it. I couldn't tell one from the other. When they took off their Stetsons, I could see they were downright handsome—curly dark hair, blue eyes, rugged features. Unfortunately, everyone had warned us they were about as mean as any men could be. As they strode up to the bar, shakin' the water off their backs like wet dogs, one of 'em—I didn't know if it was Jed or Nick—growled, "Whiskey."

They didn't toss any coins down, but Eugene hurried to pour a coupla shot glasses for 'em.

The one closest to us—the one who hadn't spoke yet—looked at Billy, and his eyes kinda narrowed. He smirked, and I knew what he was thinkin'. He liked what he saw. "I don't believe we've been introduced, friend."

"You can call me Billy. My friend here is Joe."

"Name's Nick." The man looked past Billy at me and seemed to like the look o' me too. "My brother's Jed. You're kinda new here, ain't you?"

"Just a few weeks," I said. I was kinda surprised at how he was eyein' us like that in front of the whole saloon—like he wanted to see us both unshucked. It was one thing for me and Billy to be that way with each other in private, but we wouldn'ta been caught dead doing that in front of people. Nick didn't seem to care, and all the fellas around us was actin' like they weren't seein' nothing special. Maybe they were used to it.

"Billy here is the new sheriff," Eugene said helpfully.

Nick's eye twitched. "The sheriff, huh? I heard about you. You're some kinda sharpshooter, ain't ya?"

"I'm pretty good."

"'S that so?" Jed asked, squinting at him. "I'm pretty good with a revolver myself. Ain't that so, Eugene?"

Eugene's head went up and down like a fishin' float. "That's right, Jed! Nobody shoots as good as you!"

A muscle twitched in Billy's jaw—a sure sign he was gettin' annoyed. Not much riled him, but he was proud of his shootin' ability. And up 'til now, everyone in town had been sayin' he was the best they'd ever saw. I was pretty sure Eugene was just tryin' to stay on Jed's good side, but just in case, I decided to intervene afore Billy did somethin' stupid like challenge Jed to a shootin' match.

See, I figured that couldn't turn out right for us, either way. If Billy lost, he'd get all morose about it. And if Jed lost… well, from what I'd been hearin', we didn't want to make enemies of the Cassidys.

So I tugged on Billy's sleeve and said, "I'm gettin' real tired."

"Reckon it *is* pretty late," Billy said. "We should turn in."

"Together?" Nick asked, givin' us an unpleasant smile.

Billy ignored the question. "We was thinkin' about taking a look at the mine tomorrow. We still ain't seen it."

"Not much to see. But, heck, Jed and me is headin' back there tomorrow. Why don't you stay and have a drink with us? We'd be happy to take you up to the mine in the morning."

Billy knew as well as me it was time to get outta there afore things got ugly, but we couldn't just walk out after an invite like that. He nodded at Eugene. "We'll have one more."

Nick laughed and slapped him on the back. His hand stayed there a mite too long, but Billy didn't say nothing about it. When Eugene refilled our shot glasses, Billy picked his up and said, "Here's how!"

We all repeated the toast and downed our whiskey, which worked to get Nick's hand off Billy's back.

"Joe and me will be real happy for your company tomorrow," Billy said, "but we're real tired now. So, if you'll excuse us…." He nodded and sauntered away from the bar. I followed him.

Nick snorted, but he didn't try to stop us again. He just said, "Later, my friends."

But I had the unpleasant feelin' he weren't done with us yet.

It was a couple hours later I woke up to someone pounding on the door of the sheriff's office. "Hey, sheriff!" a man shouted. I didn't recognize the voice, 'cause he was kinda slurring his words. "We need help out here!"

"Christ almighty," Billy muttered as he staggered from the cell to the door in his skivvies. In the dark I could barely see him grab his gun belt and cinch it around his waist. He threw back the bolt and opened the door, something he normally wouldn'ta done dressed like that, 'cept Para Siempre didn't have no women to worry about offending. "What's all the ruckus?"

Soon as the door was unbolted, someone pushed it open wide. The rain must've stopped, 'cause the cloudy sky was lit up with moonlight. Then two men walked in, and my stomach clenched. They was just dark shapes against the clouds, but I knew who they was—the Cassidys. They stank of that rotgut Eugene passed off as whiskey.

"Sorry to wake you, sheriff, but Nick here's got an emergency."

"What's the matter?"

One of 'em closed the door, making the room dark again. I stood and found my way to the desk, where we had a kerosene lamp and some matchsticks.

"He's had just a mite too much to drink," Jed said.

I struck one of the matches, and everybody was lit up by the flame. I didn't like what I saw. Jed was standin' real close to Billy, kinda looming over him, and Nick was leaning against the door, blocking it.

Billy looked at Nick and said, "Don't you got someplace for him to sleep it off?" He probably didn't want Nick taking his cot for the night, and I sure didn't want either o' those fellas hanging around for long.

I lit the kerosene lamp and shook the match out.

"I don't think he wants to sleep," Jed said.

"No." Nick reached back to throw the bolt on the door. "I sure don't."

Billy glanced at me, and I could tell he was gettin' nervous. I was about shittin' my skivvies. All we had was Billy's gun against these two brutes, and they both had guns of their own. I had one too, but my gun belt was hanging on the wall near Nick.

"See, Nick here is a little… skewed. Most fellas, when there ain't any womenfolk around… we have to improvise. Some of us are willin' to help each other out." Jed shrugged. "What happens between friends in the dark… well, that ain't nobody else's business. But Nick actually *likes* it that way. You get my meaning?"

Billy folded his arms across his chest. "Yeah, I do. But like you said, that ain't none of my business."

Nick sniggered at that. "Come on, pretty boy. You know exactly what we're talking about. We been hearin' a lot about you since you came to town. Your gun's not the only thing you been shootin' off in here."

Billy gritted his teeth but didn't say nothing. So I said, "I thought you said that ain't nobody's business."

I could tell right off by the grin that spread across Nick's face that I shouldn'ta said that. I'd pretty much admitted what he suspected.

"We ain't here to judge you," Jed said, stepping forward 'til he was no more'n a few inches away from Billy. "Nick just wants to be friends. And since he's my brother, it's my job to make sure he gets what he wants."

Billy looked him directly in the eye. "Meaning what?"

"Meaning I'd be much obliged if one of you—or the both of ya— could show my brother a good time tonight."

"No."

"Now, don't be hasty," Jed said, holding one hand up. "He don't wanna cut in on your… friendship. He just wants a little fun. Nothin' to be jealous about. And he'll make sure you have fun too."

"The answer's still no."

"Maybe you want both of us," Nick said quickly. "He'll do it, if'n you want."

His brother didn't look none too happy about that idea, but he shrugged.

But even though they was both pretty good-lookin', I didn't want nothing to do with 'em, and neither did Billy. He rested his hand on his gun and popped the leather strip off the hammer, so's he could draw if he had to.

Suddenly I was looking down the barrel of Nick's revolver.

"I'd take your hand away from your gun, if I was you," Jed told Billy.

Billy glanced my way, then took his hand away from his gun real slow.

Jed took the revolver outta Billy's holster. "That's better. Now, you wanna think about our offer again?"

"We ain't interested," I said, glaring at Nick. I was scared, but I weren't no coward.

"Find somebody else to have fun with," Billy said.

Nick looked kinda hurt and surprised, like he couldn't fathom why anyone would turn down a tumble with him.

But Jed just sighed and shook his head. "If that's the way it's gonna be," he said. He walked to the door and unbolted it. Then he turned back to us. "We were just bein' friendly. But you had to insult us. It's bad enough you insult me, but you insulted my brother. You're gonna regret that."

I started to protest. "Nobody insulted—"

"I ain't gonna let this go," Jed interrupted. He looked directly at Billy. "You think you're such a hotshot with a gun, you meet me outside this door tomorrow at noon. We'll see how good you are." He hung Billy's revolver on one of the wooden coat pegs by the door by the trigger guard. "Come on, Nick."

Nick looked like he wanted to put a bullet in my face, but he backed up until he was near the door. Then he holstered his gun and followed Jed outside.

Billy jumped forward and shut the door, bolting it. "Christ, those two are off their nuts!"

I couldn't say nothing at first. I was shakin' too much. I sat down on my cot and said, finally, "We need to get outta here, Billy. Jed's gonna kill you! Then he's gonna kill me!"

"Nobody's gonna kill us." Billy came and sat beside me and gathered me up in his arms. I was a quiverin' mess. "I'm better'n him. They cheated, just now, pointin' a gun at you. Otherwise I wouldn'ta backed down."

That was the problem, I reckoned. Billy always played fair. But the Cassidys wouldn't. I knew that sure as I knew anything.

THE NEXT mornin' was dry and sunny, though the ground was covered in mud. Billy and me ate some o' the apples and biscuits we got from Teddy's, wishin' we had some hot water for Arbuckle's. But that woulda meant building a fire in the alley out back, and it was too wet for that.

We went over to Eugene's and washed our breakfast down with some whiskey. It tried to burn a hole in our guts, but it sure woke us up.

Eugene and everyone else there was lookin' at us funny, like they was surprised to find us still alive. When Billy asked for another one, Eugene sloshed some whiskey in his shot glass, and said, "On the house. But don't let yourself get fuddled."

"I don't intend to."

We was too antsy to hang out in the saloon for long, so we took a stroll around the town. Para Siempre was a miserable place—nothin' but empty, half-caved-in buildings, mud and dirt, and brown grass. But we'd come to like it there. The fellas in town were mostly good folk, 'cept the Cassidys, and didn't seem to worry 'bout what Billy and I might be up to in private. We'd lived nicer places where folks treated us worse.

"What're we gonna do," I asked, "after you kill Jed?"

Billy laughed. "Well, I don't reckon Nick's the forgivin' type. And they got friends in town. We'll probably have to get out fast."

"Probably," I agreed, though I weren't happy about it.

By the time we got back to the sheriff's office, there was a crowd gathered. I didn't own a watch, but our shadows were about as short as they could get, so it had to be close to noon.

Billy stopped walkin' for a bit. "You listen to me," he told me under his breath. "I know I'm better than this blowhard, but... if something should go wrong...."

"Nothin's gonna go wrong."

"No. But... just in case it does... you do whatever you have to, to survive."

"I ain't gonna fuck Nick Cassidy!" I practically yelled, pissed that he'd even consider I'd stoop to it.

"I ain't sayin' I *want* you to. I'm just sayin' nobody could blame ya."

"Nobody's *gonna* blame me, 'cause I ain't gonna do it!"

Billy smiled, and I could tell he was glad, even though it could get me killed. "All right. Then you run. Get the heck out of town afore they can catch you. Don't hang around here. You got that?"

"I got it." But as we started walking again, I muttered, "Just you shoot that son-o'-bitch, so I don't gotta worry about that."

"I will."

As we got closer, the crowd parted, and Jed Cassidy stepped forward with Nick on his heels. "You see, boys?" he said with a wide grin. "This here sheriff ain't a coward like the last one. I told you he'd show."

From the looks on their faces, I reckoned Eugene and Teddy was hopin' we'd run. I was kinda wishin' that myself. But Billy was too proud.

"I'm here," Billy said. "How you wanna do this?"

"I say we just step out into the street, and Teddy can count down for us."

"Me?" Teddy asked, lookin' like a coyote caught in a trap. "I don't want no part of this!"

Nick gave him a shove. "Don't be such a yellowbelly! All ya gotta do is count down from three. If I do it, you'll all think Jed and me is cheatin'."

Teddy weren't at all happy about the situation, but he finally let hisself be talked into it—'specially after Billy said it was all right with him. Eugene made everyone go back inside the saloon, so's they wouldn't get hit by stray bullets, but I refused. I needed to be out there to see what happened. So I stood on the front stoop of the sheriff's office, and tried to keep myself from shakin'.

"Mind if I stand here?" Nick said, saunterin' over.

I'd as soon stand next to a grizzly bear, but I just shrugged and looked away. Nick leaned against the wall, smirkin' at me. But I ignored him, my eyes on the street.

Billy and Jed stood about fifty paces apart, both relaxed, their hands hoverin' near their hips.

Teddy stood nervously by the saloon door, clearly wishin' he was inside. But he raised his voice and said, "I'm gonna count down from five. Draw on one. Understand?"

"I understand," Billy said.

"Got it," Jed said.

"All right, then. You ready? Five... four... three...."

All o' sudden, bullets was flyin' everywhere. Not Billy's, and not Jed's either. They never reached for their guns. But shots was fired from the abandoned houses on either side of the street—more than I could count—and Billy jerked and twisted and flailed his arms as his body was shot to pieces.

"Billy!" I tried to run to him, but Nick grabbed me from behind and pinned me.

Billy fell to his knees and looked over at me, his teeth gritted in pain.

"Christ almighty!" Teddy cried out. I weren't lookin' at him, but I heard the saloon door slam shut, so I figured he'd run off.

My eyes were full of tears, and I could barely speak, but I shouted every cuss word I knew at Jed and Nick and kicked hard at Nick's legs. But he was pretty strong and had my arms folded up behind my back, so I could barely move. Jed ignored me. He just strolled over to Billy, his revolver pointed right at Billy's head. Billy tried to draw, but his arm was shot up. The Colt fell from his bloody fingers and landed in the mud.

"I warned you," Jed told him, drawing near and pointin' his revolver right between Billy's eyes. "Take one last look at your boy. 'Cause he ain't yours no more. We're all gonna have a piece of him."

Then he pulled the trigger.

I barely heard the gunshot over my own scream.

I'M NOT sure how it happened, but somehow I ended up tied to one of the hitching posts in front of the sheriff's office. There were men helping Nick truss me up—men I didn't recognize—but I was sobbing too much to really be aware of what was happening. I know Nick undid my belt and yanked my trousers clean off. He grabbed at my ass and cock while his men laughed.

But they didn't try to fuck me. I heard Jed call Eugene outta the saloon and tell him, "We're goin' up to the mine for a while. Nobody touches that pretty boy sheriff while we's gone, you hear?"

"We can't just… leave him there…."

"Nobody touches him!" Jed barked. "If I find him moved when I come back, I'll shoot every last one of you! The same goes for that deputy he was cornholing. You leave him just as he is. We'll see how stuck-up he is after a day o' that."

I didn't hear much else, 'cause I was crying my eyes out, and all I could think about was Billy's last moments, and how he was just lyin' there in the mud, and I couldn't get to him. I couldn't imagine any hell in the afterlife worse than what I'd just seen and what I was feelin' right then.

I cried myself dry. The sun was beatin' down on me and burning my ass and legs, but I hardly knew it. If I turned my head, I could see Billy's boots and legs lying out there in the street, but I couldn't see his face. I didn't think I'd be able to stand it, if I could.

At some point I musta passed out, 'cause I lost track of time. I heard Eugene talkin' all quiet, like he didn't want nobody to hear. "I can't stand it no more. You gotta at least have some water. It's hot as blazes out here."

A tin cup of water was pressed against my mouth, and I sucked it in without a thought. My throat was so dry, it hurt going down.

"I can't cut you loose," Eugene said. "They'll kill me if I do. I'm sorry."

I was barely able to talk, but I said, "It don't matter."

And it didn't.

NIGHT CAME, and I heard horses ride up. Men was laughing, and I think I heard someone kickin' at poor Billy.

"Someone gonna take that gun off him? Looks like a nice piece."

"You leave that there." That was Jed. "It's mine. I'll get it in a bit."

A hand slapped my ass, and Nick said, "Hoo-boy! You look red. We'd best get you inside before you ain't no good to me."

I s'pose it stung, but I hardly felt it. I weren't feeling nothing much by that point. Someone cut the rope holdin' me to the hitching post, and I fell down on the ground. Nick rolled me over so I could look up at his grinning mug.

"You's all mine now, deputy." He reached between my legs and jabbed a finger in me, making me grunt in pain. "I can do whatever I want."

A shot rang out, and Nick's eyes went wide as a spray of blood spit out the side of his head. He fell heavy on my chest and the breath was knocked outta me.

"Nick!" Jed screamed, and I saw him in the corner of my eye, drawing his revolver and turning in a panic. He didn't make it all the way 'round. Another shot, and he went down like a sack o' potatoes.

I couldn't see much of what was happening. I could barely move, anyway, and 'sides, I had a mangy cur lyin' on my chest and bleedin' all over my shirt. But I heard lots of screaming and shouting and gunfire.

Someone cried out, "He's alive! How—" A shot cut off the rest.

Then everything went quiet.

Sounding real far away, Eugene said, "Christ almighty…."

Someone walked toward me, and then I almost screamed myself as a pair o' bloody boots came into my sight. Billy's boots. For a second I thought, *Maybe he's still alive. Maybe he was just fakin' being dead all day, lyin' there in the mud.* But I knew it weren't true. Billy was dead.

I looked up his bloody trousers and shirt, shot full of holes. I saw his face lookin' down at me. 'Cept he wasn't really *looking*. His eyes were glassy and not really focused on me. Blood trickled down into one from the bullet hole in the middle of his forehead.

"Billy…." My voice broke, and I couldn't say nothing more.

He reached down and grabbed Nick by the shirt collar. Then with more strength than he'd ever had when he was alive, Billy lifted Nick's body with one hand and threw it out into the street. I gasped, not knowing what to expect next. I knew Billy would never hurt me, but… I couldn't be sure this was really Billy.

He didn't do anything to me. He just turned and walked into the sheriff's office.

I struggled to get up, and after I fell back on my ass, making me cry out in pain, Teddy and Eugene came to help me. They got me on my feet, though I couldn't stay there without them holding me.

"What in Sam Hill did I just see?" Teddy asked, staring wide-eyed at the open door to the sheriff's office.

Nobody answered him. Eugene shouted, "Somebody find his trousers!"

"I don't give a goldarn 'bout my trousers!" I snapped. It'd hurt like the blazes to put 'em on, and they'd all been starin' at my Johnson all day, anyway. "Take me in there."

"I ain't goin' anywhere near that door," Teddy said.

I growled, "Take me in there! Billy was my… my friend. I gotta see him."

"I don't know what that is," he said, "but it ain't your friend."

"He saved me from those curly wolves, didn't he?"

Teddy didn't have an answer for that, but he kept his peace while Eugene steered the three of us to the doorway. Inside, Billy was sitting at his desk. He weren't moving—just slumped in his chair, staring at nothing, one hand resting on the desk. We watched him for a long time, but he didn't move nor blink.

"He's dead," Eugene said. "He's gotta be. Look at all the holes in him."

He and Teddy wouldn't move no closer, so I pulled away from them and staggered to the desk. I had to grab it when my legs gave out from under me, but I edged around it on my knees 'til I was near enough to touch Billy's hand. It was cold, and I shivered at how the skin didn't really feel like skin no more. But I'll be darned if it didn't move to slide over my hand. I nearly screamed and pulled away, but I forced myself to keep my hand there. His fingers closed lightly on mine.

"Billy?" I looked up at his face, but he was still staring at nothin'.

I didn't know how it was possible. Billy was dead. I could see that, plain as day.

He just hadn't stopped moving yet.

OVER THE next several days, the fellas cleared all the bodies outta the street. I didn't know what they did with 'em, and I didn't care. If it'd been up to me, I probably would've done things to 'em I'd've been ashamed of, so… it was good I stayed out of it. I did order all the guns and ammo brought to me, and nobody fought me on that. I guess I was considered to be the sheriff now, since I'd been Billy's deputy.

I also got his slouch hat back. It had fallen off in the street when he'd been shot. It had mud and blood on it, but I scrubbed that off and set it on Billy's head. With the brim pulled down in the front, I could pretend there weren't a bullet hole in his forehead. Then I figured, if I was gonna go that far, I might as well clean him up. So I stripped him, washed him, and put his other trousers and shirt on him. And, yeah, it was every bit as awful as it sounds. But I did it.

Nobody would go near the sheriff's office—nobody but me. Billy sat in that chair, unmoving, day and night. Well, he moved his hand, whenever I put mine beside it. Some nights I just sat beside him 'til the wee hours of the morning, lettin' him hold my hand. I wouldn't take his hand—that would be too much like just holding on to the hand of a corpse. No, I'd put my hand down and let him reach for it. That told me Billy was still there in some way.

Eugene and Teddy and all them other fellas… they just went about their lives like Billy wasn't there. They still talked to me and drank with me and played cards with me. Teddy still let me take my share of goods from the store. But nobody talked about the dead man in the sheriff's office.

Leastwise, not 'til Billy got up one night and walked into the saloon.

How it happened was like this. Old Jake Warner drank a little too much, as he was wont to do. Then he got to arguin' with… well, just about everybody. Finally Eugene had to ask him to leave. Only Jake wouldn't go. I was there, so I reckoned I should do something about it, bein' the deputy sheriff and all. But afore I could get outta my chair, the whole place went dead quiet.

I looked up, and Jake was standin' in the middle of the room, white as a sheet, 'cause there was a gun to his head. Billy's revolver. And Billy was holding it. He was standing stock-still in the doorway, his arm outstretched to point that gun at Jake. Otherwise he could've been a statue. He weren't even looking at Jake. He was starin' at nothing, like he always did.

"Billy," I said softly. "We don't wanna kill our friend Jake just for gettin' a little rowdy…."

Billy's gun hand jerked a few times, like he was sayin' *this way* to Jake.

"Oh, Jesus," Jake said, kinda sobbing a little. The front of his trousers was wet.

Billy's hand jerked again, afore going back to pointing at Jake's head.

"Jake, I think he wants you to start walking."

"Where?"

"The jail, I reckon. That's where he would've took you when he was… when he was alive."

"He's gonna shoot me! Please, don't let him shoot me!"

I honestly didn't know if Billy was gonna shoot him or not. But I took Jake by the sleeve and slowly started walkin' him to the door. Billy stepped aside to let us through, then followed behind us as I led Jake to the jail. Soon's I put Jake in the cell and closed the door, Billy holstered his gun and sank into his chair in exactly the same position he'd been sitting for the past week.

I had one of the fellas from the saloon bring me a pair of clean trousers for Jake to change into. I had to pick 'em up at the saloon, o' course. If those fellas weren't scared of Billy before then, they sure was now.

In the morning I let Jake out of the cell, and he hightailed it out of Para Siempre that afternoon. Over the next few weeks, a lot of fellas left town. I couldn't say I blamed them. But both Eugene and Teddy stayed. They said they was too old to uproot now, and it didn't look like Billy was gonna bother nobody, long as they obeyed the law. I think part of it was they'd liked him when he was alive and kinda felt like they shoulda done more to help him and me against the Cassidys.

Some of the other fellas stayed too. Most camped up by the mine, so they wouldn't have to see Billy. But he rarely left the sheriff's office. Once a rabid coyote wandered into town, so Billy went out and shot the poor thing. One bullet, clean through the forehead. That was about it.

Eugene even made a joke about it, now and then. "Lots o' towns have dead sheriffs," he said. "No reason Para Siempre should be any different."

THAT WAS all 'bout fifty years back. I'm the only one left in this ghost town now—me and Billy. The mine played out not long after Billy died, and all but a handful of men left town. The rest wandered off after Eugene died of a heart attack and the saloon shut down. Teddy was the last one to go. He stuck with me s'long as he could. He figured I'd go crazy out here by myself with nobody but Billy to talk to, and him not ever answerin' back.

But eventually he moved to Santa Fe to be with relatives. He was gettin' too old to be away from doctors and loved ones. He arranged for a nephew to drive out here once a month with supplies for me, since I refused to leave. Then, about twenty or twenty-five years back, Teddy passed in his sleep. His nephew told me about it, and he brought a bottle of whiskey with him, so we could toast Teddy with it.

The nephew—his name's Wyatt—kept bringing me supplies over the years. He's a grown man with a family of his own now, but he still makes that wagon ride once a month. Said the ghost of his Uncle Teddy would never let him rest if he allowed me to starve. And he believes in ghosts, 'cause he seen Billy.

Billy ain't changed at all since he died. He ain't rotted—thank goodness—and he ain't aged. He looks exactly the same. But he still takes my hand when I sit beside him. And sometimes when I wake up in the morning, he's moved to sit on the floor beside my cot.

I think back a lot to that day he told me he was givin' his soul to me. That weren't just a joke. Billy meant it, and he did it. I just hope, when I die—and it won't be long now—he'll find a way to follow me. It'd break my heart to think of him left behind, sitting in this dingy office for the rest of the days of the earth.

Epilogue

From the diary of Wyatt Long, July 21st, 1927

I PROMISED Uncle Teddy I'd never talk about his friend Joe Brady until Joe was safely dead and buried. I never even dared write about it, in case somebody found my diary. But the time has come. I went out to Para Siempre yesterday and found poor old Joe dead in his cot. He hadn't been there more than a day or so, thank the Lord. His companion, if you can call a corpse a companion, was lying on the floor beside him.

The corpse belonged to Billy. I don't know Billy's last name. Nobody ever told me. I don't know much about him, except that he was killed fifty years or so ago in a gunfight. As insane as this sounds, that corpse never decayed. He still looked like a strikingly handsome young man of about twenty. I don't know how that's possible, but it is. And that's not even the craziest thing about it.

I'll get to that in a minute.

Old Joe had left me instructions, ages ago, that when he died, I was to build a pyre right in the street in front of the sheriff's office and cremate him on it. Since the town was a ghost town, I saw no harm in this. Hardly any of the buildings remain standing, anyway.

So I did as he asked. It took me until near sunset to build a big enough bonfire from the remains of the nearby buildings, and it was dark by the time I'd laid Joe's body on top of it. I set it on fire and said a prayer for his soul as the flames engulfed him.

He'd wanted me to drag Billy's corpse out and put it on the pyre with him before I lit it, but when push came to shove, I just couldn't do it. I couldn't bring myself to touch that unnatural thing. What I should have done, thinking back, was build the fire inside the sheriff's office. Then I could have burned the entire building to the ground with both bodies inside. But I didn't think of that at the time.

What happened next... I can barely find words to describe. In fact, the more I think about it, the more I think I'll just tear this page out of my diary and throw it away. The last thing I need is for someone to stumble across this entry and question my sanity.

But I'll write it down once, at least, just to try to make sense of it.

As I watched the flames climbing higher, the door of the sheriff's office opened and Billy's corpse shambled out. I swear to God! A dead man walked across that street right toward me! I stood there, staggering back, but too frozen with fear to run away. Fortunately the thing didn't seem to have any interest in me at all. It approached the bonfire, and then to my horror, it climbed up the pyre. Its clothing ignited as it climbed, until the entire... man... was on fire! But still it climbed, until it reached Joe. Then it... Billy... lay down beside him and wrapped an arm around him. A moment later, they were both engulfed in flames.

I ran back to my car after that and drove straight back to Santa Fe. I suppose I'm lucky I didn't go off the road or hit anyone, I was shaking that badly from fear. But it's over with now. And in a way, maybe it was a good thing. Joe wanted to be with Billy for his entire life, and I guess Billy felt the same. And now they're together in death.

May they find peace there.

The Mill

Author's Note

THERE IS an author's note at the end of this story, explaining the origins of the song I quote at the beginning of each chapter. I'll simply add that I lived near the Cocheco Mill in Dover, NH, for over twenty years. Like most of those old mills, it's been converted into a mall. Though the old wood floors and ceiling beams are preserved, giving it a much nicer atmosphere than modern malls.

Apart from the Cocheco Mill Fire in 1907, the bit of history I find most fascinating, in connection to it, is when the Cocheco River flooded in 1896. It was midwinter, and the river was full of massive chunks of ice that hammered away at the Central Avenue bridge, then called the Bracewell Block. The bridge is flat and crossed by the road and sidewalks, but unlike today, there were three stores built along it. Yes, actual buildings. Somebody thought this was a good idea.

At about 4:30 p.m., the bridge was crawling with thousands of people who wanted a good vantage point from which to watch the foot-thick ice chunks hammering into the bridge underneath them. The city marshal—a man named Fogerty—had the sense to realize this was a bad idea, and he ordered everyone off the bridge. They went, reluctantly, and a moment later, the entire bridge shuddered and sank into the torrent. Two little boys had lingered behind, and when the center of the bridge sank into the water, they scrambled up the incline to street level and barely made it before the entire thing collapsed.

If you think that bit of drama won't appear in a future story of mine, you are much mistaken.

Chapter One

Was in the town of Hawley
When the people was burned and killed,
In a textile manufactory
Called as the Hawley Mill.

THE SECOND floor of the mill building was a cavernous space so large Frank Carter's flashlight beam nearly vanished in the darkness, casting only a vague blur of illumination against the far walls. The wooden floor had been replaced a hundred years ago, after the fire burned the first floor to ash in 1907, but the renovators hadn't refinished it yet. The floor was varnished, though the sheen had been worn off by eighty years of footsteps until the mill was shut down in 1989. Grooves in the oak and holes for bolts still marked where rows of massive cast-iron sewing machines once whirred and clattered, filling the chasm with an earsplitting din.

Now every step Frank made in his sneakers could be heard, the slightest squeak of his rubber soles echoing back from the void. He switched on his night-vision goggles and pulled them down over his eyes. The entire empty expanse appeared in all its glory, as if it were bathed in a sickly greenish-gray light.

Hawley Textile Mill had been empty since the last serger was hauled out of the building in the nineties. There had been an attempt to renovate the property as a shopping mall, but a series of injuries, accidents, and overall bad luck plagued the construction crew until the investors withdrew. For almost twenty years now, the mill building had remained untouched.

"I'm not seeing anything on the infrared, Houston," Junior reported over the headset.

"Are you still on the fifth floor?"

"I'm just finishing my sweep."

"Where are you, Savannah?"

"Third floor."

"Anything on EMF?"

"Sure enough," she drawled, "if electrical wires get you all excited."

"We were warned the building still had juice to keep the security systems active."

"I know, sugar."

"If anyone's interested," Frank interrupted, "I'm currently on the second floor with the goggles. Not that it's important or anything. Maybe I'll just go stick my head in a bucket of water. Would you like me to go and stick my head in a bucket of water? God, I'm so depressed!"

Houston laughed at the *Hitchhiker's Guide to the Galaxy* reference. "Keep your head dry, Baba. You'll short out the headset if you get it wet. What have you got?"

"Nothing. Just checking in."

They'd all insisted on adopting ridiculous nicknames when they founded C-Troop Paranormal. Or more specifically, everyone but Frank had insisted on it. Frank thought it was lame. Savannah—Tamicka Jones—her nickname was pretty obvious. She wore her Savannah accent as a badge of honor. But Houston had never lived in Texas. His nickname came from manning the consoles for all the cameras and coordinating communications and data collection, as NASA's base in Houston did for the astronauts. Junior was fresh out of college—Frank's younger brother, Louis.

Houston had inflicted the name "Baba" on Frank, supposedly because he fussed over everybody too much. "Baba" was Russian for "old woman." Frank hated the name, but once Louis had gotten wind of it, there had been no escape.

"I'm on the fourth floor now," Junior announced. "I smell something."

"Did you fart?"

Junior snorted into the mic. "No, asshole. It smells like burning."

That was worrisome. The building had been inactive for almost two decades. The only thing Frank could think of that might smell like burning was faulty wiring. "Junior, are you sure you're smelling something burning? Maybe it's something else—cleaning chemicals or—"

"No, Baba. It definitely smells like… smoke. I don't think it's electrical…."

"Maybe it's an apparition," Houston suggested. "After all, there was a fire here in 1907."

Maybe. But Frank didn't like leaping to paranormal explanations when there might be something more mundane—and in this case, potentially more dangerous—causing it.

"Guys!" Junior exclaimed. "You should see this. The infrared's lit up like a Christmas tree!"

"What do you mean?"

"Everything is showing hot—*real* hot. All the walls, and the floor, and the sewing machines…. But I don't see anything when I look with the naked eye."

"Wait a minute," Frank said. "All the sewing machines were taken out in the nineties."

"That can't be right. I can see them right in front of me."

"Camera seven is pointed right at you, Junior," Houston interjected. "You're standing in the middle of a big ol' empty space."

"But I can *see* them."

"Child, what are you smoking down there?" Savannah asked.

"I've got the camera recording. You can see them for yourselves."

Frank was inclined to believe him. Junior had a good head on his shoulders, and a vision of something from the past was hardly unusual for the type of work they were doing. But Frank doubted anything would show up on the camera. Whatever Junior was seeing, he wasn't likely to be seeing it with his eyes—not directly.

"Hold on," he said. "I'm coming up there."

He strode across the empty expanse toward the stairwell at the back, but before he was halfway there, Savannah reported, "I'm in the stairwell, going down. I smell something too."

"What?" Houston asked.

"Junior's right. It smells like… something's burning. I could swear it's *smoky*."

"You see smoke?"

"Well… I don't know. It just sort of… *feels* smoky."

Frank broke into a run. "Junior! You've got the infrared. Do you see any heat sources on that floor?"

No answer.

"Junior?"

Still no answer.

Houston said, "What are you doing, Junior?" A pause. "Junior!"

Frank heard a sound. It was incredibly faint, but he thought it might be a scream—a man's scream. Junior's scream. It wasn't coming over the headset but from somewhere high above him, muffled by distance and two floors. He ran harder and slammed through the door to the stairwell, smashing it against the wall.

Smoke. There *was* smoke in here. He could smell it too. "Goddamn it! What—"

He didn't get to finish the thought. A door slammed open high above him in the dark stairwell and Louis was screaming. Frantic footsteps stumbled down the metal stairs, and as if from a great distance, Savannah shouted, "Junior!"

Frank ran up the stairs as his brother's footsteps came clattering down toward him in the dark, dissolving into a cacophony of noise— the sound of a man falling down a flight of metal stairs amid shattering technical equipment. The agonizing scream ended abruptly as Louis's body crashed into the landing with a sickening thud. The fragments of his headset and camera rained down around him.

FRANK STAYED with Louis while they waited for the ambulance, clutching his hand to reassure himself that Louis had a pulse. He had no idea how to assess his brother's injuries. He could tell he was still breathing—that was it. Otherwise he was unresponsive. He was bleeding and it looked as if his leg might be broken, judging from the sickening way it twisted underneath him.

Please, God, don't let his back be broken....

Savannah turned on the lights in the stairwell and came to sit with him while Houston made the 911 call. He kept checking in with Frank while they waited for the ambulance.

"I don't smell it anymore," Savannah commented quietly, holding one of Junior's limp hands in both of hers.

Frank looked at her, uncomprehending. Then slowly it dawned on him. The smoke. He couldn't smell it either. Not a trace of it.

He tried to speak, found he couldn't, and then cleared his throat to try again. "His face looks burned." The side of it Frank could see was puffed up and red.

"He'll be all right, sugar. Just hang in there."

When the paramedics arrived with a stretcher, Frank and Savannah got out of their way. The only thing Frank could learn from them was that Louis didn't appear to have a broken back or neck, but he had several injuries to the head and body that were potentially life-threatening. And yes, his leg was broken.

Though he felt he was barely holding it together, Frank insisted on helping Houston and Savannah do a quick lock-up of the building while the ambulance took Louis to the Hawley Memorial Hospital. The team couldn't leave until everything was secure, and after what had happened to Junior—whatever *had* happened to him—Frank couldn't bring himself to leave anyone alone in the building. But as soon as that was done, they all piled into the company van and went straight to the hospital.

THEY SPENT the next three hours in the ER waiting room, hearing nothing about Louis's condition. Had Louis been conscious, Frank might have been allowed into the ER with him, since they were family. But with Louis unresponsive and possibly needing surgery on his leg, Frank had simply filled out reams of paperwork about Louis's medical and family history, praying he hadn't forgotten about any allergies to medications, and then been told to wait.

"I don't know what happened," Houston said, keeping his voice low. There was an old woman napping in a chair by the television set. "He was waving his hand in the air in front of him, like he was trying to touch whatever he thought he was seeing. Then he started freaking out—waving his arms around, hitting himself, and staggering back. He ran through the door to the stairwell."

"I know," Frank said. They'd been over it a million times. The camera equipment was packed into the back of the van, too difficult to reach without unpacking everything in the hospital parking lot. They'd have to review it later. But the three of them were all roughly on the same page. It appeared Louis had seen a vision of the fire—perhaps he'd felt he was *in* the fire. The way Houston described it, Louis may have thought his clothes were on fire before he panicked and ran for the exit. Then it appeared he stumbled blindly down the stairs and fell.

The camera footage might tell them more, but Frank doubted it.

Junior, Frank thought, *you'd better come out of this. I want a full report, you little pipsqueak! No lying down on the job.*

He didn't know what he'd do, if…. No. He refused to think about that. Louis would be fine. He had to be. He was the only family Frank had.

Around two in the morning, Savannah put a gentle hand on his arm to pull his attention away from an insipid miracle sponge infomercial. The doctor was approaching.

"Are you Frank?" the woman asked, smiling and extending a hand.

Frank shook it. "That's me. I'm Junior's—Louis's—older brother."

"I'm Dr. Khambatta. First, let me tell you your brother is doing well. He hasn't yet regained consciousness, but his condition is stable."

"Can I see him?"

Her smile turned wistful. "It's well past visiting hours, but I can take you back for a short time to see him. Your friends may see him during visiting hours tomorrow."

"Do you think he'll be all right?"

"Yes, I do. He has a mild concussion, and we had to operate on his leg to reset the femur—it was broken in two places—but he should recover fully."

"What about the burns on his face?" Savannah asked.

Dr. Khambatta appeared confused. "Burns? No, there are no burns. His face is fine."

Chapter Two

At seven o'clock the firebells rang
But oh, it was too late,
The flames they were fast spreading
And at a rapid rate.

"THE TOWER signifies a massive change." Toby held up the tarot card, which depicted a tower being struck by lightning and collapsing while screaming people tumbled from it to their deaths. "It could be for the worse. It could be for the better. But in any case, it's likely to be life-changing."

Mrs. Hawley pursed her lips primly. "I don't like the Tower. It's such an unpleasant-looking card with all those poor people falling to their deaths, don't you think? Change it to something else, please."

Toby gaped at her a moment, uncertain whether she meant it or not. Mrs. Hawley did own half the town of Hawley, which had grown up around the mill that made her grandfather enormously wealthy in the first half of the twentieth century. She was used to having her way. But not even the wealthiest patrons could command the fates to obey their whims.

He caught the twinkle of mischief in the old woman's eye and realized she was pulling his leg. That was more in line with the woman he knew. "I'll have a stern word with the deck later, Mrs. H."

She'd insisted upon him calling her that after their first session together. For all her money, she was very down-to-earth and approachable. Though Toby had been warned by other people in town not to cross her. She wasn't above throwing her weight around if she was angered.

The woman reached out to pluck the card from his hand. "Reminds one of a mill fire, doesn't it?" she asked, examining the picture closely, her forehead creased in concentration.

"Yes, it does." Toby knew the history of the mill as well as anyone in Hawley did. "But this doesn't represent the distant past. Its position in the reading indicates something in the present."

"Is last night close enough?"

"What do you mean?"

Mrs. H. set the card down on the table. "A young man fell down a flight of stairs in the mill last night. He wasn't killed, thank the stars, but he's currently in ICU. His condition is serious but stable."

"That's horrible! How did it happen? Did he break in?"

She fluttered her hand in the air. "No, no. He was there because I hired him. Well, technically I hired his brother's… agency. The two work together."

"Doing what?"

"Well…." Mrs. H. glanced around as if to be certain they wouldn't be overheard. They were alone, of course—Toby had renovated the closet of his store specifically to provide an isolated, private space for readings. "I hired them to investigate for signs of spiritual activity in the mill."

Toby repressed a snicker. "They're ghost hunters?"

"Not the ones on television! The *last* thing I need is to have their investigation broadcast for the entire world to see. They call themselves 'paranormal investigators,' and they've promised to be discreet. I was hoping they'd conclude there was nothing there so we could release a report and quell the rumors. I need to sell that accursed building! Or renovate it as a shopping mall. It's been empty—and costing me money in property taxes—for far too long."

It wasn't that Toby didn't believe in ghosts. On the contrary, he frequently communed with the dead for his clients. But ever since the— admittedly entertaining—show *Ghost Hunters* took off, everybody who could afford to buy an EMF meter was out there claiming to be an expert. Now it appeared to have gotten someone seriously injured. "Is he going to be okay?"

"Louis? I'm afraid nobody knows for certain. I'm paying for any medical expenses not covered by their insurance, of course, and I'm allowing them to take as much time off from the investigation as they need—I'm not *entirely* without compassion, regardless of what the gossips in town may say." That glimmer of humor returned to her eyes. "But they want to cancel the contract!"

"I can't say I'm surprised, under the circumstances."

"I can't have that! I need the investigation completed so appropriate steps can be taken."

Toby doubted the wisdom of what he was about to say but decided a psychic needed to tell the truth, regardless of whether clients wanted to hear it. And that included advice. "Mrs. H.... there is always the possibility their investigation won't get the results you're hoping for. If the mill building *does* turn out to be haunted, what will you do then?"

"That's another problem with these investigators," she replied with a sniff. "They simply diagnose. They don't *cure*. They're so wrapped up in their scientific toys—meters and field readers and whatnot—but there are no scientific methods for getting *rid* of spirits if they're found, are there? Of course not! That's where I was hoping you could help me."

Toby's eyes went wide and he straightened in his chair. "Me?"

"Yes, of course, dear," Mrs. H. told him sensibly. "You don't think I really came to get a reading, did you? I already know I'm a filthy rich bitch who always gets her way. I don't need the cards to tell me that."

Toby stared blankly at her a moment, until she went on without him.

"I was hoping to engage your services as a medium," she said. "Once his team succeeds in *finding* whatever spirits might be haunting Hawley Mill, Frank—they all have silly nicknames I wouldn't be caught dead using—needs someone who can persuade them to *leave*."

Toby found his voice at last. "And you think that should be me?"

"Absolutely! Who in town is better qualified to commune with spirits?"

He would be able to talk to the spirits, if anyone could. Of that Toby had no doubt. Spirits had been visiting him since he was a child. But most were friendly. "I'm honored that you would consider me, Mrs. H., but was it the spirits who injured this poor man last night?"

Mrs. H. tapped her bottom lip with one beautifully manicured index finger. "I'm uncertain of that. Louis—that's the younger brother—apparently panicked and threw himself into the stairwell. Frank believes something in the mill convinced him he was on fire. So I suppose you could say, if it was a spirit, it caused Louis to injure himself."

"That's often the way spirits cause harm—by affecting our perceptions. Most aren't powerful enough to affect the physical world directly. Though poltergeists—"

"There!" Mrs. H. exclaimed, clapping her hands together in delight. "You see? I knew you would be the best man for the job! Please say you'll do it. I'll pay you handsomely, of course."

Toby's small New Age shop barely scraped by, selling books and herbs and the occasional psychic reading. Even Mrs. H.'s weekly patronage, while appreciated, didn't help much financially. Toby charged her the same rate as all his other clients, regardless of her wealth. This was the first time she'd tossed him a bone.

"How does…. Frank? How does he feel about me joining his team?"

"I'll have a word with him." Mrs. H. gathered up her purse and stood. Apparently the reading was over. "Truthfully, he might not be in favor of it. These scientific-types would rather depend upon electromagnetic readouts or whatever they call it. They're suspicious of old-fashioned mediums. And honestly, who can blame them with all the frauds out there today? But I trust you, dear. And so will Frank and his team, once they get to know you."

Toby wished he had her confidence. He moved to open the door for her and then escorted her through his shop to the front door. The place was empty, apart from the young woman attending the front counter.

This was moving awfully fast for Toby. He would have liked more time to think about it. But if he'd learned anything about Mrs. H. in her weekly visits, it was that she never hesitated once she'd made up her mind.

"If they agree to let me join them," he said, holding the door open for her, "I suppose I'm willing to do what I can."

"Wonderful! I'll call you later with the details."

And then she was gone, leaving Toby with the feeling he'd been fast-talked into something he might regret. He noticed Cassandra watching him from the counter. She was a tiny young woman—still in college, studying art—dressed all in black with heavy black makeup around her eyes. Even her fingernails were black. The only color she displayed was her bright red hair, wreathing her head in tight ringlets.

"Has anybody come in?" Toby asked, more for conversation than anything else. He knew what the answer would be.

"Nope. We did get a shipment of dried herbs. I already put them in their bottles."

"Great. Thanks."

Then, because he couldn't stand to leave a reading unfinished, Toby went back to the reading room. He drew the final card and placed it on the table in the position signifying the future. Then he frowned at it. Given the context of the reading and the discussion he'd just had with Mrs. H., it might not be a particularly fortuitous card—not for a woman whose family business had once been responsible for the deaths of ninety-seven mill workers, almost all young women.

It was Justice.

Chapter Three

They were men and women there
And children too, I'm told,
Who might have been saved from out of the flames
If the truth was only known.

FRANK DIDN'T like psychics. He understood what he did was the same thing with different methods—communicating with spirits. But the field of parapsychology was attempting to gain credence in the scientific community using instruments to gather data and evaluate the evidence rationally. Every time he saw a television psychic tricking an audience member into giving him information to regurgitate back as "a message from beyond," Frank envisioned respect for his field going farther and farther down the toilet.

So he was less than thrilled when Celia Hawley called his cell phone to inform him she was sending over her personal psychic to assist with the investigation of the mill. He'd already told her he wanted to back off the investigation. One near casualty was more than enough for him. Junior still hadn't regained consciousness. Frank hadn't gone into parapsychology to get his brother or anyone else killed. But the woman was impossible! She told him what she wanted done and expected him to do it. No arguments. It was like arguing with his mother.

And that was how he found himself back at the Hawley Mill building on Tuesday morning with his crew—minus Junior. Dr. Khambatta had assured him Junior's leg was doing as well as could be expected, and the concussion…. Well, that could take anywhere from a week to three months to heal. But the MRI had found no signs of brain damage. Why he hadn't yet regained consciousness was a mystery. In the meantime, Junior was being moved out of ICU that afternoon.

The building loomed over them as they unloaded the van in the parking lot, its dark windows ominous even on that sunny July morning. The windows on the lowest two floors had long ago been boarded up to keep out people looking to steal what little had been left behind or see for themselves whether the stories of ghosts were true.

"We could just bail," Houston suggested as he helped Frank lower one of the heavy equipment cases to the tarmac. "She may be rich, but she's not gonna hunt us down, is she? It's not like we've stolen anything of hers."

Houston was Junior's age—they'd been best friends and roommates in college. His hallmark way of dressing—one Frank kept after him about, since it was unprofessional—was a pair of low-hanging jeans that revealed about two inches of his boxers and a baseball cap that never seemed to face front. He was full of attitude, but underneath that he was loyal and passionate about the team and what they were doing. It was hard not to feel protective of him, the same way Frank felt protective of Junior.

"You don't have to do this, Houston. Neither does Savannah. I'm going back in there because Mrs. Hawley said she'd help with Junior's medical expenses, and... well, the job just isn't done. But that doesn't mean I want anyone else hurt over it."

Houston snorted and punched Frank lightly in the upper arm. "Fuck that! We're a team."

"That's right," Savannah interjected from inside the van. "You don't seriously think we'd let you go back in there alone, do you?"

She was older—closer to Frank's age. Unlike the boys, who'd started tagging along with Frank on his investigations before he'd gone professional, Savannah hadn't fallen into his lap. She'd been working with another group down in Georgia and already knew her way around EMF readers and thermal imagers. She specialized in researching the histories of locations, which could be challenging for someone like Frank, who didn't know his way around town property records. He'd met her through an old army buddy, and it had taken a year of wooing and salary negotiations to convince her to come work for him.

"I won't be alone," Frank replied. "Not technically. Though God knows what good this so-called psychic will do me."

Houston laughed. "Maybe you can trip him when the monster is chasing you to buy yourself some time."

"Houston!" Savannah scolded. "There's no need to be mean-spirited. And don't think I didn't see you smirking, Baba."

"Who, me?"

Savannah raised a hand to hush both of them as a small dark blue Honda Civic pulled into the parking lot. The car looked as if it were on its last gasp, dented in places and sporting patches of Bondo. It parked near them and the driver climbed out.

He was beautiful. Frank supposed some might call him handsome, since he wasn't particularly feminine, but there was a softness to his features that made Frank think of silk sheets and languorous caresses. He was probably in his late twenties, with a head of wild, dark brown curls and a thin mustache and beard—not wispy, like a teenager struggling to grow his first facial hair, but he would probably never have a heavy beard. It softened an otherwise angular jawline and chin and emphasized his full lips. Most striking were his eyes, when he removed his sunglasses. They weren't brown as Frank had expected from his coloring, but a warm, emerald green.

This had to be the psychic. He confirmed it by looking directly at Frank and saying, "I'm Toby Reese. Mrs. Hawley said she'd tell you to expect me."

"*Ordered* is more like," Houston muttered as he pulled another crate out of the van.

Savannah glared at him, but Reese quirked up a corner of his mouth and said, "Yeah, she's kinda used to getting her way."

Frank stepped forward, offering his hand. "Frank Carter. They call me Baba. And this is Savannah. The kid with no manners is Houston."

FRANK CARTER was ex-military. Toby knew that from the briefing Mrs. H. had given him over the phone last night. It was obvious from his swagger—he had to be either military or police. What she'd neglected to mention was that he was gorgeous. Muscular and broad-shouldered, he had a slightly freckled complexion and short strawberry blond hair— though not a crewcut. It was just long enough to be sticking up in all directions, as if he'd crawled out of bed that morning and couldn't find a comb. It was adorable and an odd contrast to the neatly trimmed beard he sported. When he shook hands, he regarded Toby with wide, baby blue eyes.

Toby attempted to shake hands with the others. Savannah accepted his hand graciously, but Houston chose to act like a punk and pretend he hadn't noticed Toby's hand hanging pathetically in the air. The older members of the team frowned and exchanged glances, but nobody said anything.

Toby withdrew his hand and asked, "Do you need help unloading?"

"Nope," Houston said.

Frank overrode him. "Sure. You want to climb in the van and get the other end of this crate?"

"I'll get it!"

"You deal with the case you've got in your hands, Houston. Let Toby help me with this one."

Houston shot Toby a hostile look but did as he was told.

Oh boy. This is going to be fun.

When they'd unloaded everything and locked the van, Toby helped the team carry the equipment into the foyer of the mill building. Though he'd lived in this town for most of his life, driven past the sinister, abandoned building nearly every day, and even snuck peeks in the windows when he was a kid, he'd never actually been inside.

It was disquieting, even in daylight. From the empty foyer, he could see an enormous room opening up to the north, dark apart from slanting shafts of light coming in between the boards on the windows, and nearly empty. There were chairs strewn about and piles of debris nobody had thought worth salvaging when the mill shuttered its doors. The far wall was lost in darkness.

Worse than the way the mill appeared to Toby's physical senses was the way it *felt*. Even if he hadn't known the building's history, there was a sickness in the place. Toby had never experienced such a powerful sense of dread. It seemed to envelop him and settle into his body like a virus, making him queasy and disoriented. He gripped the wall to prevent himself from falling over.

"Are you okay?" Frank asked.

"This place… it's affecting me."

"Do you need to sit down?"

"Maybe you should go home," the punk muttered as he placed a large flat-screen monitor on what must have once been the receptionist's desk.

"Houston!" Frank snapped. "Just do your job, please?"

Toby was dimly aware Frank had him by the elbow. He waved the man off. "Thanks. I'll be all right. I just need to put my wards up."

He breathed deeply a few times to calm himself, then envisioned a beam of white light coming down from the sky and up from the earth, meeting in the center of his chest to form a glowing ball of pure energy. With each breath, he felt the ball expanding, pushing the darkness out of his body and beyond, until the oppressive sick feeling faded. In his mind's eye, he saw himself standing in the center of a protective sphere of clean, pure white energy that pushed the darkness of Hawley Mill away from him, keeping him safe.

When he opened his eyes, he found all three of the team members looking at him as if he'd just farted.

"Oookaaay...." Houston said, shaking his head in disbelief and turning back to the monitor.

"I'll get the extension cords," Savannah said. She seemed to be avoiding looking at Toby as she went outside.

Toby frowned at the sour expression on Frank's face. "I'm fine. I just needed to ground myself."

"What exactly do you intend to do here, Mr. Reese?"

"Toby," Toby insisted. "And Mrs. H. hired me to talk to any spirits your investigation turns up."

"What good will that do?"

"If I can establish communication, I might be able to persuade them to move on."

Frank made a low noise in his throat that sounded a bit like a growl. "Do you intend to 'communicate'"—he said the word as if it were something he found disgusting—"during our investigation?"

"No. I expect I'll just help lug things around and whatever else you tell me to do." He added, to make it clear, "Besides getting lost. She's not paying me to sit in the car outside all night."

Frank regarded him thoughtfully for a long, uncomfortable moment. Then he said, "I think we need to have a little chat—alone."

Chapter Four

But oh, the villains that locked the doors
And told them to keep still,
It was the bosses and overseers
That burning Hawley Mill.

"WAIT HERE a sec."

Frank went out to the van to retrieve the small case containing the team's EMF readers. He might as well take one with him, if he was going through the building. He left the case in a corner of the foyer, grabbed one of the readers for himself, and then told Toby, "Follow me."

They entered the factory floor from the foyer entrance, and Frank led the way into the dark, ruined landscape. The light wasn't so dim he couldn't see his surroundings, but he was grateful for the button on the EMF reader that lit up the display.

"Have you been in the building before?" he asked.

"Never. I've only seen it from the outside."

"I assume you know about the fire?"

"Of course," Toby replied. "Everyone who lives in Hawley more than a few years hears about the fire, eventually. It's our… communal heritage, I suppose."

Frank and his team lived in Portsmouth, so they'd never heard the story before accepting the job. The mill had employed almost two-hundred-and-fifty people in 1907, almost all young women in their late teens or early twenties. Ninety-seven of those workers perished in the fire. There had only been two ways out of the building at the time, and the back exit had been locked for some reason—perhaps to prevent workers from sneaking out on unauthorized smoking breaks or union organizers from sneaking in. Most of those who exited through the front door made it out alive, but those who went down the back stairwell had been trapped.

The cause of the fire was still unknown.

"Savannah dug into the history of the mill before we came out here," he said, casually noting the EMF level on the factory floor as they strode across it. It was fluctuating a bit, but very low. It never rose above one milligauss. "There were some reports of workers sensing an angry presence after the damage was repaired and the building became operative again—about three years after the fire. But nobody took it seriously. Who works in a building where almost a hundred people died and doesn't feel creeped out by it, now and then?"

Toby snorted, but he didn't say anything, so Frank continued.

"Then when the mill shut down in the late nineteen-eighties, things heated up. It was as if the building no longer wanted people in it—or so the construction workers claimed."

"Maybe the spirits were disturbed when everything changed."

Frank stopped walking. Toby took a few steps without him, then noticed he was alone and turned to look back.

"What?"

"Houston is being kind of rude to you," Frank said. "I'm sorry about that. He's taking what happened to Junior hard—they've been best friends for a long time. But you should know he picked up a lot of that attitude about psychics from me. I don't really like… spiritualists."

Toby grinned at him, displaying some of the most perfect white teeth Frank had ever seen. "That's okay. I don't like parapsychologists much."

"Why not?"

"You first."

Frank had to smile at that. "Okay. Well… we can start with a very long history of fraud by people claiming to have the ability to communicate with the dead."

"Granted. The only response I can offer is that I am not a fake."

"So you say."

"Yes."

Frank continued walking toward the far end of the room, and Toby fell into step beside him. "So if you go into a room and get a sense of, say, a malevolent entity watching you, how can you prove it isn't your imagination?"

"Only by receiving information from it that can later be verified," Toby admitted.

"Exactly! But so often it's information you could easily have gotten from a little research, or people who knew the spirit when it was a living person. I have yet to see a psychic produce something that could only have come from a spirit—something verifiable, that is. What things are like in the afterworld doesn't count."

Toby laughed. "You have high standards! Something I couldn't have learned from books or talking to people, but can later be verified by reading books or talking to people? How is *that* supposed to work?"

He had Frank there. It would be nearly impossible. "What if it was something like the location of an heirloom nobody could find?"

"That's very precise. Would you accept that as verification of psychic ability?"

Frank shrugged. "Maybe."

"Then I'll do my best."

He was being condescending, which was irritating. But Frank had initiated this conversation—Toby hadn't asked for a professional critique—so he couldn't really blame the guy. "All right. But fair's fair. What's your beef with parapsychologists?"

"My 'beef' is mostly with the ghost-hunting variety of parapsychologist," Toby said with an annoying smirk.

Frank refused to take the bait. He raised his eyebrows as if to say, "And?"

"What you're doing is searching for physical anomalies," Toby went on. "Take that device in your hand—"

"It reads electromagnetic fields."

"Yes. So let's say you find a spot with a high EMF reading, and you're able to verify the spike isn't being caused by wires in the walls or a fuse box or anything like that. Why do you then conclude the EMF spike was caused by something paranormal?"

"I don't, necessarily," Frank protested. "But one theory is that EMF spikes are caused by the presence of spiritual entities—"

"Why? Where did that theory come from?"

"From reports. People who claim to have seen ghosts often report electrical disturbances accompanying the experience—lights flickering, batteries being drained, electrical devices turning on or off by themselves…."

Toby laughed again. "Anecdotal reports? From laymen? How can you base a scientific theory on those?"

"You have to start somewhere."

"So some people say they see ghosts while electrical anomalies are occurring near them, and you conclude electrical anomalies equal ghosts? What if electrical anomalies make people *think* they see ghosts?"

"It's a possibility," Frank admitted. "One theory is that the feelings of dread people often associate with a particular room or location might be caused by proximity to electrical transformers."

"So when your EMF reader finds an unexplained electromagnetic anomaly, it's possible there's no spirit presence at all—just some kind of natural, but unexplained, fluctuation in the electromagnetic field that could *cause* people to think they're seeing or feeling a ghost. In other words, you don't know whether you're finding the *result* of a haunting or the *cause* of a haunting."

Frank frowned at him. *Wiseass.* Though to be fair, he was more annoyed that Toby was better at this game than he was. "I'm beginning to think you're a plant."

"A skeptic sent here undercover as a 'psychic' so I can sabotage your investigation?" Toby didn't seem at all bothered by the insinuation.

"Maybe."

Toby spread his hands in a gesture of peace. "I'm not. You'll just have to trust me and Mrs. H. on that. But are we done calling each other frauds now? It's getting old."

"Agreed."

FRANK GAVE Toby a tour of the entire building, pointing out locations where people had reported seeing or hearing things in the past. Toby suspected the tour was as much to get him out of the way while Houston and Savannah set up the team's equipment as anything else. That was fine with him. He needed to get a feel for the building, in any event. And although he would never admit it to Frank, he was glad not to be wandering these cavernous rooms by himself. Up above the second floor, the windows weren't boarded up—except for some individual panes that had been replaced by wood after local kids used them for target practice—so there was more light. But it only helped a bit. There was something bleak and desolate about the mill. It wasn't merely the years of emptiness and neglect. Despite the wards he'd put up, Toby could still sense something foul in the building. There was something *wrong* there, something sick. It permeated the brick walls, the iron fixtures, the massive wooden crossbeams.

He didn't feel inclined to comment on his feeling about the place as they walked. He knew Frank's low opinion of psychics now, so there was no point in inviting his disdain.

The elevator—a rickety-looking thing with tarnished brass fixtures and a metal safety gate instead of a proper door—made him extremely uncomfortable. It felt almost as if it were angry at him. Fortunately he wasn't forced to step inside it. The electricity had been cut from all but the security systems. The elevator wasn't going anywhere, so they had no choice but to take the stairs.

On the fifth floor, Frank took him to one of the windows, a massive thing taller than a man with several glass panes set in an iron framework. On the other side of it was the fire escape. "So many people tried to climb down the fire escape," Frank told him, "it collapsed under their weight. It took out the fire escape just below it as it plunged to the ground."

"Jesus…."

"When the flames got too hot up here, workers just started leaping out to their deaths. I guess they thought it would be quicker than burning. Also, that way their families could identify their bodies for proper burials."

Toby made a face. "Ugh! That's okay. I don't need all the gory details."

"Sorry. But I wanted to point out that workers claimed to have heard the sound of the fire escape collapsing when they've been up here, along with the screams of young women. One man said the whole building felt as if it was shaking."

They visited the basement last, apparently because Frank thought it was the least interesting part of the building. It was dark enough down there to make Frank pull out his pocket Maglite to light their way. "Nothing's ever been reported down here," he said. "And our scanners haven't detected anything unusual."

But Toby sensed something *very* unusual. As they approached the mammoth furnace and boiler used to heat the mill—now stone cold and empty—he felt a wave of fear wash over him. He reached out to steady himself and take some deep breaths. After a moment he realized he'd grabbed Frank's forearm. The man hadn't shaken his hand off or glared at him. He was just watching Toby calmly.

"Sorry," Toby said, yanking his hand away.

"No problem. Are you… having another… attack or whatever happened in the foyer?"

Toby took another breath and wiped his palms against his shirt. They were damp with sweat. "I guess you could call it that. There's something here—something about this furnace. It was strong enough to break through my wards."

"Something like what?"

"Fear." Toby stepped forward, extending his hand out to touch the metal side of the furnace. But to his surprise, the contact didn't produce any strong sensations on a psychic level. "Something's weird, though. Is this the original furnace?"

It was the size of a small car and made of metal, but it seemed oddly modern. Toby would have thought a furnace from the early nineteen-hundreds might be coal-burning—not that he was an expert on that subject—but this appeared to be powered by propane.

"It isn't," Frank replied. He waved the EMF reader in the air around the furnace, pressing the button to illuminate the display. "The original had to be replaced after the fire. It's possible the cause of the fire was the furnace exploding or burning out of control. Nobody really knows. But the first floor above this part of the basement collapsed. Everything had to be replaced. The furnace you're touching is an even newer model put in place after the Second World War."

"Do you get a reading?"

Frank shook his head. "A bit higher, thanks to the metal, but not really significant."

"Something happened here."

"Like what?"

"I don't know. But I get a stronger sense of fear in this spot than anywhere else in the building."

Frank sounded a bit impatient when he said, "Savannah hasn't come up with anything about the basement. Nobody's known to have died down here, and none of the workers reported any phenomena here in the past."

"I'm telling you, something happened here," Toby insisted.

Frank shrugged, his expression noncommittal. "If you say so. Our equipment hasn't picked up anything. That's all I'm saying."

Chapter Five

The first scene was a touching one
From a maid so young in years,
She was standing by a window and
Her eyes were filled with tears.

"HE'S A nutjob," Houston said for about the tenth time. "That's all there is to it."

He and Frank were standing in line at the Taco Bell down the road from the mill building, waiting for the food they'd ordered for themselves, Savannah, and Toby. Frank needed to check that the twenty-four-hour 7-Eleven nearby had a public restroom. There were no working facilities in the mill building, and this stuff tended to go right through him.

"Yeah, well… a lot of people think *we're* nutjobs."

"True," Houston said.

The team members had retreated to their hotel rooms for some nap time during the afternoon, and Toby had hopefully taken a nap at his home, wherever that was. It was going to be a long night.

"Just give the guy a chance," Frank said. "I don't think he's any happier about being shoved into the middle of our investigation than we are, but Mrs. Hawley is paying the bills. He doesn't seem so bad, really. He let you drive his car, didn't he?"

Toby had been more than generous about letting Frank and Houston use his car to visit the hospital and make a food run. The van was needed at the mill, since it contained an assortment of tools that might be necessary.

Houston grunted but didn't bother answering. That was probably the best Frank was going to get out of him. The guy was barely holding it together with Junior in the hospital and still unconscious when they'd stopped by an hour earlier. If he hadn't known Houston was straight, Frank might have thought their relationship was closer than he'd realized. He'd never really been sure about Junior's sexuality. Frank hadn't seen him date anyone since graduating college, and even then Junior had never brought any girlfriends or boyfriends home on the holidays. But Houston had dated a lot of girls in the past. Never for long, and they'd all been too busy for much dating since they put the team together, but still….

No. They're just really close friends. A lot of guys their age have really intense relationships with their friends.

As they carried the bags full of burritos, quesadillas, and tacos to Toby's little Honda, Frank's cell phone rang. He juggled the bags a bit to free up a hand and answered it.

"Baba," Savannah said urgently, "you might want to get back here."

"Is something wrong?"

She took her time answering. "I don't know. Your boy's acting… strange."

My boy? "You mean Toby? What's he doing?"

"I… don't know. He went out onto the factory floor. I can see him on camera one. He's standing there motionless in the dark—he doesn't even have his flashlight on. I tried to raise him on the walkie-talkie, but he didn't respond."

"We'll be right there."

TOBY STOOD in the middle of the factory floor, far enough away from the foyer that the lights of the monitoring station seemed as tiny and far away as stars, and the noise of the gas-powered generator outside the front door was a distant purr. He knew Savannah was worried, but he was still where she could see him on one of the cameras, though he'd turned off the walkie-talkie she'd loaned him.

He needed some time alone in the heart of the building before the team started wandering through and deliberately disturbing things. According to Savannah, part of their methodology was to shout things out—questions and insults—in an attempt to elicit a response. Toby supposed that made sense, if the goal was to document activity. They wanted to stir things up a bit, try to get something on camera.

But that wasn't *his* goal. He could already feel a presence in the mill. Angering that presence was the last thing he wanted to do. Mrs. H. had hired him to establish communication with it, and if possible, convince it to move on.

He wasn't afraid, though he could sense the terror and rage etched into the stone walls over a century ago. If the spirits here had any power at all, electric lights or even Frank and his team wouldn't protect him from them. The only thing Toby could count on were his wards. But he could feel them fluctuating as the pervasive darkness attempted to get at the tiny, frail human in its midst. In the back of his mind, it growled in frustration, low and ominous, like the sound of metal scraping brick.

This was what had gotten to Junior and to so many others over the decades. As he strained to listen, Toby heard the faint clattering of machines... of sewing machines. Not like the small one he had at home, but heavy iron things bolted to the floors, operated by broad foot pedals rocking back and forth, back and forth—hundreds of them churning out a chaotic symphony of pedals and pulleys and metal gears....

ChChChChChCh—

The sound came to him as if from far away... or long ago. It was elusive, like a half-forgotten memory he was struggling to recall.

ChaChaChaChaChaCha—

As if it were growing closer, the sound became more insistent. Toby closed his eyes and spread his hands wide like the branches of an old television antenna. The sound grew louder, more distinct. But it brought something dark and sinister with it—a malignant hitchhiker, writhing in the dark like an octopus in a cloud of black ink.

ChakChakChakChakChakChakChak—

Toby's wards began to crack like eggshells. He felt fear as the thing enveloped him, penetrating the depths of his mind with tentacles of smoke. He smelled burning—wood, hot iron, burning hair and clothes and flesh....

DjakDjakDjakDjakDjakDjakDjakDjak....

SAVANNAH WAS losing it when Frank and Houston hurried into the foyer. She was searching frantically through the equipment crates, but she abandoned that the moment she saw him. "Goddamn it, Baba!" she exclaimed, startling him with a rare use of foul language. "He turned off his flashlight! I can see him on camera one, but I can't go after him without night-vision goggles or a flashlight or... *something*!"

Frank held a hand up in an attempt to calm her. "What's going on?"

"Last I saw the goggles," Houston interjected, "they were still in the van, unless one of you guys moved them."

"Listen!"

Savannah reached over to one of the amplifiers and turned the volume up. That particular control was connected to the microphone near camera one, and it was extremely sensitive, so it could pick up even quiet noises within about a fifty-foot radius of the camera. The sound that came out of the speaker was quiet but distinctly human. It sounded like Toby, muttering under his breath. But it was disturbingly monotone and repetitive—and fast, like some kind of machine.

"DjakDjakDjakDjakDjakDjakDjakDjak…."

It went on and on without ceasing.

"What the fuck is he doing?" Houston asked.

"I don't know. He was quiet for a long time. Then he started making that noise."

"There was a Special Ed kid in my high school who used to go into these weird fits—"

"You two stay here," Frank interrupted. "I've got a flashlight. I'll go see if he's okay." Somehow he didn't think Toby would be making a noise like that if he was fine. Not unless it was some kind of meditation chant or something. It didn't sound particularly soothing, though. Toby was repeating the… word… in a rapid, agitated voice.

Frank walked out onto the factory floor, his flashlight illuminating a small circle of the foot-worn oak floor. Having a light with him did little to relieve the oppressive gloom of the place. It merely made everything outside the circle of light seem darker.

Toby hadn't moved. He stood with both hands splayed out, as still as a statue, and as Frank approached, the sound of his muttered chant grew louder.

"Toby?"

Toby's body remained motionless, but his head slowly turned as if to look at Frank over his shoulder. But his eyes were half closed, only the whites visible. "DjakDjakDjakDjakDjakDjakDjakDjak…."

"What are you doing, Toby? It's kind of weirding us out."

Toby's face contorted in anger, and he spoke more slowly, clipping the word until Frank could clearly make it out. "Jack…. Jack…. Jack…. Jack…."

"Who's Jack?"

"*Jaaaaaaaaaaa*…." Toby shouted, the name dissolving into a scream.

Frank took a step back, uncertain how he should respond. Before he could make a decision, Toby threw his arms over his head and collapsed hard on his knees. He was silent for a few moments except for his ragged breathing. Then he took several long, tremulous breaths and toppled to the floor.

Frank rushed to his side, terrified Toby might be dead. His skin was cold and clammy to Frank's touch, though he was breathing faintly. But he was unconscious.

"WHAT THE hell are you guys doing here? This is the second time you've called us in a week!"

"We're doing what we were paid to do by the owner of the building."

"If there was another fall like that last one—"

"He didn't fall. He passed out or had a seizure or something."

"Guys! I think he's coming around. Toby? Can you hear me?"

Toby tried to answer, but he couldn't manage more than a thin rasp. He didn't recognize the voice of the woman talking to him. He heard Frank arguing with somebody—a man—but he didn't recognize the other voice. Somebody was touching him. He felt hands on his arms and upper chest. Something seemed to be strapped to his face....

"His pulse is stronger now. Can you open your eyes for me, Toby?"

It wasn't easy, but Toby managed to pry his lids open, even though they felt as if they were glued together. Judging by the heavy iron girders directly above him, he was still lying out on the factory floor. But somebody had placed a pillow under his head and another one under his legs. Everything was lit up, which seemed odd, considering the mill had no electricity.

A young woman moved into view over him. "Good! Now I'm going to shine a light in your eyes for just a second. Try to keep them open." She shined a penlight into each eye in turn, leaving spots in Toby's vision when she pulled it away. "Pupils dilating normally. Can you tell me what your name is?"

That seemed kind of silly. She'd just called him by name a minute ago. But he knew she was testing to see if he was lucid. He cleared his throat and was able to give her a muffled "Toby" from behind the oxygen mask—still—strapped over his mouth.

She held her hand in front of his face. "How many fingers?"

"Three."

This went on for a while, before Toby was able to convince her he was fully conscious. At last she removed the oxygen mask and allowed him to sit up. But she made him stay seated.

During this time, Toby heard Frank's phone ring and saw the man drift off out of the circle of light cast by four of the battery-powered high-intensity LED lanterns belonging to his team. He was gone for a few minutes while the EMTs continued to fuss over Toby. They tried to convince him to go to the hospital, but he was adamant in his refusal. He felt fine now. His knees hurt, but he could flex them. He had no desire to waste the rest of the night in the ER.

Frank returned and asked the EMT Toby had first seen upon opening his eyes, "Is it okay if I talk to him?"

"Go right ahead. He seems to be doing fine."

Frank squatted beside Toby and looked directly into his eyes. His reddish hair was sticking up in all directions, which was kind of cute, but his face looked haggard. "Do you remember what you were saying, just before you passed out?"

"I remember... a presence," Toby said slowly. "It felt like a man. I thought I could keep him out, but he was incredibly strong—boiling over with rage."

"What else do you remember?"

"Nothing."

"Do you remember a name?"

Toby concentrated. Gradually, something took shape in the back of his mind. "Jack," he said. "I think it was Jack."

"But you don't know who Jack is?"

"No."

"Nobody named Jack died in that fire. Savannah has a database she put together when she was researching it, and I had her check while the EMTs were tending to you. Only about twenty of the victims were men, and none of them was named Jack. There was a James. I suppose it's possible he was nicknamed Jack, but...."

Frank sighed and frowned, glancing down at the phone still in his hand. "Anyway, I might have brushed it off. You seemed kind of out of your mind while you were chanting. Maybe you were just hallucinating. Except Dr. Khambatta called me from the hospital. Louis—Junior—woke up about half an hour ago. But only briefly. He's unconscious again."

"I'm sorry to hear that."

Frank rubbed his chin with the back of his hand. "The point is... he said something when he woke up. Screamed it, really. It sounded like a name. He kept screaming it over and over again, until he passed out." He paused. "The name was Jack."

Chapter Six

She cried, "Oh, save me! Save me!"
She called her mother's name,
But her mother could not save her
And she fell back in the flame.

SAVANNAH HAD managed to find a list printed in the *Hawley Sentinel* of all who perished in the 1907 fire the day after the disaster, but not everyone who worked for the mill died. Some had escaped, and still others just hadn't been in the building at the time. But those names weren't a matter of public record.

Still, a company as large as Hawley Mills had to keep books. Federal regulations in 1907 were largely nonexistent—income taxes weren't in effect at the time, and there were few safety regulations—but the company itself would have tracked payroll. More than a hundred years later, those records might have been destroyed… if it hadn't been for William Ezra Hawley, Celia Hawley's grandfather, the man who built the factory. He'd been meticulous about the bookkeeping, and he'd kept all the records.

His son hadn't shared his obsession for storing everything, so he'd destroyed most of the older records. However, he'd been contacted by a man from Maine, Thomas Deacon, who had a fascination with the old New England industrial mills of the late nineteenth and early twentieth centuries. Thomas purchased many of the old records, particularly those around the time of the fire, which had been a memorable event in New England— memorable enough to have had a folk ballad written about it, in fact.

Celia had apparently been in contact with Mr. Deacon for a number of years, since he was always interested in gathering more information. She told Savannah he'd passed away in 1994. But he willed all of his papers, everything he'd collected over the decades, to the town library historical room where he'd lived.

It was because of this chain of events C-Troop Paranormal found themselves on a long-ass road trip to Boothbay Harbor, Maine—about three hours. Frank chose to ride with Toby, despite his concern Toby's car might fall apart en route, while Houston and Savannah took the van. Technically there was a third seat in the van—an extra one Houston had rigged up just behind the driver's seat—but it was uncomfortable and more than a little risky with all the team's equipment packed into the back.

"I apologize for not having a working radio," Toby said as they pulled onto Route 27.

The lack of air-conditioning was more of an inconvenience than the radio, but Frank merely rolled down his window and said, "That's not a problem. I don't really like listening to it, anyway."

"I didn't think so. I pictured you as more of an I-spy-with-my-little-eye kind of guy."

Frank gave him a sour look, but the smirk Toby was wearing made it obvious he was pulling Frank's leg. Frank snorted and settled back in his seat. It was going to be a long ride.

They'd already had a discussion about the stupidity of Toby wandering out onto the factory floor by himself in the dark. He'd surprised Frank by admitting he'd misjudged the danger, and then apologizing for what he put the team through. So… fine. No point in harping on it. At least it had produced an interesting lead.

Searching for something they could talk about, he settled on, "So what made you go into your line of work?"

"Running an occult bookstore and herb shop?"

"I guess I meant doing psychic readings," Frank amended.

"I don't know. I've always felt a connection to the spirit world, ever since I was a boy. We had an elderly neighbor who passed away. I was too young to fully grasp what death meant, at the time, and I was puzzled that everybody acted sad about it. Because I still visited with him in his garden every day."

Frank laughed. Then he quickly stopped himself, afraid he might have offended the guy. "Sorry."

But Toby didn't seem offended. He smiled and said, "A lot of people might say I was just fantasizing, the way a lot of kids do, but I'm convinced I was really talking to Mr. Paulsen. He was happy to be reunited with his wife. I'd never met her, since she died before I was born. And he said he just wanted to make sure his son and others who loved him would be all right, now that he'd left."

Frank wasn't sure that was convincing. Those were typical sentiments people always claimed to hear from the dead—things are good on the other side, people are reunited with loved ones, but they're concerned about those they left behind. Stock psychic mumbo-jumbo. He didn't feel Toby was trying to scam him, exactly. He liked the guy. He seemed okay, for the most part. But was he fooling himself about his ability to commune with the spirits? Maybe.

Except he got a name for us. One that could pan out.

They'd just have to wait and see on that, Frank supposed.

"What about you?" Toby asked. "What got you into ghost hunting?"

There was a note of humor in his voice that Frank found irritating. "I know what you're thinking," he said. "I watched one too many episodes of *Ghost Hunters* on television and thought, 'Gee willikers! I could do that!'"

Toby laughed. "Well... maybe."

"No. What really happened was Louis and I lost our mom to cancer when he was just five years old."

"I'm sorry."

The stricken look on Toby's face was almost funny. Frank waved a dismissive hand. "We were both devastated, of course, but Louis was falling apart, and I knew I had to be strong for him."

"You couldn't have been more than ten yourself."

"I was eleven." Frank shrugged. "Anyway, one of the ways I dealt with it was reading him ghost stories. Not scary ones, but cute ones about ghost families and children who are ghosts like *Ghosts Who Went to School*. It made him feel better to think about Mom becoming a friendly spirit who might be looking over us. As we got older, we started reading about real-life hauntings and poltergeists. It just kind of developed from there."

Toby gave him a quick smile before returning his attention to the road. "That's really sweet. You're always looking after everyone, aren't you? Not just Louis, but your whole team."

Frank was a bit embarrassed by that, so he just grunted noncommittally and glanced out the window at the passing greenery. Route 27 was just a two-lane road carved through the forest—paved but not exactly a highway. At this time of year, it was a nice drive.

"NORMALLY," MRS. Montgomery said, setting the heavy bound volume on the table with a *thud*, "we only allow one of these to be checked out at a time. But I suppose, since Celia Hawley called on your behalf...."

"It would help us a lot if we could each look through one," Savannah told her sweetly. "We've only booked into the B and B for one night."

The elderly librarian smiled and nodded. "I'll bring out the others."

It was boring work. Toby was used to keeping the books in his shop, but that was child's play compared to going through the seven bound volumes of paperwork from Hawley Mill. Most of it was handwritten, faded, and illegible, and it was only roughly ordered by date. No attempt had been made to separate payroll from receipts or shipping invoices.

Frank and Savannah dug into the task like the professionals Toby now considered them to be, but Houston quickly got on his nerves. He had the attention span of a gnat. His constant fidgeting and talking finally got so annoying, Frank snapped at him. "Houston! If you can't focus on what you're doing, find something else to occupy yourself."

Houston looked wounded. "Like what?"

"I don't know. I'm starting to get hungry." Frank looked at Toby and Savannah. "You guys want some food?"

"Sure."

"I guess so."

Frank pulled out his wallet and fished out a couple of twenties. He handed them to Houston. "Go find a McDonald's and get us each a cheeseburger meal or something. You're not vegetarian, are you?" The last was directed at Toby.

"No. Triple cheeseburger for me, Baba."

Houston looked offended by his use of Frank's nickname, but he merely gave Toby a sour look. He took Frank's and Savannah's orders and left.

"If looks could kill," Savannah muttered under her breath.

Toby smirked and shook his head. "So much for the slumber party I had planned tonight. I'd been counting on doing our hair and painting each other's toenails." When Houston had booked rooms at the Briarwood Bed and Breakfast, only three had been available. So he'd given Frank and Savannah their own rooms and booked himself and Toby into the room with two single beds.

"Aw."

Frank sighed. "I'm getting tired of his attitude. He can have my room tonight. I'll room with you."

"Okay."

"Unless you want the single."

"No," Toby said quickly. "I don't mind sharing a room with you." He was surprised at how pleased he was to learn Frank would be bunking with him. It might not be such a good thing, considering Frank was straight. He'd have to stay on his best behavior.

Mrs. Montgomery would have a fit if they ate McDonald's food in the historical room, so they'd all have to take a break when Houston returned. That meant they needed to focus while he was gone, so they stuck their noses back in the books. Fortunately, without Houston distracting them, things went much easier.

"I've got something!" Savannah exclaimed about a half hour later.

"An employee list?"

"No. But we're looking for a 'Jack,' aren't we?" She slid the book across the table to him. "Take a look at this."

It was a handwritten note, addressed to someone named Mr. Roberts and signed with an almost illegible signature. It might have said, "Stephen Latimer." But the text of the note was fairly easy to read.

> *Mr. Roberts,*
> *We may have to do something about Miss Quinn.*
> *There are rumors around the floor that she's taken up*
> *with the new shift supervisor, Jack Bishop. Have a word*
> *with the man, please. If he and Miss Quinn have been*
> *sneaking off together, fire the girl. Mr. Hawley does*
> *not want his reputation tarnished by that sort of thing*
> *among his seamstresses.*
> *Cordially,*
> *Stephen Latimer*

The note was dated just two days before the fire.

"Fire the girl, of course," Toby muttered. "No word about disciplining the boyfriend."

Savannah leaned across the table to flip the page. "Then there's this."

> *Mr. Latimer,*
> *I've spoken with both Bishop and the young*
> *woman in question. She insisted that she is not involved*

with Bishop in any way. I have to say, I found her
convincing. I shall leave the matter to your judgement.
Please advise.
   Cordially,
   Henry Roberts

"That one's dated the morning of the fire," Frank observed. "Was that the end of it?"

"Apparently," Savannah said. "I don't see any more notes about it. And there was a Rosaleen Quinn on the list of those who died in the fire, so the poor girl wasn't dismissed—not that day. It's too bad. It would have saved her life. She was only eighteen."

Frank looked at Toby. "Does that name sound familiar? Jack Bishop?"

"I don't know," Toby replied. Truthfully, he didn't remember much about what had happened the evening the name "Jack" surfaced. "I could try to contact him. Or Rosaleen."

Frank shifted uncomfortably and glanced away. "If you think that'll work."

Chapter Seven

The next scene was a horrible one
Just as it caught my eye.
They were leaping from a window
From up so very high.

THE BRIARWOOD B and B turned out to be very quaint. It had a common area downstairs that reminded Frank of his grandmother's house—lace doilies and antimacassars draped over all the chairs and couches and an absurd number of porcelain figurines taking up every available inch of shelf space. His grandmother had been partial to rabbits, but the owners of the Briarwood obsessed on seagulls, lobster traps, buoys, and an infinite variety of seashells. Beyond the living room, a breakfast area with three small tables looked out upon the harbor.

The owners, Mr. and Mrs. Libby, had a sixteen-year-old son—a thin, shy boy named Gale who spoke in a quiet mumble. He escorted the visitors upstairs to their rooms, dropping Houston and Savannah off on the second floor, then continuing up to the third floor with Frank and Toby in tow.

Houston had looked irritated when Frank informed him of the room change. It wasn't because he had any desire to room with Toby, Frank knew. But Houston had specifically given Frank the largest single room. Frank was the boss, and in Houston's eyes that made him the most important member of the team. He was very big on people respecting the boss, which Frank often found cute—not that he'd ever said that to Houston. But Toby had been hanging around with them for almost a week, and apart from taking a risk he shouldn't have, he'd been cooperative and friendly the entire time. Houston's automatic dislike of the guy was getting old.

Frank could have insisted Toby take the single room, but he knew that would *really* get Houston's goat. No need to stir things up that much. Frank had roomed with less pleasant guys in college, and it was just for one night. Hopefully Toby didn't snore.

The room was small, but not uncomfortably so. In the front, where the roof slanted down, two dormer windows looked out upon the bay. The beds were to the left of the door, one flush against the wall, and the other more or less in the middle of the room. In keeping with the general décor of the B and B, the beds had old-fashioned metal frames painted in white enamel, and were draped with white crochet bedspreads covered in rows of... whatever those raised patterns were called. Frank knew next to nothing about crochet. The patterns were diamond-shaped, if that meant anything.

"There's a bathroom across the hall," Gale said, almost inaudibly. "Just a toilet and sink. If you want to shower in the morning, you'll have to use the bathroom on the second floor. Mom doesn't like it if people run around in towels or their underwear, so make sure you're dressed when you go back and forth."

"Okay, we will. Thanks."

Gale backed out and closed the door, leaving Frank and Toby alone.

"Do you want the wall or the middle?" Toby asked cheerfully.

"Take your pick. I'll be fine with whatever."

Toby dropped his travel bag near the foot of the bed near the wall. He flopped down on the mattress, causing the frame to creak ominously. "Oops! Guess we'd better not get too athletic."

Frank had never seen a man blush before, but he did now, as Toby grasped the implications of what he'd just said. He gave Frank an embarrassed smile and then quickly looked away.

God, you are too cute.

Frank hadn't seen any indication Toby was gay, so he figured it was best not to let his thoughts stray in that direction. He set his bag down in the corner, out of the way. "So how do you plan on contacting Jack Bishop? Do you just go off and meditate like you did the other night?"

"That sometimes works," Toby answered. He shrugged. "Or sometimes I hold a more formal séance, if others are interested in participating."

Franked huffed out a laugh. "Jesus! Don't let Houston hear you say that. He'll flip."

"Why?"

Frank came over and sat down on his bed across from Toby. "The thing you might want to keep in mind is... we started this whole thing, C-Troop Paranormal, as a scientific endeavor. Yeah, I know some people would think that's funny, maybe even you—"

"No," Toby said sharply. "I know you take yourselves seriously, and you're trying to be scientific, even if I'm not convinced on the science."

Frank nodded. "Well, good. But your... methods... are different. I'll be honest. Before I met you, I wouldn't have wanted our group associated with a psychic."

"But you do now?"

Toby was looking at him with that wry expression he wore when he was yanking Frank's chain. But Frank didn't rise to the bait. He just smiled.

"Maybe. I guess I've taken a liking to you, at least."

"Thanks."

"But Houston hasn't."

"No shit."

"And talking about séances and channeling and shit like that.... It's just gonna make him nervous about where things are going with our group."

Toby raised his eyebrows and nodded slowly. "Okay. Good to know. What about you? Do those things make *you* nervous?"

You *make me nervous*. "I'm still trying to make my mind up on that subject."

"Fair enough."

Frank glanced around uncomfortably, not knowing where to take the conversation next, until his eyes settled on the alarm clock—a baby blue relic from the fifties with hands coated in a yellow-green paint he hoped was phosphorous instead of radium. Just past nine thirty.

They'd stayed at the library for another hour or so, hoping to find more information, and then wandered along the wharf for a while. Frank's grandparents had lived in York, so being near the ocean didn't seem like a big deal to him. But Savannah had never seen the area. She'd dragged the boys to every silly bric-a-brac store she could find—not to shop, thankfully, but just to do the tourist thing. She'd finally insisted they stop at a place that sold lobster, because she'd never tried it. And wasn't that what tourists were supposed to do in Maine? Eat lobster?

Frank hated lobster. But he indulged her.

"I think I might turn in," he said. "All that running around wore me out."

No! Don't! Stop it! Stop it! Stop it!
   Help me!

I can't breathe! I can't breathe! Oh God!

"Help me!"

"Toby! What is it?"

He thrashed about, his arms caught in the bedsheets, until strong hands gripped his shoulders. But that just made him panic more. He punched at the blankets and kicked his legs, trying to free himself. "No!"

The hands released him. "Toby! It's just me—Frank. I won't hurt you."

"Help me," he sobbed.

"It's okay. You're safe. I'm gonna turn on the light."

The room lit up with a click from the small table lamp between the beds.

Even as he became aware of the room, Frank, where he was, Toby couldn't stop sobbing. He finally freed his hands and brought them up to cover his face.

He felt the mattress sink as Frank sat on the bed beside him. "Are you okay?"

Toby tried to answer, but he couldn't. His entire body was trembling. He'd never been so frightened, so lost.

Frank touched his shoulder again, tentatively. When Toby didn't resist, Frank gathered him into his arms and held him tight against his broad chest. He was bare-chested and the warmth of his skin was soothing. He smelled good, a combination of the musky scent of his skin, Old Spice, and the fresh smell of sea air he'd picked up on their walk that day. Toby lowered his hands and instinctively pressed his face into the comfort of Frank's embrace.

"Did you have a nightmare?" Frank asked.

He finally found his voice, saying weakly, "More than that."

"Do you want to talk about it?"

"Tomorrow." Toby felt exhausted. His body wanted to drift off again, yet he was afraid to give in to the weariness—afraid of what might be waiting for him in the darkness.

To his surprise, Frank lifted a hand to stroke his hair. "Can you go back to sleep?"

"Don't leave me." He sounded so pathetic. But he felt so vulnerable right now, he hadn't been able to stop himself.

Frank said, "How about if we just lie down for a bit?"

He shifted his body around so he could lie back against Toby's pillow. Toby was embarrassed to hear himself whimper as Frank moved him, but the man didn't release him from his arms. He adjusted their positions until they were lying side by side with Toby nestled against him, his face pressed snugly against Frank's warm side and Frank's arm draped protectively around his back.

"Do you mind if I get under the covers?" Frank asked quietly. He sounded embarrassed. "It's kind of chilly."

"No."

Frank arched his back to lift the blankets out from under him. A moment later he was in the bed, his hip against Toby's crotch, and Toby finally registered they were both in their underwear. No wonder Frank had been self-conscious. Toby prayed he wouldn't get a hard-on, since it would be obvious in this position.

"You want the light on?"

"No. You can turn it off." He felt safe now.

Frank stretched and a second later the room was dark, except for the pale glow of moonlight filtering in through the windows.

"Good night," Frank said.

Then he kissed the top of Toby's head.

Chapter Eight

And the only means of their escape
Was sliding down a rope,
And just as they were half way down
The burning strands they broke.

THE MORNING was embarrassing.

Frank was a bit disoriented, at first. There was a naked man lying against him, warm and smooth in his arms, making his body tingle. Frank's cock was hard in his underwear, straining against the fabric, and the man was grinding his crotch against Frank's hip as their legs intertwined and caressed each other.

Then his memory came back to him, and he realized just who he was in bed with.

Oh shit!

He stopped his legs from their unconscious attempt at morning frottage, but Toby whimpered in his sleep and continued dry humping his hip. Fortunately, now that Frank was fully conscious, he could feel Toby's underwear rubbing against his skin—he wasn't completely naked, after all. He was, however, very erect. And as good as it felt to lie with him like this, Frank needed to put a stop to it.

"Toby," he said gently. "Toby. Wake up, man."

Toby made a sound that shot straight through Frank's throbbing cock—a sensual moan like a man being caressed—and slid his hand down Frank's belly until his fingers were cupping Frank's erection through the thin cotton of his briefs.

"Okay, that was really not what I was hoping for." Frank groaned. He reached down and pulled Toby's hand off his crotch. "Toby! Wake up!"

Toby started and gasped. "Wha...?"

"It's morning. We fell asleep."

The poor guy seemed really out of it. He looked up at Frank with his face scrunched up like an adorable child, his dark brown curls a tangled heap on top of his head. "Did we have sex?"

Frank's eyes opened painfully wide. "No! You were upset. I just… you didn't want to be alone…."

"Oh. I remember now."

The way he'd asked about having sex was so casual, as if he wouldn't have been surprised. *Is he gay?* The thought did nothing to ease Frank's state of arousal. But he couldn't think of a way to ask without sounding like he was making a pass.

"I thought I'd get up in a few minutes," Frank said, "once you'd gone back to sleep—go back to my own bed. But I fell asleep too."

"It's okay." Toby rolled away from him, and Frank lifted his arm to let him free.

Frank took that as his cue to get the fuck out of the bed. He slipped out from under the sheets and stood up, only then remembering he had a huge hard-on. He covered his crotch with his hands and was surprised when he brushed against a wet spot on his hip. He looked down at it. "Um… did you come on me?"

Frank watched in fascination as Toby slid his hand down underneath the covers and felt his crotch. His face flushed crimson as he withdrew it, glanced at the palm, and then wiped it on his chest. "Uh… not exactly. I just… leak a lot. Sorry."

"Oh. Well… that's cool. You know, it happens. Can't really control morning wood…." *Or morning dry humping.*

"Christ, this is embarrassing."

Frank laughed nervously. "I had a boner too, bud. It's okay. We're just lucky nobody was here to film it and put it on YouTube." *And you have no fucking idea how much I want to crawl back in that bed with you, right now.*

"I'm really sorry about how I behaved last night," Toby said, rubbing his face with one hand. "I'm not usually such a baby about bad visions. This one just kind of snuck up on me in a dream…."

"Do you want to tell me what you saw?"

"It was too chaotic to make much sense of. There was fear and anger and… someone forcing me down onto a cold, cement floor…. Oh God! I was raped!" Toby's hand trembled as he lowered it. He took several deep breaths and blinked his eyes rapidly. "I mean… *she* was… I… I need to get up."

He seemed to be having trouble sitting up, so Frank held out a hand and half lifted him to a sitting position. Toby let go and sat on the edge of the bed, hugging himself and rocking slightly.

"I'll be all right. I just need to…."

Then he was sobbing, and Frank had no idea what to do. He wasn't sure if he believed in the "vision" Toby had had, but it was clearly real to him, and it had traumatized him severely. It tore Frank up inside to see him like this. He kneeled in front of Toby and placed a tentative hand on his forearm. "Toby…."

"Jesus, Frank! I *felt* it! I felt him slamming into me! I had no idea it could hurt so much! And… *ugh*… she *trusted* the fucker! She thought he cared about her!"

"Do you know who she was?"

"Rosaleen," Toby said, clutching at his hand. "Rosaleen Quinn. She didn't die in the fire, Frank. She was raped in that basement—and I think she was murdered!"

"I WENT online last night to see if I could find any more information on either Rosaleen or Jack," Savannah said at breakfast.

The four of them were eating downstairs in the Briarwood's dining area. The food was good—pancakes, bacon, and eggs prepared by Mrs. Libby and served by Gale. The orange juice wasn't exactly fresh-squeezed, but it was a decent brand. And the toast used fresh bread from a local bakery. The windows presented them with a gorgeous view of the harbor, sparkling in the morning sunlight.

Toby had filled Savannah and Houston in on the details of his vision the night before. Thankfully it was already beginning to fade, or at least to become more distant. It no longer felt as if the rape and murder had happened directly to *him*, though it was still difficult to talk about. In a way, this made it clearer. He could now recall details about the events he'd witnessed—details he'd been too emotional to think about earlier.

Still, he knew he'd never forget what he'd experienced. He didn't want to.

Someone has to remember.

"The *Hawley Sentinel* is archived back to 1900," Savannah went on. "But I couldn't find any obituaries for them. No funeral notices, nothing. That isn't really unusual. The families were probably too poor to be putting paid notices in the papers. They'd let their family and friends know by word of mouth."

"Where does that leave us?" Frank asked.

"Nowhere, really." She placed a hand over Toby's where it rested on the table. With his nerves as badly frayed as they were, he was grateful for the comfort. "I'm not saying I don't believe that vision you had, sugar, but… if her body wasn't found until after the fire—or never found at all—there won't be any record of a murder anywhere."

Houston glanced up from his pancakes and asked with his mouth half full, "How could they say she was killed in the fire if they never found her body?"

"Oh, sugar, they never found most of those poor girls' bodies. Only the ones who jumped out windows or asphyxiated from the smoke in the stairwell. Most were burned up. It was like a furnace in there."

"Jack might have survived," Frank insisted. "What if he killed her and took off? The fire started later that morning, and it covered his tracks. He would've gotten off scot-free. He'd have to be dead by now, unless he's almost a hundred and thirty, but he could have died any time between then and, say, 1997."

"So you just want me to search eighty years of archives for the name 'Jack Bishop'?"

"No," Frank said, giving her a wry smile. "Jack may have moved away. That seems likely."

"Ah, I see. You want me to search the archives of *every* newspaper in the United States over an eighty-year time period for what is probably a fairly common name." Then she added with a sweet smile, "Aren't you just precious?"

Frank grinned back at her, but he was saved from answering by the ringer of his cell phone. He pulled it out of his pocket and glanced at it, his smile vanishing. "It's the hospital."

They all froze and looked at him in trepidation.

"Frank Carter." He listened a moment, a scowl coming across his handsome face. "Another one?" Pause. "Well, what's his condition now?"

The conversation went on for a minute or so, during which Toby watched Houston out of the corner of his eye. The young man swallowed his food and stared hard at Frank, his knuckles whitening as he clutched his fork tightly. For the first time, Toby sensed something from him—a powerful anxiety radiating from his body like heat.

He's at the breaking point, Toby realized.

When Frank hung up, Houston pounced on him. "What did they say?"

Frank seemed weary as he slowly set the phone down and glanced across the table at him. "Nothing's really changed. He's still unconscious. Though she said it was odd—his brainwaves are very active, like a man in REM sleep. Not typically what they would call a coma. But he won't wake up."

"If nothing's changed," Houston persisted, "why did they call? What did you mean when you said 'another one'?"

Frank sighed. "He had another episode around two o'clock in the morning." He looked pointedly at Toby. "Which was the time the clock read when you had your nightmare."

"An episode?" Toby asked, almost afraid of what the answer might be.

"He started shouting. Something like, 'You fucking got me in trouble, you stuck-up bitch!'"

Chapter Nine

Christ, Christ, what a horrible mess,
They were mangled, burned, and killed,
Six stories high and falling from
The burning Hawley Mill.

FRANK'S MOOD was dark as they finished their breakfast and packed for the trip back to New Hampshire. Louis's brain being in REM, instead of a comatose state, seemed like a good thing. But it made no sense he was even in a coma to begin with. Sure, he took a bad fall down the stairs, but the MRI hadn't shown any sign of brain damage. He should have been on the mend already.

His mood didn't improve any when Houston took him aside just as they were about to head out.

"You and I need to talk."

Shit. What fresh hell is this? "What is it, Houston?"

The young man frowned as he fidgeted with his jacket zipper. "Savannah and that Toby guy have been talking about doing a séance to learn more about 'Jack and Rosaleen.'" He said the last two names in a mocking tone of voice.

Fuck. Frank had warned Toby about letting Houston hear about that. "And?"

"Are you fucking kidding me? A séance, Frank?"

Frank shrugged and spread his hands. "I know. It's not scientific. It may not produce any data we can verify—"

"We don't even know if there ever was a Jack! Yes, we know there was a supervisor named Jack Bishop and he was having an affair with a worker named Rosaleen Quinn, who later died in the fire. Anything else is speculation. Toby's making all this shit up, Frank! You know he is!"

"No, I don't know that," Frank said. "I know it's tenuous, and we might ultimately have to throw it out, but from what I've seen, I think he's a decent guy. I don't think he's a fraud. At least, not a deliberate one. *Deluded*, maybe. He could be wrong about these 'visions' he claims to have—"

"Did you sleep with him?"

That caught Frank off guard. He stared at Houston in disbelief for a moment. Then shock was supplanted by anger. "I don't recall prying into your sex life, so what the fuck makes you think you can pry into mine?"

Houston flinched as though he'd been slapped. He tugged at his zipper and looked at the ground like a chastised puppy. But he wasn't ready to give up just yet. "He's fooling you. That's all I have to say."

Frank bit back an angry retort. Houston was acting like a child, and Frank wasn't in the mood. But he took a breath and forced himself to say calmly, "If you don't want to participate in the séance, you don't have to."

"I don't. I want to go to the hospital. Louis needs me."

That curtailed Frank's anger. He nodded. "Maybe you're right. We haven't had much time to sit with him since the accident. If you go, you can try reading to him or something. It might get through."

"You'll let me go?"

"Of course."

"Can I stay the night with him?"

That request was a little surprising, but Frank saw no reason Houston couldn't, if the hospital allowed it. He clapped a hand on the young man's shoulder. "I'll call the hospital and see if I can arrange it."

As he turned to go back to the car, Houston dropped the bomb on him. "I love him, you know."

Frank turned slowly back to him. "Love? As in *love*?"

Houston nodded, holding his chin up as if he expected Frank to rail at him.

"I thought you were straight."

"So did I," Houston said uncomfortably. "Until a year or so ago."

"What happened then?"

"I don't know. I just realized I didn't want to be with anybody but him."

"Does Louis know that?"

Houston shook his head, and Frank thought he might be tearing up. "I was afraid to tell him. I kept putting it off. I didn't expect…."

Frank took a hold of his jacket and tugged on it. Houston put up no resistance as Frank pulled him into an embrace. "Tell him when you sit with him," Frank said quietly into his ear. "They say people in comas can sometimes hear you. I don't know if he feels the same, but… don't count on getting another chance."

FRANK SEEMED to be brooding when he got into the car for the trip home, so Toby let him ride in silence for a while. But when they passed Gardiner, Frank said, "When you woke up this morning, the first thing you wanted to know is if we had sex…."

"Oh," Toby said. "Are you about to tell me we *did*?"

He certainly couldn't remember it, if they had. All he remembered was Frank holding him after the nightmare. Though Frank had kissed him….

Frank looked at him closely. "You think it's a real possibility?"

"What are you asking, Frank? I wasn't trying to imply anything about you, if that's what you mean."

Frank grunted and shifted in his seat. "Sorry. I don't do this very much. The thing is… I *am* gay. And I was wondering if you might be too."

Toby suppressed a laugh at his seriousness. "Yes, I am. And if your next question is, 'Do I find you attractive?' then the answer to that is also yes."

"Oh. Okay." Frank glanced out the window. "I think you're attractive too."

Toby did laugh at that. "Now I'm regretting letting you escape from my bed this morning."

"Yeah, me too."

They rode in companionable silence for a few miles, neither bringing up the possibility of something happening between them now. Toby was certainly open to the idea. He found Frank sweet and interesting and adored the way he looked after everyone in his charge—even an uninvited psychic having nightmares at two in the morning. He was a good man, solid, dependable… and cute as hell.

Toby wasn't sure what he could offer in return, though. Oh, he was decent-looking. He was vain enough to acknowledge that. He could probably offer Frank a good time in bed. But beyond that? They had a shared interest in the occult, but they were coming at it from opposite directions.

Well, we'll just have to see how it goes.

"So," Frank said, breaking into his thoughts, "do we want to take this somewhere?"

"I certainly do."

Frank gave him an adorably shy smile. "The team should probably have some downtime tonight. Houston... has some things he needs to work out. And Savannah would research till she dropped, if I didn't order her to take a night off now and then. What are you gonna be doing?"

"I'm hoping to have dinner with you."

AFTER CHECKING in on Junior at the hospital and making sure Houston had whatever he needed, Frank went back to the hotel to shower and dress. Then he drove the van to pick Toby up at his apartment—a nice little space he rented above his shop. Frank had been both curious to see it and dreading it. What if it turned out to be some kind of psychedelic pad with a shrine to the Fox Sisters or something like that? There was only so far Frank was willing to bend on the "psychic" thing. But it was just an apartment, neat and sparsely furnished. There was what looked like a Wiccan altar on the dresser in the bedroom, but Frank could handle that. A man's religion was his own business. As long as he didn't worship the Cottingley Fairies.

They'd have to have a talk about that at some point.

But it was hard to give the apartment much more than a glance when his tour guide was looking so incredible. Toby had showered, so his loose curls were a bit wet, which Frank found surprisingly sexy. He'd dressed in a pale blue button-down shirt that hugged his torso deliciously, complemented by tight gray slacks that displayed a perfect, tight ass to magnificent effect. Frank was already sporting a semi and they hadn't even begun the evening.

Hawley wasn't exactly known for its gourmet cuisine, but Manchester was only a half hour away. Toby directed him to a Nepalese restaurant called Café Momo on Hanover Street.

Frank's eyes went wide when he looked over the menu—not because of the prices, though they were steep, but because of the food itself. "Boar?" he asked. "Goat? Buffalo? Where the hell do they even *find* those around here?"

Toby laughed. "There's a buffalo farm in Dover, about fifty miles from here. And goats are everywhere."

"Wild boar?"

"I think they get that from a ranch in Texas. We don't have to eat here, if you don't want to."

Frank shook his head. "No, I didn't say that. I just… don't recognize anything on the menu."

"To me, it tends to taste like an interesting combination of Indian and Chinese. A 'momo' is a lot like a Chinese dumpling. Some of the chicken dishes taste somewhat Indian, but the spice isn't quite the same. They also have fantastic mojitos. Go figure."

Frank passed on the mojito, since he was driving, and the company van was finicky enough to handle sober, but he couldn't pass up an opportunity to eat buffalo momo and something called "Lamb Nepali Way." He was delighted to discover they had mango lassi on the drink list.

After they'd ordered, he looked across the table at Toby's beautiful features illuminated by the candle in the center of the table, and couldn't help saying, "You look incredible."

Toby smiled shyly. "So do you."

"I'm all right, I suppose." He'd showered, trimmed his beard a bit, and put on some clean clothes. Nothing fancy. "But I've been wanting to tell you ever since I first saw you getting out of your car—you are a beautiful thing to look upon."

"Thing?"

"Sorry, I'm not very good at expressing myself."

Toby's smile broadened, and he reached across the table to slide his fingers over the top of Frank's hand. "I'm teasing. It's been a long time since anyone's said anything that sweet to me. And I find you very handsome… and dead sexy."

Frank looked away, embarrassed. Fortunately the waiter arrived with their drinks and saved him from having to come up with a response. He was out of his element here. He was used to telling people where to go, what equipment to set up, what data to collect. The last time he'd dated was… he couldn't remember. A long time ago. And even though this date seemed to be going pretty well, he was still afraid he'd screw it up somehow.

"Thank you," Toby said when they were alone again, "for what you did last night."

"What? Oh… that." Frank shifted self-consciously in his seat. "It wasn't very professional."

Toby gave him a sour face. "It was what I needed, at the time. And what was unprofessional about it? You didn't grope me or try to take advantage of me."

"I should have put my pants back on." It had been so... *erotic*.

"Please," Toby said. "It was two o'clock in the morning. We were both awakened from sleep and we just wanted to get back to sleep. Don't make it sound sordid. You were taking care of me, like you take care of everyone."

Frank didn't know what to say to that, so he withdrew his hand from under Toby's fingers—it hadn't occurred to him to break the contact before then, even as the waiter had deposited their drinks—and fiddled with the cloth napkin in his lap. "You have a nice place," he said, trying to divert the conversation.

"Thanks. Where do you live? Is it far from Hawley?"

"Only about an hour away from here, in Keene. Louis and I still live in the same house we grew up in."

"That doesn't surprise me."

Frank looked up sharply. "Why not?"

"I just mean you seem like a very... settled person," Toby responded. "Most of us are drifters. We live in one place for a year, move to another, live there for a year or two.... We keep hoping to find a place we can settle in, but there are always jobs or other circumstances forcing us to move on. You're not like that."

"Well... after I got out of the service, I had to take care of our dad. He'd been kind of... frail... ever since Mom died, but he had a stroke while I was in Iraq. Louis took care of him as best he could, but he was going to college—still living at home, but you know, he couldn't be around all the time. So I did my stint and came home, worked nights doing security when Louis was home. After Dad passed away, Louis and I just kind of kept going the way we'd been. I never even thought about moving out. I don't know about Louis."

"How long ago was that?"

Frank had to count back. "About five years, I guess." It didn't seem like much of a life, now that he'd summed it up. But he didn't regret any of it. And he'd been happy, more or less—still was.

As long as Louis wakes up again. Frank had dropped Houston off at the hospital that afternoon and made arrangements for him to stay the night. Fortunately the other bed in the room was empty at the moment. But Louis's condition hadn't changed.

"How do you find time to do the paranormal investigation?" Toby asked.

Frank shrugged. "It's usually just a night here and there, when I'm not working. We don't charge, generally, so I pay Savannah out of my own pocket—she has a day job at Barnes & Noble in Portsmouth. Plus we got a little bit of inheritance from Dad. It's not much, but we get by. Louis and Houston are willing to work for meals. Houston stays in one of our spare rooms."

"Mrs. H. is paying you, isn't she?"

Frank laughed. "Oh yeah. I didn't even have to ask. She just had her secretary call me and dangle a wad of cash in front of me, plus expenses. I feel like a gigolo."

"Don't," Toby said seriously. "That mill is a dangerous place. You've already seen how dangerous it can be."

The smile faded from Frank's face. "Yeah. I have."

DINNER WAS wonderful. Despite Frank's initial hesitancy over the food, he seemed to enjoy it. After dessert, he took Toby back to his apartment, parking in front of the shop.

"I had a good time," Frank said, smiling.

Toby didn't like the sound of that. It sounded like a prelude to "Good night," and he wasn't in the mood to end the evening just yet. "Would you like to come inside for a bit?"

"What for?"

Toby blinked at him. Nobody had ever asked that before. "For a drink?"

"I can't. I have to drive."

"Yeah…. Maybe we could just talk for a while?"

"That would be awesome, but I should probably get back to the hotel."

Was that a brush-off? Maybe. "I guess…." Then, almost without being able to help himself, Toby blurted out, "Why?"

Frank looked puzzled. "Well… it's getting kind of late."

"I mean… you could always stay here tonight."

"I don't want to put you out—"

"Oh, for fuck's sake, Frank! I'm offering you sex! Do you want it or not?"

Frank's baby blue eyes went wide, as if he'd just realized a train was coming and he was parked on the tracks. "Sex?"

Toby suddenly wanted to run upstairs, crawl under his bed, and die of embarrassment. What had possessed him to blurt it out like that? Now Frank probably thought he was the kind of guy who spread his legs for every man who bought him a mojito. "I don't… I mean—"

"Okay."

They regarded each other in silence for a long moment. Then Toby opened his door and climbed out of the van. He waited while Frank did the same and then checked all the doors to make sure the van was secure for the night.

"Is it okay to leave it here?" Frank asked. His voice seemed a little shaky.

"Sure, it's fine." Like most of Hawley, the road in front of the shop was unmetered.

He led the way into the entry next to the shop door, and up the stairs to his apartment. Inside, he went straight for the small rack on his kitchen counter that had a couple of bottles of decent wine in it. "Red or white?"

Frank hesitated a moment, perhaps debating whether he should still refuse a drink, then replied, "White."

"Well, it's actually pink."

"Fine."

Toby retrieved wineglasses from the cupboard and poured for both of them. When they each had a glass, he took a sip and said, "I made things really awkward. I'm sorry."

Frank sipped his own glass—or rather, downed half of it. Then he took a deep breath. "If you hadn't, I'd be on my way back to an empty bed at a cheap motor inn and pissed off at myself for not having the balls to make a move."

"Really?"

"Really."

"You can make a move now, you know."

Frank took Toby's wineglass, set both glasses on the counter, and then pulled him into his arms to kiss him. Toby was amazed at how soft and warm his lips were, despite the prickling of his beard. They were close to the same height—Frank was maybe an inch taller—but Toby felt as if his entire body was wrapped in Frank's embrace. He'd never felt so safe and protected.

They explored each other's bodies, caressing every inch of their backs and sides through the cloth of their shirts, then yanking the shirts up to touch hot, bare skin. Frank was wearing a simple brown T-shirt under an open flannel shirt, and it looked incredibly sexy on him, but now Toby wanted it *off*. Frank put up no resistance as Toby slid the flannel shirt off his shoulders and let it drop to the floor.

"Take it off," he murmured into Frank's mouth.

Frank laughed but stepped back long enough to remove the T-shirt and reveal a tight, muscular torso. He had a fine dusting of reddish chest hair and a delicious trail leading down into the waistband of his underwear. "You too."

"Let's go into the bedroom," Toby insisted, reaching down to caress the growing bulge in Frank's jeans. Frank growled in frustration but followed him out of the kitchen.

In the bedroom Toby allowed Frank to unbutton his shirt and slip it off. Frank groaned when he saw Toby's chest and stroked the skin of his abdomen while he dove for Toby's left nipple. Toby had never had a guy pay much attention to his nipples before, and it surprised him how good it felt to have a hot tongue tickle the sensitive nub. When Frank bit it gently, he arched his back in surprise and gasped. "Ah! Jesus! Do that again."

Frank moved to the other nipple and showed him why it was good to have two. After a minute Toby was dry humping his crotch against Frank's thigh. Before he could suggest they try something else, he found himself lifted off the floor by Frank's strong arms and spun around so Frank could lay him out on the bed.

Frank was on top of him in an instant, kissing his way up Toby's neck to claim his mouth once more. He was a damned good kisser, and Toby opened himself to Frank's probing tongue with enthusiasm. Then Frank slid his mouth over to Toby's ear, nipped his earlobe, and growled, "I want you naked."

"Yes!"

Toby didn't have to do a thing. He lay there entranced as Frank stripped him. Then, when he was stark naked, his achingly swollen cock jutting up obscenely between his open legs, Frank stepped back to look at him. His expression was admiring, lustful, as he yanked his belt open and shoved his jeans and underwear down. His cock stood almost straight up from its nest of red-gold pubic hair.

Toby didn't usually like to be fucked. Half the guys he'd been with didn't do it right and he just ended up sore afterward. But looking at that cock, he knew he wanted it inside him. Now.

"Will you fuck me?" he asked breathlessly.

"Do you have condoms?"

He did. And lube, of course. He retrieved them from his nightstand and sat on the edge of his bed, pulling Frank in close. Before he put the condom on, he couldn't resist taking Frank into his mouth. Frank didn't seem to mind the detour. He groaned and stroked Toby's hair while Toby worshipped him, exploring the length and breadth of that beautiful cock and teasing the tip with his tongue, tasting the sweetness there. Toby himself was leaking pretty severely now, as he'd done when they were sleeping together. He could feel it as the head of his cock moved against his inner thigh, leaving a trail.

At last Toby pulled away, ripped open the condom wrapper, and rolled it onto Frank, stroking him as he gently urged the condom down his shaft. Then he dabbed some lube on it and watched Frank shudder as he coated its length.

Toby lay back on the mattress again and urged, "Fuck me, Frank. Please."

Frank growled again as he climbed onto the bed and positioned himself between Toby's thighs. He took some of the lube onto his index finger and for a couple of delicious minutes, Toby luxuriated in his gentle probing. But it wasn't enough, and Toby soon pleaded, "Do it."

Frank entered him then, slowly, filling him up. Then he leaned forward and merged his mouth with Toby's as he gently began to move within him. Toby whimpered, but when Frank hesitated, he whispered, "Don't stop. That's just the sound I make when I'm in heaven."

Frank chuckled. "Well, then I hope to hear more of it."

He did. A lot more.

Frank came first, since Toby had largely forgotten about his own cock. All he cared about was what was happening in his ass. He felt Frank shudder and his entire body stiffen. Then his cock seemed to grow larger inside Toby, and Toby felt it bucking over and over again with his release. Frank let out a long, shuddering sigh when it was over.

Toby was unhappy for a moment when Frank pulled out of him, but Frank slid down his body and drew Toby's neglected cock into his mouth. "Oh God!"

Frank was good at that too, it turned out. Toby felt the head of his cock engulfed in warmth and started when he realized just how deeply Frank was taking him into his throat. He shuddered and came while Frank swallowed again and again, not pulling away until Toby was completely spent.

Then Frank crawled back up his body to kiss him. Toby could taste his own come in Frank's mouth, and he found it an incredible turn-on. He wondered how soon they might be able to go at it again.

At last, Frank broke the kiss to say, "I hate to spoil the mood, but I really gotta take a leak."

Toby snorted. "Charming. It's behind there." He pointed to the bead curtain that covered the entrance to the bathroom.

Frank climbed out of bed and pushed it aside. He peered into the small space on the other side. "No door?"

"'Fraid not. The previous tenant kicked it in—God knows why. My landlady has been saying she'll replace it for the last five years."

"You should sue."

"I should, but she knows I won't. If you have to do anything you're embarrassed about, I'll leave the room for a few minutes."

Frank quirked an eyebrow at him. "If I had to do *that*, I'd... never mind. I don't. Be right back."

He slipped into the bathroom, did his business, and returned. But to Toby's disappointment, he didn't come back to the bed. He wandered naked around the room, taking in Toby's poster of *The Lord of the Rings*, his small rock waterfall, and his collection of meditation CDs. Eventually, he came to the Wiccan altar on Toby's dresser—two small statues of a naked, horned god and a similarly naked goddess, a chalice, and a ritual knife, all laid out on a blue cloth with a gold pentagram printed on it. Toby held his breath. Not everyone understood Wicca. Frank might think he was into black magic or Satanism.

Frank turned to him and raised that eyebrow again. "How do you feel about the Cottingley Fairies?"

"You mean those fake photos of fairies two Victorian girls took, using cutouts from magazines?" Toby asked.

Frank smiled and slid back onto the bed. "We might be able to make this work, after all."

Then he kissed Toby long and passionately, until they were both worked up enough to go for another round.

Interlude

"SHOULDN'T HE be on a feeding tube or something?" Houston asked.

The nurse smiled sympathetically as he made up the other bed in the room for Houston to sleep in and said, "You see that tube going into his nose? That goes all the way down to his stomach, and that's how we get food in. It's not as efficient as the large feeding tubes you might have seen on TV, but it's safer, for a lot of reasons. Especially if he might wake up at any moment."

Houston took a deep breath, held it, and let it out slowly. Maybe this wasn't such a good idea. Louis looked awful lying there, his skin pale and waxen, his hair greasy and messed up. It was a horrible thing to look at. But Houston knew this was where he belonged.

"If you need anything, there's a buzzer right here," the nurse said, indicating the small button hanging from a cord on the bedframe. Then he laughed and added, "Don't get carried away. The bathroom is right over there and you can get your own glasses of water. It's for emergencies."

"Got it."

"You have a good night."

"Thanks."

Then, at last, Houston was alone in the room. He tried to tell himself he wasn't really alone. Louis was right there. But it didn't feel that way. It felt as if Louis were on the other side of the moon.

"I've got something to tell you," Houston said to the unconscious figure. "It seems kind of pointless, since you can't hear me, but Frank says I should tell you." He slid the uncomfortable plastic chair he was sitting on closer to the bed and reached out to take Louis's hand in his. There was no response. The hand was warm, but otherwise there was no indication at all it was alive.

"We've been friends a long time," Houston went on. "Like.... Jesus. Eight years or so. You never made a secret of the fact that you were bi. You used to tease me—tell me I had a cute ass when I was in my underwear, shit like that. I never knew if you were serious. It didn't matter. I had my girlfriends, and you had a couple too. But you remember when you slept with Rob that night our senior year? And we got into that huge fight the next day? Well… I didn't get what was going on with me then—why I was so pissed off."

He paused, afraid to go on, even knowing he was probably just talking to himself. "I finally pieced it together about a year ago— sometime last summer. Maybe that night we went skinny dipping at Otter Brook Dam. The way you looked, naked in the moonlight…. You were so… fucking… beautiful, man. Or maybe the night we fell asleep on the couch together watching that stupid horror movie marathon…."

He took a breath, held it a moment, and then let it out in one big huff. "So this is the way it is. I'm in love with you. I've been trying to think of a way to tell you all year, but… well, I kept chickening out. I mean, sure, we're best friends. But you've never really acted *interested*. But…. Frank says I should tell you now, so I'm telling you. I love you."

Louis's hand flexed in his, the fingers closing slightly.

"Louis?" Houston stood and peered down into his friend's face. "Louis? Can you hear me?"

But there was no response. Louis's fingers stayed curled around his, but there was no other movement, and Louis didn't open his eyes.

After a few moments, Houston removed his baseball cap and placed it on top of Louis's head. "Here, you need this more than I do. Loser."

He sat back down, lifted Louis's hand to his lips, and kissed it. Then he settled back, wondering if he'd remembered to pack his Kindle. It was going to be a long night.

Chapter Ten

But I hope their spirits has fled
To a better place far still,
Up high, up high, up in the sky
Above the Hawley Mill.

TOBY AND Savannah seemed to have decided the matter of the séance, whether Frank was on board or not. He didn't put up a fight. Maybe they'd learn something; maybe they wouldn't. There was no harm in trying—he hoped. The last thing he wanted was to have to make another 911 call. But Toby insisted he could guard against that.

Famous last words.

Just before sunset, while Frank and Savannah were unloading equipment from the van—just enough to cover the foyer tonight—a car drove into the lot. Frank looked up from his work, expecting to see Toby's Civic, but was surprised to see a brand new BMW instead. Mrs. Hawley was at the wheel. Toby was in the passenger seat, and a young woman with scarlet hair was in the back.

"Frank!" Toby called with forced cheerfulness the moment he was out of the car. "I hope you don't mind me inviting Mrs. H. along."

His anxious expression suggested he'd done nothing of the sort.

"A séance!" the old woman exclaimed, clapping her gloved hands together in delight. "I haven't been to one of these since my second husband died without telling anyone where he'd hidden the safety deposit key, the paranoid old fool."

Toby came close to Frank and said under his breath, "She called me to check on progress, and I made the mistake of mentioning my plan."

Frank smirked at him. "I forgive you."

"*You* can try talking her out of it, if you like."

"Not on your life."

"Am I allowed to kiss you in front of Savannah?"

"Go for it."

Toby kissed him tenderly on the mouth, enough to get his motor revving but no more, and then turned to introduce the red-haired girl. "This is my assistant at the shop, Cassandra."

"Pleased to meet you, Cassandra."

"Mr. Carter." Out of the car, Frank could see she was dressed all in black—even her lipstick and fingernails—and she had sort of an Egyptian kohl thing going around her eyes. She accepted his outstretched hand with a limp wrist, as if she expected him to kiss it, and an air of Victorian affectation he found amusing.

"Cassandra's Wiccan, so I invited her to assist with casting the circle and setting up wards."

Ah. Magic. That was Toby's plan for protecting everyone. It made Frank distinctly uncomfortable, even while he acknowledged that his belief spirits *could* attack wasn't far removed from Toby's belief that a Wiccan circle casting could protect them from those attacks. They both believed in psychic energy. It was whether living humans could consciously control it that they differed on.

Give it a chance, Frank reminded himself.

"We're going to be recording the whole thing on video and audio," he said. "We'll also be monitoring EMF and thermal in the room. Our team still has to document any activity."

Toby didn't seem to have any issues with Frank's setup. "Good. No Houston tonight?"

"He'd rather chew broken glass," Frank replied. "But that's fine. I told him to keep an eye on Junior at the hospital and text me during the séance if he says anything or reacts in any way."

Toby nodded. "Sounds like a plan. But please keep your phone on vibrate, so it doesn't completely yank me out of trance."

The thought of Toby going into a trance state made Frank a bit uncomfortable—less out of fear than because he was growing fond of the guy and didn't want to watch him make a fool of himself—but all he said was, "Will do."

As he turned to lead the way into the building, Frank caught Savannah watching the two of them with a knowing smile.

"Did you have a comment to make?" he challenged her.

"Me? I would *never*."

TOBY KNEW casting a circle would be the best way to protect all of them from whatever malevolent force had attacked him—and probably Frank's brother, as well—a few days earlier. It invoked forces more powerful than anything he could raise on his own. But he fretted about Frank's reaction. The man seemed to understand Wicca was simply an alternative religion, and not something evil or Satanic, but that didn't mean he was really cool with it.

Still, Toby knew what had to be done.

"I'm going to draw a circle in chalk inside the reception area," he announced to all present. "If you need to bring in more equipment while I'm doing that, go right ahead, but please try not to smudge the circle. When we actually cast it, everyone will need to be inside the boundary I draw and stay there until the séance is done."

The floor of the reception area was carpeted—a short pile with an ugly brown pattern that had faded over the past few decades until it was nearly indistinguishable. It also smelled of mildew, now that he was close to it. He drew the circle by hand with pastel blue "lecturer's chalk," the kind used in street painting. It didn't need to be geometrically perfect. Technically the circle didn't even have to be drawn, since the actual circle was created from psychic energy, but Toby wanted something concrete to give Frank and the others a clear idea of the boundary.

While Frank and Savannah set up their own equipment at the receptionist's desk, Cassandra and Mrs. H. brought in the supplies Toby needed. He was going all-out this time, and he couldn't deny it was partly for show. Not only did it need to be impressive enough to convince everyone present the circle was real, but it also needed to convince the spirits of the mill he meant business. Magick—even real magick—took place where the human mind interfaced with the Universal Mind, and therefore was always part psychological.

Cassandra used a compass to determine the four directions and placed colored candles at each point: yellow in the east, red for the south, blue in the west, and green in the north. The candles were jar candles, for safety. Since there hadn't been room for a folding table in the trunk of Mrs. H.'s BMW, they would all be sitting on the floor. He did, at least, put down a heavy blanket and meditation pillows for the five of them. He'd been a bit concerned about Mrs. H. having to sit on the floor at her age, but she'd insisted she was in perfect health and could manage.

They brought in a few more accoutrements, and then there was nothing to do for several minutes but wait until Frank and Savannah had everything running on their end.

FRANK KNEW he was dragging his feet, taking more time to get setup than he really needed. He wasn't thrilled with this whole séance thing.

But after he'd tested the sound on the mics for the tenth time, he glanced up to find Savannah watching him, arms crossed like an irritated parent. He turned around and saw that *everybody* was waiting for him.

Oops.

"Sorry. I guess I'm a little nervous."

Toby gave him a knowing smile and extended a hand. "If both of you can come inside the circle, we'll begin."

Savannah smiled and cocked her head at a jaunty angle, crooking her arm at him. She tended to wear her thick, jet black hair pulled back in a tight bun to keep it out of the way as she worked, but in that pose, she suddenly looked like a debutante waiting for her date to escort her onto the ballroom floor. So Frank stood, bowed, and escorted her into the circle.

Watching Toby go through the casting was... challenging. Intellectually he knew it was just another religion. Instead of one god, Toby and Cassandra worshipped two. Instead of saints, Toby called upon "elemental spirits." But even though he wasn't particularly religious, Frank had been raised Catholic, and this was decidedly not Catholic—or even Christian. It would definitely take some getting used to, if they decided they wanted to keep this thing between them going.

Cassandra lit the last candle—the green one—and intoned, "Guardian of the North, element of earth, power of strength and endurance, we call upon you to bless our circle and protect us during our working. Please join us!"

Toby was standing behind her, a small knife pointed at the edge of the circle with his right hand, crossed in front of his body so he could walk clockwise. In his left hand, he held a censer up high, burning frankincense and myrrh. He claimed those were for protection. But there was also something called elecampane in it. Frank wasn't familiar with that herb, but Toby told them it aided psychic ability. Whatever. The whole mixture was pretty overpowering in the closed room. By the time Toby reached the east again and declared the circle complete, Frank was feeling a bit nauseated.

"Sit, please," Toby said, indicating the small circle of cushions on the floor.

Frank offered a hand to Mrs. Hawley, who seemed a bit creaky, despite her insistence she could run circles around all of them. Then he took his place between her and Savannah. Toby settled into a half lotus position, his back straight and his hands in his lap.

"I'll ask you all to remain as quiet as possible until I come out of the trance. Cassandra will be asking me questions, and you may hear Frank's phone buzz. If it does, he'll relay what the text message says. But apart from that, please don't say anything… unless the spirit asks you a direct question. Otherwise it may bring me out too soon."

Frank quietly took his phone out and placed it on the carpet in front of him.

Toby watched him, nodded slightly, and then closed his eyes. Nothing much happened for a long time. Toby breathed slowly and evenly while the others tried not to fidget.

At last his eyelids flickered open part way, but not enough to reveal his pupils.

Cassandra quietly reached out to an unlit candle in the center of their circle and lit it with a butane lighter. "Spirits of this place, we welcome you in peace. May the light of this candle guide you to us. Come speak with us."

There was a long silence. Then Toby asked in a slow, quiet voice— almost a whisper, "Who… are… you?"

Cassandra seemed to be considering her answer carefully. Then with a glance at Mrs. Hawley, she said, "The current owner of the mill."

Toby jerked his head to face Mrs. Hawley, though his eyes were still nearly closed. "A woman?"

"Yes."

Toby turned slowly back to face the candle. "Why do you bother us?"

"Us? How many are here?"

"Many."

"Is one of you Rosaleen Quinn?"

"She is here."

"And Jack Bishop?"

Toby let out a sharp, unpleasant laugh. Frank didn't believe in demons, but the malevolent grin Toby wore as he continued to chuckle at some private joke chilled him to the core. "Not here. But near. He tries and tries to escape… but we will never… let… him… go…."

HOUSTON HATED this. He couldn't believe Frank had fallen for all this psychic medium bullshit. Sure, Toby was a good-looking guy, and kind of nice. But he was either a nutcase or manipulating Frank for some reason. Money, most likely. Mrs. Hawley was paying him, wasn't she? Maybe he had plans to write a book. *The Hawley Mills Horror*. Catchy. He might even get a movie deal.

And he's gonna make us all look like fucking idiots.

Still, in the back of his mind he wondered. *If Toby's a fake, why does Louis shout things every time he goes into a trance? How could he fake that?*

Well, that's what Houston was there to find out. Frank had just texted him they were beginning the séance. The doctor had been notified, and even though she was reluctant to go along with it, she'd agreed to let the on-call nurse know not to interfere if Louis started talking—not unless his heart rate shot through the roof or he was otherwise in danger.

Several minutes had gone by, but all was still. Junior appeared to be sleeping peacefully. Houston kissed him gently on the forehead—that was okay, wasn't it?—then opened his Kindle and went back to rereading *Firestarter* by Stephen King. He'd been reading *Doctor Sleep* before Louis's accident, but... he just couldn't deal with that one right now.

Just when Houston had convinced himself nothing was going to happen, he heard something. Something like heavy breathing.

He looked up, startled, and found Louis *watching him*. Well, he couldn't actually be watching—not with his eyes rolled back like that so only the whites were showing. But his face was turned toward Houston.

"Louis," Houston gasped before he remembered he wasn't supposed to interfere.

Louis didn't appear to hear him. He "stared" at Houston for a moment longer. Then his face contorted in anger and he hissed, "Let... me... go...."

FRANK'S PHONE buzzed, and he glanced at the text message from Houston. Even though he'd been expecting it, it still disturbed him to read *Louis awake but not awake. "let me go."*

"Junior just said 'Let me go,'" he told Cassandra quietly, trying to keep his voice from shaking.

Toby was still grinning in that disconcerting way. He laughed again and shook his head.

"Is Jack with Louis?" Cassandra asked.

"Part of him...."

Cassandra's eyes widened. "Where is the other part?"

Toby—or whatever was speaking through him—seemed to find that uproariously funny. When it finally stopped laughing, it replied, "Where it should be...."

SHE WASN'T dead—not yet. He'd left her unconscious on the cold cement floor of the basement, perhaps thinking she was dead. But she awoke, coughing and gagging for breath. The air there was always difficult to breathe because of the smoke from the massive coal-burning furnace, but never had she found it so painful to open her throat and take in air. The pain was the worst she'd ever felt—her neck, between her legs, all over her body where it had been scraped and bruised against the floor.... She tried to cry out, but she couldn't. She couldn't move or make a sound. For a few seconds, she had hope she'd survive, that she'd be able to crawl up the stairs to safety. But then she heard him returning.

"Christ! You're still alive?" He kicked her.

She cried out, though she knew it would do no good. She knew how loud the machines were when they were all going at once. Even now, she could hear their endless clattering through the heavy oak floor over her head. Nobody would hear her.

"I'm not havin' you go whining back to Roberts." He grabbed her wrists and pulled, dragging her across the floor, scraping her hip and leg across the cement, shredding the already worn fabric of her dress. She whimpered for him to stop, but he ignored her.

She felt the heat of the furnace and saw how the floor was blackened with soot and coal dust before she realized where he was dragging her, what he intended to do.

"No! Jack! You can't!"

He kicked her face hard, and she tasted blood.

It was impossible to open the cast-iron door without first donning the heavy canvas gloves used by the maintenance workers, and while he was searching for these, she attempted to crawl away. But she didn't get far before he came after her and dragged her back. She heard the scrape of the massive latch and the squeal of the door as he opened it.

The heat forced him to step back a moment. Then he lifted her, in those strong arms she'd once admired, while she struggled and screamed—

"No! ENOUGH! *Enough*!" Toby screamed.

Frank couldn't help himself. He leaped forward, toppling the candle and the bowl of water in the middle of the circle in order to catch Toby as he fell over backward, his fists digging into his eyes. "Toby!"

He was vaguely aware of Cassandra making sure the candle was out, but he was focused on the man in his arms.

"He killed her!" Toby gasped. "Stuffed her into the furnace! But then he stoked the furnace too high to make sure… everything burned. The flames got out of control, climbed up the chimneys. It's what started the fire."

"Jack Bishop?"

"Yes."

"Frank," he heard Savannah say, but he ignored her.

"Where was he when the place went up?" he demanded.

"On the first floor. He made it out alive."

Figures.

"Oh God! He left by the stairwell exit… and *locked it behind him*!"

"Frank!" Savannah shouted.

He looked up and saw instantly what she'd been trying to draw his attention to. Through the glass doors that led to the factory floor, something was moving. It was still dark in there, but there were shafts of moonlight coming through the gaps in the wooden boards, along with light from the halogen lights in the parking lot. And against this dim backdrop, Frank could see shadows, as if people were moving about… walking slowly toward the foyer.

Frank struggled to lift Toby to a standing position. "We need to get out of here. Now."

"They're coming closer," Cassandra said, her face ashen.

"I see them. Try to take some of the equipment with you."

They grabbed what they could—laptops, cameras, monitors, microphones. Other things, like power supplies, cables, and surge protectors, Frank ordered them to leave behind. Toby could barely walk on his own—the séance seemed to have drained him of all his strength—so Frank just shoved him out the door.

When they were loading things into the van, Cassandra asked, "Where's the old lady?"

They all froze. Mrs. Hawley was nowhere to be seen.

"She must still be inside," Savannah said.

"Goddamn it!" Frank growled. "Get everything packed up. I'll go back for her."

He ran back to the foyer, but Mrs. Hawley was nowhere to be seen. With a growing sense of dread, he walked to the glass door leading onto the factory floor. The shadowy forms were still there, still indistinct in the dimly lit interior. But they'd stopped moving. They seemed to be focused on a single point a hundred feet or so away from the door, a tiny form standing alone in their midst—Mrs. Hawley.

Frank tried the door. It was locked.

"Mrs. Hawley!"

LEANING AGAINST the side of the van, barely able to stand, Toby could feel the evil of the mill radiating off the building. Or perhaps not evil, but *anger*. And hatred. Hatred for Jack Bishop, for what he'd done to Rosaleen, for what he'd done to *all* of them when his violence against her expanded to take almost a hundred other innocent lives.

But something didn't add up. Jack had survived the fire. Why was his spirit tied to this building? Guilt? But he was apparently trying to escape. How did he get trapped there, if he hadn't *died* there?

Because he *did* die there. Somehow.

But Toby had seen him leave the building in his vision when the fire alarm was first sounded.

He's there. I know it!

Toby pushed himself away from the van, staggering but managing not to fall—barely. Savannah and Cassandra moved toward him, but he waved them away. "I need to go back inside!"

FRANK WATCHED in dismay as the heavy UPS bounced harmlessly off the glass door without even cracking it. Did he have anything heavier? The chair? Not likely, but he'd try it. Mrs. Hawley hadn't moved, as far as he could see. He wasn't even certain the spirits could harm her directly. But what if they possessed her as they had Louis?

He reached for the chair just as Toby staggered through the front door. Or rather he was half carried through the door by both Savannah and Cassandra, one arm draped around each of their shoulders.

"Jesus Christ!" Frank snarled. He dropped the chair and moved forward to take Toby's arm from around Cassandra. The girl looked relieved to be out from underneath his weight. "I told all three of you to get the fuck out of here!"

"He insisted," Savannah said, rolling her eyes.

"I've got him."

Savannah relinquished Toby's other arm. "Cassandra can go back outside, if she likes. I'm staying as long as you two are in here. And Mrs. Hawley. Did you find her?"

"Yes and no," Frank said. He nodded in the direction of the factory floor.

"Why haven't you gone after her?"

"Because the goddamn door refuses to let me through. You try it!"

Savannah gave him a puzzled look, then walked over to the door and pulled on it. It didn't budge. "Is it locked?"

"No. If you look closely, you can see the bolt isn't engaged." The door lock was a simple mechanism. Turn the key to the right and a metal bolt slid into place; turn it to the left and the bolt slid back. There was empty space where the bolt would have been, if it had been locked.

"Help me get near it," Toby ordered him.

Frank didn't want to obey. He wanted to drag Toby's sorry psychic ass back outside and toss him into the van. But he did as Toby asked.

When they were near the door, Toby extended his hand and pressed it against the lock. That was all. Then he grabbed the door handle and pulled.

The damned thing opened.

"What the fuck did you do?"

"Take me in there, please. Now."

Frank growled and hoisted Toby's arm to a more secure position over his shoulder before moving forward. "You keep bossing me around, I might develop a fetish for spanking you."

Out of the corner of his eye, he caught Toby smirking. But they didn't have time for that now. Frank helped Toby cross the distance between the door and Mrs. Hawley's position. To his annoyance, Savannah and Cassandra flanked them.

Goddamn it!

Well, he supposed he had to respect them for not being afraid—at least, no more than he was. The shadows were still there, impossible to see clearly, but moving around them silently in the darkness. In his peripheral vision, Frank glimpsed what looked like women in drab, dark dresses, but they were never there when he tried to look at them directly. He could *feel* them, though. Their anger seemed to radiate off them, making the air feel hot and suffocating. It was hard to breathe.

"Mrs. H.," Toby said quietly.

The old woman turned to them, apparently surprised to see them there. "I've been trying to reason with them, but they won't listen."

"Reason with them how?"

"I've told them if they don't want the building turned into a mall, I'll just tear the monstrosity down! It's no use to anyone as it is. And I certainly can't subject others to what we've gone through." She looked pointedly at Frank. "You'll still get your pay, dear, but I don't think we need bother with your final report. I have no doubt the building is indeed haunted."

Cassandra snorted, then looked apologetic and quickly covered her mouth.

"Mrs. H.," Toby said, "they don't want the building torn down."

"Whyever not?"

"Because they've committed a murder, and they don't want it discovered."

Frank looked at him, puzzled. "A murder?"

"Jack Bishop. He returned here, years after the fire—perhaps after the mill was shut down in 1989. That would make sense. Nobody reported much psychic activity here until then."

"Why would he come here?"

"Well… not guilt. I don't think he had much of a conscience. Perhaps just curiosity. And the spirits who'd more or less lain dormant here for over seventy years were enraged by his presence. It isn't easy for a spirit to move objects in the physical plane. But ninety-seven angry spirits could manage it. They killed him. And they know if the building is renovated or torn down, his body will be discovered."

Frank could have sworn he felt a ripple go through the air surrounding them, as if the spirits were disturbed by what Toby had just said.

But Celia Hawley scoffed at it. "If they *did* kill Bishop, why on earth would they care about his body being discovered? It's not as if they can go to prison."

"They've been holding him prisoner," Toby responded. "If his body is discovered, his spirit will be free. And they can't stand it!" He raised his voice, looking around at the restless shadows. "But Jack isn't the only prisoner here, is he? You've all been trapped here for more than a century! Your families, your friends—they've all passed on. But you're still here, trapped in your worst nightmare, with the monster responsible." He paused, and Frank could feel how near he was to collapsing. "This is hell. But it's a hell you've created for yourselves. It's time to set yourselves free…."

For a long time, nothing happened. Then Frank felt the darkness easing. The air no longer seemed as oppressive. He could see into the darkness, where the shadows had seemed too deep just moments before.

Something metal crashed, and they all jumped. A whirring noise drew their attention to the far wall. The elevator safety gate was open. As they watched, the elevator moved upward until it was almost out of sight, revealing the gaping black hole of the elevator shaft underneath.

"That's it," Toby whispered. "They frightened him and he ran. They herded him right into the elevator on the fourth floor, and he was so terrified he didn't see until it was too late."

"He's at the bottom of the elevator shaft?" Savannah asked in a frightened voice.

"Yes."

Chapter Eleven

WHEN THEY were back outside in the relatively cool—and certainly less oppressive—evening air, Frank's cell phone buzzed. He looked at the text messages and found: *Come to the hospital. Now.*

Shit.

Frank tried calling Houston's cell, but it just rang a few times and went to voicemail. "Houston, this is Frank. We're on our way. Call me when you get this message."

He tossed his phone to Savannah. "Hold on to this, please. Answer it if Houston calls back."

"Will do."

Cassandra and Mrs. Hawley were helping Toby into the back seat of the BMW. The guy still looked awful. Frank waited for the women to step aside, then leaned in and gave him a gentle peck on the cheek. "Are you gonna be all right?"

"I'll be fine," Toby assured him. "I just need to sleep for a few days."

"Houston texted me to go to the hospital. I don't know what's going on."

"Then go! Mrs. H. will take me home."

Frank kissed him once more—on the lips this time—and ran back to the van.

IT WAS past visiting hours, but the nurse at the front desk had been flagged to page Dr. Khambatta if Frank showed up. A couple of minutes later, the doctor was hurrying down the hall toward him and Savannah, and Frank's heart started beating again—she was grinning.

"Your brother is awake!" she exclaimed. "He woke up about a half hour ago, and he seems very lucid. All of his vitals are good."

"Oh my God."

He had to extricate himself from Savannah's embrace before he could follow the doctor down the hall to the elevator. This time nobody seemed to mind Savannah tagging along. Frank doubted she'd listen if they tried to keep her out, anyway.

They entered the room and found Houston leaning over Junior's bed. Frank didn't know much about medical stuff, but he was pretty sure what he was doing wasn't CPR.

"That explains why you haven't been answering your cell phone."

Houston jumped a mile. Then he had the good grace to look sheepish while he wiped his mouth with the back of his hand.

"Hey, Frank!" Louis said cheerfully. "Savannah! How's it going?"

"It's going all right. Some of us have had to work while you've been napping."

Savannah practically shoved him out of the way to get to Louis's bedside. She gave him a warm embrace. "Oh, honey child, you have no idea how much we been missing you!"

Louis put up with her hugging him and roughing up his greasy hair with good humor, but to him it probably felt like the day after he'd fallen down the stairs. If he even remembered that much.

Suddenly Savannah pushed him away, holding him at arm's length. "So what's all this we just walked in on?" She cocked an eyebrow at Houston.

Junior grinned and looked up at Houston. "I don't know. I woke up, and the first thing I thought was, 'Houston loves me!' I didn't even get a chance to say much. He started hugging me, and the next thing I knew, we were making out."

Houston blushed. "Yeah, well… I *must* love you to kiss you with that week-old morning breath."

Dr. Khambatta interjected, "We broke up the make-out session so we could examine Louis. Though it certainly didn't take them long to get back to it."

"What about Casanova's broken leg?" Frank asked wryly.

"Still broken, of course. And he still has a minor concussion, though everything is healing well. The nurse put something in his IV for the pain after we examined him."

"Yeah, I'm feeling pretty good," Junior said cheerfully.

"No wonder Houston's looking good to you." Frank clapped a hand on Houston's shoulder to make it clear he was teasing. The poor guy looked like he might pass out from anxiety. Then Frank sat on the edge of the bed and took Louis's hand. "You had us worried, Junior. You had *me* worried. I wouldn't know what to do with myself if anything happened to you."

Louis squeezed his hand back. "I had a lot of... fucked-up dreams. Nightmares. About the mill, and the fire, and... some stuff I don't want to talk about right now."

"It can wait. I think I know some of it."

There was a quiet knock on the open door and a young man in a nurse's uniform addressed Dr. Khambatta. "I was told the patient needed a bath."

The doctor nodded. "I think he'd appreciate that. A bath, a shampoo. And he needs to brush his teeth."

"Sponge bath?"

"You can take him into the shower."

"This promises to be totally humiliating," Louis said. Then he smiled up at Houston. "But I should have fresh breath soon, if you want to stick around."

TOBY STAYED in bed for a couple of days. He felt like a total slouch, but whenever he tried to get out of bed longer than it took to go to the bathroom or eat some yogurt, exhaustion overtook him and he had to lie down again. He knew he wasn't ill in a physical sense. But psychic work often took a toll on him, and this had been a very rough ride. Fortunately Cassandra was more than capable of running the shop. She had to expand her hours to cover both days, open to close, but Toby fully intended to give her a bonus for that, as well as the work she'd put in at the mill. Regarding the latter, she seemed to have enjoyed it. The exact phrase she'd used was "bang up to the elephant"—not that he had any idea what that meant.

The best part was when Frank came by to tell him the good news about his brother, Louis, waking up out of his coma. Not only was Toby delighted to hear that—and the bit of gossip Frank dropped about Louis and Houston somehow stumbling into each other's arms—but Frank stayed with him for a couple of hours, cuddling. Toby hadn't had a boyfriend who enjoyed cuddling since college. It was... nice. Very nice.

On the third morning, he was able to drag his ass out of bed and shower, then wander downstairs to see if Cassandra might like a break from manning the cash register. He stumbled across Mrs. H. grilling the girl about which essential oils were best for arthritis.

"There you are!" the old woman exclaimed when she saw him.

"Good morning, Mrs. H. If you need something for arthritis—"

"Never mind that now," she said, waving a hand dismissively. "I have something to tell you. The police have been to the mill. Guess what they found at the bottom of the elevator shaft?"

"A body?"

"Well… a skeleton. And rotten clothing, plus a wallet with identification. It was Jack Bishop, all right!" She seemed delighted. "Miss Jones—Savannah?—she did some more research and managed to track him down. He'd been living in Manchester until he was reported missing in July of 1990—right around the anniversary of the fire. Now listen up, both of you. This is very important. If anyone asks, Toby did *not* know where the body was. We were all doing some ghost hunting and someone shined a flashlight down the elevator shaft. It looked as if there might be something down there. That's all. Got that?"

"Why?" Cassandra asked.

Mrs. H. sighed and crossed her arms, tapping the gloved fingers of one hand against her elbow. "So that Toby isn't accused of murdering Mr. Bishop, my dear, and leading us to the scene twenty-five years later. That's why. The police aren't very imaginative when it comes to the workings of the psychic plane."

"I appreciate you looking out for me, Mrs. H.," Toby said.

"Think nothing of it. Now, I must run. I have a meeting with my stockbroker. But I'll see you at the usual time on Monday for my reading?"

Considering how much trouble her last reading had resulted in, Toby had to suppress a shudder at the thought of doing another one. On the other hand, it had led him to Frank. He smiled and gave her a nod. "I'm looking forward to it."

Epilogue

THE MILL was torn down that August, and by early October fresh turf had been laid down to convert the grounds into a park. In the center, though the pipework was still being installed, a marble fountain had been erected with brass plaques at intervals around it, listing the names of the victims of the fire on July 17, 1907. One woman, Rosaleen Quinn, had a plaque of her own, though the reason for this was known to only seven people—seven people sworn to secrecy.

The discovery of Jack Bishop's body made the local papers, and there was much speculation about how it had ended up at the bottom of the elevator shaft. Where it had ultimately been laid to rest, Frank didn't know... and didn't much care. That monster's fate was in the hands of God or karma or whatever controlled men's destinies after death. Though he technically died in the mill, his name was not listed on the fountain plaques.

"I need to rest," Louis said. His arms were trembling as he hobbled over to a bench near the fountain on his crutches. Houston guided him down into a sitting position.

"You shouldn't push yourself so hard," Houston said.

"Oh, come on! It's barely a hill."

"The doctor said the leg needs rest in order to heal."

"I'm resting right now. See?"

Houston groaned but apparently decided he couldn't win this argument, so he just kissed Louis to shut him up.

Frank watched the exchange with amusement. It had been wonderful to see the two boys so happy over the past two and a half months. Savannah had declared that, between them and how sickly sweet he and Toby could be, she was going to have to get her blood sugar checked. Frank glanced at his boyfriend and thought she was probably right. He'd started singing along with the radio whenever they were in the van. He'd never done that. Not before Toby.

Toby had picked out the flowers he and Savannah were planting around Rosaleen's plaque today—heather for protection and white roses for love. The chrysanthemums and other decorative flowers Mrs. Hawley had ordered for the fountain would be planted by the florist later that week. Technically the park was still closed for construction. It would open in another week.

"May you find peace at last," Toby murmured when they were finished, placing his hand on the plaque.

Savannah added, "You'll always be in our hearts, honey child."

It was good to watch the two of them together. They'd grown fond of each other over the past several weeks, whenever the C-Troop team was able to visit Hawley and hang out with Toby and Cassandra. Even Houston seemed to have gotten over his initial dislike of Toby.

Frank and Toby had talked about doing more investigations together, with Toby as part of the C-Troop team, and Cassandra had been pestering both of them to bring her along too. Frank had been hesitant to propose the idea to the others, but they surprised him by approving of it. Oh, sure, Houston was still uptight about keeping things scientific, and Frank kind of agreed with him. But maybe they could find room for both approaches.

Savannah and Houston were family to Frank, almost as much as Louis. It would have been difficult to keep seeing Toby if they'd disapproved. He would still have done it, of course—nobody told Frank Carter who he could or could not love. But it was nice to have everybody on the same page. His and Toby's jobs kept them apart during most of the week, especially since Frank tended to work nights, but Keene was only a bit more than an hour's drive from Hawley. It hadn't been too difficult to arrange time together.

Frank came up behind them and wrapped his arms around Toby's middle. "We're gonna have to head back soon. We have an investigation in Peterborough tonight. Do you want to grab something for lunch?"

"Mmm. That sounds nice." The way he was caressing Frank's forearm made lunch sound like a dirty proposition. Maybe it was.

Apparently Savannah thought it might be. She gave the two of them a smirk and said, "You two go on. I'll watch after the Hardy Boys."

"Sounds good."

As they walked across the grass to where Toby's car and the van were parked, Toby asked, "Hardy Boys? Do they have another nickname now?"

"Who knows?" Frank said. "This group comes up with nicknames at the drop of a hat. At least they seem to have given up calling me 'Baba.' God, I hated that name!"

"They haven't proposed any nicknames for me, have they?"

"They're tossing some around." Frank gave him a mischievous grin. "'Psychic,' 'Psychicboy'...."

Toby groaned. "Gods, it makes me sound like a superhero!"

"I've seen you in the bedroom," Frank laughed. "It might apply."

"Me? You're the animal in the bedroom. Maybe I should come up with some nicknames for *you*. How do you feel about 'Tarzan' or 'Deep Throat'?"

Frank snorted. He reached out to pull Toby close and glanced back over his shoulder to make sure nobody could overhear them. "How about we keep that one to ourselves?"

Author's Note

The Burning of the Granite Mill

THE HAWLEY Mill fire is based upon real events that occurred not once, but several times in New England at various textile mills—the Granite Mill in Fall River, Massachusetts, in 1874, the Cocheco Mill in Dover, New Hampshire, in 1907, and most famously the Triangle Shirtwaist Factory fire in New York City in 1911, which cost the lives of 146 people, most young women between sixteen and twenty-three years old. And there were more. The lack of safety precautions in these mills often meant it was impossible to escape if fire broke out.

The verses heading up each chapter in this story are taken from a ballad originally written about the Granite Mill fire sometime before 1890. There were many variations on it, so I don't feel I'm breaking with tradition by adapting the verses to my fictional Hawley Mill. But here is the original ballad in its entirety.

The Granite Mill Fire

Was in Fall River City
When the people was burned and killed,
In a cotton manufactory
Called as the Granite Mill.
At seven o'clock the firebells rang
But oh, it was too late,
The flames they were fast spreading
And at a rapid rate.

They were men and women there
And children too, I'm told,
Who might have been saved from out of the flames
If the truth was only known.
But oh, the villains that locked the doors

And told them to keep still,
It was the bosses and overseers
That burning Granite Mill.

The first scene was a touching one
From a maid so young in years,
She was standing by a window and
Her eyes were filled with tears.
She cried, "Oh, save me! Save me!"
She called her mother's name,
But her mother could not save her
And she fell back in the flame.

The next scene was a horrible one
Just as it caught my eye.
They were leaping from a window
From up so very high,
And the only means of their escape
Was sliding down a rope,
And just as they were half way down
The burning strands they broke.

Christ, Christ, what a horrible mess,
They were mangled, burned and killed,
Six stories high, and falling from
The burning Granite Mill.
But I hope their spirits has fled
To a better place far still,
Up high, up high, up in the sky
Above the Granite Mill.

Keep reading for an excerpt from
Saturn in Retrograde
by Jamie Fessenden.

JOSHUA STOOD as the door to the conference room opened, unconsciously wiping his right hand on the pant leg of his suit in case he had to shake hands. The bearded, silver-haired man who entered was dressed casually in a maroon sweater and jeans, and his pleasant smile put Joshua at ease.

"Dr. Bannon?" the man asked, extending his hand.

"Joshua."

"Call me Max."

Max gestured for Joshua to be seated again, as he took another chair on the same side of the glass table. Max sat in his chair for a long moment, looking at his hand as he rubbed his fingers together, apparently toying with his wedding ring.

"I've brought a copy of my CV," Joshua said at last, growing uncomfortable with the silence. He slid his curriculum vitae along the table.

Max made no move to pick it up. "Yes, I've read it. So has Dr. Riley. It's fine."

He leaned forward, tapping his index finger on the tabletop. "What we're more interested in is your doctoral dissertation on post-selected closed time-like curves in quantum mechanics."

Joshua looked at him, dumbfounded. "You've read it?"

Max gave him a quirky half smile that looked vaguely familiar, though Joshua couldn't figure out why. "Dr. Riley and I are friends with Professor Garcia. He pointed us at your dissertation when we were at his house for dinner a few weeks back."

"It was largely based upon Dr. Riley's published research," Joshua said. The thought of Patrick Riley actually *reading* it was mind-blowing.

"I know." Max sat back in his chair again. "Patrick was flattered that you were so well-versed in his work. And he was impressed by your ability to extrapolate on his data."

Joshua cleared his throat nervously. "I'm sure he's already thought of everything I came up with."

Max didn't respond, merely smiled at him calmly. Apart from his age, he was handsome enough and seemed to have nice eyes behind the glasses he wore. Not really Joshua's type, though. Especially with that beard. If anything, Max reminded Joshua too much of his father.

"Why don't we go inside," Max said, standing abruptly. "Patrick's looking forward to meeting you."

This wasn't the way Joshua had expected the interview to go. He'd been prepared to argue that his work in Professor Garcia's lab qualified him for the open position at Dr. Riley's lab in the Eloi Institute, but when he reached for his CV, Max dismissed it. "You won't need that. Follow me."

Joshua left the stack of papers on the table and followed the man through the large double doors.

Max led Joshua through a maze of long corridors, pointing out various other labs in the building and giving Joshua a quick rundown of the work they were doing. The Cambridge, Massachusetts-based lab had connections to MIT and UMass Boston. Eloi's cutting-edge reputation—and Dr. Riley's rockstar-like status in the field of quantum research—had made the lab a popular destination for grad students from both universities.

Max brought Joshua past the men's locker room, and said, "I recommend keeping a change of clothes in your locker. We don't have many spills in the physics lab, but all-nighters aren't uncommon, and who wants to start another day without taking a shower?"

They stopped at a large door, where Max swiped his security card and pressed his hand against a scanner. The door hissed and slid aside.

The laboratory was enormous. Steel girders crisscrossed high above their heads, reminding Joshua of an airport hangar. Computer stations and lab equipment took up every bit of space along the four walls, and the center of the room was dominated by a sphere of metal with pipes and other apparatuses jutting out from its surface. It was surrounded by a circular walkway with a metal staircase curving gracefully up to it.

"We call this contraption 'Saturn'," Max commented, as they approached it, "because that's what that circular catwalk around it puts us in mind of."

Standing on the walkway was Dr. Patrick Riley, a pioneer in the field of quantum time effects and the man whose career had shaped Joshua's life since high school. From the moment he'd come across an entry in his physics book providing a brief summary of Dr. Riley's work, alongside a photo of a surprisingly handsome man with wavy ash-blond hair and soft, intelligent gray eyes, Joshua had been fascinated by the physicist. He'd looked up everything he could find on Dr. Riley in the school library and soon graduated from reading watered-down descriptions of his experiments in popular magazines to reading the original abstracts in physics journals.

Joshua had never told anyone about his "celebrity crush" on the handsome physicist. He'd come out his sophomore year, and his family had been cool about it. But telling them that he was harboring a crush on a *physicist*? That seemed epically geeky, even to Joshua. Not that it had stopped him from carrying a small picture of Riley in his wallet, snipped out of one of the journals.

Patrick Riley's attention was on something in his hand, but as Joshua and Max approached, he thrust the object into his lab coat pocket and closed the curved hatch on Saturn's side. Then he removed his safety goggles and leaned over the railing, those amazing gray eyes looking directly at Joshua. For a split second, the man seemed… Joshua wasn't sure. Surprised? But then Riley smiled, revealing dimples in his cheeks that made him seem far younger than his fifty years.

"Dr. Bannon, I presume," he said with mock formality. "Welcome to Eloi."

THE FIRST thing that struck Patrick was how strikingly handsome the young Joshua Bannon was. His penetrating blue eyes were set in a face as perfectly sculpted as a Roman statue, and his high brow and angular features were softened only by the sensual curve of his mouth. Even his short, golden-brown hair reminded Patrick of a Roman senator. But almost as quickly as Patrick noted all of this, he sternly admonished himself.

He's far too young.

True, Joshua was twenty-five and already had his doctorate. There was nothing technically wrong in Patrick finding him attractive. But he felt like a lecherous old man, nonetheless.

"Dr. Riley," Joshua said, looking up at him. He seemed a bit awestruck, and Max had already warned Patrick that Joshua was a "fan." Which was yet another reason to put on the brakes. Flirting with a naïve young man with a case of hero worship was *definitely* not something Patrick felt comfortable doing.

He descended to floor level and offered his hand to Joshua. "Please call me Patrick. If we go around 'doctoring' each other all day, it will drive me insane."

He laughed, but Joshua didn't seem to find it that amusing. The young man was still holding his hand and looking intently into his eyes, until Patrick was forced to look away uncomfortably.

Patrick tried again, taking his hand away and putting it in the pocket of his lab coat. "Did Max tell you that I read your dissertation on P-CTCs?"

"It was largely a summation of your work," Joshua replied.

"Up to the point at which we seem to be stuck." Patrick began walking, and Joshua fell into step beside him. "We've succeeded in creating a temporal distortion inside Saturn that fluctuates for a few nanoseconds, but the net result is always null. I thought your ideas on the subject were very fresh, and I'm hoping you'll give our research a boost."

"I hope so."

"Why don't I give you the grand tour, and then we can discuss what your duties will be over lunch?"

Joshua glanced over his shoulder, perhaps noticing that Max had deserted them. Then he asked, "Do you have other applicants to interview?"

It was a fair question. The research associate opening had been posted all over the physics department at the university. But the other applications had been set aside upon receipt. There hadn't been any interviews, apart from this one.

Patrick simply said, "No. The job is yours."

JAMIE FESSENDEN is an author of gay fiction in many genres. Most involve romance, because he believes everyone deserves to find love, but after that anything goes: contemporary, science fiction, historical, paranormal, mystery, or whatever else strikes his fancy.

He set out to be a writer in junior high school. He published a couple short pieces in his high school's literary magazine and had another story place in the top 100 in a national contest, but it wasn't until he met his partner, Erich, almost twenty years later, that he began writing again in earnest. With Erich alternately inspiring and goading him, Jamie wrote several novels and published his first novella in 2010. That same year, Jamie and Erich married and purchased a house together in the wilds of New Hampshire, where there are no street lights, turkeys and deer wander through their yard, and coyotes serenade them under the stars.

Visit Jamie: jamiefessenden.wordpress.com
Facebook: www.facebook.com/pages/Jamie-Fessenden-Author/102004836534286
Twitter: @JamieFessenden1

DREAMSPUN
DESIRES

SMALL TOWN
SONATA

Jamie Fessenden

Can the trusted town handyman
rebuild a broken pianist's heart?

Can the trusted town handyman rebuild a broken pianist's heart?

When a freak accident ends Aiden's career as a world-renowned classical pianist, he retreats to his New Hampshire hometown, where he finds the boy he liked growing up is even more appealing as a man.

Dean Cooper's life as handyman to the people of Springhaven might not be glamorous, but he's well-liked and happy. When Aiden drifts back into town, Dean is surprised to find the bond between them as strong as ever. But Aiden is distraught over the loss of his career and determined to get back on the international stage.

Seventeen years ago Dean made a sacrifice and let Aiden walk away. Now, with their romance rekindling, he knows he'll have to make the sacrifice all over again. This time it may be more than he can bear.

www.dreamspinnerpress.com

Jamie Fessenden

Murderous Requiem

A Brethren Novel

Jeremy Spencer never imagined the occult order he and his boyfriend, Bowyn, started as a joke in college would become an international organization with hundreds of followers. Now a professor with expertise in Renaissance music, Jeremy is drawn back into the world of free love and ceremonial magick. The old jealousies and hurt that separated him from Bowyn eight years ago no longer seem significant.

Then Jeremy begins to wonder if the centuries-old score he's been asked to transcribe hides something sinister. With each stanza, local birds flock to the old mansion, a mysterious fog descends upon the grounds, and bats swarm the temple dome. During a séance, the group receives a cryptic warning from the spirit realm. And as the music's performance draws nearer, Jeremy realizes it may hold the key to incredible power—power somebody is willing to kill for.

www.dreamspinnerpress.com

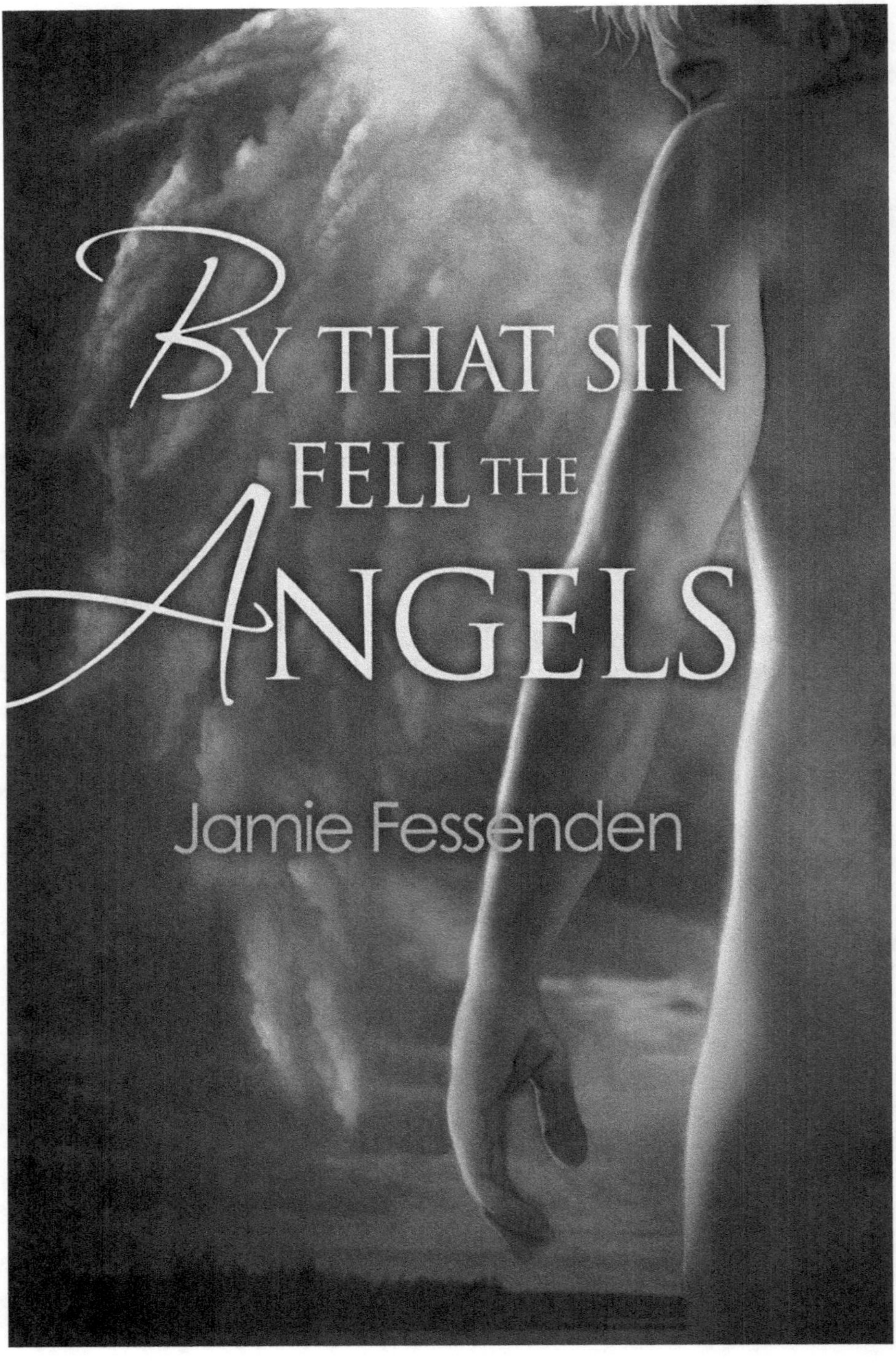
By That Sin Fell the Angels
Jamie Fessenden

It begins with a 3:00 a.m. telephone call. On one end is Terry Bachelder, a closeted teacher. On the other, the suicidal teenage son of the local preacher. When Terry fails to prevent disaster, grief rips the small town of Crystal Falls apart.

At the epicenter of the tragedy, seventeen-year-old Jonah Riverside tries to make sense of it all. Finding Daniel's body leaves him struggling to balance his sexual identity with his faith, while his church, led by the Reverend Isaac Thompson, mounts a crusade to destroy Terry, whom Isaac believes corrupted his son and caused the boy to take his own life.

Having quietly crushed on his teacher for years, Jonah is determined to clear Terry's name. That quest leads him to Eric Jacobs, Daniel's true secret lover, and to get involved in Eric's plan to shake up their small-minded town. Meanwhile, Rev. Thompson struggles to make peace between his religious convictions and the revelation of his son's homosexuality. If he can't, he leaves the door open to eternal damnation—and for a second tragedy to follow.

www.dreamspinnerpress.com

Screwups

JAMIE FESSENDEN

In 1996, Jake Stewart is starting his third year at the University of New Hampshire. Even as a successful business major, he is absolutely miserable. Not only is Jake pursuing a field he hates when he'd rather study art, he is utterly terrified of what will happen if his father finds out he's gay. When he finally gets up the courage to move into the creative arts dorm on campus, his new roommate, Danny, is openly gay—and there's no denying the attraction between them.

Danny Sullivan has been out since high school, and he appears comfortable with his sexuality. But something happened in Danny's past—something that gives him nightmares he refuses to talk about. Unknown to Jake, the way he mistreated his friend, Tom Langois, when Tom came out to him in high school, is mild compared to the way someone very much like Jake treated Danny.

It may be too late to fix the mess Jake made with Tom, but if Jake wants to be with Danny, he's going to have to fix the mess made by another closeted jock he's never even met.

www.dreamspinnerpress.com

Connor is a netrunner: a hacker who ventures into cyberspace to steal data from corporate computers. As he hides out in the slums of Seattle, he's attacked by a street gang and, incredibly, rescued by one of the members. His rescuer is a man named Luis, who has decided Connor needs his protection.

But instead of providing safety, Luis's presence wreaks havoc with Connor's online identity, and they find themselves hunted by a lethal security force. While they attempt to escape the city, Connor finds himself struggling to survive with the most lethal killer ever pitted against the corporations that control the FreeCorp—and he risks losing his heart to the same man.

www.dreamspinnerpress.com

FOR **MORE** OF THE **BEST** **GAY** ROMANCE

www.ingramcontent.com/pod-product-compliance
Lightning Source LLC
Chambersburg PA
CBHW060927030726
47503CB00003B/500